The
Adventures of
Elizabeth Fortune

The Adventures of Elizabeth Fortune

A NOUVEAU WESTERN

K. Follis Cheatham

BLUE HERON PUBLISHING

WES
Cheatham

The Adventures of Elizabeth Fortune
By K. Follis Cheatham

Blue Heron Publishing
1234 S.W. Stark Street
Portland, Oregon 97205
503.221.6841
www.BlueHeronPublishing.com

Blue Heron Publishing is a division of A-Concept, Inc.

Interior design and production: Daniel Urban
Cover illustration: Nancy Rush
Cover design: Dennis Stovall

ISBN 0-936085-44-4

Printed and bound in the United States of America
Printed on pH-balanced paper.

First Edition, February 2000
9 8 7 6 5 4 3 2 1

DEDICATION

This book is to the memory of my grandparents, Lida and Charles Blackburn; to Mark Twain, Zora Neale Hurston, John Steinbeck, Chaucer, Leslie Silko, Homer, and other great storytellers. They furbish the tale that has been condensed to insignificance or hidden by purposeful omission. A storyteller rarely misses a chance to glorify the mundane, and what is merely a paragraph in a text book becomes a rich portrayal of real events. Without these people, history would be drab and trivial; with them, the past will forever be heard.

I am trying to uphold the tradition.

K. Follis Cheatham

Acknowledgments

Thanks is given to my friends and colleagues in the Nashville wRiters' Alliance: (Madeena Spray Nolan, Jim Young, Alana White, Nancy Hite, Martha Whitmore Hickman, Michael Sims, Phyllis Gobbell, Ronna Wineberg Blaser, Amy Lynch, Steven Womack, Sallie Bissell) for keeping me focused and for their diligent critiquing; to authors/historians Jeanne Williams (who encouraged this project) and Susan Butruille (who introduced it to Blue Heron Publishing). And to my children, Nisah and Onika who always said "Don't stop writing."

Valuable information was obtained at historical sites Fort Larned and Fort Lyon (now a VA Hospital), and from the regional history special collections in the public libraries of Trinidad, Colorado, and Ellsworth, Kansas. Oberlin, Ohio, (my birthplace) I constructed from memories.

PROLOGUE

May 9, 1870. On an overcast spring afternoon in northern Ohio, Elizabeth Fortune set her books on the corner of the wide wooden stairs that led to her room with no thoughts of the future beyond studying for upcoming exams. Yet an incredible alteration to her life had already occurred. She took off her gingham bonnet and pulled a few wooden pins from her brown hair, letting the mass of waves fall down her back. Weariness tugged at her. She had been up since dawn, feeding chickens, serving breakfast, and helping with the laundry here; then the hike to the college. The classrooms were two miles away, and the walk back was mostly up hill. She unbuttoned the waist-length blue jacket she wore over a tailored blouse, and looked forward to getting out of the small bustle and two petticoats that were deemed proper under her soft gingham skirt.

The scroll-legged hall table, which sat under a pale artist's rendition of Walden Pond, held two pieces of mail. Elizabeth stepped forward to read the names on the envelopes. She hoped for a letter from her father, Samuel, who served in the cavalry on the western frontier. It had been three months since she had heard from him. One envelope was addressed to her. She grabbed it up, but her heartbeat quickened with apprehension. The letter was from her grandfather, Wilson Clark. Her grandfather had never before written her. She broke the seal and opened the envelope, thinking of her grandmother. When Elizabeth had been home in April, Etta Clark had been pale, and tired easily. Elizabeth had wanted to stay in Terre Haute to be with her, even though an additional housekeeper had been hired to see to the woman's every need. Now, less than three weeks later, this.

The word *funeral* leapt off the page Elizabeth unfolded, blinding her to other words that would truly change her life. She closed her eyes, remembering her last farewell to Etta Clark. "I'll be back soon, Grandmother," Elizabeth had said, clinging to the small soft hands.

"Not to worry. It's all right, now," Etta Clark had said, a gentle smile on her face.

"I'll be home soon," Elizabeth had reiterated.

"Certainly, Anne. Not to worry."

"Anne", Etta Clark had called her. Elizabeth's mother's name. A mistake Etta had frequently made in the last year; not that Elizabeth resembled the lavender-eyed, sable-haired Anne Clark Fortune.

Elizabeth opened her eyes and blinked away hot tears. She looked again at the letter. *We are holding my dear wife's funeral today...* Quickly, she read the letter's date: 3 May 1870. "Six days ago!" Indignation swept her. "He deliberately didn't let me know until it was too late to be there," she declared. She clenched her fists, squeezing the letter in the process.

In the kitchen, russet=haired Mrs. Holcum heard Elizabeth's outcry and hurried into the hall. "Elizabeth, what is the problem?" she asked. She owned this house where Elizabeth lived and worked for board.

"My grandmother has passed," Elizabeth said, caught in a mix of dismay and outrage.

"Oh, my," said Mrs. Holcum. Of all the young lady boarders she had over the years, she felt a special warmth for Elizabeth.

"And Mr. Clark—" Elizabeth put a fist to her mouth. "I had saved the money—would have paid my own way." Why? Why cut me out of this, too? she lamented. "He should have sent a telegram when she was failing," Elizabeth went on. "I would have been there."

Mrs. Holcum, not totally understanding Elizabeth, took the crumpled letter from her hand. "Goodness!" Mrs. Holcum declared, reading the letter. "He's turned you out!"

But Elizabeth didn't hear the woman. She had already whirled to the front door and bolted outside. She dashed across Vine Street, and called to the woman who hoed a large garden next to a fine red barn. "I have to borrow a horse, Mrs. Parsons. I won't be long!" Without awaiting an answer, she ran through the open barn, out the back, and into the paddocks where three of Mr. Parsons' large work horses lounged near the fence. Quickly she grabbed up a tether rope and fashioned reins for the halter of the dark brown gelding. She led it through the rail gate, and after closing it, used the rungs to clamber onto the horse's broad back. Her gingham skirt bunched up and showed white petticoats beneath and ankle-high button shoes over white stockings. With an urging from her heels, the brown lumbered along Vine Street, and across the Plum Creek bridge.

Down Main Street they went, passed the hardware and livery, passed the barber shop. Elizabeth slowed the horse only when she neared the bank. She angled the brown around delivery carts that stood along the edge of the park-like town square, and illegally jogged the willing creature under the maples and elms, crossing the park on the diagonal until she reached the far corner. Here, rows of buildings housed the academia of Oberlin College, where Elizabeth attended classes. Elizabeth barged the big horse along a small lane until she reached a cottage dormitory for men. She slid from the horse before it stopped and ran it to the hitching rail, looping the reins with a deft toss. She rushed to the cottage door.

"Scott!" she yelled while knocking on the door. "Scott, I need to talk to you!"

The door opened quickly and several young men stood before her, eyes wide.

"Where's Scott?" she asked.

"Scott?"

"Yes. Scott—uh, Clark."

But someone else was already calling: "Hey, Scott! There's a lovely at the door for you, and she's really got her dander up. What have you done this time?"

Several of the men were snickering and studying Elizabeth's wind-blown appearance.

"You're Miss Fortune, aren't you?" one of them asked. "I met you once in Wellington. At the train station." He was eager, and his face held a flushed smile.

Elizabeth gave a slight nod. When she spotted a medium-built fellow in blue trousers and checkered shirt, exiting a far door, she held her skirt and darted around the building. "Scott, please!" she begged.

He stopped and turned, his lavender eyes nearly black with rage.

"You have no business over here. No business at all!" he began. His fine features looked a lot like Elizabeth's, although his skin was more pale; his light brown hair glinting blond.

"You knew, didn't you? And didn't tell me. About grandmother." Dismay made her voice sad.

"Shush." He grabbed her elbow and whipped her off toward a formal garden that stretched along the side of the house.

"Shush nothing!" she said, jerking from his grasp. Anger caused green flecks in her brown eyes.

"I was told not to tell you, so I didn't." He looked over his shoulder, scanned their surroundings, and urged her further into the garden. "Grandmother went easily, in a sleep she had been in for two days," he said softly. "She didn't seem in any pain."

Elizabeth swallowed hard and an unbidden tear slid down her cheek.

Scott went on, "Houston has gathered up most of your things—took them somewhere, I don't know."

"Houston? You were both there?" she asked, knowing the truth. "Grandfather telegraphed you and you went home. And you didn't even let me know!"

Scott sighed. "Let's not go into histrionics over this."

"You're as cruel and heartless as he is, Scott Fortune."

He grabbed her shoulders with both hands and shook her. "Don't call me that!"

"I will call you that," she said, seething. She had avoided him on campus, never made comment when he took the train home on a different day so he wouldn't be seen with her. "I'm not like you," he had told her six years ago when he was fourteen, Elizabeth a year younger. "I'm white, like grandfather Clark—like our mother. I will not be sullied by you bantering your dark-race heritage."

Now Elizabeth glowered and declared in a hoarse whisper, "You are Scott Fortune. Samuel and Anne's second child, and I'm ashamed to say, my brother."

He flung her aside. Elizabeth lost her footing and fell into a tall hedge, her brown hair swirling around her shoulders. He started toward her, his hand raised, menace on his face. Elizabeth leapt up, fists clenched, ready to defend herself as she had done so many times when

4

they were younger and he would try to beat her up.

A voice stopped Scott's advance. "There she is. She rode the farm horse over here," someone said. Scott whirled around. Elizabeth could barely breathe, she was so tense.

A town patrolman in a hard-billed cap and a blue suit with a metal star on the pocket, came toward them, followed by young men from the dormitory. Scott stalked out of the garden, pushing away his curious friends.

"My, my," said the patrolman. His eyebrows raised with surprise. "Hardly what I expected for violating town rules."

"Miss Fortune is a student here," said the friendly young man who had been at the cottage door. "Perhaps she didn't know—"

"Nonetheless, it will have to be reported." He gave a chivalrous bow, indicating the path back toward the street. "Come along, Miss—what was the name again?"

"Fortune," Elizabeth said, standing straight and looking sorrowfully to where her brother had disappeared. "Elizabeth Fortune."

That evening (after being fined by the town police, referred to the college administrators for discipline, and thoroughly fussed at by Amos Parsons), Elizabeth, in a muslin nightdress, sat cross-legged on the polished floor of her room. In the glow from the coal-oil lamp and with her long hair in two braids, one over each shoulder, her "dark race" heritage became obvious. Cherokee showed here, but Elizabeth and her siblings were also Negro—both races from their father, Samuel. In a breathy voice, Elizabeth sang a mournful chant as she had for the last hour. Outside the door, Mrs. Holcum stood a moment, stricken by the grief she heard. She had cleared the supper dishes herself so Elizabeth could have some personal time. Now she retreated downstairs, deciding not to ask about the sweet, smoky smell that came from Elizabeth's room.

Elizabeth placed more sage in the small fire that burned in a plate-sized seashell in front of her. The shell had come from North Carolina, had been her grandmother's—her Cherokee grandmother, Jannie Fortune. The words Elizabeth chanted were also from the Fortunes. She had sung them with the rest of her Fortune family: first when her mother died, the next year when Grandpa George was killed, and again eight years ago when Jannie passed on. Elizabeth hoped her grandmother Clark wouldn't mind a southeastern, mostly Cherokee, lament to her departed soul.

Her tears had dried to salty lines on her cheeks; she finally let the smudge ash out.

Her nightdress shrouded her slim body when she got up and stepped to the small desk near the door. She looked again at her grandfather's letter:

> *Elizabeth:*
>
> *We are holding my dear wife's funeral today. This school year has depleted the funds from the sale of the Minnesota farm, and you are ten months beyond your eighteenth birthday. When the term is over, do not bother to return to this house. I take no more responsibility for you.*
>
> *Wilson Clark*

He had always been hard on Elizabeth, telling her she was rebellious like her mother—a statement that only made Elizabeth more haughty. Now he had disowned Elizabeth as he had his daughter after her marriage to the black-Indian, Samuel Fortune.

Elizabeth laid the letter aside and sat in the desk chair. She drew in a long breath. "I can survive this," she muttered.

Taking up her pen, she opened her diary and wrote: *"I know nothing will ever be the same again."* Then she took a sheet of clean paper from the desk drawer and began a letter.

> *Dear Houston,*

Houston was her oldest brother, four years her senior.

> *...Scott made some comment that you had gathered my things. Thank you. Mr. Clark was probably going to burn them.*

Five years earlier, Houston had left Terre Haute, taken back his Fortune name, and now dealt cards on an Illinois riverboat. Yet even Houston had been called home for Etta Clark's funeral, emphasizing all the more Wilson Clark's dislike of Elizabeth.

But I will not mope around about this. First, I find it hard to be-lieve that the money Daddy left from selling our farm is gone, what with my paying my own board and all. And I also can't but wonder what else Mr. Clark hasn't told me—told us. Like all those letters from Daddy he never let me see when I first got to Indiana.

I must find out about Daddy. It's been too long since his last letter, and I've written him several times—especially when Grandmother became ill. He should have responded. I even wrote the War Depart-ment to learn more about where he is. But they're as slow as winter molasses. No answer yet. So I've decided to go out there.

She gave an emphatic nod, pleased with her decision.

My funds are a bit low, after paying some stupid town fines, but after exams I'll earn some extra strawberry picking at Godette's. Then I'm headed west. Fort Union in New Mexico Territory is where Daddy's last two letters came from. If you would forward my belong-ings there, I'll pay you back as soon as I can. And I'll write. Not to worry.

Her grandmother's often-used phrase. Elizabeth bit her lip, and the clinging sweet fragrance of burnt sage eased her pain. She went back to the letter, her youth and innocence evident in what she next wrote:

It shouldn't take too long to find Daddy.

ONE

(From Elizabeth's diary) A horrid day. If it weren't such a use-less effort, I'd have myself a long hard cry.

31 July [1870]

Elizabeth rolled across the warped floorboards, scooted behind the bar, and grabbed up the double-barreled shotgun the bartender had dropped when he was shot. A pistol shot careened off a nickel-plated beer spigot, sending the six bystanders closer to the walls.

"She's been playin' you for a fool all evening!" came a rough voice from ten feet away. "You can't let her kind better you, Johnny."

Elizabeth gritted her teeth and checked the load on the gun. Both breeches were ready. She had learned firearms eleven years ago, at age eight. Her father taught her, and always insisted that guns were tools to provide food and to protect against varmints. Right then, the long-haired blond in striped denim pants, leather chaps, and gray calico shirt was a varmint.

She could taste blood on her lower lip, feel the warmth of it along her chin, and was again astounded that this drunk—that anyone!—had hit her. Even her grandfather Clark, with all his bitterness, had never struck her.

Two more shots whizzed from the single-action Colt. One smashed into the floor, the other cracked the four-foot mirror above Elizabeth's head. Glass tinkled and fell, and a sliver spiked the back of her hand. As her blood welled, Elizabeth's anger erupted to action. She came up with the shotgun leveled at the drunk and his mean-eyed friend. Five men bolted away from the nearby poker table.

"Get her, Johnny!"

"Don't. Please don't!" Elizabeth protested. Her heart pounded. She had never before aimed a firearm at a person. She eased the barrels to the right of the man.

The blond grinned and pointed his pistol at Elizabeth, arms outstretched, legs wide. He cocked the hammer. Elizabeth clenched her teeth and pulled the trigger.

Boom! The roar of the shotgun filled the big room and the man lurched and spun back as if jerked by a rope. His pistol thunked on the shot-pocked wall after skidding out of his hand. That hand swung crazily, too, two fingers shattered, white bone protruding; then blood soaked the arm of his shirt and flowed off the thumb like water from a red icicle.

Elizabeth felt queasy as the assailant's head lolled back. His stocky companion caught him as he fell. The sound of the big gun echoed and blue smoke meandered out of the barrels. To Elizabeth, it suddenly weighed a ton. Four of the bystanders scrambled for the door while a bird-like woman in a beige linen-and-lace gown screamed at Elizabeth: "My God! What have you done!" She was Faye Wentworth, Elizabeth's boss.

"She killed him!" the dark-haired thug declared.

Elizabeth shook her head, certain she hadn't. The blond moaned and leaned against the other man as he tried to sit up. The loud mouth bent to give comfort, and Elizabeth, her nerves tingling like drawn piano wire, hurried to the bartender who still lay motionless near the faro table. Blood trickled from his thinning black hair. She put her hand on his chest, grateful to feel the steady rise and fall of breathing through his leather vest and striped cotton shirt.

"Get away!" Lady Faye's hazel eyes snapped with anger as she yelled at Elizabeth. Light brown curls flopped around her thin face when she stooped to the man.

The shattered mirror reflected Elizabeth's tall form in pieces when she stepped back. She propped the shotgun in its corner against the bar. She couldn't believe she had really shot someone! She pressed the back of her hand to her cut lip and frowned at her two adversaries. It was their own fault, especially the dark-haired man; he was the one who had started the trouble.

The tough jerked up from where he had propped the fallen man on a bunched jacket. "You red-bone bitch," he growled, glaring at Elizabeth.

Elizabeth flinched from the hatred she heard. He was thick-set, with lank brown hair hanging around his square jaw. He reached for the gun in his waist band. Someone screamed.

Three men crashed through the green-painted bat wings, delaying the tough's revenge. "Hold it!" the tallest of the newcomers ordered. He held a sawed-off shotgun, butt to his shoulder, and wore a six=pointed star on the pocket of his dark shirt. "You'd think at seven p.m. a man could stop and get a meal, even if he is the county sheriff," he said. "What the hell is going on?"

The angry man, his gun still in his belt, pointed a stiff finger at Elizabeth. Hatred filled his voice when he declared, "That tramp just shot my brother!"

Elizabeth drew an alarmed breath. His brother! She thought it might be nice to be the fainting type right then, but she wasn't.

The Sunday shooting really drew people's attention, especially in Ellsworth, Kansas, a town sorely lacking in activity. Excitement had flurried the previous week when David Hastings arrived with his caravan of fifteen wagons filled with wool and copper ore. David once owned a store in Ellsworth, but sold it just that spring for a move to Trinidad, Colorado Territory. Since people knew him, they held genuine curiosity when he came all the way back to Kansas for supplies. And he had been attacked by Kiowas along the dry branch of the Santa Fe Trail, one of his teamsters killed. But even with this personal interest, the information came second hand, while the shooting of Johnny Tillison was here and now.

Elizabeth had been in Sheriff Sieber's office only ten minutes when Nathan Suggs pushed through the clot of citizens gathered outside. Suggs, slender-built with narrow shoulders, ran the two-week-old (and floundering) Ellsworth *Chronicler*. He still had a napkin tucked into the waist of his suit pants. A large crumb of cornbread nestled in the long beard under his dark mustache. Elizabeth looked away, surprised to find something amusing in this evening.

"I say, Sheriff. Someone's shot young Tillison?" Elizabeth was certain Suggs' precise way of talking was fake. "I trust you've apprehended the floozie who did it. Can't have decent citi—."

"Johnny Tillison is an upstart," the sheriff growled. "And it was self-defense. He had already knocked Miss Fortune, here, around; and he clipped Lester Nims."

Suggs looked at Elizabeth for the first time. "*She* shot him?" He stepped back and took in Elizabeth: brown hair pulled neatly into a twist on the back of her head, wearing her college glee club dress: a dark blue challis with white piping around the peplum, white ruffles at neck and sleeve. Elizabeth wore it to work just to make certain the customers didn't take her for one of the other women at Lady Faye's. "Why, she doesn't look the type," Suggs concluded.

The cornbread swayed in its dark, hairy nest. Someone chuckled and Elizabeth covered her twitching lips with the damp cloth that the dance-hall swamper, Lost Johnson, had given her.

"I was told that Hank said his brother was shot by some dance-hall tart and for no reason!" Suggs said, sidling toward the sheriff's desk.

"Well, if you've already put that to press, I'm sure Miss Fortune here will want you to print a retraction."

"No! Of course I haven't." He coughed into his hand. "And what caused the altercation, Miss—ah—Fortune?" The cornbread fell to the floor, and with it the slight humor Elizabeth had felt. From the pocket of his poorly-made suit coat, Suggs pulled out a pad of cut foolscap and a stubby pencil.

"Johnny lost at her table a few times and accused her of cheating," Sheriff Sieber answered for her.

"You're a dealer?" Suggs' eyebrows rose.

"Yes. And only a dealer!" Elizabeth replied.

Suggs asked questions in more detail than those of the sheriff. She gave vague answers about how long she had been in town and where she came from. Her stomach soured over the remembrance of how her grandfather had turned her out. Nathan Suggs sounded like a doctor when he gave a long and detailed rundown of Johnny's injuries. The sheriff nodded wearily; outside men coughed and scratched and spit. The smells of tobacco and too many people smothered Elizabeth. She leaned her hands on the dusty desktop, her head aching. Suggs addressed her again.

"It's a good thing you're a poor shot, Miss, or you'd be a murderer." Suggs eyed her resentfully, probably wishing she had killed Johnny; it made better press. "Shooting a man at that range. You even drew blood on his brother."

"If I'd intended to kill the man, he'd be dead," Elizabeth muttered.

"How's that?"

"Nothing."

A clean-shaven man standing nearby snickered. Elizabeth frowned at him. He grinned, brown eyes mischievous. She turned away, morose and achy.

"And how are you going to explain this to Gabe Tillison?" Suggs was saying to the sheriff.

"Gabe's not in town, thank the righteous." The sheriff stroked his long mustache, frowning over the deposition Elizabeth and the two most sober witnesses had signed.

"Sheriff Sieber," Elizabeth started. The throb in her head grew worse.

"But that bunch he's got working for him is tough," Suggs went on. "The Tillison name carries a lot of weight, from here all the way to Texas. What if they expect some legal action—some retribution?"

"Like what? Johnny started it. There were witnesses."

"Sheriff?" Elizabeth leaned on his desk.

"Sheriff Sieber." The brown-haired man who had snickered spoke loudly to get the sheriff's attention. "Is there anything else? The other witnesses have been allowed to leave and Miss Fortune's had a rough time of it." His boiled white shirt looked bright under a dark broadcloth vest. Suit trousers.

Elizabeth gave the man a tight smile, not wanting to be beholden for his help.

"Uh. I need where you're staying," the sheriff said to her. "It ain't the dance hall, I take it."

"Certainly not!" She held her head higher. "I'm at Larkins House. Room two-oh-four."

He scrawled that on the edge of the deposition. "Thank you, Miss. You can go."

The helpful man put on his dark brown hat and started to the door with her, but she gave him a hard look. "Thank you," she said, dismissing him. He pursed his lips, then gave her a courteous nod.

Curious onlookers stepped back when Elizabeth went out. They examined her like she was a circus star, and she swept passed them, feeling weak and lonely. Dust from a passing group of riders made the July twilight murky, but the long breath Elizabeth pulled in helped to clear her head.

"Miss 'Lizabuth, ma'am?" came a drawl. "Are you all right?"

Relieved to hear a friend, Elizabeth turned, but the pain in her jaw kept her from smiling at Lost. "I believe so, Mr. Johnson."

She always called him properly, although against his wishes. "It ain't seemly for no white woman to show me courtesy," Lost had told her. "Well, I ain't no white woman," she had snapped.

Elizabeth wished she could let down her guard and allow Lost to baby her. He was a chocolate-brown man and not much taller than she, with arms like sinew—a fatherly type who was good at nurturing. A father was what she wanted right then, and if her own father's cavalry regiment had been encamped at nearby Fort Harker rather than on the hot, barren lands of the Southwest, then she wouldn't have been dealing cards at Lady Faye's and none of this would have happened.

"How's Mr. Nims?" she asked. Taking long strides, she held her skirt primly and continued down the edge of the cinder-flecked street past a group of men from the railroad.

"Doin' all right." Lost followed a half pace behind her. "Got a crease in his skull, but he's awake and back at work. But Lady Faye—." Lost sighed. "She sent me to fetch you back to the dance hall, and she's real riled."

Elizabeth's shoulders sagged. She knew Faye didn't like her. Faye's husband, Bob, had hired Elizabeth. He even gave into Elizabeth's insistence that she would only deal cards, and would never work past midnight; he even allowed Elizabeth to keep five percent of her table's take, a stipulation no one ever before got out of Bob Wentworth. Bob smiled a lot when Elizabeth was around. But tonight, Bob was over in Wichita at the Wentworth's new establishment. Tonight, Lady Faye was in charge.

Lost escorted Elizabeth into the office at the back of the dance hall and Elizabeth frowned to see her own handbag open on the walnut desk, its contents spilled out. Faye Wentworth, her thin arms akimbo and hazel eyes hard on Elizabeth, screamed: "You're fired!" and went into a tirade about Elizabeth's continual impudence, and the proper way to treat customers. "Search her!" the woman ordered.

"Now, Lady Faye. You're bein' too hard on her," pot-bellied Lester

Nims said from where he stood near the door, a wrap of white bandage on his head. Lester shifted from one foot to another and chewed the corner of his black mustache.

"I said search her!" Faye's eyes narrowed to slits. "She cheated Johnny Tillison or none of this would have happened."

"Johnny was bad drunk, ma'am," Lost started.

"You keep out of it!" Faye marched around the desk. "Where'd you hide it? Coins will be easy to feel, even if you slid them in your corset." Faye slapped her hands along Elizabeth's bodice and indignant Elizabeth shoved her away. "Don't push me, you no good," Faye snapped. "My husband gave you a job, met your terms, then you do this to us!"

Faye reached for Elizabeth, and again Elizabeth jerked away. "I'll not be pawed at!" she said. "Just give me my wages and I'll be out of your way."

"Wages! When you've been stealing from us?"

"That's a lie! And you owe me for last week."

"It'll cost that much to get the bloodstains off the wall. Hold her, Lester. I'm going to find that money."

"Now Faye," came his feeble protest. But Faye's mood made him more concerned for his job than for Elizabeth. Not much employment in this town, and he had a family to feed. So when Faye demanded, "Hold her!" Lester grabbed Elizabeth's arms and pinned them to her side. "Sorry," he muttered. Lost left the room, embarrassed.

Elizabeth wrenched against Lester's hold. She knew that if she kicked Faye in the teeth, like she wanted to, the woman would press charges. Losing her job was bad enough, but being in jail was unthinkable, and considering the racial pretense under which she had gained employment, she wanted as little digging into her background as possible. She clenched her teeth and balled her hands to fists. Faye whipped up Elizabeth's blue skirt and reached to feel in her garters. Tears of outrage stung Elizabeth's eyes. The woman ripped a petticoat and squeezed all the material around Elizabeth's arms and legs, and by the time Faye was convinced Elizabeth had nothing on her but her clothing, Elizabeth had decided to fight regardless of the consequences. But Faye stalked back to her desk and Lester's grip eased.

Elizabeth spun away from Lester and glared after Faye. "Are you satisfied?" She marched to the desk in two strides.

Faye tossed a comb and coin bag, hotel room key and gloves into the blue draw-string purse and closed down the mouth.

Elizabeth's eyes narrowed. "The derringer," she said from between clenched teeth. She would truly fight for that silver-plated pistol.

"It's probably not even yours," Faye smirked.

"My brother gave me that gun, and my initials are on the side lock!"

Faye examined the side lock, frowned at Elizabeth and took the two.44 cartridges out of the little pistol's side-by-side chambers before she shoved the gun into the bag. "Get out of here." Faye's words didn't have the punch they held before.

"My pleasure!" Elizabeth snatched the handbag and strode to the door. Once outside, she slammed the door so hard it rattled the glass chimney on the brass desk lamp.

The sun set like an orange ball on top of the dust-covered cotton-woods and elms by the river, but the July evening hadn't cooled much. From a nearby street came the clatter of a wagon, and a horse snorted from the saloon hitching rail. In the stockyard a few cows called plaintively to each other. The town seemed as sullen and depressed as Elizabeth felt. She tugged at the peplum of her dress and frowned when she fingered the place where the piping was ripped. One of her slips hung to one side, and after she adjusted the torn nether garment, she opened her bag and checked the contents. The leather coin purse still held her luggage key, but there was no money. Three dollars, gone!

She whirled to the closed door of Faye's office. Her instincts nearly rushed her back in there to confront the thief, but common sense turned her away and set her shaky steps along the street. After she crossed the tracks, she sat on a split log that served as a bench before a vacant store. A dark mass of birds swept across the sky and settled into the trees, chirping madly while despair drained Elizabeth's energy.

That's what you get for trying to pass, nagged her conscience.

Of course, if she had let people know she was black, she wouldn't have been in the dance hall—would never have been hired. Then Hank Tillison wouldn't have gotten his hate nerve plucked and she wouldn't have shot his brother. "And I'd never have earned my stage fare to New Mexico," she muttered, trying to justify her deception.

But bitter irony darkened her thoughts. She still didn't have enough money and she had lost her ill-gotten job. In the long counting purse she kept in her portmanteau, her meager stash of coins amounted to forty dollars. Enough to by a decent horse or an old wagon, or for a farm family to live on for six to seven months; but when stage fare cost twenty-five cents per mile, forty dollars wasn't enough to pay the 700-mile trip to New Mexico. Unless she could spin gold from prairie grass, she had little chance of getting southwest anytime soon.

Larkins House, where Elizabeth had leased a room, was one of many stone buildings in town. It had a wooden verandah and two gilt windows near the door. The window of her small, second-floor room overlooked Douglas Street. Spare though it was, it seemed a real haven to her then. She lit the bedside lamp and went to the beechwood commode in front of an oval mirror. Limp curtains swayed in the half-breeze from the open window. She gingerly bathed the cuts on her cheek with cool water she had poured from the glazed pitcher into a basin. How to get to New Mexico was her main thought.

Discouragement hovered around her as she pulled off the dress, the small tie-on bustle, and two petticoats. She stripped out of the frilled pantaloons, a chemise, and light corset, then put on her long muslin nightgown and combed her waist-length hair. While working her long legs out of the dark stockings, she thought bitterly about her grandfather. Elizabeth blamed everything wrong in her life on him.

Actually, she might have looked back earlier than that—back to 1846 when the fair-haired Anne Clark with an eager, curious mind—Anne, who liked to ride fast horses—met the pecan-brown Samuel Fortune with the quick smile and soft voice—a man who read Rousseau essays in the evenings after they had both finished day work on the new school in the Roberts community. That was in Indiana. An industrious colony started by North Carolina slaves and Indians who escaped the tyranny of their old home.

She flung the cotton stockings toward her luggage. He could have at least waited until I graduated, Elizabeth thought. Although college graduation probably wouldn't have altered her circumstances any.

She wrote a brief line in her diary and laid it aside. "I can survive this," she muttered while cleaning the pen. With her thick hair pushed loosely into a sleeping snood, she turned out the lamp and laid back on the bed.

Elizabeth had a dream that night—one that had often flickered through her brain. A memory actually: *Grandmother Clark smiles, so eager to see her, holding out her arms for a hug as if Elizabeth were still a toddler. Her father unloads her belongings from the pack horse. Five men travel with him. All Minnesotans, off to join the first colored regiment allowed in the war. "Oh, Elizabeth!" Etta Clark's arms enfold her. "How wonderful you're here!" The powdery embrace crushes Elizabeth to the woman's lacy dress collar. Already as tall as Etta Clark, Elizabeth accepts the pale woman's hug, and over the woman's shoulder she sees her grandfather on the side porch, glowering; a sandy-haired boy stands beside him, his expression equally as harsh.*

"Are you sure, Elizabeth," her father's voice asks. Elizabeth turns to him. She keeps her chin high. "Yes. I'll be all right," she says, glancing at her stern grandfather. "For the Union." She forces a smile to her father. He disappears like morning fog under an August sun—fading, floating away. "For the Union," says her father's voice from the ebbing mist.

Elizabeth frowned and tossed on the bed, pulled toward wakefulness by the discomforting dream—and by something else. Something scuffed on the bare floor. Another strange sound. Elizabeth bolted up. A thick-knuckled hand clamped across her mouth, then someone slugged her in the stomach.

"Lousy nigger bitch."

Fear tumbled through Elizabeth like a waterfall.

"I don't like it none, Hank. It ain't right to do this," came a slow-spoken complaint from near the window.

"She's a nigger."

"She looks white to me. And you surely can't go around treatin' no white woman like this."

The ability to breath had barely returned to Elizabeth when Hank Tillison wrenched her backward across the bed.

"She ain't white. I seen enough woodpile niggers down home to know one. Hold her arms!" he ordered.

A third man grabbed Elizabeth's arms and forced them above her head. Her hair tumbled loose from the net bonnet as she twisted and fought. She strained to yell, but it came out as a gurgle when Hank stuffed the edge of the bedclothes in her mouth. She nearly gagged from the lump of material holding down her tongue; she tried to kick, but he sat on her legs and ripped at her nightdress down from the throat.

"Look at that long hair." A rough hand stroked her head. She jerked away. "Got skin like them Mexican wenches," the lean man said. His long-jawed profile had a prominent beaked nose. He easily held both her wrists with one large hand and gave a nervous laugh. "All creamy—"

Elizabeth flailed against his grip.

"I don't know, Hank," came the slow wheedling tone again. This from a huge bulk of a man silhouetted by the window who had never stepped further into the room. "Even if she ain't white, it don't seem—"

"Get out of here then, if you don't want a piece. Johnny had his arm cut off tonight 'cause of her. She owes us."

"'Twas Johnny's arm, Hank. I—"

"Shut the hell up!"

Hank undid the buttons on his trousers, slid his suspenders off his shoulders. He ripped Elizabeth's nightgown further, his fingernails scraping her skin. Elizabeth writhed with desperation. The tall man began tying her wrists to the bedstead.

And a knock came at the door.

The three men froze stock still, but Elizabeth moved when the second knock came with a soft call she knew to be Lost's. "'Lizabuth?" She made as much noise as she could with her mouth gagged and squirmed harder, hoping to unseat Hank from her legs so she could really kick. Hank smashed his hand onto her mouth, and jammed the back of her head into the pillow. He lay on her now and leaned his face close to hers. His breath smelled of whiskey and old food and hate.

"'Lizabuth!" Lost's voice had more insistence. "Are you all right?"

Elizabeth bucked her body, twisted her head under Hank's forbidding clamp. His other hand fumbled below her waist.

Because of her previous squirming, the tall man hadn't fastened her left arm securely and she pulled loose. Her fist connected with the tall man's whiskered face and he couldn't squelch a cry.

The giant jolted to leave and kicked the chamber pot into a table leg before he lumbered through the window. Elizabeth pulled Hank's hair, clawed hard at his ear, her nails gouging across his jaw.

"Goddamn!" Hank gasped.

"Let's go!" the third man insisted, tugging Hank's shoulder. Hank fell off the bed, his legs sticking up, trousers around his knees exposing a dingy cotton Union suit.

Elizabeth groaned as loudly as she could and started pulling at the stuffing in her mouth. Hank Tillison struggled up, rubbing at his bleeding face with one hand; he backhanded Elizabeth. Her head jerked to her shoulder; darkness flooded her mind but only for a second. Hank had just gotten onto the porch roof and Lost was still at the door when she regained her senses.

Feet skidded on the tar paper and knocked shingles to the street. "Who's out there?" came a call from another hotel room. But the three men got away without being seen.

Even after Elizabeth yanked the sheet from her mouth, the scream she intended wouldn't come. She gasped against dizziness and the pain in her jaw. The knotted leather that held her right arm finally gave way to her persistent fingers and she spilled herself from the bed, wrapped the sheet around her and made for the door.

"Oh, Lordy! What they done to you, 'Lizabuth?" came Lost's stunned whisper when she opened the door. "Oh, Lord!"

"You saved me, Mr. Johnson. Knocking on the door when you did. Please, I still need your help." She closed the door down to only a crack, and peeked out at Lost, acutely aware of her undress.

From the first floor, a groggy voice asked, "What's going on up there?"

Elizabeth and Lost jerked up tight, knowing they shouldn't be observed as they were. Lost being in the hotel this late would cause problems, and Elizabeth certainly couldn't speak to his credit dressed only in a sheet. If the night clerk could have heard thudding hearts, he would have gone upstairs to investigate, but silence sent him back to his cot in the small room off the downstairs hall.

"I'll fetch Dr. Duck," Lost whispered after they heard the door close.

"No! They didn't—. You got here in time." Had it been daylight, Elizabeth's cheeks would have shown bright crimson. "But I can't stay here."

"I'll get the sheriff, and then—"

"No. Mr. Johnson. Please. I can't remain here. I'm going to pack my things. Please." The fright and anger of the situation left her thoughts jumbled, but Elizabeth knew one thing: she couldn't spend the rest of the night in that room.

Lost nodded and thought. "You'll go to my place. My wife Phyllis will know what to do."

"Yes. Thank you." Just what she needed—comfort from another woman.

"I'll have a buckboard down at the back door in a flash," he said.

"Thank you."

Elizabeth closed the door; her knees wobbled. Fear locked in her chest like a vise. Only the heavy wooden door on which she leaned kept her upright. She blinked back hot tears and stared at the window, still open. She staggered over and forced it shut. After pulling together the dusty draperies, she fumbled for the lamp and lit it. The soft yellow glow relieved her only a little bit, because the smell of whiskey and stale to-bacco from those men, Hank Tillison especially, lingered. She scrubbed at her arms with the bed sheet, wanting to be rid of his touch, his odor. A sob wrenched from her and she slammed her fists onto the night table. Then she drew in several deep breaths, swallowed hard and started dress-ing.

By the time her luggage was packed, she had ordered her terror to subside and functioned with an outward calm that belied her anger and desolation.

Two

...This family [Johnson] *is truly special, and I'm certain if my mother had lived and the Fortunes stayed intact, we would have exuded the same warmth and generosity.*

2 August

It's a lucky thing Elizabeth was so honest and proud. If she had been like her brother Scott, she would never have had Lost Johnson for a friend and Lost wouldn't have come by the hotel when he got off work to warn her that Hank Tillison was talking and drinking himself into revenge. Nor would Lost have driven a buckboard to the back door of the hotel and packed Elizabeth and her luggage off to his house where his wife nursed Elizabeth's wounds and tucked her into bed like she was one of their own children.

Elizabeth had met Lost three weeks earlier when the train stopped in Ellsworth and she stepped out of the baggage car as if from her own private carriage, a stylish hat perched securely on her pinned-up dark hair. She was frightened, but refused to let it show. She dragged her overstuffed portmanteau and carried her hat box and valise, keeping her shoulders straight so as not to show the strain the luggage caused her. Several men rushed to aid her, but she ignored them. Lost Johnson had been there with three of his boys, watching the train come in. They were the only blacks there—the only blacks in Ellsworth—and Elizabeth had walked up to him, relieved and hopeful. She looked him right in the eye and said: "Your pardon, sir. Would you perchance know a place where a sister could find employment in this town?"

Lost looked her right back, just as honest. "You don't show what you're sayin', ma'am, so your best chance of findin' a job here would be

22

to hide what you're braggin'." He had his boys grab up her bags, and they led her to the respectable part of town.

Because of that meeting, Lost Johnson much admired Elizabeth Fortune and spoke highly of her to his wife Phyllis, even when Elizabeth let other people treat her white. Elizabeth found this deception as distasteful as burnt hominy, and Lost kept the act going better than she did, it being his suggestion. So now when she really needed one, Elizabeth had a friend. A family of friends.

The Johnson farm nestled in a fertile dale between humped hills a few miles from the Smoky Hill River. Behind a picket fence near the farm road, the main house was built of the native red sandstone, and a series of neat buildings spread back to cultivated fields.

That third morning at the Johnsons', Elizabeth roused herself from bed and washed up to the sound of an ax whacking into wood, and Phyllis Johnson humming in the next room while she kneaded bread dough. A dog barked excitedly. Elizabeth looked from the window and watched Mandy, a dark-skinned, sloe-eyed six-year-old, laugh and call to the brindle-colored dog she played with. Jemma, a brown-skinned girl with thick shoulder-length braids, came around the house with her hoe and ordered Mandy back into the fields. Jemma was nine. She waved to Elizabeth. Elizabeth smiled.

"Todd! You keep a better eye on Boudine," Phyllis called from the front of the house. "He's climbing into that hog pen again."

"Aw, Ma! Get the girls to do it." Todd, tall for his age, was ten. He wore a blue bandanna around his head to keep sweat from his eyes.

"They's busy in the cornfield. Let him stack wood for you."

Four-year-old Boudine, a tea-colored boy with looping brown curls, was a foster child. So was Jemma. Children left like excess baggage at the Johnsons' door, and the family's charity allowed them to take them in, as they had Elizabeth.

A few minutes later, Elizabeth entered the kitchen wearing her dark brown calico work dress. Corsetless and without a bustle, she felt comfortable. She had pinned her two long braids across the top of her head. The angles and planes of her face really stood out. Phyllis gave her a bright smile. "Well! You's lookin' much better today."

"The sleep made all the difference in the world," Elizabeth said. She rubbed at the healing scrapes on her right wrist—the ones from the leather thongs. "But now it's time you set me to work, Mrs. Johnson. I feel I've been malingering."

"Oh, pshaw, girl. After what you been through?" A short, dark woman, Phyllis wasn't fat, but carried a lot of bosom and even more hip, making her clothes always hang askew. Her wide face and flat, thick features were far from attractive, but her smile was radiant, and her voice rich and full of caring.

"You fly with crows, you get shot at," Elizabeth said. "I should have known better."

Phyllis laughed and put the bread dough into a crockery bowl and covered with a cloth. "Don't see how you's done nothin' wrong. A person's got to make their way how ever they can in this-here world."

"I've got to make my way southwest," Elizabeth said. "All my belongings have been shipped there. And my father is there. The only family I've really got," she muttered as she sat down at the table. Fear had edged her thoughts since her grandfather's letter. Would she ever again have a home? Family? Security? She picked through the sewing basket and took up one of Jemma's old dresses that needed to be hemmed for Mandy.

"Well, maybe you can get a job as a laundress out at the fort." Phyllis wiped her hands on her big plaid apron.

"That would take me months to earn enough money! Back east, stage fares are so low! I never knew it would cost so much to go west." She threaded a needle and started hemming.

"It's the distances," Phyllis said. "And the roads are rough on both the coaches and the horses."

"That must be why they charge by the mile. But it makes for outrageous prices." She sighed, pausing in her work. "Dear Houston. He sent me half of his savings before I left Oberlin. And spent money sending my trunks to Fort Union, too. I hate to tell him about this predicament."

"From what Able says." (Phyllis always called Lost by his rightful name of Able). "The town's still talkin' about how you shot that Tillison boy. It gets grander with each tellin', and folks would be even more on your side if you'd report to the sheriff what those men tried to do to you."

"I don't want to discuss that." A shiver of dread coursed through her. "I couldn't prove who they were anyway, so it's best not mentioned." She resumed her mending.

"The sympathy might help you get a job."

"Maybe." Elizabeth hadn't forgotten what the newspaperman said, that the Tillisons carried a lot of weight in the area. She knew just as many people thought her in the wrong as felt the shooting was justified. "I guess I'll have to keep on with this charade and check some other town for a clerking position."

"What you mean, charade?"

"Pretending to be white," she said through clenched teeth.

"Umm, um!" Phyllis shook her head. "You's the strangest high-yella gal I ever met. Most is aching to be thought white. Only Negro in you is your daddy's daddy, right?"

"Yes, but—"

"Goodness, you's more white than black, what with your mama and all."

"Mrs. Johnson, you know perfectly well society doesn't see it that way. Besides, I know the kind of girl you're talking about. I met some of them when I went to Fisk." That had been Elizabeth's first college experience. Her grandfather had hoped to marry her off to "one of her own kind." It almost worked.

"I think some of them did want to be white." She shook her head. "I certainly don't."

"Well, with the straits you's in now, only you knows what you is, and you look like a white girl," Phyllis declared. "Might as well take advantage when you can."

Elizabeth scowled. "I suppose." She closed off her stitching and cut the thread with her teeth.

"From what you've said, it sounds like your pa is into sodgerin' real good. So what you gonna do wid yo'self after you find him?" Phyllis asked.

"Well, there are schools at the forts. Daddy said they're required at the Negro garrisons. The fort chaplains run them, and I'm sure if they don't need help, the nearby towns do."

"And you know for sure your pa is at Fort Union?"

"His last two letters have come from there." Doubt nagged at Elizabeth. She set about rethreading a needle, not wanting to think about where her father might be or what information her grandfather Clark had withheld from her. "He keeps being sent on special assignments. At first he thought it a compliment because he was literate. Now he thinks its to keep him out of the politics. He's written letters to Congress, and had one printed in the *Washington Post* about the prejudice the troopers have had to face." Elizabeth smiled with pride.

"All those Southern territories was Confederate, too," Phyllis said. "Treatment must be awful. Why, right here in Kansas, they had terrible fights. Black and white sodgers tryin' to kill each other, even."

Elizabeth wielded the needle and thread as if work would cancel Phyllis's words. Even though she hadn't been with her father all these years, she couldn't imagine life if he were killed. The long letters he sent her had been like August rains to a parched prairie. And now over four months since the last one.

"He'll be glad to see you, I know, since you his only chil' left to him." Phyllis clucked her tongue. "I can't believe your grandpap would steal those boys off like that."

"The summer after my mother died," Elizabeth said. "I'll never forget." Elizabeth knew why she hadn't been kidnapped. She didn't look right. In Minnesota, her skin had been weather-tanned to a toasted-almond coloring that constantly reminded Wilson Clark of his daughter's rebellious marriage. Urban life had faded Elizabeth's sun coloring, and now her skin just had a mellow hue, rather like fresh dough. "And Daddy made trips to Indiana to get them back, even borrowed against the farm to hire lawyers." Elizabeth bit the inside of her lip, wanting the memories of those futile efforts to stop.

"But grandfather Clark—Mister Clark, I had to call him—that man is as unbending as a railroad tie," Elizabeth said, her voice tight.

"Your daddy must have been hard pressed to turn you over to him."

"No place else for me to go." She shrugged her shoulders straight. "Grandma Jannie died winter of '63 and the area men had already planned their join up." She sighed. "Grandmother Clark had been writing him to send me since the Santee Uprising." She picked up the blue cotton twist and rethreaded the needle. "My grandmother—." She shook her head, feeling the pain of her grandmother's death. "She always told me I was like my mother."

The Johnson's dog started barking and Phyllis looked past yellow ruffled curtains out of the window. "Well, looks like Philip home already, and it's only mid-morning."

Phyllis stepped out of the door. Elizabeth went, too, knowing Philip had planned to work all day with Able, Jr. at Sanderson's livery. Mandy and Jemma, standing in the big cornfield where the tasseled plants towered over their heads, had stopped hoeing to stare at Philip's running figure as he passed. Little Boudine dropped a piece of wood on Todd's foot; the older boy fussed, but only halfheartedly as he watched twelve-year-old Philip sprint out of the sunny east along the rutted road from town.

"Ma! Ma!" Philip dashed through the picket gate, his dark brow furrowed with concern. "It's the Tillisons," he panted. "They come to town to cart Johnny home, and the old man's lookin' for you, Miz 'Lizabuth. Junior sent me out to warn you, in case they ride this way."

The current issue of the skimpy tabloid Nathan Suggs called a paper held a front page story about the shooting, complete with a crude drawing of Elizabeth with a shotgun and Johnny blasted against a wall. Elizabeth knew this, and gruesome possibilities about a confrontation with Gabe Tillison harried her thoughts. She could imagine the spiteful things Hank had told him, and the Johnsons had informed her Tillison was an ex-Confederate.

"I have to leave," she said as she hurried to the girls' bedroom.

"Leave? Don't be redicalous," Phyllis said.

"I can't get you involved." Elizabeth dragged out her portmanteau and began stuffing in clothing.

Phyllis stood at the bedroom door. "We got our own selves involved. Besides, you really think they'd ride out here?"

"If you had seen that Hank Tillison." Elizabeth shook her head. "If he's an example of that family's attitude, they will come here. They must know that Mr. Johnson could know me. Where is Mr. Johnson?"

"He took a load of vegetables out to the fort." Phyllis frowned.

Elizabeth gathered her brush and a handkerchief. "I don't want any indication that I've ever been here. Tell the children. They've never heard of me!" She closed the portmanteau.

"And what you gonna do?" Phyllis didn't wait for an answer. "You go traipsin' up the road with that stuff and they git you for sure. We'll hide you."

"But Mrs. Johnson—" Elizabeth gripped her purse.

"We got a place," Phyllis said. "Philip, get her baggage out to the hay rack, cover it up good."

"Yes'm.

"Todd, go up on the rise and keep watch." He took off running.

The girls hurried over, eyes wide. "What's wrong?" Mandy asked.

"Well, let's say, we might be under attack," Phyllis said, her dark face frowning. "You know what to do, Jemma."

"Yes'm." She grabbed up Boudine.

"And Mandy, you take the basket." Phyllis handed the younger girl a basket that held a jug of water, a blanket and some jerky. The two girls trotted off toward the orchard, Boudine in tow.

Todd called, "I can see 'em! Six, seven riders maybe!"

Elizabeth put her hand to her mouth, imagining Hank Tillison already in the yard.

"Land o' mercy," Phyllis said. Perspiration dotted her brow. "Come on in here, Todd, and see to Miz 'Lizabuth. And Philip, tie up that rackety dog." She pushed Elizabeth toward the smaller house in the Johnson spread. "Don't you worry none. We done dealt with angry white folks before." She scanned the farm critically. "Git on with you." Phyllis picked up a broom and started sweeping Elizabeth's footprints out of the front house and the dusty yard.

In the old one-room soddy that served as the boys' bedroom, Todd drew back a rag rug and opened up a hatch in the floor. He went down the short wooden ladder into the root cellar. Elizabeth followed. The area was large enough for eight bushel bags of produce, or for several children to hide in during Indian attacks or tornadoes.

"Back here," Todd said, signaling her into the dark behind two baskets of potatoes.

Elizabeth stopped short, peering into the underground crawl space. Todd whisked heavy cobwebs from the dark entrance. "Go back there, and then push up the wooden floor piece to cover the hole," Todd instructed.

Elizabeth hesitated, unable to evade thoughts of poisonous spiders. Rattlesnakes liked cool dark dens in the summer, too.

"The tunnel go all the way out to the orchard where the girls is," he said. "But you jest stay here."

Elizabeth licked her lips, drew a long breath. The dog set up a terrible racket. The faint chink of spurs and metal horse equipment carried to

Elizabeth as the horsemen jogged their mounts up to the Johnson gate.

"They's here!" Todd said. He waved her toward to dark hole. She gathered her skirt tightly around her legs, drew in air. "Hurry, Miz 'Lizabuth!" Todd whispered.

She quickly stepped over the baskets and scooted into the space, pulling her body to a tight crouch to get beyond the wooden floor piece. Todd was already up the stairs. He closed the hatch. The dark was like looking into a boot. Elizabeth pushed up the fake wall. Silky threads of web brushed her face when she squirmed around to put her back to the wall. A moldy smell filled her nostrils, and she closed her eyes to keep them from straining against the dark. Her knees and skirt bunched by her chin, she shifted to find a more comfortable position. When her hand touched a moist, rotting potato on the dirt floor, she nearly screamed. She shrank against the earthen wall to her left, and clutched her purse, feeling the hard lump of the derringer within. Not much defense against six or seven men.

Maybe they aren't the Tillisons, she thought. But then she heard loud talking and Phyllis declaring she hadn't seen anyone. "Maybe they'll just believe that and leave," she whispered into her clenched fists. But next she heard the horses' footfall, the creak of leather, could even feel the vibrations when they passed close by, walking over where the escape tunnel extended under the yard. Dust sifted like powder along Elizabeth's hideout. The horses stopped, then—.

"I tell you, she's got to be out here!" Elizabeth recognized Hank's voice and bit her knuckles to squelch her fear. "That swamper buck at the dance hall was real friendly with her."

"Maybe he just rode her into Salina." Although muffled, Elizabeth knew that slow, wheezy voice was from the giant. "Him and the wagon is both gone."

"That's probably it, Gabe. Ain't no dance-hall woman gonna stay on this dirt farm with these spooks." She didn't know that voice, but it held a distinctive Southern drawl. If she could have seen the narrow-eyed man dressed in black, her fears would have doubled.

"She's one of 'em, I tell you!" Hank insisted.

"I don't know, Hank," labored the big man.

The horsemen moved off, but a commotion started and Philip yelled.

A pail toppled and the chickens clucked with alarm. A pig squealed some outrage and Elizabeth prayed for the girls and Boudine to stay hidden—for no one to get hurt. Someone entered the soddy, she could hear the beds being moved. She took hold of her derringer. Something crashed above her, then footsteps scuffed on the cellar steps. Elizabeth pressed her back on the wooden wall.

"Ain't nothin' down here," was a call. Retreat on the steps. The hatch banged into place.

When a carbine shot sounded outside, her heart froze. She had no way of knowing Todd's gun had fired into the air when Gabe Tillison lurched his horse into the boy. Tears of anger and fear burned her eyes.

In front of the main house, Gabe's brown, hawk-like eyes studied the farm from under bushy eyebrows. His mutton-chop whiskers jerked slightly as he clenched his teeth. He could tell that harming the stubby woman before him and her children, even if they were black, wouldn't make him any friends in Ellsworth. These farmers carried their own weight and would be respected for that, if nothing else. If they had been down-in-the-mouth begging types, he would have shot at least one of them out of spite.

"I know you know where she is," Gabe said to Phyllis as she gathered Todd to her. "So you jest tell that thar Fortune gal I'm gonna git her fer what she done to my boy. I'm gonna git her or—or sic the law on her. She'll pay!" Gabe belched and spit. "Let's go!" He wheeled his huge steel-dust horse toward the road.

This ugly confrontation was just a long silence to Elizabeth before she heard two more shots, these from pistols, followed closely by a shot-gun blast. Chickens cackled with hysteria. The dog's bark became more fierce and horses whinnied. Elizabeth clenched her hands so tightly her nails imprinted little curved lines on her palms; her mouth was dry. Through the earth she could feel the horses loping away, rumbling the ground.

The farmyard noises subsided, except for the chickens, and Todd came and yelled down to her that no one was hurt. Elizabeth released a tense sob of relief. Phyllis came and muttered something about, not much longer. "We ain't takin' no chances," she said. "Philip's out on the hill now, makin' sure they don't come back."

After ten long moments, Phyllis returned. "Philip counted all the horses and they's nearly to town already," she said as she pulled back the rug and opened the cellar door.

Elizabeth scooted from the wall, let it fall and scrambled out. "What were the shots? I was so frightened for you?" Elizabeth asked as she climbed into the soddy. She breathed in fresh air and brushed herself off. Her hands trembled.

"Oh, that fool Todd grabbed up his carbine, actin' tough." Phyllis shook her head. "I'm surprised that Tillison didn't shoot none of us. I ain't seen such a mean man in a long time."

Elizabeth hugged Phyllis. "Thank you," she whispered, thinking of all the tragedies that could have happened.

Lost returned from Fort Harker in late afternoon (his vegetable baskets empty and coin in his pocket), and only a broken window and trampled radish tops revealed there had been a problem at the farmhouse—and the unusual mid-week smell of stewed chicken. The children talked over each other, each wanting to tell the adventure and who was most brave and how it really happened. Todd kept showing the huge knot on his arm from when the horse knocked him down. Elizabeth said nothing, could only worry over the danger she had brought them. Even Philip's brag on how she had fixed Todd's trade gun didn't lessen the guilt she felt for what had happened.

"Seems anything to do with her hands, she does well," Phyllis said when Todd showed his father the carbine. "Cards, guns, and you should see the hem she took on a dress this morning."

"Where'd you learn gunsmithin', 'Lizabuth?" Lost asked. Boudine hugged his leg and Lost picked up the boy.

"My daddy did the work back in Minnesota. Learned it from Grandpa Fortune." She had already bragged to the Johnsons about George Fortune, a tinner and a gunbuilder. "The year of the bad drought, we made our seed money by traveling around repairing firearms. I helped him."

"Well, I'll say, that's a handy talent. Not so usual for a girl, though."

"No."

A girl should master sewing, be useful in the kitchen, and, according to her grandmother Clark, play the piano and quote a bit of Keats. Elizabeth didn't mind doing any of that, although the piano didn't appeal to her too much, and she preferred the contemporary John Greenleaf Whittier to the tragic Keats.

> *"Here is the place, right over the hill*
> *Runs the path I took;*
> *You can see the gap in the old wall still*
> *And the stepping-stones in the shallow brook."*

The vivid description in "Telling the Bees" so patterned her Minnesota farm, Elizabeth had been moved to tears when she first learned the poem (and she didn't cry readily); and *"Mistress Mary...dead and gone!"* became the farm and her father and all the good times past when she had done not only domestic chores, but had guided big mules to harrow straight in the fields, herded cattle, gone hunting, and ridden bareback on a frisky pony through bright, early snows.

Jemma told again how the girls had hidden with Boudine in the orchard and heard the shooting, and how they ran back when it was over.

"Papa. Papa," came Boudine's husky voice. He patted Lost's chest. "Papa. I was scared."

The little boy's words were like a slap to Elizabeth and she pinched her lips together, knowing she had to leave here as soon as possible.

"But the Tillisons have already been by here. They won't come back," Phyllis said later. The boys were tending outside chores, the girls in the bedroom folding clothes. Lost slowly ate the unplanned chicken dinner before he went to town for his night's work at the dance hall.

"They've got friends in town where I intended to find work. If they learn I'm still around, they'll be back, I'm sure of it. I have to leave the area as soon as possible." Elizabeth took bread from the oven, her hand wrapped twice with her apron, and set it on the cooling grate by the window.

"One of the boys can drive you back to Salina come morning. That'll be safer for you," Lost said.

"That's the wrong direction, Mr. Johnson, and it would add another five dollars to my stage fare south."

"Or maybe you should go into Topeka," Lost went on. "One of the Negro aid societies might could help you. That's what they're set up for."

"They're to help homeless freedmen," Elizabeth declared. Homeless and free seemed an odd blend to her. "I would never impose on that charity." She frowned out of the window.

Able, Jr. had gotten a ride from town with a friend and now slid from the back of that boy's mule. The friend laughed and waved, and Able called a farewell as he came into the yard, inspecting it with keen eyes. He scowled at the garden, waved to the younger boys and hurried on, not even stopping to pat the dog that frolicked around his feet. Long strides, suspenders over broad shoulders under his sweaty brown shirt. Elizabeth opened the door for the fourteen-year-old. He and Elizabeth were eye to eye.

His relief at seeing her made him grin. He looked a lot like his mother, buckeye brown with broad features. "Glad to see you're all right, Miz 'Lizabuth."

"A big thanks to you and Philip for that, Junior."

"'Twas just luck I overheard them like I did."

Mandy and Jemma bustled in, eyes bright, and anxious to tell their brother all that had happened. They fidgeted in the doorway.

"Papa, Mr. Sanderson wants me to work some more tomorrow and says for Philip to come, too. They's got a big order for Mr. Hastings. You know, who moved away this spring. He's takin' a load of supplies to New Mexico."

"I don't know why that man had to traipse off to start a store in the mountains," Lost said.

"It's 'cause his wife and little'n got took by sickness. Bad memories here," Phyllis said.

"Ummm. Well, things is bad down there, too. And I saw him at the fort today, trying to beg troopers to ride escort with his wagons," Lost said.

"Can't be sparin' no troopers for private freight what wid the Cheyenne kickin' up a fuss jest west of here." Phyllis sniffed with disdain.

"Oh, Junior. I brought you back more papers. *Topeka Commonwealth* and the *Times and Conservative* from Leavenworth."

"Thanks, Papa!"

"You got chores before them papers," Phyllis said as Philip went out.

"You can show off your readin' after that."

"Yes'm."

Phyllis beamed at Elizabeth after Junior left. "He been readin' since he was eight. Taught me. Taught the other children. Even Mandy can read a bit." Mandy grinned at her mother's praise. Phyllis went on. "And he wants to go to college!"

"Miz 'Lizabuth can read," Mandy said.

"She been to college, too," Jemma put in.

"Not too many folks travelin' west got the cree-dentials you got, 'Lizabuth," Lost said.

"But that schooling isn't doing me a whit of good," Elizabeth said glumly. Dealing cards, like Houston taught her, and repairing guns—the things men did—would get her by in the West.

Those thoughts and watching Junior at the pump, caused an elaborate plan to blossom.

THREE

*...I'm imagining me in a gossamer gown with a silk chemise,
lying in a hammock sipping lemonade. Ha!*

4 August

When Elizabeth Fortune took a notion to something, few people could get her to change her mind. To someone who really knew her, it would have seemed moderately predictable for morning to find her rolled in a blanket, sleeping on parched land near the Ellsworth stockyard. But when she told her plan to Phyllis and Lost Johnson, they were beside themselves with shock and disbelief.

Lost had come home from work at two in the morning, and under the shimmer of stars and wisp clouds, he believed he saw one of his boys leaning on the well wall. When he challenged the reason for being out at this hour, Elizabeth, dressed in some of Junior's clothes, wearing Philip's old brogans and with a bed-roll over her shoulder, turned: "It worked, Mrs. Johnson. I told you I could fool him."

"Lordy, 'Lizabuth. What you gone and done?" Lost said, jumping off his mule.

Phyllis came from the house shaking her head and carrying a coal-oil lamp. "She done cut off all that pretty hair and bound herself smooth under her shirt."

"This disguise will fool the Tillisons *and* get me a job." Elizabeth's voice was filled with zeal, although deep inside fear lurked like worms in the cabbage patch. "I'm going to sign on with Mr. Hastings' wagons. Work my way to New Mexico," Elizabeth told him. "When I can, I'll send you money for the damages done to your farm because of me."

"'Lizabuth, this is the most redicalous thing!"

35

Elizabeth knew this was as risky as hunting bear with a slingshot. But with her determination to reach New Mexico and avoid the Tillisons, this seemed the only way.

"I'm as tall as most boys around. I'll just inform people that I'm fourteen or fifteen since my voice isn't too deep."

"And you ain't got whiskers," Lost put in.

Elizabeth went on as if she didn't hear him. "I used to be quite good with a mule team. It will come back to me."

"No doubt," Lost said peevishly. "But it ain't right, actin' mannish."

"Only until I'm out of the Tillison territory."

Back in the house, Elizabeth stuffed a few more things into the blanket. "My luggage will be going with me—marked for E. Houston. I've left money for the freight charge."

"Junior's going to take the bags by to Hastings in the morning when he go," Phyllis said.

"Sounds like you in favor of this nonsense, Phyllis," Lost snapped.

"Oh, Able, I done talked myself near to death tryin' to undo her thoughts. Most we can do is help her all we can."

"You've done more for me already than anyone has in a long time," Elizabeth said. She hugged the shorter woman and then Lost, again impressed with her own height and having confidence the plan would work.

By morning, however, Elizabeth's confidence had ebbed. Sleeping on the ground wasn't anything. She'd done that before; but morning made her more than a shadow in the night. Now she had to walk, talk and act like a boy. The previous night, she had contemplated all this on her way into town and even practiced different walks until she found one she felt comfortable with. Trying to get her voice low in her throat had her muttering to herself. Luckily the road was empty, or people would have thought her daft. But now, the day seemed to dry up all that like it burned off the mist that hung over the stubby cottonwoods by the Smoky Hill River.

With a tight rein on fears riding in her, Elizabeth got up and folded her blanket, turning her back to the two men who were pissing near a fence post some ten yards to her left. She couldn't duplicate that male accomplishment. She jammed the straw hat onto her uncombed hair and sought a privy. The one near the railroad round house was noxious and fly filled. She held her breath while she used it, then started into town.

One huge thoroughfare ran east and west in Ellsworth and the railroad track cut it right down the middle, so it was called as two streets: South Main, with the dance-halls and saloons, was flanked behind by the river, while North Main, on the north side of the tracks, marked the edge of more respectable merchant and trade establishments and the rest of the town.

Elizabeth had seen enough of the south side of the tracks, so she kept to North Main, crossing Lincoln Street and then turning up Douglas, concentrating on how to adapt, concentrating so much that she bumped into a little girl who clutched a woman's hand. She mumbled an apology when the woman scowled, then remembered too late she should tip her hat to be proper. Stand aside for the ladies, she coached herself. Open doors, tip your hat.

But when she got near Mayer Goldsol's Old Reliable House, she neglected those manners. The brown-haired woman in a pale yellow dress sashaying from the general store was none other than Faye Wentworth. Elizabeth stopped directly in the woman's path.

"Rude boy. Get out of the way," Faye demanded.

Elizabeth moved slightly, and glared the hat box as Faye swept around her toward her buggy. Elizabeth wanted to rip it from the woman's hand and fling it into the street, certain the purchase had been made with the money Faye had stolen from her.

An elbow caught Elizabeth in the side as the hack started off. "She's a looker, ain't she?" a grubby man said. He reeked of dirty clothes and stale beer. Elizabeth's stomach flip-flopped, but she grunted "yeah" before she headed into the Goldsol's store. Her heart beat double-time when she thought of what could have happened if Faye had recognized her. But the disguise worked, she thought, after berating her lack of prudence.

The store, dimly lit by window light and hanging coal-oil lamps, had farm equipment hung from one wall. Musty smells came from the various bags of grains and flours, but the majority of the store consisted of rough planks propped on old barrels that held an exceptional variety of apparel and sundries. Elizabeth rummaged around and found herself another pair of britches and an oiled canvas rain poncho. Dealing cards for three weeks had softened her hands, so she splurged on a pair of pigskin work gloves. She bought a good pocket knife, and in all (including the money she had sent with Junior to pay to get her luggageput on the wagon train), had spent nearly half of her forty dollars.

Back outside, she felt more comfortable with her pack and her identity. She crossed the rutted street, long stepping over muck and enjoying the ability, with no worry that a petticoat might drag through the smelly excrement. At Beede's, a bigger general store, a boot display dominated one window. Philip's brogans, with cloth scraps stuffed in the toes so her heels wouldn't rub, had already relieved the usual pinch of women's dress shoes, so she wasn't tempted to make a purchase. But at the window by the door her fancy was caught by the array of firearms, from knuckledusters to a .50 caliber Hawkens, behind the iron grill. She admired the rich woods and intricate designs on the patch plates of the old long rifles and fowling pieces. Unable to resist, she made a pragmatic move and went inside. She needed a more trustworthy weapon than her derringer when she traveled with the freight wagons.

The fat-stomached gunsmith who rented this spot from Beede sat at a barrel-and-slat table off to one side. The rasp of his metal file as he worked chirred into Elizabeth's mind, reminding her of the nights she and her father would work on guns by lamp light after they finished farm chores. She stared through the glass cabinet at two authentic Deringers with curved walnut butts and wrought-iron barrels, then moved past an assortment of revolvers. She needed a rifle, a.44, so she could interchange cartridges with her derringer. She eased by a cow herder with run over boots and faded clothes. Of the various rifles and carbines under the glass, an iron-framed Winchester '66 drew her attention. Houston had once won one in a card game, and it had been all she could do to keep from begging him to give it to her. Not that her grandparents would have let her keep it. They hadn't even liked her having the derringer.

"May I see the Winchester, please," she asked, then silently rebuked herself. She shouldn't have sounded so timid; should have phrased the sentence as an order: Let me see that Winchester!

The long-bearded gunsmith looked her over. He shifted his tobacco chaw and snapped a suspender. "This ain't no curio shop, sonny," he said.

"I'm shopping to buy," she retorted.

He got up slowly, buttonholes of his drab shirt strained at his belly. "Well, I got some Springfields and used Remingtons down here. Might be more in your price range."

"I want to see the Winchester."

Elizabeth's stubbornness furthered her role as a boy, and right then she had her jaw set so it squared up her face, which was dirt smudged from her night on the ground and still held a bruise from Hank Tillison's knuckles. Her brown eyes glared with discontent. The gunsmith opened the display case and with greasy hands, pulled out the rifle.

The other customer looked at her and snorted. "What you want with a fine gun like that, kid. You don't need it to be an errand boy." He laughed.

Elizabeth glared at him.

"You lookin' to join with a cattle herd, ain't no one in this town hirin'," the gunsmith said.

Elizabeth ignored them both and examined the stock and action of the rifle. The chamber and magazine were empty, so Elizabeth put the neatly curved butt to her shoulder and sighted along the smooth barrel into a dark spot on the plank ceiling, pulled the trigger, levered it, sighted again. It wasn't heavy like many rifles, and not much more than a yard in length from barrel tip to butt. She squinted at the firing pin, noting that the gun had been used. She ran her fingers along the polished wood of the stock and examined the magazine and bore grooves.

"How much?" she asked slowly, recalling how little cash she had left.

The gunsmith frowned at her, and rubbed his whiskered chin. "I'm askin' twenty."

"Twenty?" She was shocked. The one Houston had won had been appraised at thirty-five. But she kept her head. "This isn't a new gun." She tried to sound as indignant as possible.

"That's why it's only twenty," the man quipped. He spit tobacco juice into the corner, certain this wouldn't be a sale. He had been trying to get rid of that rifle for two months, hoping a cattleman or even a villain would come through and buy it.

Elizabeth swallowed hard, her thoughts about having to fight bandits or Indians along the Santa Fe Trail all wrapped up with her desire for this piece.

"I knew you couldn't afford it." The man shook his head and reached for the gun. Elizabeth pulled back.

The cowboy chuckled low. "Git yerself a brass-framed Henry," he said. "That's all a Winchester really is—with a few changes."

She knew a Henry would be less expensive, but the longer she held the Winchester, the more she wanted it. "You include a hundred rounds and you have a sale," she said.

Five minutes later, Elizabeth walked out of the store and a rifle barrel and stock stuck out from either end of the bed-roll. The brass cartridges made heavier the old haversack Lost had given her. She had the bill of sale in her pocket, and one dollar plus change. Although her stomach growled from hunger, she headed toward the livery office to get her job.

Elms and broad-leafed cottonwoods shaded that part of town, their morning shadows stretching toward the river. The town's business buildings thinned out and she passed a neat yard of a small boardinghouse. Around the corner by the blacksmith shop, she headed south to the livery, but when she got close to the small, stone-front office, what she saw stopped her like she had been cast in bronze. The "Men Wanted" sign that had been in the window all the previous week was gone.

Worry caught in her stomach, making a hollow feeling. She glanced around the street, then moved under the trees which shaded the door of the slope-roofed building.

From inside came an angry voice. "You tol' us there'd be military along!"

A gravely growl started up. "Them Commanch is just out there waitin' for the Goddamns. We'll be sitting ducks."

This turmoil made Elizabeth hopeful. Pushing her hat lower on her forehead, she scowled and went in the open front door. A small window let in dim light, barely showing the side door that led to the corral area. The office was crowded by the two long-whiskered, sun-burnt men who harangued with a stocky man in a three-piece suit. From Lost's description, Elizabeth knew this was David Hastings. The short jacket of his coat stopped at his hips and his auburn whiskers flared across his jaw, touching the corners of his mouth.

"I hain' about to lose ma scalp to no fuckin' injuns at this date. You's only got twelve wagons. That hain' even enuf for a decent *co* rral." The speaker was in his late forties—pocked and grisly. "Five years ago you couldn'ta taken a train on the trail with less'n fifty wagons."

"An gittin' to Santy Fee before September's half through—! Ain't no way to make it, leavin' so late," the other man said.

"We've got a five span for each tandem, grain to feed them, and better rigs than any freight company," Hastings insisted.

"Yeah, but I hear tell you ain' got the money to pay us with after we git there."

"Who told you that? I'll have your pay and then some!"

The men shook their heads. "Nope. Count me out," the gravely-voiced one said.

They slouched for the door, flanking Elizabeth in a scent of unwashed barnyard, sweat and tobacco. She managed not to gag, and squelched a sudden panic over her plan. But here was her chance.

"That puts us to eleven drivers," a rangy, slit-eyed man said. Pure sinew and muscles, he wore leather pants, a dark calico shirt, and tall boots. His face, framed by graying hair to his collar, was scarred, weathered and tanned like a well-used saddle. His waist belt held a revolver and a Bowie knife hung in the sheath by his left hand.

"I realize that, Joe." Hastings paced and tossed down the cigar he had been worrying. He stopped in front of the desk, his stocky form blocking light. "Damn! I wish I knew who scared off my other drivers."

"Most likely it's rumor. Nothing planned," the walking whip cord said.

"Well, someone has to turn up. We've got to move out of here tomorrow!" The middle-aged freighter nodded, eased around a straight-backed chair and went out the side door, his Mexican spurs ringing. "We've got to," Hastings muttered to himself.

To Elizabeth, this paralleled her getting the job as dealer at Lady Faye's, where Lost had informed her one man had just quit, another had died from dysentery a week earlier. In she had walked. With her courage renewed she now said: "I've come to sign on."

Hastings did a quick turn and fixed her with a harsh scowl. "I need mule skinners, son. Not stable boys."

"You need fighters, too, and it isn't necessary to have the cavalry at my side for me to ride a trail."

Not at all the speech pattern of a trail-bred lad. Lost had told her she spoke too proper. To compensate, she kept a rugged stance, with her legs slightly apart, thumb hooked in the rope belt on her borrowed pants. "I got a good rifle and—."

"What's your name?" Hastings snapped.

Elizabeth blinked. This was one thing she hadn't thought to do—decide a name for herself. She surely couldn't say Fortune. "Clark." It came out spontaneously and she fumbled for a first name. "Uh. Zee Clark," she added.

Zee for Lizzie, the teasing name Houston always called her. The name her grandfather hated.

"You have family around here?"

"My—my mother's dead. My dad's in New Mexico. I'm headed south to be with him." She was glad she didn't have to lie about this, although reviewing her situation made her ache inside.

Hastings pondered her a while, then took up his cigar and paced to the other side of the room. "No no, son. This is going to be rough trip. I can't be responsible for—."

"You feed me, I'll work. If I work hard enough, you give me wages, too. I have to get south, Mr. Hastings." And I only have a dollar! railed her thoughts. Her heart bumped double-time in her chest.

Hastings studied her a moment, then said. "What do you think, Pritchard?"

Only then did Elizabeth notice another person in the room. He sat in the shadowed corner behind the desk, his feet propped on the wall. Slowly he lowered his legs and leaned forward into the faint light from the small window. He twirled a toothpick between his fingers and perused Elizabeth. Her insides went hollow as she took in the dark brown hat pushed back over wavy brown-yellow hair; she had seen him before. That he was somehow connected with the shooting last Sunday nagged at her.

He gave a slight laugh, then asked. "How old are you, kid?"

"Four—fifteen." Her voice caught a bit. "Got to get south to the rest of my family. Figure this is the easiest way."

"Easy!" Hastings shook his head and grimaced.

Casey Pritchard covered his smirk by pretending to cough. "Working a freight wagon isn't easy."

"I know that! But it's better than walking the trail alone." And that's surely what I'll have to do, Elizabeth realized. An alternate plan began in her mind.

"You've handled mules before?" Hastings went to the desk, still in doubt. He struck a match, drew the flame to his cigar, then lit the lamp on the desk edge. The dingy light only marginally brightened the room, but Elizabeth felt the men's scrutiny as if she were standing by a bonfire.

"A foursome on a Conestoga," she said.

Hastings scowled at her again. "I don't know."

Pritchard unfolded his 6'2" frame and strolled to the front of the desk, his intense brown-eyed gaze never leaving Elizabeth. A faint smile played on his lips. He was dressed like a teamster: tall boots, canvas pants, blue shirt. He had a wide purple bandanna tied at his neck, a Bowie knife in his belt and a pistol strapped to his waist. He wore it with the engraved silver butt plate on the walnut handle forward on his right hip.

With his arms folded over his broad chest, he scowled at her. "Do you know how far it is to Santa Fe?" Pritchard didn't wait for an answer. "We'll be going through harsh country with snakes and all kinds of bugs."

Elizabeth shrugged, confused by his sarcasm. Hastings blew air through his thin lips.

"Maybe Zee Clark can do the hookup work," Pritchard went on. "It would be good to have another herder. Less strain on the teamsters. You think you can handle that, kid? Watching the mules; cleaning up after them in camp; scraping crap out of their hooves before we get rolling?"

She acted like she didn't hear this man's taunting words, and Casey Pritchard sighed heavily and said, "Well, you might as well hire him, Dave. I get a feeling he'll be tagging along behind the wagons anyway."

He seemed to know Elizabeth's thoughts, and she gave him a startled look. She often wished she could read people's minds and this was one of those times.

"Uh," Hastings glowered at her. "If you say so, Pritchard. I guess I'd rather have him in the camp than spooking the animals by hanging out in the shadows." He went around the big desk. "Here, Clark. Sign in. You'll get a dollar a day, paid out when the train reaches Santa Fe."

"I thought muleskinners got paid more than that," she said.

Casey Pritchard snickered.

"You aren't a muleskinner," Hastings said. His disgusted tone made Elizabeth hesitate and clutch the strap on her bed-roll.

Hastings looked up, impatient. "You got to sign or make your mark, son."

"I can write," Elizabeth declared. She strode to the desk.

Pritchard didn't move—was so close to her left side that her shirt brushed along his pants. Without removing her gloves, she dipped the pen nib into the inkwell and signed, *Zee Clark*

"What does Zee stand for?" Pritchard asked.

"Zebulon."

The quickly concocted Zebulon Clark shook hands with Mr. Hastings, and was relieved that Casey Pritchard didn't offer his hand.

"Here's a credit authorization." Hastings handed her a paper.

"Sir?"

"Go to Beede's and buy yourself some decent boots; they'll come out of your pay at the end. The rest of your gear looks okay. I've got a trail cook, so you don't need any mess supplies." He pulled a watch from his vest pocket, glanced at it, then snapped the cover closed. "Be back at the corrals by two this afternoon."

"Yes, sir."

Relief made Elizabeth's legs rubbery. Her pulse raced as she left the building and headed up town to buy boots and spend her dwindling cash on breakfast. But she had her job! She managed not to swing her hips and leaned forward over her knees, certain someone was watching her.

She was right.

Casey Pritchard set a muscular shoulder on the door frame, brown eyes intent on her.

"He might prove up. Got spunk," Hastings said, coming beside the taller man.

"Yep. Spunk." Pritchard scowled. "That's the hellfire truth if ever I heard it."

Set in the rolling humps of land along the Smoky Hill River, Ellsworth doesn't get the continual wind like in Wichita or even Salina. Sometimes summer heat seems to collect over those hollows like a cap, stilling the air and letting every smell and grain of dust linger and cling to the skin and clothing.

It was that kind of afternoon when Elizabeth reported to work at the wagon yard. Perspiration dribbled from her hairline along her jaw, traced the curve of muscle on her neck before getting absorbed by the cotton shirt. The padding she had wound around herself to smooth out womanly curves on her chest made her look brawnier, but it itched and was uncomfortable. A rough bunch of teamsters stood in the shade talking and laughing and spitting. Their voices were deep and harsh; most were unshaven; their clothes already grubby even though they were in town.

Elizabeth gritted her teeth. What have I gotten into? she thought.

"Clark!" called the whipcord wagon master she had seen earlier. "Rig out that new mule there," Joe MacGrin said. He walked away as if unconcerned.

Elizabeth shivered a bit even in the heat as she eyed the beast that stood straddle-legged near an empty Dearborn wagon in the corral. She had worked mules before, albeit it was seven years ago, and knew she couldn't walk up and toss leather and chains on a green mule without a real battle. While she examined the traces, tightened the strapping and lined out the guide poles of the complicated rigging slung over the corral fence, she recognized something that comes to most folks as they age: caution. She had no desire to get battered and stomped by a half-ton creature, a circumstance she couldn't remember worrying about when she was twelve. She tried not to worry about it now, either, because she had to do this and had to do it right. The equipment was nearly as expensive as the mule, and if she wrecked either of them, her new job would vanish like snow in an oven.

Elizabeth looked the mule over when she entered the corral, its size convincing her it must have had a draft horse for a mother. Nearly sixteen hands high, its nose was as long as Elizabeth's forearm with ears to match. It scrunched up its big lips when she came into its space, showing green-stained teeth as it brayed a warning. Elizabeth was going to see a lot of that ugly face, because the first rule on this job was to stay far away from the mule's back end. Elizabeth had always been convinced that if a mule had toes, it could stand on two of them and do all kinds of acrobatics with the rest of its body, each move designed to repel what the ornery beast wanted no part of, which in this case would be any human.

By the time Elizabeth got the animal roped and snubbed to the bronc post in the middle of the corral, she appreciated her padding. The butts and shoves she received from the mule's big head would leave her sore, but she wouldn't bruise. Her legs would surely ache as much as her shoulders and arms, because she had to sprint away from angry kicks while she got it contained. She barely had the energy to handle the halter and rigging after that, but she did, gasping for breath, sweat soaking her shirt and the waist of her pants, hat gone and wisps of hair sticking to her forehead. The mule pivoted, even with the confining hobble she had tied, and knocked her flat into the dust. She bolted to her feet, and while she was latching it to the guy poles of the wagon, she realized why muleskinners used so much profanity. Words formed in her head as she glared at the beast and finished her work. She only hoped she hadn't taken longer to do this than Joe MacGrin expected.

The strain withstanding, she grabbed her hat and batted the dust from it. "Shall we let him at it?" she called.

The audience her work had drawn stunned her. All the teamsters, and David Hastings looked on, and a tall sullen-looking kid who sneered when she looked his way. Philip and Able Jr. hung on the far side of the corral and she prayed that if they recognized her they wouldn't give her away.

"Yep. Let 'im fly," Joe said after eyeing the rigging to see that Elizabeth had it properly set.

Elizabeth undid the hobble and took up the end of her catch rope. She backed off and gave a single tug which released the mule from the post. She was on the off-side of the creature and knew it would circle inward, wanting to fling its powerful legs and hoofs in her direction. It couldn't. Elizabeth coiled the rope and kept her tired pace steady to the corral fence while the animal yee-hawed and tried to escape the trailing wagon.

The teamsters and Joe MacGrin seemed satisfied; but Casey Pritchard came over to her as she got a dipper of water from the barrel beside the livery office. Elizabeth swallowed a sudden fear and acted like he wasn't there, even when he leaned on the wall only a foot and a half in front of her.

"Just what are you trying to prove?" he asked. His keen eyes scowled at her and his tanned face held a frown.

"I'm doing my job. What's it to you?" She started away.

He stopped her with a hand on her arm, his fingers creating just enough pressure for her to know he could exert more. Her aching muscles quivered under his slight grip. "Let me put it another way." He glanced around, then said. "I know who you are."

Elizabeth's pulse throbbed in her throat and temples. She tried to act offhand and shrugged away from his touch. "I guess you do. You were in the office when I signed on this morning."

"Right. And I was in the sheriff's office Sunday—Miss Fortune."

She looked up at him, meeting his brown eyes. This was the man who had interceded for her so she could leave the office. Her nostrils flared slightly and she glared at him. "What I do or why is none of your concern."

"That's true, but I like a mystery. Do you really think you can pull this off?"

"I'm doing all right so far." Doubt of her abilities was something Elizabeth couldn't bear.

"You've only had the job for three hours. It's going to take over a month to get to Santa Fe. Seven weeks of work like you just finished and worse!"

Elizabeth's stomach kinked up like wet wool. Seven weeks with these loud, smelly men. Nearly two months! But she didn't show her fear when she retorted. "Maybe longer if you keep me from my work."

As if given a cue, Joe MacGrin called to her, pointing out a slew of harnesses he wanted readied for the mules. "Yes, sir!" She forced her tired legs to move toward the cart he had indicated. Pritchard kept step beside her.

"I can't believe you cut off your beautiful hair." His hand played along the shorten locks at the back of her neck. "You're a remarkable looking woman, Miss Fortune."

She stopped and faced him. His hand stayed on her shoulder and if she hadn't been too upset with him to notice, his admiring look might have made her flush.

"The name's Zee Clark, and I have a question for you, Mr. Pritchard. One the teamsters are probably asking themselves right now." She kept her voice low and fixed him with a scowl. "Do you always go around trying to seduce young men?"

His hand came away from her like she was a glowing forge, and his worried eyes scanned their surroundings. No one had paid them any attention.

"All right—Zee. You can do what you want."

"And be who I want?" Pleading wasn't her style, but she would do it if that was what it would take for him to keep his silence about her.

"Right. Be who you want, like any other free white American."

"I'm not white!" she growled.

Her spontaneous words took her breath away and caused Casey Pritchard's gaze to sharpen. She had overreacted to a common phrase of the day, a phrase most people said without even thinking. Her brother Scott teased her with the words, knowing his acceptance of the white world infuriated her. Elizabeth's hands went cold thinking her hair-trigger response might send Pritchard running to Hastings.

A smile played on Casey's lips. "Okay—Señorito Clark." His hand went up as if to tip his hat, but he caught himself and rubbed the back of his neck before he started off, shaking his head.

Elizabeth let out a long, relieved breath as she continued to the work Joe had assigned her. She glanced at Casey strolling off. He didn't look back, and she wondered if he would keep his word and how much of a hassle he would give her during this trip.

The binding around Elizabeth's chest chafed under her left arm and she worked her shoulder, peeved by the discomfort. Then she remembered the part she was playing, reached boldly inside her shirt and gave a relieving scratch. The advantages to this role started building up in her mind: She could belch or scratch whenever she felt like it, and she could perspire all over her clothes and not care. She'd be expected to lean on counters, use a toothpick, not clean her nails; and wearing britches let her bend and kick and climb without exposing anything unseemly.

During the first days on the trail, however, she learned she also had to listen to ribald stories, be the brunt of teasing that always came to young men, and hold back her bodily functions until she could sneak to some secluded bush. She had to hear men fart and make jokes about it, and laugh over their sexual exploits. She got friendly whacks on her shoulders that left bruises, glimpsed men's private parts more than she ever cared to, and was exposed to profanity that far outdid what her brother Houston used.

When darkness settled, Elizabeth got skittish, afraid someone other than Casey Pritchard knew her identity or that he told someone. He wasn't with the wagons those first days, and she hoped he wouldn't show up at all. But she kept her derringer handy and stayed out of people's way as she cleaned the Winchester over and over. She even leveled it at a stocky shadow who came on her too quietly.

"Easy there, Button," the man said, backing off.

Elizabeth worried about his approach and her own jumpy nerves, and when she rolled into her blanket that first night (derringer at her fingertips) and the camp became quiet, she listened to the night sounds and stared at the star-littered sky. Tears crowded her eyes and she blinked them back, thinking how, right then, her father might be in some far-off soldier camp studying the same stars.

FOUR

...I could find this amusing if it weren't so dreadful. It surely would be nice to come upon an outhouse in this spectacular terrain. I have bites in the most impossible places.

6 August

"Stretch em' out!"

That call from the rangy wagon boss, Joe MacGrin, started the train moving in the mornings, but it was by no means the start of the day. Before dawn, the other day herder rousted Zee Clark from "his" blankets. Without even a sip of coffee, Elizabeth would shake out her boots and pull them on, tying her belt as she went. She would grab up a heavy rope and stumble about in the dark, hazing the mules toward the wagons.

This was no easy task. Eight Conestoga tandems, which carried nearly thirty-five thousand pounds of farm seed, food stuffs and sundries to stock Hastings' new store, needed five span—ten mules—each. Then four J. Murphy wagons each held four thousand pounds of cabinetry, as well as machinery and lengths of piping Hastings had contracted to take to the reopened copper mines south of Santa Fe. These wagons needed four spans each—another thirty-two animals. The Mexican cook, Jorge Estévez, drove the mess wagon with attached supply cart, using another four mules. Eighteen extra critters, just in case, along with ten riding horses, so the herders rounded up over 120 animals every morning.

That first night on the trail, after covering only ten miles, many of the animals had been picketed to their wagon tongues so they wouldn't head back toward Ellsworth and grain and civilized lights they seemed to have a yen for. But as each plodding mile carried them farther from structured civilization, the animals were let to roam, with the night herder keeping them moderately contained.

Elizabeth also aided teamsters with hookups, and hauled water to fill the barrels strapped on the sides of the mess wagon, and she ran more errands than she thought possible. "Zee! Go out there and scrounge firewood for our next meal!" would be an order, or "Hey, kid, get your ass over here and put liniment on my mules while I take a leak." "Zee! We need water over here for the strappings!" "Where's that hammer I asked for, Clark?" Elizabeth's head ached from the amount of cussing and heehawing by the muleskinners and their beasts (they each seemed to know how to do both) and the incessant barking of the cook's piebald terrier, called Dog by the teamsters.

By the time Joe called "stretch 'em out!" and the teamsters snapped their long whips over the lead mules' ears, sometimes two or three hours had passed, all without food. Elizabeth learned real fast to tuck away a piece of hardtack from evening meal to munch on in the morning, because after the wagons finally started, two abreast on the trail, Joe MacGrin kept them at it until after midday.

Those first days out, the scant clouds were high and pale like streaks of steam. Within her new gloves, Elizabeth's hands formed calluses across the palm, and in her new boots, her feet blistered. These were over-the-ankle, lace-up boots. The store keep had convinced Zee Clark they'd be the best since she—he—had such narrow feet, and the man insisted a size larger would be better since feet of a young man like Zee would still be growing. The tongue kept slipping. Elizabeth already had raw spots along her heels and the extra socks she wore made her feet sweat more than the rest of her, which was considerable. Mosquitoes and flies bit. Swarms of gnats gusted up from thick patches of buffalo grass. She was glad she could scratch without recrimination, because she had to do that a lot.

When they camped, the smells of unwash wafted from everything: mule sweat, mule shit, dirty men, grease, tobacco, urine. She tried to bathe her face and neck at each nooning and always brushed her teeth, but the itching was the worst. While walking along the broad, rutted trail, she kept alert for any chickweeds, wild onions or other herbs she knew could relieve her misery. Jannie Fortune had taught her about herbs.

By the second evening they had gone twenty miles more to Walnut

51

Creek near the Great Bend of the Arkansas. This was where the military road from Ellsworth joined up with the Santa Fe Trail. They camped at old Fort Zarah which had been vital when wagon trains of 100 or more vehicles used the trail, and the Osage and Kiowa made sport by terrorizing travelers. But those days were gone and the fort had been closed the previous year. Its abandoned sandstone buildings reminded Elizabeth all the more how desolate this trip was going to be.

The Arkansas River, a few miles on and filled with very little water, looked desolate, too. Elizabeth, familiar with the waters of the Wabash, the Mississippi and the Cumberland Rivers, was taken aback by this wide trough where sandbars, often covered with grass and weeds, humped from the center like boggy islands. At some points she could have walked nearly the full width of the river without getting her ankles wet. Pools stagnated under clouds of mosquitoes, and beyond this stretched the plains. Elizabeth and her *compadres* were specks crawling along this paunch of relentless brown land where shoulder high grass undulated in the steady breezes, and rippled smooth light-brown under the sun's glare.

"The critturs are pullin' real good," muleskinner Seth Landers said during the nooning the third day out. He looked the part of his profession, with his blue shirt and long hair and brawny arms. His full brown beard reached nearly to the middle of his broad chest.

All the wagons had stopped in the shade of Pawnee Rock. The broad sandstone cliff with a grassy top that poked over seventy feet above the prairie, sloped north and if her feet hadn't hurt so much, Elizabeth would have climbed the prominence to look out over the vastness and various trails, much the way Indian scouts did when they planned attacks on the wagon trains back in the mid-'60s. But her feet throbbed, so she stayed put.

"Ground's hard, road's in fine condition." Landers poked at the side meat on his tin plate with a rolled tortilla. The flat cornmeal rounds Jorge Estévez made were new to Elizabeth, but like the men of the train, she enjoyed the added flavor they gave to a meal.

"If the weather holds, we can make twenty miles a day, easy," Joe MacGrin said.

"The moon's in its growth and rising early. Keep pushing past sunset," Hastings said.

Elizabeth and a few others glanced toward Mervin Gaynor, who had already protested working on Sunday. Mervin, who looked too puny for the amount of work he did, and Don Suther sat away from the others, Mervin holding open his Bible and talking. If Mervin hadn't mentioned it, however, Elizabeth would not have remembered the day of the week.

One week ago, she shot Johnny Tillison.

The shocked horror in his eyes occasionally flashed to her mind and made her draw a sharp breath. Then Hank Tillison's face would appear, filled with hate, his hot breath on her neck as he pressed her against the bed. She couldn't keep herself from cringing.

"If the animals hold up, go till nine or ten o'clock," Hastings continued. "Maybe get over twenty-five miles a day. I brought enough grain, so they don't need to graze a lot."

The teamsters nearby didn't seem to bat an eye at Hastings' order, but the thought of not stopping until ten that evening galled Elizabeth. By the time they unhitched and settled the animals, set up sleeping quarters and ate, it would be close to midnight before she'd get into her blanket.

"How are you doing, son?" Hastings asked from across the ragged circle that included her and the eight other people who made up the first mess.

Elizabeth shrank from the question, wanting to stay unnoticed.

"He's doin' a good job," Joe answered for her. "But you need to take care of those feet, Zee. I seen you limping some."

"Get out of them boots while you're resting. Let the sun bake up the pus," Pete Hayward suggested. Except for his coloring, Pete Hayward was a lot like Lost Johnson. Small, wiry but with obvious strength and a real good heart. He had given Elizabeth a big bandanna the first day out to tie around her neck and protect it from sunburn. Pete tossed part of his tortilla to Dog who sat on the perimeter just hoping for a handout.

"That sun's about to bake us all into the ground," Willie MacGrin said. "Barely got enough water left in me to piss."

Willie was Joe's son: tall like his dad, with straight dark hair that he kept pushing back from his face with big hands. He had sneered at Elizabeth at the corral when she was tested with the green mule. Although he was sixteen, three years younger than Elizabeth Fortune, his reality saw him a year older than the boy, Zee Clark, and he was real glad to have Zee around to take some of the ribbing off him. He threw a rock at Dog. "You like this kind of heat, Zee? You get this kind of heat where you come from?" he went on, glowering at her.

Elizabeth concentrated on eating. In some ways the openness did remind her of Waseca County where she grew up in Minnesota—where the wind continually blew and the hills were just small lumps against the horizon. Minnesota had more water, with lakes and creeks and natural springs. And the people there were a whole lot different. People of color. The farm next to the Fortune's was owned by French Chippewas, and one black family in the next county had been there for three generations. Her Grandma Jannie always said it reminded her of the Roberts settlement in the first few years. Indian and black people living and working together. Elizabeth wondered about her old neighbors, and hoped the hate hadn't touched them as it had the Roberts settlement—as it had her own life.

"So. This easy way to get south is doing you fine, huh boy?" The teamster beside her chuckled. A squat, muscular man with scraggly brown beard and wide-set gray eyes, Al Guzlowski had signed on after Elizabeth, the twelfth driver, and his accent marked him as a recent immigrant not just to the West, but to the continent. Scarred hands and thick knuckles proved he had been a rail layer for the Kansas & Pacific; the prejudice of some of the Irish workers had made him change jobs. Like Willie, he was glad not to be the object of ridicule and easily turned it on someone else.

He poked Elizabeth with his elbow as she lifted her tin cup to take a drink of coffee. A hot dollop soaked into her dusty pants. Willie guffawed.

"Huh, Zee? I hear about that," Guzlowski said.

David Hastings had told that story, but not knowing this, Elizabeth wanted to glare at Casey Pritchard. He had shown up sometime during the night, and when Elizabeth saw him that morning, her pulse thumped heavily with wonder of when he would expose her. Right now, however, he stood at the picket line, checking a hoof on his unique black spotted white horse.

"Mebbe we ought to get Zee up there on one of them bad-assed nigh-wheelers, let him handle the whip a awhile," Dodie Watson's gruff voice crackled. He grinned from behind his thick gray beard. Dodie had been the shadow Elizabeth had aimed her rifle at the first night out.

"When are we starting up again?" Hastings suddenly asked Joe. His tension brought a silence to the others. They stuffed their mouths with the end of their meal.

"After the heat slows, as usual," Joe said.

"It's one and a quarter now. I want to be moving no later than three o'clock," Hastings said. He snapped closed a silver watch and pushed it into the little pocket on his leather vest before he got up and strode off to join Casey Pritchard.

Forks scraped on tin plates. Someone belched. No one said a word, although they all knew David had high expectations for this trip.

Elizabeth could have told David something about fate changing expectations (not that he would have listened) like the hard times that forced her father to sell the Minnesota farm after the war; and her grandfather kicking her out *before* she graduated college; the high cost of stage fare. Then losing her job at Lady Faye's—and why. Elizabeth was used to things never going as planned.

David Hastings should have been used to that, too. This whole freight-wagon trek from and to New Mexico occurred because things hadn't gone as planned. Hard times in Ellsworth made the Hastings brothers decide to move their establishment, and the younger Jake took his new bride southwest in search of a more productive location. *Trinidad* he wrote David last November. *An active stage route, and the railroad coming.* Jake settled on a small homestead and also bought a store—or at least he thought he had. *A good building with stock included not too far off Commerce St.*, he informed David. But by the time David had sold the Ellsworth business and made financial arrangements, packed his two young children and elderly house-keeper, and set off for southern Colorado Territory, the whole scheme of things had changed, forcing this return trip which had been a disaster. Things certainly hadn't gone as planned, yet David still wasn't realistic about the hazards of the trail.

Ash Creek, a puny cut in the landscape, was August dry. It ran a ragged trough across the trail about five miles south from Pawnee Rock. Over five feet deep and chocked with protrusions of rock and root, the banks were grooved at two distinct levels from rushing water. Thin-trunked trees outlined the banks and offered some of the only shade in over three miles.

Most people had managed a nap during the nooning, Elizabeth included; but as the others moved easily along under the hot sun, she struggled, bothered by her abused feet. In the welcome shade by the empty water course, Elizabeth sat on the flat of shale as teamsters guided the sure-footed mules down the steep talus and across the dry ford. Wheels crunched and bumped on rocks. Dog sat down beside her. Bluebirds and meadowlarks flittered to higher branches and their twitterings were lost in the creaks and screeches of the lumbering wagons. Traces clanked and the men cussed encouragement to their teams: "Git on, you club-footed sons of Satan!" came a call. Dust fogged up from the dry ground. In the hot blue sky, bright white clouds towered from the southwestern horizon like heaps of clean sheets. Hawks wavered against them, looking like distant black kites.

Elizabeth patted Dog, pulled off her boots, straightened the long tongue of the left one and put it back on.

Joe MacGrin rode by on his big sorrel horse. "Problems?" he asked, peering down. His long graying hair was tied at the nape of his neck with a leather thong and his eyes set like slits in his weathered face. Dog leaped off to chase a startled ground squirrel, a snarly bark in his throat.

"No, sir. Just retying my boot." Elizabeth kept her head down, worried by Joe's attention. Sitting with her knees apart, Elizabeth forced a belch as she tied her work boot. Joe rode on.

At the beginning of the trip, Elizabeth had fiddled with her boots so everyone else would pass her and she could find a bush to squat behind. Now her feet hurt so badly, she wished she could put on Philip's brogans. But they didn't give the ankle support she needed for walking the bumpy trail and crossing steep-walled stream beds like Ash Creek. Nor would they protect against rattler fangs, a constant worry in rough country.

She smoothed the sock on her other foot. It had stuck to blisters on her instep and fresh blood dotted the gray wool. Gingerly, she fitted the boot back onto her foot, grimacing as she secured the laces. She contemplated the days ahead of work, and endless heat and grime. Gritting her teeth, she changed focus to her father, imagining his great, open laugh and the dancing light in his brown eyes. She could hear his voice in her head, too, insisting that nothing was impossible, and how diligence to duty and honor would always bring benefits. She wasn't sure how much honor her present situation offered, but gave a grim smile because now she was fifty miles closer to Fort Union than she had been two weeks ago. That was something.

The hot breeze gusted more dust around her. Another team and wagon passed. "Haw! Can't take this god damn hill like a race track. Hold back there!" *Snap!* the whip's order.

Mules snorted and grumbled. Dodie Watson, a teamster for eighteen years, had taken to the wagon seat of his Conestoga. He stood on the rail, brake on and hauling rein on the big nigh-wheelers that braced the weight of the tandem on the descent. The friction brake screeched; the wagon rumbled by, then the short tongue and the second wagon. Spurts of dust from the wheels made Elizabeth squint and she turned her head. The next team was already in sight. Elizabeth stood up, surprised to see it so close.

"Whoa up there, ya shit-assed, long-eared hay-burners!" Seth Landers, his long beard tan with dust, walked beside the mule on the left of the wagon tongue and wrenched at the reins.

The brakes squawked, then a loud grating sound preceded a *thunk* heard even above the noise of wagon, mules and man.

Seth hollered, "Whoa!" But under the front wagon, the brake arm trailed, putting no pressure on the iron tires. The mules skidded, working against the incline and the weight pressing from behind. "Gee! Gee!" Seth demanded. Elizabeth hobbled back from the ford as Seth tried to keep the animals along the rough slope face to lessen the downhill push. Debris slid and rolled beneath the weight of the wagons. Elizabeth held her breath, fearing the worst.

It happened.

The second wagon tipped, cracking the tandem tongue. It heaved left. The groaning crash was punctuated with high squeals of terrified mules trying to kick and run. Canvas on the first wagon caught on a tree branch and ripped. Leaves fluttered in the air like green confetti. The mules shambled on in fright, still dragging the wagons, one upright, one on its side, along the slope face. One creature floundered and went down with a high and piercing scream.

Elizabeth couldn't see Seth Landers, and the absence of any cussing convinced her he was hurt. She bounded down the slope after the wagon, slipping on rubble and ignoring her hurting feet. Elizabeth got to the front of the lead wagon and clambered over the rigging and tongue to the nigh wheeler, hollering all the time for the team to whoa. The choice expletives she used would have surprised her had she remembered them, but she didn't; and she didn't recall how she grabbed the reins, ordered the team to a nervous stop, and turned to the prone Seth just as a large carton loomed toward him from the exposed wagon bed. With outstretched arms, she lurched under the carton, jamming her palms flat on the wooden slats and straddling Seth's unconscious form. The weight was too much for her arms, and she turned and braced the big crate on her upper back and shoulders. Pain lanced up from her feet as she planted her boots against the slope and fixed her hands on her slightly bent knees. Pushing back, she gritted her teeth, squeezed her eyes closed, and prayed the mules wouldn't move.

Joe MacGrin and Dodie Watson rushed into the Ash Creek bed from the far bank. Dodie steadied the mules. Joe, eyes bugged with disbelief at Elizabeth's predicament, joined her effort and called out for help, which was already on the way. Soon two men pulled Seth to safety while four others helped Joe push and shove the huge carton to a stable position. Elizabeth slumped to the ground to comments of awe:

"How'd that button hold up that dad-blamed thing?"

"Gawd Almighty! He coulda broke his back, I tell you."

"Saved Seth's life, that's a fact."

Willie rode down and helped Dodie with the mules while Casey Pritchard knelt at Elizabeth's side, his brown eyes flashing worry. A fit of shakes hit Elizabeth, caused first by her muscles relenting from their tense endeavor, and then by thoughts about what *could* have happened. Sweat drenched her and she opened her eyes with the fright of those possibilities. Pain from her feet quickly overcame her.

"You're crazy," Casey muttered when Elizabeth gasped. Carrying her, he struggled up the steep bank to flat land.

"Put me down, Mr. Pritchard." She could feel each surge of her pulse across her feet. Men thumped past them from the other wagons, shouting to learn what had happened and what they could do.

"Getting yourself in the middle of that," Casey kept on, looking for a spot of shade away from the creek to place her in. The brown land rolled endlessly.

"Mr. Landers would have been killed." Her calf muscles knotted in spasms; a fiery insistence engulfed her toes. "Please put me down."

The sound of a big revolver exploded as someone shot the injured mule. Casey clumped toward an overhang of elderberry. "What about your own self, you little fool."

Unbidden tears stung her eyes. "Put me down, Mr. Pritchard. Please! It's my feet that hurt. I want to get out of these damn boots!"

FIVE

Mr. Pritchard's integrity far exceeds what I expected. It almost makes me feel I have another friend on this wretched trip, the first being Dog.

7 August

The excessive concern which Casey Pritchard showed Zee Clark went unnoticed in the general hoopla caused by Zee's bravery. Everyone congratulated this strong boy, especially after Casey got the boots off and they saw the condition of Elizabeth's feet. Casey carried Elizabeth to the mess wagon and propped her beside Seth Landers. Seth's right hand had been mangled under the wagon box when it skidded; the gash on his head left him only half conscious. While the men began removing the spilled merchandise and disabled wagons from the creek bed, David Hastings complained about the trip that had to be made to Fort Larned, six miles southwest along the Pawnee Fork. But the fort had a wheelwright; and the two injured could be treated at the post hospital.

Casey's concern about Elizabeth allowed him to ignore David's grumbling. She wasn't a sudden preoccupation, either. When he arrived in Ellsworth the Friday before Johnny Tillison was shot, he had toured the saloons, as many single men were apt to do, and gone into Lady Faye's. Elizabeth's hands had first impressed him. So fluid when she shuffled the cards, precise when she dealt. Strong yet graceful. Then her face, with straight nose a bit upturned, high cheekbones, alert brown eyes. Her remote expression told him immediately she didn't belong there, so he didn't speak to her, knowing she'd see him only as another bar hooligan she had to avoid.

Then the Sunday of the shooting, in Sheriff Sieber's office, he had been drawn to that fieriness that turned other men away. He had made note of her room number at Larkins House when she told the sheriff, and on Monday morning, he paid a call. When he didn't find her there, he wandered town, depressed, and scanned the streets and shop customers, looking for that regal stature and direct way of moving she had. He finally went to Lady Faye's and asked for her.

"My wife fired her, little bitch," Bob Wentworth said from behind the bar.

Those were fighting words to Casey until he realized Bob's slur was directed at his own wife.

"Why'd anybody fire a sweet girl like Elizabeth?" Bob went on. He was tired from his trip back from Wichitaw, but Faye always took Monday off.

"Gabe Tillison's gonna tear this place up when he find out," said a woman from a dark corner at the end of the bar. Three weeks earlier she had boasted to the census taker that her profession was "to squirm in the dark." Except for her, Casey was the only patron. She pushed back her short hair that had been dyed red so many times her scalp looked pink.

Casey bought a drink. "Does Tillison pull a lot of weight around here?"

"He moved up here from North Texas the year after the war," Bob said. "Runs cattle down along the Cimarron and supplies meat to Fort Harker on a regular basis." Bob spat an accurate stream of tobacco juice into the spittoon five feet away. "His boys spend lots of money, my Faye's right about that. We can't get them mad at us."

"Made a place for lots of folks that'd have nothin'!" Miss Squirm said. She had been in the area since the first hog house went up on the outskirts of Fort Ellsworth military camp. The laudanum she took by the tablespoonful four and five times a day made her speech breathy and slow. "And he don't take nobody messin' with his boys," she went on. "I hear tell they had to chop off Johnny's arm." She eyed Casey from under layers of makeup.

Casey could tell she was about to make a move and stepped back. "Do you think Tillison is going to take it out on you about his boy?" he asked Bob.

"No. Not since Faye fired Elizabeth. My God, she was a nice girl. I mean a real nice girl." Bob shook his head.

"Bet Gabe won't think so," Miss Squirm said.

It would have been good if Casey had asked these people who might be spreading rumors about David Hastings' financial predicament. David was certain that mysterious person was in cahoots with an unidentified faction that was trying to bilk him and his brother out of their Trinidad store. Casey had been hired to investigate the unusual occurrences, but Casey wasn't too convinced of collusion, and right then Elizabeth predominated his thoughts.

The red-headed woman asked Casey what kind of lover-boy he was, and when he finished his drink and left, ignoring her, she made disparaging comments about his private parts. Casey didn't care. He had other things on his mind, like what Gabe Tillison might do to Elizabeth. He worried even more when Gabe got to town on Wednesday looking as evil as Casey had imagined and with a pack of riders who seemed more like state-line bushwhackers than cow herders. And all this time he saw neither hide nor hair of Elizabeth. When she showed up on Thursday dressed like a boy and looking for work, he was so overjoyed she was safe it set him nearly in shock. He had recognized her right away, and couldn't believe no one else did. His intrigue and bafflement at her disguise had him wondering what she would try next.

Now he stood impatiently beside the cot in the Fort Larned infirmary while the post surgeon examined Elizabeth's scraped and swollen feet. Joe MacGrin stood on the other side, scowling at the floor. Even bruised, it seemed quite obvious to Casey that those smooth-skinned feet, with neatly trimmed nails and graceful arches, were not the feet of a boy. He clenched his teeth and winced when she did at the doctor's probing touch.

"Nothing broken. In fact, the worst of it is across the insteps. Improper shoe covering." He called to a steward to bring a bath of Epsom salts. "How long have they been like this?"

"Just a couple of days," she answered.

"You must have torn open a lot of these blisters when you saved that teamster, there, from getting crushed."

"Yes, sir."

Seth lay on a bed across the room out cold from the chloroform given him before Dr. Laing reset the bones in his hand.

"Mr. MacGrin was telling me about that. We probably better check out your ribs and back while you're here. Treat the bruises."

"NO!" Casey blurted that, and Joe MacGrin blurted that at the same time.

"We did that back at camp—before we carted him here," Joe said.

Watching him, Casey knew without a doubt that Joe knew Elizabeth's true identity. "Right. We, ah, didn't want to risk moving the kid if something was messed up," Casey said.

"Yeah."

"Well, we might just have a check anyway," Doctor Laing said.

"I'm fine doctor. Really!" Elizabeth's heart drummed as fast as a telegrapher's key at the beginning of an Indian attack.

The doctor frowned at her, then looked curiously at the men as he scratched his black curly beard. But neither Casey nor Joe noticed as they gave each other shrewd looks over the top of Elizabeth's head, each wondering how the other would explain his knowledge.

"I want to talk to you, Pritchard," Joe said. And his tone wasn't friendly. He headed for the door.

That Joe assumed Casey was Elizabeth's accomplice bothered Casey, yet in a way that was true. But right then, Casey wasn't going any place. While the doctor clipped torn skin from the tops of her feet, Elizabeth had unconsciously grabbed his fingers. Under her strong grip, Casey's knuckles rubbed together and hurt something fearful, but he wouldn't have pulled away for the world.

After the doctor's ministrations, they left the infirmary set in the new commissary building (the old adobe hospital had been condemned in July) and started back to their camp, just the two of them. In her perpetual stubbornness, which Casey grumbled about but greatly admired, Elizabeth insisted on walking. Her wrapped feet fit easily into the pair of old brogans she had in her haversack. Casey noticed the cherry-wood gun case in there, too, just as he had noticed the impressive Winchester she carried. Those items had him all the more curious about her, and although her independent nature might have suggested loose ways to some men, Casey felt certain she was from a strict background and maintained high standards.

Evening light made their shadows long, and nighthawks skimmed from the trees across the open areas, their pinched calls underscored by a harrumph of frogs and chirring crickets. Bats flittered. Voices wavered with the air currents:

"Shall we gather at the river;
the beautiful, the beautiful ri-ver."

Chords from a piano reminded Elizabeth and Casey of the day.

By the time Casey and Elizabeth completed the walk diagonally across the fort parade grounds, past the sandstone commandant building and to the trees at the edge of Pawnee Fork, only Dog was at the mess wagon Jorge had used as ambulance for the injured. Casey correctly assumed that Joe, Jorge and Willie (who had come along just because) had taken off for the sutler house and saloons on the eastern perimeter of the fort, which suited Casey just fine; now he could talk to Elizabeth in private. He started a small fire.

Dog, tethered to a wagon wheel, sat up, anxious for a pat. Elizabeth obliged, then hobbled around and laid out her bed-roll. She knew perfectly well what Casey had on his mind, although they had said nothing to each other during the long walk, not even to comment about the clammy, still air or the cloudy sky. Elizabeth had noted outhouse locations, and wondered if she dared gimp her way to the one behind the officers' quarters. Even with these concerns, Casey's puzzlement surrounded her like a herd of elk at a salt lick, and the blustery comment Joe MacGrin made to the doctor convinced Elizabeth that Joe was on to her, too.

Which is just what Casey said when he started the conversation. "Well, you know. Joe's on to you."

Elizabeth eased onto the blanket and sighed with relief at getting off her feet. Her stomach growled loudly. From the West, a coyote yipped and was joined by other canine voices, including a hound on the other side of the fort. Dog whined.

"He's bound to tell Hastings. You should have gone to him from the start; told him your situation," Casey continued.

"He wouldn't have given me this job."

"He might have."

"I couldn't risk it. I don't have any money, Mr. Pritchard. None at all!" She took some jerked beef out of her haversack.

"Well, talking to him now will be hard. Injured folk are a drawback to a wagon train as it is, and a woman—"

"Mr. Hastings wouldn't leave me here, would he?" Panic struck her. "There's not a town within forty miles of this fort."

"The stage comes through here headed back to Salina. Maybe you should—"

"I don't have any money!"

Casey sat cross-legged beside her. "All right," he said while she chewed on the jerky. From behind them came the lazy gurgle and slaps of water in Pawnee Fork. "Why are you doing this? Why didn't you just stay in Ellsworth?"

"Like I told Mr. Hastings, I have to get south." Elizabeth might have looked poised and calm, but below that expression panic lurked like a catamount watching a fawn. She blinked and rubbed her nose to maintain her composure.

"To meet your father?"

"Yes," she said, "He's in the cavalry."

"Where?"

"His recent letters have come from Fort Union, the last one in February. He's with the Ninth."

"That's one of the colored outfits," Casey said. Elizabeth nodded. "Well, it shouldn't be too hard to locate an officer, even in the field. We'll contact him and—."

"Officer!"

"If he's with the Ninth." Casey shrugged. "All the officers are white, even with the Colored Troops."

"Yes. I know." Elizabeth's tone could have frosted a cake. "And my father's an enlisted man, Mr. Pritchard."

Casey scowled and remembered her cryptic comment back in Ellsworth. "Oh." He plucked a sprout of wild mustard.

Casey had lived his young life in California and had seen lots of mixed blood people, but he hadn't even considered that Elizabeth could be Negro. His eyes flicked to her, looking for subtle signs that proved her heritage. Firelight gave their skin a ruddy glow which Casey noticed especially on Elizabeth. Maybe her nose he thought, seeing the slight flare of nostrils. Full sensuous lips, a gentle slant to the set of her long-lashed eyes. Her smooth skin and handsome features mesmerized him and his heart pounded.

The amorous emotions stirring in Casey were lost on Elizabeth. She barely even registered the throb in her feet, being much more concerned about this new predicament. She considered explaining how her grandfather Clark disowned her mother because of her marriage, or how he later kidnapped Elizabeth's older brothers who looked white and had now disowned Elizabeth, too. Just thinking all that was too painful, so she decided to tell Casey only about the Tillisons and why she had to take on this disguise. She hoped Casey could persuade Joe MacGrin to keep her secret.

The thoughts of telling even that twanged Elizabeth's nerves like they were banjo strings. Remembering that night at the hotel was bad enough, and thoughts of speaking it aloud, to a man, drained her strength and courage for several minutes. If she had known about it, she might have taken a swig from the bottle of "medicinal whiskey" Jorge kept in the mess wagon. Instead, she took a gulp of water from her canteen and sighed.

"Mr. Pritchard," she finally began. "Let me tell you what happened."

It wasn't hard to convince Casey of Elizabeth's plight, and an hour later when he arrived at the sandstone saloon near Henry Booth's trading post, his decision to help her took even deeper root. In the dimly lit room, at a rough-hewn table close to the bar, lounged a man dressed totally in black. Lamplight glinted dully off the copper studs of his hat band, belt and the holsters of his two guns. Casey had seen that man riding with Gabe Tillison in Ellsworth, and now, as then, he studied him a bit, thinking he knew the thin face and smooth mannerisms. At a card game at a round table, one of the men playing seemed extremely large. Casey wondered if that could be the giant Elizabeth had mentioned. Fortunately, Hank Tillison wasn't among the various soldiers and trail men who talked and laughed over their drinks, for Casey would have jumped him and pummeled him onto the splintery wooden floor before Hank even knew the reason why.

Casey started across the room, suddenly certain he could get Joe to see things his way. Joe met him before he reached the bar, a bottle in his hand and two glasses. "Over here," Joe rumbled, indicating a lonely table deep in the shadows.

Joe had barely sat down good when Casey began. "You remember that shooting in Ellsworth last Sunday?"

"Don't get me off track, Pritchard. You just explain—"

"I'm trying to. Remember the shooting?"

"Well, yeah. Got reminded of it a bit ago when that fancy dressed fellow came in," Joe said, nodding toward the man in black. "He was riding with Gabe Tillison when they came to pick up his kid. But what does that have to do—"

"Just listen!" Casey hunched over the table and kept his voice low. "The girl who shot Tillison. She lost her job because of it, then Johnny's brother and some men went to her hotel Sunday night and tried to—have their way with her." That had been the delicate way Elizabeth put it.

"What!?"

Casey continued. "A friend of hers came by and broke that up, hid her out. But when Gabe came to town, he rode his gang out to the farm and shot the place up when they couldn't find her. She was hiding in a root cellar. Her friends told her Tillison said something about making her pay some day—getting the law to do it if he couldn't."

"What a bastard." Joe shook his head. "But this doesn't have much to do with—." Joe eyed Casey suspiciously. "How do you know all this, anyway?"

"Ah, she told me."

"She tol—." He sat up straight in his chair like someone had dropped ice down his back. "This girl. I know her, don't I." He squinted his eyes and whispered, "Zee Clark?"

"Right." Casey cast a disparaging look toward the man in black.

"Lord Almighty. And I was about to light into you about withholding information and your sneakiness." Joe scowled at Casey. "What do you have in mind for this girl, anyway?"

"That suspicious tone tells me you have daughters," Casey said with a smile.

"Damn right. That's why I knew Zee wasn't who she said. I mean, you shoulda seen how she held to you when you carried her. And the way she took that pain. Just like my Lucinda in childbirth, or my oldest girl the time the billy-goat smashed three of her ribs." He shook his head

67

and wiped his long mustache with his hand. "So what you got in mind, Pritchard, and it better be admirable. I don't care what she's done."

"I agree, and I also think she's a perfect lady." Casey ran a callused finger around the edge of the glass. It totally slipped his mind to mention her racial makeup and the bigotry that caused Hank Tillison to abuse her. "She doesn't have any money, Joe, so under the circumstances, we have to—"

"Ho! Wait a minute. I see what you're getting at, but—"

"Well, what do you suggest?"

"I could spring some money for stage fare back to Ellsworth."

"It's two days before the stage arrives. You really want to leave her here at the fort?" Casey leaned toward him, frowning. "With Tillison's men already here? We've got to go along with her ruse."

Joe drained his glass of liquor. "Damn, that's risky." He poured another drink. "And Hastings'll have my balls if something flares up because of this."

"But you know I'm right, Joe. There's nothing here but this fort. No town, no place to get a job, she's got no money; and Tillison's men are lurking around here for some reason. Doesn't that seem odd?"

Joe closed his eyes for a moment, then shook his head.

"She stays Zee Clark and with the wagon train," Casey went on. "It's the only way she'll be safe."

"But if the men find out—. Teamsters ain't the most refined folks, you know. Some of 'em—."

"We just have to make sure they don't find out."

Joe tipped back his head and gave a long sigh. Casey poured himself a drink, knowing the man would agree.

Bad weather can pull down the spirits and make even a decent situation seem foul, so the rain which swept in the night Joe MacGrin joined Casey in protecting Elizabeth's identity had a real bad effect on a lot of people. Especially Willie MacGrin. Jorge Estévez had stuck with him that night at the fort and Willie hadn't been able to get drunk like he wanted to. When the drenching started at three in the morning, the wagon was already occupied by Zee Clark. Willie got sopped setting up a lean-to. The rain slowed to a drizzle by dawn, but the ground was soaked and his clothes felt clammy. Jorge prepared Zee's breakfast and carried it to him, and Willie scowled while his dad helped the kid put on a pair of brand new calf-high moccasins—the double-soled smoked-leather kind for trail wear like Willie had been wanting since they left home. All of a sudden, this Zee Clark, who Willie had been glad to see join the train to take the greenhorn hoorah off him, occupied everyone's attention, a hero, and Willie's dad led the praising pack.

Rain gusted around them when they slogged their way back to the wagon camp with the repaired wheel and three new tandem tongues. Elizabeth rode in the mess wagon along with a groggy Seth Landers, his hand bandaged and throbbing.

At a general meeting after they reached camp, the men stood in several clumps, their slickers repelling the steady rain. A canvas had been stretched to give a spot of dryness. Joe stood under it and Elizabeth sat on the wagon box, sleepy from a recent dose of some potion the doctor had sent back with her. "Don's gonna drive Seth's team till Seth's hand heals," Joe said. Don nodded. "And Mel, you'll have to take over Don's job," Joe went on.

Mel Burns, an unofficial member of the wagon-train crew, had come north with a shipment of wool. Although he had wired the money back to his family in Santa Fe, he was staying with the wagon train south so he wouldn't have to travel the barren land alone.

"And Zee will take on Mel's night herding duties," Joe finished.

"Oh, great!" Willie grunted to Bill Porter. "Hero Zee can sleep in Jorge's wagon during the day with his boots off, while the rest of us tromp along in the god damn heat."

"It ain't gonna be too cool up under that canvas. Not breeze a-one," Bill pointed out. He scratched at his auburn beard which was always just a stubble, although he never shaved.

"Shit," Willie said. He swaggered off, nearly running into Casey.

With the meeting over, Elizabeth retreated into Jorge's wagon. Seth snored from his cot over the boxes of canned goods, and Elizabeth clambered into the hammock that had been arranged for her. Jorge had even given her a flour sack filled with clean cloths for a pillow. Elizabeth was more tired than she had ever been, and with the hammock anchored on two wagon-canvas ribs, which when the wind gusted, swayed like a rocker cradle, she fell right to sleep.

"Well. Got that part of it done," Joe said to Casey as the two of them moved to another lean-to. "Now what about this chain thing?"

"Like I told David. That chain had been filed."

"No wonder Hastings was so red-faced."

"Yeah." When Casey had told David about the apparent sabotage, it was all he could do to keep the man from throwing a fit and accusing all of the teamsters of working against him. While Casey and Joe talked, David fretted in his tent with a cigar.

"When David told me he was expecting trouble, I figured it would be a war-type attack with guns, men riding in on us. Something a man could face head on and know where he stood," Joe said. Casey nodded agreement. "But it's an odd thing, what with the man who sold Jake the store falling dead and all. And now this rigged brake chain."

"Yeah." Casey scowled into the wet wagon yard. Until this happened, Casey had thought David a bit paranoid. "There's something pretty damned shifty afoot," he muttered. He had asked around Ellsworth to learn if anyone might have a grudge against the Hastings brothers and learned that Jake and David were well-liked, honest people; they left Ellsworth with good credit. Now Casey shifted his hunched position and hoped the lawyers in Trinidad were having better luck.

"I'm going to have to find out more about the men we've signed on," Casey told Joe. "Any links anyone has with Trinidad, I need to know."

"This group's not the type for that sort of thing. Not even Dawson."

War-veteran Tom Dawson, with scraggly blond hair and a quick temper, had just finished a stint in Leavenworth for aggravated assault.

A gust of wind blew rain under the canvas. Joe turned up his collar and squinted while Casey secured his hat. "Most have taken this job just to move, and the others are professionals," Joe went on.

Casey nodded. He was certain neither Watson, Ledbetter, or Pete Hayward would mess with equipment. "And old John Bradshaw told me he was looking to join up with his daughter and her husband down in

Taos," Casey added. "But I'm going to have to make sure all that's true."

"Be careful how you do it. I sure as hell don't want a mutiny on my hands. A majordomo's nightmare. And there's a lot in this bunch who would up an' run if they thought they was heading for trouble."

"I've noticed. Like Sim Chambers. And I'm not sure Porter or that Gaynor fellow would do too much fighting."

"Gaynor? Oh yeah. That quiet Bible reader."

The rain pattered relentlessly on the sagging roof of the lean-to and water filled ruts in the muddy ground. Two in the afternoon looked like nine o'clock on a moonless night. Casey looked away from the dismal environment. "There's something else you should know," he said, unsure of how his words would be received. "Looks like Willie's a bit jealous of Zee Clark." The wind picked up, sweeping the gray clouds lower.

"Damn. I don't know what's wrong with him this trip. He's supposed to be the camp hunter, and won't even get up before dawn. He was fine coming up here, but—."

Beyond camp, the green-frocked limbs of the trees along Ash Creek thrashed and then blurred in the increased tumult of rain. The mules faded to flat shadows through the deluge and when they brayed, they sounded far away.

"Check the god damn animals!" Joe called, dashing out.

"Somebody get that awning!" Casey ordered.

Gusts tugged at picket pins and billowed tents. Stakes slid out of the mushy earth. Lean-tos flapped and the teamsters scattered to secure the canvases and animals.

"I need a rope! Rope!" someone called, his words drowned in the torrent and the people nearly drowned, too. Clothing became glossy as it clung wet to the men. Bill Porter's hat flipped off and disappeared in the dense gray air. Everyone's hair was wet, looked dark, and water glistened in small streams from beards.

After fifteen minutes, the blow subsided and the mules became three-dimensional again, their eyes half-lidded, nose and ears down to show their discomfort. They shifted on their picket lines, trying to keep their tails to the steady wind. The teamsters searched out spots to sit where the water wasn't too deep. From somewhere distant came a long growl of thunder.

"Pete!" Joe called "Get some help and cut grasses we can put under the wheels when it's time to pull out of here!"

Pete saluted and set to work. Sim Chambers, a chronic complainer, fussed when Pete called on him to help, but did the work.

"Getting caught in camp in a rain is worse than if we had been on the trail," David Hastings grumbled as he peered around. The wagon wheels had already sunk a hand's breadth into the mire. Water cascaded from canvases. "If the mules had been in harness, we could have done five miles at least and found ourselves a camp on higher ground."

"There ain't much around higher than where we are," Joe said, turning up the collar on his slicker.

"It's gonna be hell pulling out of here!"

"At least we've already crossed the creek," Casey said. Ash Creek flowed a tumult of wrecked trees and sludge from upstream. The rampage scoured the banks, running four feet deep and rising.

The rain lasted through the afternoon, dulling the sky which glowed a rusty gray at sunset. They ate a cold meal that night, and everyone stayed to their tents as much as possible. For some, it wasn't possible— like Mel Burns and Zee Clark. Joe ordered them to move the mule herd to new pasture and he told Zee to stay out with the animals.

Casey winced, not wanting her out there by herself, but he knew Joe hoped to protect her identity by keeping her away from the men as much as possible. He walked to where Don limped over with a bay gelding for Zee Clark to ride.

"Saddles are in the supply wagon," Joe said, and he mumbled to Casey, "By the way she handled that mule in Ellsworth, I figure she ain't horse shy."

With the animal sheltered from the weather by a lean-to, Elizabeth got the bay bridled. The heavy cattleman's saddle gave her a bit of trouble, however, with high pommel, double girths, long skirts and toe-guarded stirrups.

"You don't seem to know this too well," Don said, limping over. Mud squished around their feet. Rain still fell.

"It's just different." Elizabeth's nerves tingled, feeling she created too much attention with this procedure. "I'm used to riding—" (Casey held his breath, thinking *side saddle*) "bareback," she said.

Don helped her saddle up, let her adjust the stirrups. She secured her Winchester in the scabbard, tied her bed-roll and a few belongings behind the cantle, led the horse in a circle a few times and pulled into the saddle like a veteran, spilling the long tail of her slicker across her belongs and the horse's rump. Mel handed her the rope for a string of mules and they went off into the rainy night.

What a woman! Casey thought as they faded into the mist.

"All the trouble Zee was havin' with that saddle, he seems sort of green," Sim Chambers muttered.

"I hope that kid ain't afraid of the dark," Horace Cross said, his wet beard looked black in the twilight. "He might get jumpy and shoot one of the mules."

"Yeah," Bill Porter put in. "Willie says he don't think Zee knows how to use that fancy rifle he's carryin' around."

Casey remembered the comment Elizabeth had made in the sheriff's office about shooting Johnny Tillison—that she could have killed him if she had aimed to. That brag had sounded like an expert, and it had been said even before she had to play this opposite-sex role. In fact, it had taken talent *not* to kill Johnny with a shotgun at such close range. He chuckled. "Oh, I think Zee knows how to use it."

Six

There's a certain loneliness I can never seem to stem. I know it started when I moved to Terre Haute, but you'd think I'd be over it by now—could stop feeling like an outsider...
                                                                11 August

In any part of the country people will say, "If you don't like the weather, just blink and it will change." It's sort of a joke, but it's really the nature of nature—unpredictable. Kansas weather plays around with the joke as good as any place, so as the night wore on and folks blinked, the weather changed. The mules didn't care. They had fresh forage in a dale with a wet-weather spring. Runoff spilled into the area, but the thick prairie grass kept the ground from being pure mud.

She drew a shaky breath and studied her surroundings to refocus her thoughts. The layers of sweaty dirt on her seemed to reek of the camp, and the nearby trickle of water caught her eye. She smiled. In that quiet night, Elizabeth had the luxury of washing all over. She did this in sections, of course, not about to take the chance of being totally undressed if the mules decided to bolt, or coyotes came around. She was thinking of the two-legged kind: Indian hunters or men from the camp.

But the risk was worth it, and limb by limb, bit by bit, Elizabeth got clean. Her moderately clean hair dried in soft curls across her forehead as she rebound her breasts, buttoned into a fresh shirt, washed the dirty one. Escaping from her prison of grime did nearly as much to restore her peace of mind as when she learned Joe MacGrin agreed to be her ally.

She kept the gelding under saddle so she could ride out every now and then to survey the herd, and made her camp near a clump of stunted serviceberry. While she wrote a few lines in her diary, the wind blew and the sky became so clear it seemed like the stars had been polished. She lay back on her bed-roll, not terribly tired, and enjoying the pleasant night. The creek chuckled its way through the dale, the sound competing with frogs croaking and crickets' chirps.

This reverie nearly lulled her to sleep, but the gelding snorted alarm; its head went up with a jerk. Quick as a lizard, Elizabeth snapped fully awake. Although she was accustomed to vast land and enjoyed seeing horizon in every direction, she knew dangers could whip up like a summer storm. She went to the horse, heart pounding, and held the animal's nose so it wouldn't nicker. The plain-looking bay stared into the wind, ears twitching like antelope tails.

The mule herd, however, was interested only in grass, and Elizabeth became less tense. She slid her Winchester from the scabbard anyway, and with a stealth befitting her Cherokee background (or maybe Ibo or Watusi—whatever African nation spawned old George Fortune's ancestors) Elizabeth eased up the rise for a better look.

A horse whicker carried easily to Elizabeth and she worked quickly along the mushy face of the next ground swell. Twangs of protest spurted up from her feet, but she bit her tongue and, half crouched, kept going. A horse was skylined on the crest of the hill near a scraggly hackberry. Only one horse, but that didn't make Elizabeth any less wary. No saddle. Maybe Indians. The steady breeze caused rustlings in the bushes and frogs croaked down near the spring while the mules stomped and blew and ate grass. But the man-shadow she saw near the crest made her fall flat and hold her breath. The wet of the ground quickly seeped into her dry clothes. "Damn," she muttered.

She eased herself up again, just in time to see the person gathering a hat full of earth clods. He wasn't Indian and he hurled a fistful of clumps, startling a hinny, but not enough to cause a stampede.

When he scrounged for more rocks, Elizabeth levered her rifle. "Put down everything you're holding and don't reach for a gun," she said.

Her stomach knotted up tight as a vigilante's noose and she kept that rifle chest high, the stock between her arm and side to keep it steady. She aimed at the middle of the tall shadow. She knew throwing rocks at mules wasn't a shootable offense, but Elizabeth couldn't be certain that was all this vagrant was up to. If he moved wrong, she planned to pull the trigger.

The man dropped the hat, eased around and said, "Whoa up there, kid."

Elizabeth recognized Willie MacGrin's voice and that gave her a brief moment of relief, until she wondered why Willie would try to scatter the mule herd of the wagon train his daddy bossed.

"What are you doing out here?" She stood the rifle butt on the ground.

Willie's whole attitude changed. "You stupid pissant! Who the hell are you to be holding a gun on me and asking questions?" Willie had started down the hill.

"Wait a minute, Willie." She gripped the gun barrel with her left hand, her right hand still clenched on it.

He kept coming. "I've had just about enough of your high and mighty attitude!"

Willie reached to grab the youngster Zee Clark by the shirt collar, but Elizabeth stepped aside and swung the rifle by the barrel. The stock of the gun caught Willie in the gut; he doubled over, and she knew if she brought the piece up hard under his chin while he was bent, it would probably break his jaw or at least knock him out. But she thought of Joe MacGrin who was working to protect her. She stepped in and kicked Willie's feet out from under him so he landed on his back.

Willie's head smacked the ground. He gasped for breath and then managed, "You broke my ribs!"

"You just got the wind knocked out of you," Elizabeth said. "Now get up."

"I can't! I hurt."

"Get up!"

Willie pushed up to his elbows, and Elizabeth kept the rifle pointed at his chest.

"You'd better leave," Elizabeth breathed shallowly. Her hands on that gun were gritty from sweat and mud.

Willie panted while he stood up, his pains slowly fading. "So what are you going to do? Tell my pa?"

"No." Elizabeth had already rejected that idea. In her current role, she had to handle this herself. She stepped back so Willie couldn't throw dirt at her and try for the gun.

He found his hat and swatted mud clots off it. "You ain't seen the last of me, Clark," he growled when he whipped up the reins of his horse.

"If you're not leaving the wagon-train, I guess that's true," she snapped.

Willie made an angry sound in his throat, threw himself onto his horse's bare back and rode off.

The clop of the horse hooves faded before Elizabeth came out of her tense stance. She put her hand to her throat, her pulse racing. A quiver of uncertainty pulled her doubts forward again, and the rest of the night, she was restless and jumpy. She blamed it all on Willie. He had spoiled her contentment, made her muddy her fresh clothes, and put her temper on a short fuse. Luckily, nothing else bothered the mules that night, for Elizabeth would have given whatever a very hard time of it.

Late the next morning, sunlight heated the air and the pale blue sky didn't hold a single cloud. Elizabeth had been awake since predawn, scanning the rolling prairie. Bees circled pipestems and daisies. Prairie hens chuckled in the shadows while wild primrose scented the morning air. "Every morning is a new beginning," her father had always said. "Just take one day at a time, and anything is possible."

With all the heartaches in Samuel Fortune's life, Elizabeth gloried in the strength of those words—their meaning. She let the growing brightness renew her positive attitude.

"Halloo the camp!" came a proper greeting at mid-morning. Elizabeth waved to Mel, relieved not to be alone. "I come to help ya get the mules back in. Mr. MacGrin's going to try to pull out by noon."

"Have things dried up that much?" she asked.

"No, but Mr. Hastings is chewing on his cigar. You know."

Elizabeth grinned, already aware of the signs of David Hastings' impatience.

They urged the mules to action, slapping ropes on the rumps of stragglers, heading them back to camp. Water flowed along every drainage like a miniature creek and when they got the mules to the wagons, the swampy footing oozed up to Elizabeth's ankles when she stepped from her horse. She glowered at the messy condition of her new footwear.

"We ain't never gonna get out of this shit," Sim Chambers complained.

"Damn foolish thing to be even tryin'," Bill Porter said. Dots of mud speckled his red stubble.

Elizabeth silently agreed. Wagon wheels sat deep in goo.

"Well, hiya there, Zee," came a greeting from robust Amos Ledbetter. Dodie Watson called a greeting, and Don. Other men smiled at her as if it helped to have a hero in camp.

"Them feet feeling better today?" Pete Hayward asked.

Elizabeth nodded. Since the bottom of her feet hadn't sustained much damage from the wrong-sized boots and the moccasins Joe had given her were gentle across the bandaged insteps, her feet did feel pretty good.

"You jest set someplace. Nothin' for you to do in this," added John Bradshaw.

Casey Pritchard grinned and asked Elizabeth if she had a pleasant night. "Must have been good not to be around these miscreants," he muttered.

His literate wisecrack made Elizabeth smile. The night herding was definitely to her advantage, but her encounter with Willie kept her quiet.

"Go on. Get off your feet," Casey said. "I'll take care of your horse." She relinquished the bay to him.

Nearby, men wrestled with a big crate to place in the wagon bed of Seth's repaired tandem. It was the very crate Elizabeth had so bravely caught.

"What's in there?" she asked. In the brightness of the day she had to squint at teamster Horace Cross, a medium height, thick-muscled man with thinning hair and even thinner eyebrows over gray eyes. His beard was gray-streaked light brown, although he wasn't much over thirty.

"Mirrors. Big ones for a bawdy house in Santa Fe." He laughed and put a sturdy shoulder under one end of the crate and pushed. With Gaynor and Guzlowski pulling, the crate slid into place. "I think you ought to stop by there and get some free pleasures for holdin' these things up. Shit. Chances are the mirrors would have broke before Seth's back did." Horace sleeved sweat off his sunburned forehead.

"I'll hafta to go with him," Seth rumbled from behind his big beard.

He had been awake since dawn and not feeling too awful. "The others told me what you done for me, Zee. So I'd jest hafta go to make sure you got treated right."

Elizabeth stared into the mud by her feet, hoping to hide her flustered expression.

Seth laughed and one-handed, he grabbed a canvas-wrapped carton by a leather strap. The bulk shifted; the carton tumbled out, cracking on one end and exposing white Valenciennes lace and folds of blue silk moire—at least that's how Elizabeth would have called the materials. She managed not to gasp over the items and hurried to keep the edge of silk out of the mud.

"Careful with that!" David Hastings called, running over. "Bradshaw, bring some nails."

"Stuff it back in, Zee," Seth said. "It's only some cloth."

"Only!" Hastings squatted beside Elizabeth, flicking specks of crating from the lace. Elizabeth quietly marveled at the exquisite cornice tatting with a broad swirl resembling a peacock tail. "A special order for an officer's wife at Fort Union. Shipped all the way from Amsterdam. They're paying me five times the price for delivering it." Elizabeth helped him rewrap the carton, then David frowned at her. "Get off those feet, son. And that's an order."

"Yes, sir." His sudden scrutiny made her tense and she got up quickly, not wanting Hastings to see through her disguise.

Another member of the wagon train had already distinguished her, however. Style of clothing and length of hair meant nothing to Dog; one sniff and it knew the truth, and Dog thought it was pretty fine to have this female-type human around. When Elizabeth squished along toward the mess wagon, each step sending spatters of mud onto her pant legs, Dog, its white hairs stiff and tinged brown from mud, trotted out to greet her with its stubby tail a-waggle. Elizabeth gave Dog a pat.

"Ah, *buenos tardes!*" said Jorge Estévez, the slight-built cook. He smiled at Elizabeth as he closed the lid on a kettle of beans. He set beans to soak every morning and by evening, it took only thirty minutes or so to cook the softened legumes.

Willie MacGrin sauntered around from the far side of the wagon. Elizabeth glared at him.

"I wanted to ask you, Señor Zee, did you see any game out there *este mañana*?" Jorge asked. He was only as tall as Elizabeth's shoulder, and his long drooping mustache dominated his face. His dark eyes were shrewd.

"How come he's *Señor* Zee and I'm just Willie?" Willie growled.

"You are like family, Willie." Jorge gave Willie a sidelong glance. "One of my own bad boys." In Santa Fe, Jorge Estévez always signed on with Joe MacGrin, a business arrangement they had assumed for over twelve years. Great luck for whatever wagon train they worked, since Joe was one of the best wagon masters around, and Jorge was by far the best trail cook.

Jorge smiled at Elizabeth. "There was game?"

"I didn't really notice," Elizabeth said. She did notice the hateful look Willie gave her, and decided not to mention the four deer she had seen in the willow thickets near the spring. Antelope had been stiff-legging their way along the flats to the south of the mule herd, too, paying her no mind at all.

"Sure would be good to have some fresh meat," chubby Clive Williams mumbled, putting his rinsed cup into the mess box. "If you can make us some, Zee, do it. Hell, I'm sick of side meat and beans."

"I'm the hunter for this outfit!" Willie declared.

"Is that so?" Clive eyed him ruefully and walked away.

"That is true, Willie," Jorge said, feigning innocence at prodding the young man. "Maybe we can have some fresh *carne* for this night?" He fed Dog a cold tortilla.

"You're damn right!" Willie tried to stomp to his horse, slipped and nearly fell in the mud. He yanked loose the reins and glowered around, daring anyone to laugh.

But the others didn't notice while they prodded and strained to get the wagons out of the mire. Two wagons had to be completely unpacked, moved, and then repacked; another had to be hitched with a double mule team to get it on more solid ground.

In the mess wagon, among the hanging ropes of garlic and dried peppers, Elizabeth pulled off her moccasins and undid the gauze wrappings on her feet so the fresh air could help them heal. She took a dose of the medicine the doctor had given her and set her moccasins in the warm shade to dry. When she lay back in the hammock, Willie's petulant expression floated in her thoughts, then blended into Johnny Tillison's face. She jerked and gritted her teeth, but fatigue and Dr. Liang's medicine overcame these back-of-the-mind worries, and Elizabeth slept soundly, not even bothered by the abundant cussing and noise of camp, nor by the steamy heat that stuck her shirt to her, drew flies and had sweat beading her top lip like dew. She didn't even notice when the wagons finally got underway in mid-afternoon.

An hour after sunset, the exhausted mules couldn't keep going even though the moon was nearly full. The wagons had managed only seven miles of muddy trail that day, and the men and Elizabeth ate a meal of side meat and beans. Willie still searched for fresh meat. But by then the wild creatures used the shadows to avoid him and they cut along the back trail of the wagons to the washes and dales that still held water. Elizabeth had the tired mules bedded on night forage before Willie returned to camp.

The temperature stayed rock-frying hot for the next two days; there was little shade and even less fresh water. Even so, Elizabeth was feeling pretty good. Her feet had ceased to hurt and the old blisters were scabbing over. Her muscles had hardened to their new tasks, and she found the open land fascinating. They passed sign of buffalo on occasion, and Elizabeth's pulse quickened at the thoughts of seeing one of the big American Bison. Wood buffalo ranged in northern Minnesota, but they weren't as big as the plains buffalo, and didn't roam in the huge herds that all the eastern magazines and dime novels wrote about.

The mules didn't find their surroundings as intriguing, and they flopped their ears a lot and fussed and nipped at each other. The men weren't much better. Mundane things got the best of them, and they grumbled loudly about their diet which still consisted of side meat and beans. Elizabeth approached mules and men with caution, realizing their rotten dispositions. Amos Ledbetter, a Missourian and Tom Dawson, who had been a Redleg during the war, had a serious fight thirty miles more along the trail, leaving Dawson with a puffy eye and Ledbetter with one less tooth. At nooning on August 11th, while the relentless sun produced a baking heat, those two still bickered, and Bill Porter and Sim

Chambers came to blows over a dipper of water.

"Shit. It's too early in the trip for all this," Joe grumbled from his meal.

"We got a bunch of slackards," David Hastings complained. "They're quick to gripe and shirk duty."

"If I could keep their bellies happy, I might be able to control them." He glowered at Willie and then asked Elizabeth. "Are you seeing any game out there, Zee?"

"Oh, no, Mr. Watson. I'm glad to leave the hunting to Willie," Elizabeth said.

She wasn't usually one to turn away from a challenge, but Elizabeth hoped to get back to that low profile she had before the wagon accident. It was a long way yet to New Mexico and she didn't intend to give anyone else a chance to see through her charade.

Willie didn't make this easy for her, however. "Yeah, kid," he sneered. "We don't need you scarin' off whatever game is out there before I get to it."

"*Madre de Dios*," Jorge muttered. "Do not aggravate him."

No one heard, and Elizabeth was already aggravated. She glared at Willie, but John Bradshaw's words made her swallow a lump of dismay.

"Well, let's do it," the slope-shouldered, gray-haired man said.

"Now, just a minute." David Hastings scowled at John. "Are you suggesting a contest?"

"You betcha." He finished his last bit of food and tossed his plate aside.

"You start shooting guns in this camp and we'll be chasing mules from here to sundown!" Hastings' logic made sense to Elizabeth and she prayed the others would listen.

"There's a spot back up the trail," Dodie's gravely voice said. "Half mile or so." He was on his feet. So was Willie. Pete chuckled. Al Guzlowski shambled off to spread the word.

"Joe! Get these fellows stopped!" Hastings said.

Joe's reply of, "Sounds fine to me." made Elizabeth's heart skip a beat. "It'll kill off some of the doldrums the men got."

"What's going on?" Casey Pritchard rode into camp as Dodie was laying out the rules.

"A shootin' contest," Ledbetter told him. "Zee's challenged Willie. It oughta be good."

Elizabeth was on her feet, dismay increasing, She shook her head at Casey to convey her reluctance for the plan.

"It'll be a two shot chance at each distance," Dodie hollered around. "Same target area."

Seth tromped over, grinning. "I'm puttin' six bits on ya, Zee." He slapped her on the back. "Anybody match that!" he called.

All the excitement drowned Elizabeth's protests. Teamsters unhitched mules so they could ride out to watch. Mel Burns had a broad grin when he brought in Elizabeth's horse.

"And who the blazes is going to guard this camp!" Hastings fumed. "You're just going to ride off and leave the wagons untended?"

"Fort Larned command said there hasn't been a hostile in southern Kansas for over four months," Joe said.

"I'm stayin'," reclusive Mervin Gaynor said from where he lay in the shade under his wagon. "I don't hold none with gamblin'."

"I'll stay, too," Don Suther said. Three others nodded agreement.

"Jorge's holding the chits," Joe said.

"And I'm staying here! *Es verdad!*" Jorge wanted to be far away from any possible fireworks.

Elizabeth gritted her teeth, knowing if she argued to get out of this now, she'd draw more attention than not. If she were really the plucky, trail-bred lad she was pretending, she couldn't back away from the challenge. Once her mind settled on that, her stubborn pride took hold and she was determined to show Willie MacGrin a thing or two.

"So, should I put my money on you?" Casey whispered as he walked his horse to where she was tightening the saddle cinch on the bay.

"I think so." It helped having Casey there. Sort of a friend she could talk to. "I've only fired the Winchester a few times, but I've got a good eye."

"You what?"

Casey's open-mouth shock didn't slow Elizabeth down. She grabbed her rifle and swung into the saddle. If her hair had been longer, she would have looked like a young Pawnee or Kiowa warrior with her tall moccasins and rifle clenched in her right fist. She was off to a battle which seemed inevitable, necessary and (as Joe MacGrin had said) a welcome outlet from the drudgery of the trail.

SEVEN

I must always be on guard, never forget my role and what, or who, drove me out here.

12 August

The land had given way to large stretches of barrenness and the dry brown grass was only knee high and dotted with sturdy yellow-flowered plants. During the short ride from camp, Elizabeth carried the rifle in her hand and it seemed to acquaint itself with her. She had tested the piece in Ellsworth the morning she bought it, going down to the Smoky Hill and assuring herself the Winchester was as sound as she assumed. She had used fifteen rounds getting accustomed to the elevation, the kick, variations of sighting which she might need for windage. Fifteen rounds after several years of no shooting at all wasn't very much, but Elizabeth had a natural ability with firearms.

The spot Dodie led them to for the contest was off the road some five hundred yards, over a slight hill where tan boulders tumbled like turnips spilled from a sack and gray-green sage brush grew out of every depression. The soil was pale with streaks of orange hard rock beneath. The bay gelding danced under her, anticipating something different, and when Elizabeth dismounted, she scowled over at Willie, hoping he would leave her alone after he had been whipped in a fair fight.

When they started the third round at a distance of forty paces, Elizabeth and that Winchester were like one unit. She'd raise it, sight, draw in a breath, judge her pulse, squeeze the trigger. *Whap!* went the empty tin cans Jorge had sent for targets. Willie grew more nervous with each shot. He finally missed at seventy paces.

Joe sidled over to Casey. "I thought Willie would win this easy," he

84

said. "This ain't gonna help at all if she beats him."

Casey gave a lopsided grin. What a woman! he thought.

But Elizabeth missed her next shot, too. The teamsters were quiet as bed bugs when Willie raised his Henry for a second try. Elizabeth rubbed her palms on her pants legs. A fly buzzed along her jaw, landed; she reached slowly and brushed it away. Willie's shot nipped the outer edge of the can and sent it spinning. Not a true shot, but his backers cheered and whooped like they'd won a race.

Elizabeth stepped to the mark. She wiped sweat from her forehead and resettled her hat. Everyone got dead still.

"I say fifty dollars the kid makes it," came a quiet tenor voice. A stranger's voice with a heavy southern drawl.

Elizabeth nearly gagged. She had heard that man before.

The teamsters, Joe and Casey jerked around, shocked that someone had joined them. On seeing who it was, Joe went rigid, and Casey flipped loose the hammer thong that secured his revolver in the buckskin holster.

"This is a wagering affair, isn't it?" asked the quiet-spoken rider dressed all in black.

The remnants of his Alabama drawl gave his words a friendly sound, but distrustful thoughts flurried among the teamsters with Joe especially wondering if this were some diversion while other men attacked the wagons. Dodie Watson, Mel Burns and Al Guzlowski had already gone to their mounts, preparing to head back. John Bradshaw started for his mule while Seth cursed his broken hand that had convinced him to leave his handgun back at the wagons.

The thud of Elizabeth's heart seemed to start in her stomach and threatened her to sickness when she heard the next slow voice.

"Aw, hell. Who don't bet on sportin' affairs?"

Elizabeth levered the action on her rifle and slowly turned from the targets. Perspiration rolled along her jaw and added to the wet darkness on the bandanna around her neck.

"Sorry, son. I guess I wrecked your concentration," Blacky said, smiling at her. He pushed back his hat from his thin, angular face.

Pure logic flooded Elizabeth and she barked a harsh laugh at her foolish fears. These men didn't know her. The giant had seen her only once in a dark hotel room when her hair had been nearly to her waist and her clothes torn off (she couldn't look him in the eye for fear of screaming with that memory), and the other man—. She had heard his voice when Gabe Tillison came to the Johnson farm. Todd and Philip had described a man like this to her: all in black, two pistols, black horse. But he had never seen her in any guise.

Once her fear had relaxed, anger took over. Anger for what they represented and over the reminder of what she had endured because of them and their friends: getting slapped around, nearly raped, taking this grubby job on the wagon train. She gripped the rifle.

Casey stepped forward, scowling at the man. "What's your business here, mister, or do you always sneak up on folks like this?" he asked.

"The name's Goodhue. Darcy Goodhue." The man kept a forced smile under his well-groomed mustache and looked around, waiting for recognition.

Casey knew the name, and his eyes widened a bit; he clenched his jaw, hoping he wouldn't have to acknowledge this dark piece of his past.

"This here is Ox Lewis." Goodhue shrugged toward the giant. "Is this some private shoot-out here along a public road?" He tossed one slim leg over the saddle and dropped to the ground.

Clive Williams put his fat hand to the .36 Navy pistol that rode in his belt at the back of his pants. He couldn't remember if he had primed the loads.

"Come on," Darcy said, looking at everyone, but with his body facing Casey. "Fifty greenbacks on the young one, there."

Not a man among them had fifty dollars to their name, not even Casey.

Goodhue's grin broadened. "Or better, one hundred that I can hit both targets at the same time from here with my *pistoles*." The revolvers seemed to leap into his hands.

Just as fast, Casey had Goodhue covered with his Adams, drawing left-handed (which got Elizabeth's attention, as well as Goodhue's). Willie aimed the muzzle of his Henry at Ox.

"Ah don't believe they think we're friendly, Darcy," Ox drawled, a worried frown on his huge face.

Tension radiated from everyone and the riding animals all fidgeted, There was no doubt that if either of these strangers moved an eyebrow, they would be plant fodder in less than a second.

Darcy Goodhue released the butts of the handguns and slowly, one at a time, fitted them back into the black, copper studded holsters. "That better?" He was still smiling, and his gray eyes focused with excitement on Casey.

Four teamsters suddenly lit out for the wagon camp and Willie snuffled a laugh, feeling good at being on the control side of this situation.

"Dawson. Willie. Scout the area," Joe ordered. "Zee, you, Clive and Landers get on back to the wagons."

Elizabeth and three others started for their mounts, more than willing to leave. Willie didn't move. "What about the contest?"

Darcy Goodhue chuckled. "The kid was gonna beat you, boy," he said. "It was obvious. He's got what you call poise." That was a word once attributed to Goodhue, written in the paper, even, the time he gunned down the two toughs in Cairo in what was supposed to be duel with one of them. It had been a trap for Goodhue, but he had kept his "poise" and killed them both.

"Go on, Will," Joe said.

"Aw, Pa!" Willie slouched to his horse, glaring at Elizabeth.

She tightened the cinch and pulled into the saddle. She didn't even notice Willie who rode out, glowering under a defeat that was never confirmed.

"You sure you don't need no help here?" Tom Dawson asked, reluctant to leave. His blond stubble gave his square jaw an even rougher appearance.

"No," Joe said. "Pritchard and me will just have—."

"Pritchard?" Goodhue cut in. His voice came out tight and hard. "That must be why you seemed familiar. Wouldn't be that you used to be a Pink, would it?"

Casey's face got tight, muscles tensing rhythmically in his smooth jaw.

"I got a real sore spot for that Pink Pritchard, if you be him," Darcy said, setting his legs apart and squaring toward Casey.

"Darcy, forget it!" Ox ordered. "The war's over and then some." The authority of his voice seemed out of place with his docile hulk appearance. "There ain't gonna be no gun play," Ox said. And as confirmation, he rode his horse right up against Darcy's back, bumping the thin dark-haired man out of his tense stance.

"Get going," Joe said again to Elizabeth and Tom. "We'll be right behind you." Tom nodded and urged his horse forward, cutting through a tumble of rocks and toward a pinched stand of cedar trees to have a look around.

With her rifle cradled over her legs, barrel toward the intruders, Elizabeth angled her gelding behind Casey and Joe. "Be careful," she said low while the gelding fiddle-stepped, anxious to be on the move.

Casey's heart swelled in his chest as he took those words to be mostly for him. Deep in her thoughts, they were, too, for Elizabeth wondered at Goodhue's hostility. All the way back to the wagon camp, she kept listening for gunfire behind her. None came.

When Elizabeth reached camp, the teamsters who had returned from the contest were expounding on what happened, and speculating on what could have happened. They surmised ridiculous anecdotes about what was then happening with Joe, Casey and those two hombres who had ridden up. "I swear, that one bastard were as big as Al and Seth clumped together!" Clive exclaimed. His brown eyes, set in the folds of fat on his face, seemed to glitter.

"Hell, I coulda took him," Seth grumbled. "Bare handed! Even with this paw in a wrap!"

David Hastings set Pete Hayward and Ledbetter as sentries, alert to anything strange, but they all relaxed a bit when Willie and Dawson rode in, telling that there was no sign of anyone else around.

"Musta had grease on those guns, they came up so fast," Clive was muttering to Don Suthers. "What the hell kind were those, anyway? Goddamn!"

"They were Coopers," Elizabeth put in absently. "Fashioned like a Colt, but double-action."

Nobody questioned her authority on the subject. Willie sneered and cut a wedge of tobacco to gnaw on.

"We saw those bastards up in Ellsworth, seems like," Dawson said. "Riding with a gang or somethin'."

"They looked to me like some of Gabe Tillison's boys," Sim said in his puny voice. Even these words sounded like a complaint. "I hear tell the Daltons is regulars at Tillison's place in The Nations," Sim said.

"You hear. Go to hell, Sim. The Daltons don't need no two-bit horse trader like Gabe," Dodie said, his voice raspy.

"I tell you, that Goodhue did a change when he heard Casey's name. Asked him if he was a Pink," Tom Dawson laughed. "The Pinkertons did a bunch of spyin' on the ol' CSA. Really helped break 'em out West, here."

A few people scowled and turned away. Bradshaw grunted and spat tobacco juice. "War's best left done an' over."

"That's the truth of it," Pete agreed.

Mel and Don had been Southern sympathizers, as were many people from the Southwest.

"I wonder if Tillison ever found that gal who shot his youngest boy?" Pete spoke up, trying to change the topic. He scratched under the armpit of his blue plaid shirt.

"Someone tol' me he wants to do a little cuttin' on her like the doc had to do on Johnny," Seth said. Elizabeth cringed. "Get a woman with a gun and you got trouble."

"Well, she had a right, I figure," Horace said. Horace Cross always spoke in declarative tones while pointing a grimy finger in the air. "Johnny plum gave her some blows and then pulled a pistol and was shootin' the place up."

"That's talk," Dawson growled.

"Hell. I was there!" Horace went on, waving his arms.

Elizabeth sat as still as a stump, her nerves like drying rawhide, getting tighter by the second.

"What'd she look like?" Willie asked from where he slumped in the shade of Jorge's wagon.

"Long dark hair. A little gal. Looked sort of foreign."

"Foreign! You got your head up your ass," Dawson said. "I hear she was a big, buxom type. Lots of curls."

"You callin' me a liar?" Cross jerked toward him.

"No, he ain't," Pete Hayward said, stepping in. Even though he was of slight build, his carriage and scowl made the two stop short.

"Get to work, everyone," Hastings said. "I want things ready to go when Pritchard and MacGrin get back."

Some of the tension left Elizabeth as the men went to their work, wary and complaining about the heat. She couldn't recall Horace Cross from that Sunday night, just as he couldn't recall her. A little gal, he had said, when Elizabeth had rarely met a woman taller than she. She gave a long sigh.

Before long, Joe and Casey rode down the trail, flanking Ox Lewis and Darcy Goodhue. The teamsters got real quiet; the strangers rode on by, Goodhue with a sticky grin on his face and Ox looking like a huge lump on his big brown horse. They passed on out the trail with never a by-your-leave.

"So what the hell are they doing out here?" David Hastings asked.

"They're—looking for someone," Joe said, his eyes sliding to Elizabeth and then away. "A woman with dark hair: tall, dressed in city clothes. They wondered if a buckboard or hack had come by the wagon train."

"Hell, ain't nothin' come by us till they showed up!" Dodie said.

Seth snorted. "City-type woman! They must still be lookin' for that dance-hall gal."

Elizabeth bit her lip and fastened a tug line on the singletree of Ledbetter's wagon, grateful to be Zee Clark. As Elizabeth Fortune, she would have been found by now: in Salina, in Ellsworth, at Fort Larned. One of Gabe's men would have seen her, and—. She shivered, thinking of what Seth had said: do a little cutting on her.

"Hey, Pritchard, did that Goodhue know you from somewhere?" Dawson asked. "He sure did a turn when he heard your name."

Elizabeth looked over at Casey, curious, but wishing Dawson hadn't brought that up again.

"Sort of, I guess," Casey said with a shrug and a pained expression.

"Looked to me he was ready to take you on right there, if it hadn'ta been for the big guy."

"Shit. I'd like to see a contest between Pritchard and that pilgrim," John Bradshaw said. He spat tobacco juice for emphasis.

"Well, I told him another time," Casey said real casual. He walked his horse to the picket line.

"Hopefully you'll never see him again," Hastings growled. "That's all I need—a gun fight."

The teamsters debated the outcome of such a confrontation while they readied the teams for the trail.

Elizabeth more conscious than ever of her role as a boy, knew she couldn't let up for even a minute with Tillison's men looking for her. Even after the wagons lined out on the dirt road, she could see two small silhouettes shimmering in the heat waves of late afternoon. Their very presence made her tense and resentful and belligerent. That kept her disguise in place as well as anything. By evening, Joe reported that the men's tracks had veered to the southeast, off the Santa Fe Trail, headed toward the Tillison ranch, but Elizabeth had no illusions that she had heard the last of Gabe Tillison.

When I get out of Kansas, maybe it will be better, she thought.

After Kansas, it would be another five hundred miles before they got to Fort Union.

The encounter with Goodhue and Lewis superseded the teamsters' thoughts of which kid with the wagons was the best shot. Willie managed to bag two deer that evening, laying low complaints about his hunting duties. For supper, Jorge cut steaks from the carcass and pit roasted a large hunk all night so it would be ready for the next nooning. John Bradshaw and Dodie Watson grumbled because Willie hadn't brought in the livers. The rest of the deer was tossed aside with the tawny hides and left to rot beside the trail. Elizabeth glowered over the waste, but she enjoyed the fresh meat, wiping grease from her mouth with her sleeve, just like everyone else. Willie wasn't pleased, however. Zee Clark still had way too much respect from this crew to suit him and he started taking his meals with the second mess to be away from Zee.

"Gabe don't have the cleanest nose around, but I don't think he's into robbing wagon trains," Dodie said.

"What would he want, anyway?" Joe asked. "Sacks of seed? Iron piping?"

"Well." David chewed on the end the unlit cigar. "The way those two rode up on you. We could get hit by Indians again."

"Not this far north," Joe said.

"Hell, it's comin' on autumn," John Bradshaw said. "Injuns won't do nothin' that might lose them the winter handouts from the government."

"Pawnee, maybe. Fort Dodge was totally routed two years ago," David went on.

"That was before the Medicine Lodge Treaty," Pete put in.

"You expect those heathens to hold to that?"

"As much as we do," Casey said.

"I thought the treaty didn't allow the wild tribes to come north of the Arkansas River," Sim Chambers said. He chewed the end of his mustache, obviously nervous.

Dodie Watson chuckled. "This close to Indian country, there's no telling when some Kiowa might be tempted to add to his tribal standing or impress a young maiden by making off with a horse or two." Sim got more nervous. Dodie grinned. His comments got to Elizabeth, too, causing her to frown. She had read articles in *The Saturday Evening Post* about massacres, and still recalled the frightful details of the Minnesota Santee Uprising when she was ten.

"And the fact that forts Larned and Dodge are so close would make the theft even more of a coup," Bradshaw added.

"All the more reason we need a tighter watch in this camp. There's too much fooling around with games and festivities," David complained as he stalked off to his tent.

Sort of an overstatement. A couple of men sang tunes along with Horace Cross's mouth harp, and that was about as festive as they got, what with the heat and mosquitoes.

Elizabeth stared at the plains around them, suddenly distrusting the view. Bandits could be waiting to rob them, Indians might sneak out of the night. She jumped when Casey moved up beside her.

"I really don't think anything will happen," he said. "We'll set a watch, keep most of the stock with the wagons. Just precautionary stuff."

She gave him a weak smile.

"Mules aren't considered much of a take, anyway, unless someone were really hungry."

Elizabeth nodded, but continued to watch the prairie.

That night Mel Burns sat out with Elizabeth on night herd duty, and it helped her nervousness to have someone else around even though they weren't that far from the wagon camp. By swapping off rides around the herd, she was able to get her needed privacy. Mel, only a year older than Elizabeth, talked mostly about his family down in New Mexico Territory. He was lanky and narrow-shouldered, but kept himself clean and didn't get into spinning lurid yarns or spitting tobacco, although he did use snuff. They played a couple of hands of cards about two in the morning. Mel wasn't feeling too well, he said, and finally fell asleep, which was good since Elizabeth was about to suggest a betting game. He was such a push over, she would have cleaned him out without even thinking.

Casey rode by one time and asked how she was doing. She said fine. He asked how her feet were healing, that he hadn't seen her limping much. She said they were healing, pleased by his concern and curious about this man who had not only kept her secret but convinced Joe to help her, too. Elizabeth wondered about his many sojourns out of camp and exactly what his position was with this wagon train. He didn't drive, he didn't hunt, and David Hastings never yelled at him. And then there was the man in black—Goodhue—and his instant animosity at hearing Casey Pritchard's name. But Elizabeth kept her wonderment to herself, knowing one of the codes of the West was that a person's business was a person's private business.

If she had indicated any interest at all, however, Casey would have gladly spent the evening sitting right there with her, talking away. From east coast to the west, Casey had wooed and won several women, but his strong feelings for Elizabeth were different, and they spooked him. Maybe because she was so different. Tenacious, a risk-taker, intelligent. While he mused over why she was out here, he never thought about her mixed-blood heritage. Instead, pushing past the idea of holding her—of feeling her warmth mingle with his—was the possibility of himself as a settled family man. That thought had previously seemed laughable since he never expected to find the right woman. But now he was realizing with each moment how sincerely he was attracted to Elizabeth Fortune.

EIGHT

To deny my growing fears would be ludicrous. The land itself is
relentless and unpredictable, and then these teamsters...

13 August

The next day, out on his morning scout, Casey hailed down the east-
bound stage nearing the end of its fifteen-day run from Santa Fe to
Salina. The region was quiet, the driver reported, all the way through to
Fort Lyon.

"Got road agents up that-a way. You might want to get you a escort
from the fort," the mustached man said. He spat tobacco juice into the
dust.

This small coach carried mail and only one bleary-eyed passenger. It
would be one of the last coach runs along this section of the Santa Fe Trail.

"Bandits, huh? Are they organized?"

"Seem to be. I ain't lookin' forward to switchin' to that Kit Carson
run next month. No sir-ee." That was the new line the Barlow and
Sanderson stage company was adding on. The stage would meet up with
the railroad in Colorado and go south from there.

"Any name to these outlaws?" Casey asked.

"Which group? Got to be four or five workin' between Denver and
Raton Pass."

Casey groaned, dreading the possibilities ahead.

"Git yerself a escort. That's what the damn blue coats is out here for."

Casey only nodded as the stage rumbled off. Dust spurted in steady
plumes from the wheels.

Casey reported the information to Hastings, and rather than worry
about it, David seemed to rush to it. By taking advantage of the bright

moon and driving the teams once until midnight, the wagon train managed to be near Fort Dodge by the end of the second week in August. Heat and a gritty series of dust devils had continued to plague them, and even with fresh meat, the sullen men were at the edge of their patience about everything. Willie avoided Elizabeth, although he dreamed of a fight to the finish (he never lost in his dreams). Elizabeth suspected as much and was glad to have little contact with the surly youth. When she and Mel took night duty with the mule herd, she kept her gelding in plain sight since it had proved to be a good sentry, and her rifle was in her hand even during the day when she slept in the narrow hammock in the mess wagon (a fact which kept Jorge a bit nervous).

Early on August 13th they passed white-washed signs with faded warnings about the area's splenic fever epidemic.

"Goddamn that fever crap!" David cursed. Under his nervous hands, his grullo gelding pranced before the sign. Elizabeth, who had just climbed into the back of Jorge's wagon for her morning sleep, thought David was going to rip the sign out of the ground. "Cost me half my profits! Having to buy these confounded mules."

"Government thinks his oxen brought the fever in when we came up here," Pete Hayward said from his wagon seat. His wagon was behind Jorge's and off to the left, and he talked to Elizabeth over the mules' ears. "Put the whole bunch in quarantine."

"What's the splenic fever?" Elizabeth called. She pulled off the bandanna Pete had given her and wiped the sweat from her brow. The morning sun was so bright she had to squint.

"Some sickness brought in by Texas ticks. It drops cattle in their tracks."

"And I'm gonna insist on fair market value for those beeves," David was raving. "Get my money back somehow."

Elizabeth shook her head, amazed how David Hastings could always find something to fuss about. She sighed and wiggled her toes to the warming air. She was tired. The last few nights, Mel hadn't looked too good and Elizabeth had let him sleep, wondering what ailment he had. Even now, sitting his horse behind Horace Cross's wagon, Mel looked pale and seemed to slump in the saddle. Elizabeth frowned and laid back in the hammock, certain her sleep would be short. Mel was the one who should be in taking a rest.

Well before the nooning, David Hastings rousted her. Mel stepped off his horse directly into the mess wagon, his skin pale and clammy. Elizabeth, gritty-eyed and weary, pulled on her moccasins and rode Mel's horse off to the remuda. The heat seemed like a weight on her.

Later that day, under a glaring sun, they took a road that curved and sloped through more contours of land than Elizabeth had seen since Ellsworth. Large swells marked the river near Fort Dodge. Clumps of dark green marked various copses. The thought of shade kept everyone plodding with little comment. A town hadn't been established, but hide hunters and mustangers were steady customers to the wretched little dram shops set in the dale near the river. The ring of hammers and rasp of saws drifted to the wagon train, evidence that more permanent structures were being built.

But Joe kept the wagons going, passed the hovel of outbuildings; the teamsters prodded the animals along the road until even the sandstone and adobe structures of the three-company fort were out of sight behind humps of hills and bristly stands of scrub oak and cottonwood.

"Shit. I wanted to go inta the fort," Horace Cross complained.

"Yep. Belly up to a bar and cut the dust from our throats," John Bradshaw added.

"Hell, ain't no more civilization for put near a hundert 'n fifty miles," Dodie said. Other men cussed and growled their displeasure.

Elizabeth ground her teeth together. But she knew she couldn't quit the train now, not with Gabe Tillison's men looking for her.

"I was thinkin' of hittin' one of the cribs," Seth Landers said, leering. "It's the main business down there besides the saloons and hide buyers. They got to have some interesting gals around there."

The big man's comments further squelched Elizabeth's thought of quitting the train.

"What with the fort and all, a woman'd be plenty well-used by now," Bill Porter said.

"Sorta like plowin' in and out of a smoke stack," Dawson said. "Me. I like 'em tight."

Elizabeth moved to the other side of the mess wagon so she wouldn't have to hear the talk.

"I have to ride in and talk to Fort Dodge command," Casey was saying to Joe. "So I'll re-check the trail information."

"Perhaps I can go with you," Jorge said. "Go into the commissary for *un poco de*—."

"You'll stay here. Tell Casey what you need," Hastings interrupted. He fiddled with a fat cigar. "I want to be moving again by seven o'clock," he said.

"We're not moving anymore tonight," Joe responded. He wiped his face with a bandanna and tied it back around his neck. "Got six mules with loose shoes, several with sore frogs, bridles to repair, twelve of the critters are chafing since you've been pushing them ten and twelve hours. They need a solid rest."

"We've got to make up that time we lost at Ash Creek!"

"We can't do it if the mules are lame, Dave."

"Mel seems to have a touch of the ague, too," Casey said.

"I don't like camping this close to the fort," Hastings grumbled. "Can't afford to lose men to drink and brawls."

"Well, we're setting right here 'til morning," Joe said. "Don't worry. I'll give orders that no one's to leave camp." He turned to Elizabeth. "Go tell the men to unhitch."

Elizabeth nodded, not really wanting to be around the other men, but she did as she was told.

They had about half the mules unhitched when Dog signaled the approach of riders. They seemed to rise up out of a draw in the southeast, the forms like mirages, all wiggly in the late-day heat. Blue coats, brown horses.

"Wal, I'll be damned." John Bradshaw shifted his quid and watched the troopers.

The teamsters stared and seemed to move in slow motion, but Elizabeth stepped quickly toward the apparitions, her heart pounding in anticipation. The afternoon sun shown directly onto these people and the cavalrymen were black.

In 1870, the Negro cavalry and infantry (two regiments of each) made up more than thirty percent of the western forces, but that meant thirty percent of the three to four thousand men who kept martial law from Mexico to Canada, from the Missouri River into the Rocky

Mountains, so it wasn't surprising that not everyone had seen a Negro trooper.

"Uh. Brunettes at Fort Dodge?" said Clive Williams.

"Some was stationed nearly three years at Fort Larned," Dawson put in.

"Sure as hell glad they wasn't there when we was," Seth Landers grumbled. "Can't stand to be around niggers. They smell funny."

This conversation went unheard by Elizabeth. She had already moved beyond the wagons, staring with awe at the men. The yellowish McClellan saddles seemed bright in the late-afternoon sunlight.

The neat double column stopped fifty yards or so from the wagons and the white officer loped his horse over to where Hastings, Joe, and Casey clumped. Elizabeth, numb to all other goings on, walked out to where the troopers had stopped, squinting from under her straw hat at their faces and hoping beyond hope that one of these men would be Samuel Fortune.

One of the troopers chuckled and grinned down at Elizabeth. "What is it, boy? Ain't you never seen a Buffalo Soldier before?"

"Are you with the Ninth?" Elizabeth asked.

"Naw! Git on. I said we was Buffalo Soldiers." The talker pointed at the insignia on his sleeve. "Tenth Cavalry." If a voice could swagger, his would have.

But Elizabeth was let down, sort of like Christmas had come with no presents. Her shoulders drooped; she started away.

"What you know about the Ninth?" came a question.

The man asking was as fair complected as Elizabeth, but with brown kinky hair cut close to his scalp and an abundance of freckles across his cheeks and nose. From his full, round features, he peered at her, certain he was seeing a "brother."

"I know someone—down in New Mexico." Her voice trailed off. "Fort Union. Have you been there?"

"We been lots o' places, kid," said the braggart.

That's when Elizabeth knew for certain that just because her father's letters had come from Fort Union, he wasn't necessarily there. She wished she could reread his letters from several years ago; she had forgotten the name of the fort that garrisoned the Ninth. But those letters were packed in her trunk—the big trunk Houston had sent to Fort Union.

"Yeah, but this beats sittin' around down at Fort Stockton, waitin' fo' de Pacheez to make a raid," said another.

"Is that where the Ninth is garrisoned?" she asked.

"Naw. They're further south in Texas, at Fort Davis."

Elizabeth was stricken with a strange sense of betrayal. Even with no map to whisk out and see exactly where Fort Davis was, Elizabeth was certain it was hell and gone from Fort Union.

"You ever think about joining up? It's a prideful occupation," the light-skinned man said.

Elizabeth stared at him, considering what he said, and if the Johnsons or even Houston had been there right then, they would have been holding their breaths with fear for how she might answer.

But Elizabeth said, no, and was about to ask if they knew any people in the Ninth when Seth Landers called, "Zee! Get the hell in here and help unhitch this goddamn team!"

Seth was more worried about young Zee Clark getting contaminated by these black folks than he was about the mules. If he had known all the truths about Zee, he'd have died of apoplexy.

While this was going on, the cavalry lieutenant, Ballard, was talking with David Hastings, Joe MacGrin, and Casey. Seeing the Negro troopers refreshed Casey's memory of Elizabeth's predicament. He had already asked if these troopers were from the Ninth Cavalry. He was disappointed for Elizabeth's sake, although it despaired him to think that if her father were here, she would probably leave the wagon train and he wouldn't see her again. He wondered what her father would be like, and glanced at Elizabeth, again slightly amazed that she could be Negro. Not that he hadn't seen near-white Negroes before. He had: in South Carolina, in California, in Illinois. He hadn't thought much of it then, but now it complicated his emotions a bit. He frowned and returned his attention to the conversation at hand.

"You shouldn't have any problems west of here," Lt. Ballard said. "We're headed into Colorado Territory, but up north. Some trouble at the mines near La Porte. But the post commandant wanted me to tell you about this gang. They shouldn't be in this area, but if you saw anything of them back east, he'd sure like to know."

This "gang" the lieutenant referred to was a new group that had sprung up, not the Youngers or Daltons which harassed eastern Kansas and western Missouri, not the Rocky Mountain renegades that the stage driver had mentioned to Casey. The lieutenant had even brought a flyer put out by the sheriff in Wichita.

WANTED FOR ROBBERY AND ATTEMPTED MURDER, A GANG OF FOUR MEN MASKED AND HEAVILY ARMED. NO DISTINCTIVE MARKINGS OR HORSES. BELIEVED TO WORK FOR THE DANCE-HALL WOMAN ELIZABETH FORTUNE, WHO WAS INVOLVED IN A SHOOTING IN ELLSWORTH AT THE END OF JULY.

Joe MacGrin looked at the flyer and his squinty eyes got wide. He handed the paper to Casey who read it and snickered, then turned away to cover a guffaw. He shook his head, but as the words sank in, he got mad. When he looked back at Joe, his eyes were as flinty as the majordomo's.

"What's this gang done again?" Casey asked, interrupting David's interrogation about conditions along the trail.

"Hum? Oh. They robbed a saloon keeper and his wife last Sunday."

"That'd be the Wentworths, I'll bet." Casey folded the flyer and stuffed it in his pocket.

"Matter of fact, I think that was the name. And held up their other saloon in Wichita. The Wichita sheriff suggested it was a revenge motive of some sort."

"That's the Lord's truth," Joe muttered.

"They also hit the stage from Junction City just this week. No one killed or anything; they got over twelve hundred dollars and the mail pouch."

"It's no concern of ours unless they come west," David grumbled. "It's ahead I'm worried about. Any word of thugs up the trail?"

The lieutenant reassured David the way was clear through to Fort Lyon.

"Where did this flyer come from?" Joe demanded. His anger made his voice rough, and the lieutenant frowned at him, not sure of this hostility.

"A rider came into the fort yesterday. Had a stack of them."

Joe rolled his eyes and turned away. "That bastard," he growled.

Since Elizabeth had been with the wagon train on the times of these happenings, both Joe and Casey reached the quick conclusion that Gabe Tillison had staged all this to give Elizabeth a bad name and flush her out for his own revenge. Neither of them considered that Elizabeth could have hired men to do this work while she was someplace else, as some people may have thought. Like Sheriff Sieber.

It had been only a day since the Ellsworth County sheriff rode out to the Johnson's farm pursuing a tip he had received about Elizabeth Fortune. Sheriff Sieber remembered Elizabeth and was skeptical about this Fortune Gang business, even though Faye Wentworth swore the robbers told her it was revenge because she had fired Elizabeth. Nonetheless, he wasn't a man to shirk duty, and he rode to the Johnson's, arriving about two hours before Lost returned from his usual vegetable run to Fort Harker. Phyllis honestly said the young woman had stayed with them a few days, but she didn't know where she was now. Able, Jr., the only of the children who knew anything about Elizabeth's plans, since he had put her luggage on the freight wagons, was working in town, so the other Johnson kids vouched for their mother. Sheriff Sieber made a desultory search of the farm and left, more than glad not to find anything incriminating.

If Lost had already returned, however, the story might have been different. August, 1870 was just a month before Perry Hodgsen became U.S. Postmaster and express agent in Ellsworth, so all the mail for the town's people went through Fort Harker. That was why the post commandant (whose wife always bought vegetables from Lost) handed in person to Lost a package addressed to the Johnsons. When Lost opened it on the way home, he was astounded to find a U.S. mail sack containing $100.00 and a ring (which had been stolen from Faye Wentworth).

"Lordy, Able. That must be why the sheriff come by here," Phyllis said. "It couldn't possibly be from Elizabeth, though, 'cause she's with that wagon train goin' west."

"Somebody's tryin' to frame the poor girl," Lost said. And they both knew who that someone was.

They burned the mail sack, dropped the ring down the well, and hid the currency in the little box on the loft in the hen house where they kept their savings for Able Jr.'s schooling, and that was the end of that!

Back at Fort Dodge, Casey tried to work off his bad mood about the Tillison scam by helping with the camp setup. The conversation around him, however, heightened his discontent. The men talked about the cavalry and bad-mouthed Negro troopers and black folks in general. This time Elizabeth heard it all.

"What got me is how those Johnny Rebs could put up livin' with all of them," Seth grumbled. He was taking a chance, here, not knowing the war sympathies of some of the other men. "Havin' them in the house and cookin' the food and all," he went on. His face was florid from the heat. Sweat trickled from his hair, beside his eyes and into his beard.

"Aw, shit, Seth. That's what they're bred for," Cross said. He waved his hands for emphasis. "Put the big bucks in the field; the others in the house. Hell, they can be real devoted."

"Sorta like dogs," Sim put in. He fanned himself with his hat, then put it back on his head, squinting at the late afternoon sun.

Guzlowski, who had already been the brunt of New World prejudice, stared hard at his work wile others nodded. Casey's nostrils flared. He found the conversation offensive, and he also had this notion he had to protect Elizabeth. He clenched his teeth, too embarrassed to even glance at her.

But the talk wasn't anything new to her and she had learned to cope. When people accepted her as Negro, she found that whites liked to talk like this to aggravate her; when she got mistaken for white (like when she was at Normal School and now) they just rambled along with no personal malice intended. Elizabeth found it easier to ignore stupidity than a direct taunt. She was also caught up in worry over her plans. She wondered about the stage costs from Fort Union to Fort Davis. What had seemed such a simple trip when she started was suddenly getting very messy. She waved away a big group of gnats, blinked against the dust that swirled in the steady breeze, and was struck with a sudden weakness. Her father could be anywhere in the vast Southwest; she could wander and travel and search—. No, she rebuked herself. I can survive this. I will find him. Her hands shook while she kept on examining mules' feet like Joe had ordered her to. The teamsters continued with their philosophies.

"But I tell you, with all this freedom stuff—them ridin' around in uniforms and everythin'—you know what they're goin' after next," Sim said, portent filling his voice. They all knew what he meant, even Elizabeth, especially when Sim executed the age-old sign language with his fingers.

"Hell, I met a little number in Fort Riley who didn't care what she diddled," Seth said. He rubbed at his bearded chin with his bandaged hand. "Me and some boys let her know real fast what she had to stop doin'."

Now the talk was getting to Elizabeth, and if it had happened a week ago, she might have thought twice before rushing to Seth's aid when the wagon overturned.

"Right. Don't nobody want to dip their wick in a well that's been fouled," Horace said.

Elizabeth glared at the men, her face reddening.

"That pretty bitch couldn't work for a few days when we got done with her, but she was sure careful after that about who she bedded," Seth went on.

"Well, that's one hell of a lesson!" The words popped out before Elizabeth could stop herself, and the comment surprised everyone, especially Casey who was all knotted up and close to taking a swing at someone. Elizabeth kept on, her contempt obvious. "I mean, she must have thought real hard about what man to be with after that. The colored boy who probably didn't do her any harm, or you white low-lifes who beat her up."

The sarcasm wasn't lost on anyone, but Seth straightened up and studied Zee Clark with narrowed eyes. Anger and shock filled his face, as he realized Zee was *one of them.* "God damn it! God DAMN!" Seth stomped off.

Elizabeth knew what had happened. She had seen it before. People being nice to her and openly declaring their prejudice, then having to either eat those words or claim she was some sort of exception when they found out she wasn't white. Most of those people didn't like being made to feel a fool, and Seth was reacting in a classic way and certainly wasn't going to admit to anyone his error. He punched a mule in the ribs with his good hand. The animal squealed and went to bucking. Seth raised his hand to club the beast on the nose.

"What the hell are you doing?" Sim rushed to him (the mule was part of his team). Sim and Seth started shoving and arguing.

Casey was just then recovering from Elizabeth's speaking out and he didn't know whether to try and calm down Seth and Sim or hustle Elizabeth to some other part of camp. Cross's words interrupted his decision-making.

"I know! Your folks must have been real abolitionist people," the man said to Elizabeth like he'd solved a riddle. "Well, hell. I was a free-soiler, myself, but that don't mean I want them black souls livin' next door. Not them or these funny talkin' Polacks that's been showin' up of late."

Al Guzlowski whipped Cross around by the shoulder. His big fist shot out, clipping the other man on the chin. The brawl was on: Sim and Seth, Guzlowski and Cross; Dawson and Ledbetter resumed their dispute, and sickly Mel Burns took that opportunity to holler at Willie about helping with their tent. Willie socked him. By the time Joe dashed over from the make-shift forge he had set up, almost everyone had taken sides in one fracas or another. Pete hurried in to help break things up, and Hastings shook his head in disgust. Jorge set up the tripod and kettle that held the dinner beans on the far side of the mess wagon so it wouldn't collect dust while the men hollered and brawled. He called Dog with him while he arranged the fire, and the curious terrier laid down under the wagon, its bright eyes keen on the fighting.

Dust was plentiful as the men lambasted each other. Mules kicked and brayed. Elizabeth was calming two of the animals when Sim Chambers grabbed her arm. "This is all your fault, you little jackass!" Sim's fist was like a boulder in front of her face, looming too fast for her to react.

Whack!

Her thoughts went bright, then black…

Casey saw her get hit and ached to rush to her, but he was hanging on to Al Guzlowski's big shoulders to keep him from ramming Horace's head into the hub of a wagon wheel. Joe was yelling at Seth who, after pushing Sim out of the way, was indiscriminately punching mules and men alike with his healthy left hand. Bill Porter and Clive Williams shoved at each other while Dodie and John Bradshaw chuckled and made wager on who would be left standing when the dust cleared. Don Suther and Mervin didn't get involved.

Cross put an elbow to Al's groin and that got them apart. Casey turned to aid Elizabeth just as Dog licked her forehead, bringing her around. Casey was about to kneel over her with pampering comments when Willie MacGrin sauntered by. "Looks like *Señor* Zee finally ran into something he couldn't handle," Willie sneered. He had bloodied Mel's nose and felt pretty good.

Casey swallowed hard. "You okay, kid?" he managed to get out without his emotions bursting through.

Elizabeth wasn't too sure what was going on, since she had lost four minutes. She sat up, and when the split skin under her left eye started stinging, she recalled what had happened. Her head ached, and swelling was quickly closing her eye. Anger and dismay got all mixed in with her pain and she wanted to curl up some place for a good cry. Even Dog's whine of concern seemed too loud, and she shoved him away.

Beyond her, Ledbetter knocked Dawson down with a quick series of blows, but that fight wasn't over. Dawson pulled a knife. "Oh, no," Elizabeth said, pointing. Casey turned. When Dawson reared back to throw his Arkansas Toothpick at Ledbetter's back, Casey drew his gun and fired.

The bullet churned dust where it hit between Tom Dawson's spraddled legs, but it was close enough to get the man's attention. He whirled just as everyone else calmed to see what was happening. The mules were still carrying on something fierce.

"You lousy bastard! You coulda killed me!" Dawson dashed to Casey, fists balled and face scarlet with anger.

"You're still alive, Dawson, which is more than Ledbetter would have been if your knife had found its mark."

"You nearly shot me in the balls!"

All Elizabeth could see were boots, but when one foot took a long step forward—the heels rundown, mud smeared on the ragged cuffs of denim pants—she grabbed the ankle that went with it and yanked. "Just shut up," she said, all sense of propriety burned from her.

Dawson fell hard. "Damn you, boy!" he yelled, but when he started to get up, Dog bared his teeth and set up a fearsome growl. John Bradshaw and Pete Hayward stepped beside Dawson with looks that would have scared a moose.

"Let it go, Tom," Pete said. Dawson just glowered.

Elizabeth strode to the mess wagon, Dog close on her heels.

Casey looked a bit dazed, but only because he was again stunned by Elizabeth. What a woman! he thought. He was getting ready to tell her that, but Joe MacGrin called him, ordered him! to Hastings' tent.

At the mess wagon, Jorge studied Elizabeth with wide eyes. "Aye, caramba! Señor Zee. I feex a poultice. There is *mucho dolor?*"

Just as Willie's comment had kept Casey from revealing Elizabeth's true identity, so the nearness of this sincere man helped Elizabeth maintain her pose. I can survive this, she insisted to herself.

What she desperately wanted was a hot bath, clean hair and a soft bed; then getting up in the morning to have breakfast at a table with a cup of rich tea rather than coffee, a china plate full of scrambled eggs, a thick slice of ham, and scrapple with syrup. She leaned on the wagon wheel and laughed at her ridiculous thoughts. A laugh without humor.

Hearing that laugh reinforced Jorge's notions about Zee Clark. Here was the coldness that befitted a killer. His hand shook when he held out a damp cloth that smelled of witch hazel. "Sim Chambers. He didn't mean it. He is *hombre pequeño*; no need to hurt him."

This made Elizabeth guffaw (something she had learned to do in the past nine days). "Me? Hurt Sim?"

The cool cloth Jorge gave her felt good on her cheek and Elizabeth held it there while perusing the wagon yard. Jorge backed away and when he got to his cook pot on the other side of the wagon, he crossed himself and muttered a prayer.

Joe MacGrin had ordered the teamsters to settle the spooked mules and then come to Hastings' tent. People still harangued with each other even as they picketed the jittery animals. Seth was groaning like a wounded bear. He had forgotten himself and whacked out at something with his bandaged right hand. By the time Joe managed to calm the men and give a stern lecture about fights staying clean and no use of weapons (a reprimand not directed at Casey), Jorge had a hot meal ready, complete with fresh *sopapillas* and his special cactus jelly, which always sweetened a mood. Casey looked for Elizabeth, but under orders from David, she had already left camp, taking forty healthy mules with her to a quiet spot a mile east.

NINE

I should write to Houston, but explaining all this to anyone seems painful.

14 August

To Elizabeth, alone with the mule herd, the golden dusk seemed filled with heavy portent. Dark birds careened over the tree-lined Arkansas River; they snapped up insects. In the amber light that drenched the landscape, prairie dogs barked warnings. Even at this distance of two miles or so, she could hear an occasional wild, but human, cry erupt on the night from Hide Town, usually accompanied by slaps of gunfire. The mules seemed to be drawn to these feral sounds which also meant stables and grain. Elizabeth hobbled eight of the mules, hobbled and picketed one gray hinny that often caused trouble, and tethered the rest of them on picket pins so they wouldn't wander toward the fort. She also purged her distress with a good ten minutes of tears. Her horse nuzzled her curiously when she picketed it, and she pulled herself together, her eyes feeling swollen and hot.

Just after moon rise, while the sun still hung on the western sky, the hard gallop of several horses reverberated through the ground. Elizabeth stepped back from the small fire she had just built, rifle in hand. The horsemen sped past unseen beyond a set of low eastern hills.

The brown land cooled. Hunter and hunted began their evening stealth: owl after snake, snake after vole. Tarantulas snuggled in sandy pits awaiting hapless beetles. Elizabeth wasn't after anything but some peace and quiet. She considered herself neither hunter nor prey, although in some ways she was both. Just as was Casey Pritchard who rode in the general direction of Fort Dodge.

As he rode through the bright twilight, Casey was hoping to get word at Fort Dodge about the legal questions involving Hastings' new store, and he was also planning to send some wires, put out feelers of his own, about Jeffery Bragg, now deceased, who had sold the store to Jake Hastings and whose wife was denying the sale was ever made. Yet beneath these professional concerns surged more basic thoughts. Rather like the bison bull twenty-three miles northwest, the one whose tail slapped the air as it trotted along the stretched-out herd, head raised, bellowing ascending-tones to lure a mate. Casey wasn't bellowing. Most human males aren't so overt. And he was much more discriminating than the bison, not wanting just any old snorted response. He could get that in the cribs around Fort Dodge. No, Casey had one particular female in mind and homed in on her now as the hot-coal sun began to dissolve toward the ash-colored horizon.

The mules, oblivious to sunset or sex, ate stiff grass. Casey spotted them and the flicker of a tiny fire near a stubby hackberry. A bay horse was tied off to the left, unsaddled, head up and peering at him. He guided his horse down the slope, currently the hunter. "Halloo the camp!" he called.

"Mr. Pritchard!"

This statement came from a depression twenty yards to his left and, surprised, Casey jerked in the saddle; his horse side-stepped and snorted.

"I expected Mr. Burns," Elizabeth said, standing from her tense crouch, rifle at ready.

"You surely do have a way of sneaking up on a fellow." A double truth, that comment. Zee Clark was stealthy, and two weeks ago Elizabeth Fortune had caught Casey's emotions unaware. "How are you doing? Joe and I were worried."

True words, but Joe hadn't suggested Casey ride out to see about her. In fact, if the older man could have seen the eagerness with which Casey dismounted, or noted how the man's heart was pounding like he'd just run a race, Joe might have taken a whip to Casey.

"All right, I guess. Is Mel too sick to come out?

"He's got a smashed nose and that ague he's been fighting for the past few days."

With a gentle touch on Elizabeth's chin, Casey turned her head so he could examine her injury in the dwindling daylight. "I thought it was going to be worse than this." He could make out the dark coloration above her cheek bone, but the eye wasn't shut tight the way it had been when she left camp. Casey thought nothing of her red, puffy eye rims.

"Mr. Estévez gave me something for it. Thank you for your concern, Mr. Pritchard." She backed away from him.

"Casey. Call me Casey." Her hesitation prompted him to add, "Zee Clark ought to, you know. It seems odd your calling everyone so formally."

"Yes. I suppose…Casey." She started for her camp fire. "Have things calmed down back there?"

"I reckon. Dawson's still pretty mad at me for shooting at him."

"People tend to get upset by that." An image of Johnny and Hank Tillison chilled her.

"Teamsters tend to get upset by *any*thing." He tied his horse near the bay gelding, his back to Elizabeth. "But, I swear, the way Seth and Horace were talking, it's hard to believe the fifteenth amendment got passed this year." He turned to her, his arms at his side. "I'm—I'm sorry about them."

Elizabeth wished she could make out his expression in the evening light. The number of common laborers, West or East, who knew about Congress granting full suffrage to Negro citizens could have filled a small saloon where they would have gotten drunk lamenting the ratification. Elizabeth had already guessed that Casey wasn't a common laborer, and his manner of telling his unexpected knowledge put her at ease. She was certain he didn't expect a response.

In her Zee Clark role, she welcomed his company as a friend. She untied her moccasins and pulled them off. The cool air was refreshing on her nearly-healed feet. "I've admired that revolver you carry," she said.

Casey joined her by the rock-lined fire, not needing its warmth with the internal heat he was experiencing. His pulse jumped on seeing her naked toes.

"I take it, it shoots true," she went on, oblivious to his frustration. "That's why Mr. Dawson isn't dead."

"It shoots true. A fine piece." He handed it to her, and collected his wits while she leaned toward the firelight and made an expert examination of the British-made Adams.

"This is why you're with the wagon train isn't it? Or are you part owner?"

"I'm not a hired gunman or anything," he said defensively. He wasn't sure how much to tell her, and propped himself back on his forearms while he thought. Stars began to twinkle on the darkening sky. "I'm trying to solve a mystery for David Hastings. It's my business."

"Do you still work for Mr. Pinkerton? I mean, you did, didn't you? Like that gunman said."

"Yes. I did."

Her curiosity overcame the code of the West, and she asked: "Where did that fellow know you from? Is he wanted for something?"

Casey was quiet a long while, then sighed. "Pinkertons did a lot of the scouting of the Confederate headquarters in Arkansas," he said. "The Union forces went in—." He sat up, smoothed back his hair. "They closed the place down, and the tactics weren't the greatest." His discomfort was obvious. "All in all, it's something I wish I hadn't been involved in, not even marginally."

Elizabeth filtered through all the things she had heard about the war. Of this she was ignorant.

"Do you still work for Pinkerton?"

"No. I'm on my own now. I plan to set up a really good detective agency in Santa Fe."

"Your own agency! Fancy that." Zee Clark's persona had slipped away with the sunlight. "There's a need for such down there?" Elizabeth's voice was light as goose down and she wrapped her arms around her knees.

"Yes, indeed. What with mining disputes and robberies, missing persons to find."

"Missing persons. Huh."

"Heirs to wills, mostly."

"Or rich families trying to locate wayward kin," Elizabeth said sarcastically.

"You sound disapproving," he said.

"Oh, no. It's just that private detectives' scruples are often wanting." In the ensuing silence, Elizabeth quickly judged that she had offended him and hurried to make amends. "I don't mean you! But I've heard of detectives who get paid by the week and follow people around for months before they inform their clients." That had happened when Houston left home—before Grandfather Clark knew Houston had become a gambler. Elizabeth had known where he was the whole time.

"I'm sure that's often done, but I ask payment only for the results, not for the time involved."

"You could lose money that way."

"Not since I know what I'm doing." His confident, almost boastful tone made Elizabeth smile; but his next words reversed that. "I know I'm prying, but—. Is your family looking for you?" Again, a poignant silence. Casey pressed on, spurred by his professional curiosity and his attraction to this woman. "It seems odd you'd be out here without proper finances and all."

Elizabeth nearly asked if he were hoping for reward money, but his sincerity was so concrete it squelched the thought and locked her into tense despair. Her need to confide was as urgent as a thrush to morning song.

"My grandfather turned me out," she confessed. Casey blinked with surprise. "My grandmother passed on in May—. She was the only reason he did anything for me. I guess I remind him of how he thinks his daughter went astray in her marriage. I show my Fortune heritage much more than my brothers do. He could accept them, but—"

"You have brothers?"

"Yes. Two of them."

"Oh!"

"Goodness, I'm not some romantic mistake! My parents loved each other. Were married!"

"Well, if I had a sister, I'd surely not let her roam the West unattended!"

"Oh." Elizabeth shifted uncomfortably, not knowing how to defend her brothers. She sighed. Then words tumbled out about Minnesota and the farm she so loved. She didn't tell how her parents had been forced to move away from Indiana because in 1846 mixed marriages were illegal in that state, and in Ohio, and in Illinois. But Elizabeth did tell about Grandfather Clark kidnapping the boys when she was seven and leaving her behind; and how Scott liked being a Clark; and all the complications that led up to her being in Terre Haute.

"I tried to fit in, but it never worked. I was at Normal school when I heard the war was over." She sighed and remembered how pretending she was white made her stomach hurt the whole time she was there. "I ran off when the news came. Got a ride back to Terre Haute on a farm wagon so I could be there when my father got home. I thought we'd go back to the farm in Minnesota, but everything went wrong. Mr. Lincoln got killed, the cost to start farming again when the land had been fallow so long was too much; Daddy sold the land and reenlisted with the Western cavalry. So anyway," Elizabeth finished. "I'm on my own."

Venting the facts seemed to take a load off her although she was struck with the odd awareness of how much she had revealed to this man. Embarrassed, she snugged her legs closer to her chest.

Casey was stunned by her situation and impressed by her daring. She was a refugee, a pioneer, an orphan, and he still found it hard to believe her brothers had abandoned her, too. "But what about your brothers?" he asked.

"Scott's in college," she said, wondering if Scott even cared where she was.

"And the other?"

"Houston gave me half of his savings for this trip. It paid my way to Kansas." She smiled sadly, thinking of her brother. "He taught me how to deal cards when I was thirteen. Right now, he's in charge of a casino on a Mississippi riverboat." And, she thought, a job he wouldn't have if they didn't think him white.

"Really! My mother has a casino in her hotel." Casey was happy to turn the conversation, sensing depression coming over Elizabeth.

"She owns a hotel? Where?"

"In Chicago. I didn't grow up there, though."

"I know you don't have any sisters, but—"

"How do you know that?"

"From what you said earlier, but what about brothers?"

"Nope. Just me. My father disappeared when I was a tike."

"Disappeared?"

"During the gold rush in California. There was a land slide one winter. All the bodies weren't found. My mother likes to think that he survived and went back to the Rockies. He was a mountain man once."

Casey never believed he survived; never even believed his father was a mountain man although he firmly maintained the story his mother, Susan, always insisted. When he was little, her lie confused him, but in later years he realized it helped create her defense against the approach of other men: that promise that her husband would soon return. He actually thought his father had been some shiftless sort whom she may have been glad to be rid of. He was almost right. It was Susan who had been lured by the gold rush. She panned gold until Casey was nine, fending off claim jumpers and suitors and worse, until she accumulated enough money to buy her first hotel. Now she was an elegant, refined member of Chicago's elite. Casey loved her dearly, but she had set quite a standard of independence by which he viewed other women. No one had measured up—until now.

"That's where I got my name," he went on. "Casey. Kay Cee. For Kit Carson. Mother always insisted my dad and he were friends."

"Kit Carson Pritchard?"

They both laughed, and then they talked about mountainmen and trapping, with Elizabeth telling about a wolverine hunt she went on with her father when she was nine.

"You know, sitting here in the dark talking about casinos and guns and wild critters almost makes me forget who I'm talking to," Casey said. "You can be a pretty convincing boy, some times."

And at other times... The implication went unsaid, but not unheeded. Sitting alone in the dark with this man—with this attractive man—this young attractive man she respected and who had similar interests and dislikes—set Elizabeth's heart to pounding with a mix of pleasure and dismay. Deep below her stomach throbbed a sudden need. If the sun had materialized overhead and cast them in midday glare, Elizabeth wouldn't have felt anymore aware or vulnerable than she did right then.

Casey wasn't caught unaware. For days he had been enduring what she had just recognized, and like that buffalo bull, if he had taken to song it would have been low and guttural, filled with sensual growls and blaring desires.

The fire flared and popped. Casey lurched up and rubbed the back of his neck. "Well!"

Elizabeth got up, too, resisting the urge to wrap herself in the tarp for protection. To quell her continuing desires, she began planning her defense, noting the closeness of her rifle, the edge of her moccasin that she could grab and whack Casey with; she had her derringer in her pocket.

Nothing probably would have happened, had it been daylight. Casey's own trail-worn appearance would have made him shy, and he could have seen her clearly: standing there in her dusty boy's clothes, barefooted with a bruise on her cheek. In fact, they both might have gotten a chuckle out of the situation. But it was night.

Casey touched her shoulder with intentions for a simple little kiss, a brotherly sort of thing. He maintained a firm resolve to do no more than that, and a good thing, too, because the hunter became the hunted.

His lips brushed on hers. All of Elizabeth's trepidation washed away and she gripped his shirt front and responded to his kiss with more passion than Casey anticipated. Up on tiptoes to reach him, she moved her mouth on his like she was sucking a peach. Her tongue traced his moist lips, probing slightly and he couldn't hold back a moan of pleasure. Their bodies together, with his left thigh between her legs and he cupped his hands around her tight buttocks and held her closer.

But Casey's plans for Elizabeth were greater than an illicit roll in the hay (or scrub grass, as was this case) and so he pulled away, breathless, hot and hard. Only then did Elizabeth want to dissolve like sugar in a rainstorm because of her brazen actions.

"Oh! Oh, dear!" she said. She drew a deep breath and squeezed shut her eyes, then snapped them open, afraid of what Casey might do next. Fleeing into the darkness seemed her only solution, but when she stepped off the tarp, hard rocks poked her bare feet.

"You really must go, Mr. Pritchard." She stood on the edge of the ground sheet, trying to sound like she was in a well-lit parlor.

Her proper address to him didn't at all seem strange to Casey. He was Mr. Pritchard, and she was most definitely Miss Fortune. The back of his hand went to his warm lips and Casey wanted to do flips of joy over her response to him. But he kept his feet on the ground and shuffled back a bit so he wouldn't go to her again. "You're right, Miss Fortune." God, more woman than I ever dreamed! he was thinking. The wrinkles he squeezed in the rim of his brown hat would be there for days. "You take care of yourself, now."

"Certainly. You, too."

He backed to his horse, not that Elizabeth knew. She stared, appalled, at her bare feet, and perspiration created a sheen across her forehead and down her neck.

"Goodbye," he said. That came out like an order, as if they wouldn't see each other for months. But because of Elizabeth's charade, they were fellow workers on a wagon train and both knew it would be a long time before they could allow this closeness to happen again. Elizabeth vowed anew her determination to uphold her upbringing and remain chaste, and Casey (sensing this) didn't want to jeopardize what he really wanted. As he shakily reined his horse toward Fort Dodge, Elizabeth stood ram-rod straight in her embarrassment. Heat lightning flickered on the night sky as if their passions had fled to the clouds; or maybe a war took place behind a distant rise of land.

Ten

Kit Carson Pritchard. He is so easy to talk to! But I have to be more careful. He has a charming smile, but I'm certain he's just playing me for a fool.

13 August

The world was the size of a walnut with only two people in it. Or so Elizabeth and Casey felt that night near Fort Dodge. Elsewhere, things weren't so simple. Vigilantes enforced law in Montana towns while Mangas Coloradas and Cochise led Apaches on bloody raids in southern New Mexico and Arizona.

The Wichita paper had an article about the Fortune Gang raiding farmers near Hunnewell, Kansas, stealing chickens and such, and yelling Elizabeth's name at the top of their lungs. In Trinidad, folks talked about the Anglo who had been shot and left for dead in an arroyo outside of town. David Hastings' brother, Jake, was recovering at his hillside house. This was grapevine news, since Trinidad didn't yet have a newspaper; and even the canniest reporter wouldn't have known how the tightening circle of law enforcement had made Gabe Tillison jumpy. On that very evening, while Elizabeth was surprising herself and Casey with her emotions, Gabe's gang robbed a trading store in Medicine Lodge where one of the outlaws was wounded and captured.

By morning, Gabe began plans to move west, and Elizabeth's euphoria, caused by her encounter with Casey, started to wane. She couldn't afford herself any womanly reveries. Being Zee Clark was a full time job, and if she slipped up for even an instant, she would be stranded on the prairie, or sent back east by over-protective men, or ravaged by a bunch of grubby teamsters. Another fact also pulled her back to reality. Casey Pritchard was white.

While Elizabeth gathered up her obstinate charges, the bright yellow dawn illuminated more to her than the fat clouds on the horizon. She recalled the planter on the stage near Clarksville, Tennessee, who had tried to buy her favors (and he had thought her white); the obscene approaches some white men made to the young women at Fisk, the rape attempt by Hank Tillison.

"I've really been stupid," Elizabeth growled. Her horse flicked its ears to her voice. She clenched her teeth, recalling too well how nice it had been to have Casey's concern about her injuries and then his embrace. She shook her head. "He figures I'll just go to him whenever he wants, especially since he's got the threat of exposing who I am to the others."

She shuddered when she thought of all those men suddenly knowing she was Negro *and* female.

The mules didn't give her any problems when she drove them down to the Arkansas for water. While they drank, she moved upstream and took care of morning ablutions and got a good look at her reflection on the water surface. The purple bruise on her cheekbone and discoloration below her eye gave renewed explanation for her horrible headache. Her appearance would have kept anyone from questioning her sex, and it made her believe all the more that Casey Pritchard was toying with her. Faint scars still marked her lip and chin from the whacks of Johnny and Hank Tillison. Her womanly feelings from the previous night blew away in the morning breeze, and she took on her Zee Clark role with grim determination.

The sun glared a hand span above the treetops when Elizabeth drove the mules to the wagon camp.

"Where the hell have you been!" David Hastings yelled as she walked the mules in a circle to settle them. Sim Chambers and Mervin Gaynor shuffled out to catch up their beasts.

David rode his horse beside hers, a thick cigar unlit and sticking from the corner of his mouth like a peg. He talked around it. "I sent Clive out and he couldn't find hide nor hair of you!"

"Closest water was the river," Elizabeth said. Wind tossed her horse's dark mane; she tightened the tie on her hat.

"You could have had the whole confounded herd stole! You don't know who the hell's lurking around these parts. Damn buffalo runners, mustangers, Indians."

He said all this as he rode off to count the mules, certain Zee Clark had lost one or two. Elizabeth ignored him and rode on to the camp.

"Don't mind him," Pete Hayward said when Elizabeth reined up at the picket line near the mess wagon. Dodie Watson and Bill Porter stood nearby chewing some jerky. Casey wasn't around. Neither was Willie. "He figured you'd run off to Hide Town, I reckon."

Seasoned teamster Amos Ledbetter ambled up, a week's growth on his narrow chin and stuffing his blue flannel shirt into his pants. "He's plumb skeered some of us is gonna git some pleasures somewheres."

"Can't see Zee gettin' no pleasures, with his face all bunged up like that," Bill Porter said, scratching his red beard.

"The whores would have to mother him, that's all. Pull that baby face all up to their tits." Ledbetter laughed and slapped his leg. "Bet you wish you'd thought of that, heh Zee?"

Elizabeth's scowl deepened. She dismounted on the off side of her horse to hide her blush from the men. Dog came over for a pat.

"Seth took off," Dodie mentioned in his raspy voice.

"Yep. Gonna find hisself some sympathy." Ledbetter's chuckle was a vocal leer.

"He broke his hand up some more with all that damn mule punchin' he done," Dodie went on.

The broken hand might have been Seth's excuse for leaving, but Elizabeth knew the real reason: he didn't want to work around that colored boy, Zee Clark. Elizabeth ducked under her horse's head, put her back to the men while she undid the latigos on the saddle.

A horse pounded in. "Don't unsaddle, Clark. We're pullin' out of here," came David's harsh tone. "You've got to run the loose stock 'cause Mel's still laid up with whatever. You men get your teams hitched!"

"Who's gonna drive for John and Horace?" Dodie asked. "They got a case of ague, too."

"It's their own bull-headedness they're suffering from," David said.

"They snuck off into town last night," Pete said, bringing Elizabeth a tin cup of coffee. "Ate some bad food, looks like."

"Hell, it's just Jorge's cookin'!" Ledbetter teased.

"I hear you, Meester Ledbetter," Jorge called from where he closed the side box on his wagon. "Tonight there will be nettles *en las frijoles solamente por usted*—only for you."

Ledbetter laughed and sliced a piece of tobacco from a block as he started toward the mules.

"Shouldn't be goin' no wheres with men sick," Bill Porter complained.

"Who's running this outfit, Porter!" David barked. "Now get to work!"

"He's pretty sore that we might have to hole up for a few days," Pete said when Hastings rode off. The man peered at Elizabeth, examining her cheek. "You don't look so bad. That shiner'll heal in no time." He started away.

Elizabeth just glowered.

With David Hastings and Joe MacGrin driving for the two sick men, they set up camp another eight miles west. Far enough to satisfy David that the men wouldn't head back to Fort Dodge. Most of them grumbled about it, especially that evening when the sun started sinking and Casey Pritchard still hadn't returned.

"He probably found hisself some little blonde-headed wonder and is workin' her real good even now," Ledbetter said with a laugh.

"And he's drinking whiskey. Lord. Bet they got more than red-eye down there."

Elizabeth tried to imagine Casey drinking in some sleazy bar and bragging about the mulatto he was setting up. His genuine smile and friendly conversation overrode this, however, no matter how hard she tried to make him a villain.

"Shit. That thar town's a piss hole. All they serve is peppered rotgut what's barely fit fer the Injuns," Bradshaw said.

"Got to go to Denver for good liquor," someone put in.

"And women! What do you think, Sim?"

Sim just shrugged since he didn't have anything to brag and wasn't imaginative enough to think up a tale. Don Suther, a strong family man, limped off toward where Mel lay listlessly on his bed-roll. Mervin

Gaynor went with him.

"St. Louis got the best whores I ever met," Ledbetter said, and he launched into a story. Willie laughed and wanted to tell everyone about his few steamy nights in Santa Fe, but he didn't since his dad was around.

Elizabeth moved off with a lantern, industriously braiding grass for a quail snare, something she had suggested to Jorge. She hoped she'd catch enough of the birds for Jorge to fix a good stew and add some variety of the fare. The work helped her ignore the talk, but she still heard more than she wanted to.

"I get me the best wimmen in a 'Rapahoe camp." Dodie Watson gave a lusty laugh. "They know how to treat a body."

"Didn't know you for a squaw man, Dodie," Ledbetter said.

"Hell, that's the best he kin do. Some greasy red bitch," spoke Clive. He and Dodie got into a name-calling session that even the mules shied from.

"Zee."

She jerked and looked up at Joe MacGrin.

"Take those mules over there out to grass," he said. "Stay with them, too. I'm hearing a lot of coyotes tonight." He cast a disparaging glance toward the main camp fire.

"Yessir."

Elizabeth wondered if Joe ordered her off to protect her from the bawdry or so he could join in without her overhearing. She had noticed he didn't swear as much since Fort Larned. While she saddled up and collected the mules, she wondered what Casey would do if he had been there, and then thought about him still at Fort Dodge, or in Hide Town, or wherever.

If Casey had been in camp he wouldn't have involved himself in the teamsters' rough talk. He never considered bordello nights as anything to brag about. But Elizabeth's imagination got active and she made up stories for him. The ideas made her flush.

These feelings weren't new to Elizabeth. By age nineteen, many women had experienced, responded, and were married with one or two kids. Elizabeth had almost done that herself. In '68 at Fisk, a brown-skinned, lean-bodied boy had courted her with ribbon-tied sprigs of forsythia and surrey rides along the Cumberland. In April, he initiated illicit kisses on the shadowed lawn beside Union Barracks. Elizabeth's internal tumult had been worse than water boiling in a sealed container, and if she hadn't the self control, 1870 would have found her married and living in Charleston, South Carolina, her husband a headmaster at one of the many Negro academies in that town. Her dread of the east and dislike of city life had helped her resist him. "You're a snob!" He had declared. "You think you're too good for me, don't you? You and your high-toned self." Although she tried to explain, his continued attack had kept her from a situation she wouldn't have been happy with for long.

But now the pot was brewing again, and she got angry because Casey Pritchard was the heat.

Elizabeth laid out her camp near a deep swag of hills, well out of ear-shot of the men, although she could see them sitting around the fire, walking back and forth, looking no taller than her hand. Where she was, deep impressions pocked the earth. Back in the hard winter of '22, kegs and boxes of goods had been buried here for safe keeping after all the mules of a wagon train died. The men had walked to civilization (which was the Illinois border back then), got more mules and returned for the goods. Over the years, erosion and natural land shifts turned The Caches, as they were called, into a setting for wagon-train stops and a point of interest for creative stage drivers to impress pilgrims with the rigors of the West. The old depressions held more moisture than the rest of the land, and locust and elderberry grew thick, making it a good place for the mules. Elizabeth looked forward to the solitude.

Right after moon rise, the low whicker of her gelding made her look down the hill. A lone figure trudged up the grass from the main camp. Only when he was a stone's throw away did Elizabeth recognize the bearded man in his mid-twenties, who looked more like mid-thirties, as Mervin Gaynor. Elizabeth put her hand in her pocket, wrapped her fingers around the stock of her derringer, wondering what he wanted.

"Hallo! I been sent out to join you. Volunteered," Mervin said as he waved. "You got a nice spot here." He plunked down his belongings and looked around.

Elizabeth gritted her teeth.

"Gettin' too foul for me back in camp, and comin' on a Sunday, at that." He fiddled with an old pipe and struck a match. The smell of sulfur wafted away on the steady breeze. "I'm glad MacGrin is keeping you away from that rabble. I seen the way he's been lookin' out for you," he went on as he sat down. "At least we won't be workin' on this Lord's Day."

Elizabeth sat sideways to the fire so she wasn't looking right into it—a tip her father had taught her. It kept her from being night blind if she had to see onto the plains. Now it also kept her from facing Mervin. She bent back to work on the grass snare.

"You keep to yourself like you're doin' and mebbe you won't get tempted to sin like those men have."

Mervin hadn't shown himself to be a Bible thumper. In fact, Elizabeth had heard Don Suther say that Mervin couldn't even read and Mervin leafed through the Bible muttering his own version of it. Other than those spiritual moments, Mervin was most times silent. Elizabeth hoped he wasn't about to change. Although she had gone to church regularly with her Grandmother Clark, she had no real fondness for the Christian religion, especially not from missionaries. Sometimes she'd try to analyze that feeling: her mother, after all, had been working with missionaries when her parents met. Yet, she knew her mother hadn't stayed with it and could remember her father talking about the hypocrisy of it all. Her main memories were of the good Lutheran Minnesotans who, because of the Sioux uprising, refused credit or service to her father and their mixed-blood neighbors. And she recalled with rancor the local Hoosiers, Christians one and all, who never prosecuted the brigands that had set fire to her grandpa George Fortune's shop and to the Roberts community church. Indiana Rebels, Grandma Jannie had called the men. George Fortune had died fighting those fires, and that happened three years before the War. Honest, true thinking, white people, like her mother, seemed too scarce to count, and what matter anyway? Elizabeth knew the Wilson Clarks ruled.

Mervin stayed quiet for a while, smoking and staring into the flames. Elizabeth finished the natural noose, laid it beside five others. She had already noted places in the hillside depressions that would be good to lay them out. She started notching the sticks she would use for the little traps.

"It's the wickedness of the flesh which draws men from the ways of Jesus," Mervin started. He had pulled a sewing kit from his haversack and was darning a sock. "You jest remember, Zee, that wimmen is a needed part of procreation. Amen. To carry man's seed, be his help mate. That's the original intent." He nodded emphatically. "But after the apple. Well. They're not the way God intended. Devil's tools, they are, whose sole purpose is to beguile and set men to sin."

Elizabeth flinched at the concept and sliced a little notch out of her left thumb. Mervin went on while she sucked at the cut.

"They talk about wimmen bein' the salt of the earth." He chuckled. "Don't know too many men who can live drinkin' brine. Do you? Now me. My pa taught me the hex signs to keep a woman from puttin' a cravin' of evil in me. I'll teach them to you."

"That's all right, Mr. Gaynor. I—"

"Oh, I don't mind. You're gettin' to that age where you need to know. Got to be in daylight, though, to make sure you get it jest right."

Elizabeth bit the inside of her lip to stifle a rude comment.

"Me though," he went on. "I ain't takin' no chances. There's a female back in Portsmouth. I'm from Ohio, you know. I'm a-sendin' for her when I can. Have her to cook and clean—have my babies. She's real dull witted and I won't have to worry none about her creatin' no devilment."

Elizabeth lurched up, not sure she could quell her disdain much longer. "I've got to set my snares," she said, starting away.

Those words would have had double meaning to Mervin if he had known Zee Clark was female. But he merely nodded thoughtfully while Elizabeth dashed up the hill.

The full moon gave her enough light to set the quail snares and then she hunched in the brush out of camp until she saw Mervin put away his mending and roll out his bedding. Quietly, she came back, but saddled up her gelding as Mervin lay down. She took a slow trip around the mules. Mervin was soundly asleep when she returned.

But she got another visitor that night. Casey Pritchard returned from Fort Dodge and rode out to see how she was. Knowing it was Casey by his distinctive horse, Elizabeth had mounted her bay when she saw him coming and headed her horse west. He pulled his animal along side hers.

"How's the eye?" he asked.

"Fine, thank you." Her reply was snippy, although remembrance of his previous night's visit gusted through her thoughts and stormed her senses with warm vulnerable feelings. She steeled herself against them, remembering her decision and her interpretation of Casey's actions.

"Did you have a good trip to the fort?" she asked, a sharpness in her voice as she recalled the speculation in camp about his activities.

"I guess. I was surprised to learn that John and Horace had been there. I never even saw them. David's really mad because they're so hung over."

"Pete thinks they ate some bad food."

"That's possible down there."

"I guess we're going to be stuck here for a while."

"I think everyone, mules included, needs a break."

"I guess. I just want to get out of Kansas and away from anything that could be related to the Tillisons."

"I can't blame you there."

Elizabeth scowled into the darkness, trying to resist her urge to talk to this man. *He's just using me, and I've no intentions of being his paramour.* This, even though Casey was doing nothing to follow up on their sensual encounter.

They had moved two-thirds of the way around the scattered mules, and Elizabeth turned, heading back, not wanting to be out of sight of the wagon camp with Casey at her side. "Thank you for coming out. With Mr. Gaynor here, I'm sure I'll have no problems."

"Gaynor? Oh, yes."

Their horses plodded along, the steady breeze lifting the beasts' manes on occasion. Her bay snorted and shook its head. Casey's horse coughed.

"Well. Goodnight."

"Oh. Yes."

Even in the darkness, Elizabeth could feel Casey's direct gaze, could sense a certain longing from him. She reined her horse away, hoping he wouldn't follow. He didn't. And after she heard his horse jogging down the hill toward the main camp, she gave a long sigh, the night pressing loneliness around her.

"Stretch 'em out!"

Three mornings later, Joe started them back on the trail, and that made Hastings loosen up a bit from his tense, fussy attitude. It also was a relief to Elizabeth who found it hard to stay in Zee Clark character when in a stationary camp. The time without work meant more interaction with the men, and one afternoon when she was talking with Don Suther and John Bradshaw, Elizabeth let slip some facts that most fifteen-year-old farm boys wouldn't have known. All about the telegraph pushing West and the Union's need for the short-lived Pony Express—things that would have happened when imposter Zee Clark was barely four years old. But in '59 Elizabeth Fortune had been eight. Her father subscribed to *The Nation*, and worked with abolitionist groups.

With the teamsters, she covered her knowledge by saying her family was into education—teachers and such. Not totally untrue. She made a mental note to keep her mouth shut, although plodding along week after week with no decent conversation wasn't a pleasant thought.

She could have talked to Casey, but naysayed the idea. She relished her night herding when she could pretty much be alone, even though Mervin continued to take watch with her. Mel slept in the mess wagon hammock, still with a slight fever and occasional chills. Jorge had concocted a tonic that Mel said was really helping.

That first night back on the trail, Mervin helped Elizabeth run out the mules. He settled down beside the fire with a harness to mend, and told her some more of the scriptures According to Gaynor: an account of how after Cain slew Able he was sent to The Dark Continent and turned into a Negro, and was the father of them all.

"Now I ain't sayin' slavery was right, mind you. But it was sort of destined to be, it seems. The sins of the father, you know."

With her teeth gritted until her jaws ached, Elizabeth excused herself to survey the herd. If Mervin noticed that she took her bed-roll with her, he didn't say anything. "I just can't take all that," she muttered to her horse. It tossed its head and snorted as if in agreement. "I hope Mel's better soon."

The night was quiet, the moon still bright, although losing some of its roundness. She tossed her things down near a spindly cedar tree on the far side of the herd and laid back to watch the sky…

Her horse whickered. The ground seemed to be moving under her. Elizabeth's eyelids flew open, and she heard a "hiaah!" from somewhere off to her right. Looking straight ahead, she could see Mervin's little fire a quarter-mile away, and to the east, a faint hint of light from the coming morning. She shook her head, disbelieving the night was nearly over. It seemed like only a few minutes since she made her second trip around the herd. She fumbled for her moccasins.

A shot rang out. Quickly to her feet, Elizabeth nearly climbed into the saddle without tightening the cinch. Her mouth was dry, eyes gritty. Another shot slapped across the night air, then a yodeling which brought her instant images of attacking Indians. Mules were running, and Elizabeth realized their hobbles had been cut. She jerked her horse toward the nearest beast, slapping it across the neck. "Get around there! Hiaah!" she yelled. Her bay reared a bit, but had little effect on the push of mules. The draft animals veered east, then toward the north. Elizabeth turned the bay to keep it with them.

Yelling came from the wagon camp, and Mervin stood up, groggy, pulling up his suspenders. Three riders galloped their mounts out from the wagons, one veering off to chase a rustler while hoof beats drummed across the prairie to the east. A rider loomed beside her. "Pretty easy, huh?" he laughed, urging the mules on.

Elizabeth swallowed her shock. Not Indians. White rustlers. They think I'm one of them! She sent her horse into the running mules, cutting away from the rustler.

A rifle shot rang out. Someone groaned.

"Shit," came a voice, all too close. Elizabeth leaned along her horse's neck and it plummeted along behind the stampeding mules. More rifle shots, and Elizabeth just prayed no one was aiming at her. She pulled the bay sharply to the left, gigging him in the flank with her heel and heading toward the firelight.

"There! Shoot the bastard!" David Hastings' voice crashed through the night.

"No! It's Zee," Mervin said. "Hold up!"

Drenched with fear, sweat, and panting nearly as hard as her horse, Elizabeth reined the beast around Mervin's little fire.

"Goddamnit boy, I nearly shot you!" David said.

"You did shoot someone. I heard him get hit," Elizabeth said.

"Fucking Indians. I knew—"

"No, sir. They were white men. I heard them. I—" She gasped again for breath and stared to where Tom Dawson was trotting up carrying a blanket, a pair of moccasins, and a rifle. That was the first Elizabeth realized she was barefoot.

"I thought he was suppose to be standin' watch," Tom growled, dropping the blanket and moccasins in front of Elizabeth's horse. Dawn was brightening everything to a dingy gray. "And it would be nice if you'd use this rifle for more than target practice." Tom tossed the Winchester to her. She nearly dropped it. Her face felt hot.

"You okay, Zee?" Pete Hayward asked, riding close and peering at her.

"Yes, sir." Elizabeth stared at her saddle horn, too humiliated to look him in the eye.

Ledbetter rode up on his mare. "Chased 'em off, Mr. Hastings. Wasn't more than three. Mules is scattered down in the breaks near the river, but we can get 'em easy come good light. Don and Horace is keepin' an eye on them."

"So which one of you was supposed to be on duty with the mules?" David growled, fixing first Elizabeth then Mervin with a hard eye.

"It was me, shoulda," Mervin said before Elizabeth could get her aching throat to let out sound. "I snoozed drivin' on my wagon today. The boy was plumb tuckered out."

"Don't take blame where it ain't yours," Tom said. "The kid shoulda—."

"They came sneakin' in real quiet, I tell you," Mervin insisted. "You know how Injuns is."

"But they weren't Indians," Casey Pritchard rode up, leading a brown horse with two white stockings. Across the saddle was the body of a tall man.

"He is not yet *muerto*, but bleeding hard," Jorge said, studying the man they laid out near the main fire. His gurgly breathing seemed loud. Everyone was up, the others having stayed at the wagon to defend it in case of an attack.

"He's going to be dead in a minute," David said. "Hoist the wagon tongue on that J. Murphy!" David pulled a stout length of hemp from the supply wagon.

"You gonna hang 'im?" Sim asked. He shifted nervously, his narrow shoulders making him look like a scarecrow.

"Damn right. Fuckin' rustler."

"Shouldn't we ought to take him back to Fort Dodge? To the law?" Mervin said.

"A waste of time," John Bradshaw said before he spit tobacco juice.

"I don't think he'd survive the trip," Casey said. He stooped beside the man and wiped the man's face with a damp cloth; Al Guzlowski held up a lantern. The light clearly showed the bloody shirt front where Hastings' bullet had ripped into the man. The ground beneath him was already stained, his pale features had gone gray, eyes closed.

Elizabeth stepped closer to the body, repulsed by the acrid smell of sweat and blood, but drawn by the man's build and features. She put her hand to her throat and swallowed hard. "One of Tillison's men," she said, recognizing the tall man with beaked nose who had been in her hotel room.

"What?" David stomped over.

"Are you sure?" Casey stood up and frowned at her.

Elizabeth nodded. "He's the one who—" Her heart pounded as she remembered his hands on her wrist, the way this man had stroked her hair. "One of the ones—." Her stomach churned, sending a sour taste to her throat and she walked away, her steps unsteady.

"I think Zee's right," Sim said, peering at the man. "At least I seen him ridin' with Gabe's boy lots of times."

Elizabeth's head began to pound and she couldn't keep a tremble of fear from her as she realized one of the other men out there could have been Hank Tillison, riding around in the dark, riding right passed her. She clutched the wheel of a nearby wagon. Casey came over, his quiet presence helping her calm.

"Yeah. His folks own a little farm down near Medicine Lodge," Sim went on.

"Been an awful lot of Tillison men in the area of late," Casey muttered.

"All because of me?" Elizabeth whispered. "I can't believe—"

"He's said to be a rogue, but this attack on the wagon train—." Casey hunched closer to her, his brown eyes concerned. "Don't worry. He couldn't possibly know you're here."

Elizabeth wasn't so sure, and she looked back to where David had dropped to one knee beside the injured man. "You! Goddamn it." David slapped the man's face. "You work for Gabe Tillison? Did he send you out here to do this? Answer me, you bastard. You're going to hang, you know."

"We can't just hang the boy without—" Bill Porter started.

"The hell we can't!" Tom Dawson said.

"Yeah. You Redlegs are good at hanging," Ledbetter sneered.

David got up and strode back to the supply wagon. He threw the rope into the back, then went angrily toward his tent. Joe knelt beside the man. "He's gone," Joe said.

Jorge crossed himself and Mervin got on his knees in the dust to mutter a prayer.

Seeing that tall man who had been involved in her attempted rape kept Elizabeth looking west, anxious to be farther from Kansas. And her humiliation about failing her duties made her resolve to never again get out of the saddle when she was on herd duty. She diligently helped round up the scattered mules, and spent the afternoon on Pete Hayward's wagon seat, repairing cut hobbles. Some of the men thought she was just trying to make up for her apparent error that had caused the near loss of the mules, but mostly Elizabeth wanted to ensure that their travel went as swiftly as possible so the miles would increase between her and anything Tillison.

Eleven

I wish to heaven I'd come up with another way to get south besides this impersonation. If I had the man-strength to go with Zee Clark, I'd clobber someone right now.

21 August

With men standing night watch and Hastings orders to drive all day and into the darkness, the grumbling was nonstop, and it seemed to increase the teamsters ribaldry, too. Add to that Mervin Gaynor's obnoxious philosophies (he had cornered Elizabeth at the nooning to teach her more warding hexes), it wasn't surprising that Elizabeth reached a point where she wanted to chuck everything, go back to the beginning and start again. This happened early Monday, her eighteenth day on the trail.

She had just run down a fussy mule and whipped the long-eared beast back in line. The creature brayed and kicked, but finally moved on with the rest. Dust roiled up and caught in Elizabeth's eyes. She winked them clean, but a few tears of bone-weary tiredness got mixed in.

"I can't take much more of this," she gasped to her gelding. It whickered and nodded. She patted its neck.

From her right came an ear-piercing scream. Three seconds later it pinched off as a jack-rabbit became breakfast for some owl. "Easy there," she said to the nearby mules. She didn't want them shambling further north like they had a bit ago. High yips and cries of coyotes came from the slopes south of the river.

"Wish I could just give you your head," she muttered to the bay. "Ride away from all this."

She was 100 miles west of Fort Dodge and more than that east of Fort Lyon. Elizabeth didn't know the exact distances, but she knew her wishing was for naught.

Her horse cocked its ears toward her when she gave a long sigh. "I thought maybe Jorge was different—him being Mexican and all," she said. "But he's the same as the others. When I asked him to teach me Spanish, he comes up with this tongue twister *pica la puta*—spear the whore. It was awful." Her bay snorted as if in agreement and Elizabeth guided it around a natural fence of prickly pear that edged an old buffalo wallow. She headed it for the small camp where Mel was sleeping. "At least I have you to talk to."

The region the wagons were traveling was flat uphill with grainy soil and litters of rock and stones humped around on the short-grass prairie like piles of huge horse turds. Real leavings from buffalo were scattered around, too, flat and chalky brown. Jorge collected the "chips," since firewood was getting scarce. They had yet to see a buffalo, however.

The fire had dwindled to a vibrant glow in the depression Elizabeth had dug for it. Mel lay rolled in his blanket, snoring slightly.

"It's nearly dawn," she said from her horse.

He was instantly alert. "A quiet night."

"Yeah."

Elizabeth stood off the gelding and kicked dirt over the embers. A hand-sized tarantula skittered from under one corner of the ground tarp when she started rolling her bedding, and Elizabeth kicked at it, too, but was immediately sorry. No fault of the creatures here that she was so miserable.

Mel stretched and scratched at his pale arms and belly before straightening his dingy cotton undershirt. He pulled on a blue work shirt, one elbow worn through, the shirttail frayed, and turned away to a nearby rabbit-bush to relieve himself.

"Damn mules," Elizabeth growled as she tied the pack behind her saddle.

Daylight crept further up the landscape, catching lavender clouds from behind and making a bright yellow aura of their edges. Squinting west, Elizabeth made out the spot of orange that pricked the dawn: a campfire at the wagon train. She pulled into the saddle. I can survive this, she reminded herself as she prepared to endure another day with men.

On this same morning, Gabe Tillison's brother, Thaddeus, received a message that the Hastings' wagons were still headed toward Trinidad. Thaddeus stayed in a ramshackle house in the intricate rise and fall of hills near the Timpas River in Colorado Territory. The location near the Santa Fe Trail gave him good access to that and the north-south wagon road from Denver to Fort Union. The steady, westward construction of the Kansas & Pacific Railroad had opened new commerce along that route as military supplies, payrolls, and stagecoaches rolled south from the rail's-end towns rather than over the slower mule road of the Santa Fe Trail. That meant profit for road agents in the area. Since moving in from a dying "business" in north Texas, Thad Tillison had become one of the area's best road agents, and brother Gabe let Thad know when a lucrative wagon train was headed southwest. They were especially interested in the Hastings' wagons. Hence this communication from brother Gabe, delivered by Billy Joe Shenby.

Billy Joe was a real good informant. In fact, he was the one who rode his horse nearly to death to get to the Tillison ranch and inform Gabe that Johnny had been shot. A tall, well set-up fellow, he exuded a certain nervousness, with eyes shifting warily around every room he entered, whiny voice, eager obedience to any tone of authority, even from forceful strumpets who said "Buy me a drink, fellow." He spent a lot of money on these girls, and then they'd usually leave him at the table while they went off to back rooms with someone else. He hadn't the courage to hire them himself, and they never seemed to want him, aware of his weak-kneed character even though his physical stature seemed to boast a different personality.

This may not have been obvious to everyone, but professional whores developed an eye for such things. And so did good detectives. Which was why Casey Pritchard had noticed Billy Joe at Fort Dodge when Casey visited there the night of his lusty encounter with Elizabeth. And he hadn't been so moonstruck that he didn't recognize Billy Joe as the same man who had been loitering around Ellsworth, Kansas playing cards with Hank and Johnny Tillison, and watching the wagons get packed on Thursday. The run in with Darcy Goodhue and Ox Lewis had been fresh in his mind, too, so Casey's curiosity was enough to make him ask questions about Billy Joe and Gabe Tillison.

No one remembered Billy Joe, but, "Tillison?" a supply sergeant at the fort said. "Yeah. We buy beef off Gabe on occasion. Only when we're desperate, you know. Winter annuities for the Kiowa and all."

"Has he ever been involved in any robberies?" Casey asked.

"Nah. We think he's responsible for some rustlings down in the Nations. We get folks from the Creek Nation Council complaining off and on. But no proof yet."

In Hide Town, after Casey dirtied up his clothes, hid his horse and acted sort of down and out, he learned a bit more. "Hey. Good customers, that Tillison crowd. A little rowdy sometimes, but if you're lookin' to hook up with an outfit." (Casey had said this—that he was looking for work.) "He does well by his boys, that's for sure." The barkeep of the stone-built bar/restaurant/hotel-brothel shrugged his beefy shoulder. His place was three rooms strung together. In the front room, he served over-cooked buffalo steaks and beans that smelled sour. Most people just settled on drinking whiskey, which he tapped from huge kegs on the wall behind the grease and dust layered counter near the door. Sleeping quarters were in the next room, with cots lined up like cross ties, and the closet-type spaces behind that were where you could take one of the wretched Indian girls he kept like slaves in a shed out back.

"Now his daddy was the one. Yessir! Old-time Texan. Rode with the Snively bunch back in '46. Nearly whipped them bastard Mexicans, they did."

Casey had kept his disparaging frown inside, having read government reports about Snively's Raiders who had tried to run the Spanish out of Texas territory and then went outlaw. The man made no mention of Thaddeus, who only robbed the richest trains, and provided liquor and gunpowder, and other things his men needed to stay perversely happy, and to give Thad goods he could resell. At one time he stocked his brother's trading posts in the Territory, but just last year he opened his own store—in Trinidad, Colorado Territory. The store the Hastings brothers thought they owned. Of course, no one knew this but the Tillison clan.

But the information Casey had received worried at him like a loose tooth. After the attempt to run off the mules and Elizabeth's identification of the dead would-be rustler, Casey felt certain Gabe Tillison was somehow involved in David Hastings' problems, and he began watching the wagon-train's back trail.

In the chill-tinged dawn of August 22nd, while Elizabeth and Mel were running the mules into camp for the hookup, Casey was riding southeast, staying low along the slight hills and scanning the distance through his brass rung telescope for wisps of gray smoke that might indicate night camps. As the sun glowed brighter behind thin clouds, Casey rode along the wagon road and checked all trails cutting across it. He sweated quietly in the thick brush behind boulders and listened, his mind meandering from various dreams about Elizabeth to worry over what Shenby's regular presence indicated, to wonderment why Gabe Tillison would be involved in any of David's troubles. Trinidad, New Mexico was a long way from Kansas. All the while, he was attuned to the sounds around him, waiting to hear just one click of hoof on stone, one little whuffle from a horse, to see one curious flick of his own horse's ears that could indicate someone might be following the wagon train. By late afternoon when the sweltering heat was beginning to subside, nothing out of the ordinary had occurred and he rode north from the banks of the Arkansas River to peruse the more barren, northerly landscape before heading back to the train.

He didn't catch up with the wagons until late afternoon, and his eyes immediately sought out Elizabeth. He trotted his spotted horse to the part of camp farthest from her, heart pounding, fingertips tingling. He wanted to talk to her. A private talk. He wanted to tell her how he felt for her. But she had become even more remote in the past few days, staying to herself and with a sullen expression that made him keep his distance. He was certain the miles and trail dust and tough work were getting to her, and he was amazed that she had maintained her charade through it all. What a woman! he thought, as he often did. He just wished there were time and place that she could relax, that he could relax with her, that they could be man and woman again.

Beyond the wagon camp by an eighth of a mile, the lumpy form of the stage stop was visible. This one-room soddy with two windows, backed by an empty rope and sod paddock, was an inelegant place and remained unoccupied until stagecoach travelers spent the night with everyone crowded in the one room and sleeping on the dirt floor. The horses would browse the sparse grass in the paddock. Firewood could be gotten on the white clay islands in the middle of the Arkansas.

"You pushed a hard pace today," Casey said reining up to where Joe MacGrin stood at the edge of the wagon camp.

"Hastings'—wants to go on after sunset, too. He's broke out more grain for the mules. They seem to be fit enough."

"Have you ridden up there?" Casey cocked his head toward the soddy.

Joe nodded. "Checked it out before the wagons were even in sight of it."

Casey nodded, but he rode up to the shoddy structure. Slight depressions were still in the earth from the rifle pits dug for the temporary outpost of Fort Aubry during the 1865 Indian War. Casey satisfied himself that neither the stage stop nor the trenches contained bushwhackers and hadn't been recently used, and then rode back to camp.

"Don't trust me?" Joe asked with a crooked grin.

"It pays to be cautious," Casey responded. He walked his horse around the mess wagon to the picket lines. Elizabeth was there, tending the bay gelding. It took a lot for him go up beside her, but he figured avoiding her would be as suspicious as not.

"'Lo, Zee. How's it going?" If he noticed that she leaned a bit into her horse, kept her eyes averted, he didn't give sign. "You're looking pretty healthy, considering what you've been through. How are the feet?"

"Fine, Mr. Prit—Casey. Thank you."

To Elizabeth his words were a tease: pretty, healthy—code words for his backhanded compliments. She vigorously brushed the bay's flanks.

"Zee's gonna wear that horse out, all that groomin'," Amos Ledbetter said. He grabbed a rag out of the big box that held the tack and started to work on a sweat-rimmed harness. "Spoil the beast."

"Who you talkin' to about spoilin' their horse. The way Pritchard dotes on his spotted critter, think it was made of gold." Don Suthers limped over.

"In this country, a good horse can mean your life," Casey said.

"Yep, can mean losin' it too, if somebody takes a hankerin' to your mount."

"Does that mean I have to watch my back?" Casey laughed.

"With this fuckin' crew—always," Ledbetter said.

Elizabeth tossed the brush into the box, walked away, never giving any of them a second glance.

The Hastings people had just started their meal when Horace spotted dust from up the trail. Up the trail meant several miles away, so Casey wasn't too worried. He looked through his spyglass and made out what caused the dust. An hour later, two rickety Conestogas pulled up to the stage stop.

The high tones of children's voices drew everyone's attention. This freight road wasn't much used by emigrants anymore, and the sound of children was like seeing an apple tree among mesquite bushes. Dodie Watson got up from his dozing and stepped to the edge of the wagon circle with Casey, Joe MacGrin, and David Hastings to peer toward the stage stop.

"What d'ya suppose?" Dodie queried, shifting his quid.

Joe shrugged his shoulders.

"I seen diseased folks cast off from caravans—kept away from towns," Dodie went on. "You suppose they got smallpox or something?"

"Uh. Probably a ploy to get at the wagon train," David said.

"Those are kids, Dave," Casey said. "Just look."

Little people flounced from the wagons like startled quail from a thicket, scattering into the brush around the building. Four adults climbed from the wagon seats and three outriders dismounted.

"Don't nobody look sick," Joe said.

Soon Joe and Casey and a group of curious teamsters ambled up there. David Hastings and Dodie went too, approaching with caution.

The eastbound wagons made Elizabeth hurry to finish swabbing tar and tallow in the wheel hubs. She anticipated seeing and talking to people other than the teamsters, and when Willie passed her on his way back from the stage stop, her curiosity kicked in.

"You need to be with that bunch," Willie sneered. "Deadbeat kids gettin' shipped back east."

The gooey lubricant seemed to stick Elizabeth's fingers together and she wiped them on the empty flour sack tied to Jorge's wagon. Still greasy, she rubbed her hands in the powdery dust of the road and then on her pants before running off to the stage stop.

"Railroad's all the way to Colorado, now," Joe was saying when Elizabeth reached the odd scene. The children's ages ranged from two to early teens. Despair etched some of the small faces and a three-year-old was wailing and stamping his feet up and down like they were on hot coals. Gnarled and gray-whiskered John Bradshaw went to comfort him. "Be easier to cart them up there," Joe suggested.

"We thank you for the suggestion, sir, but our funds don't permit such," spoke a small bird-like woman. This was Mrs. Jenkins, in charge of this wagon trek and an obvious leader. Gray hair wisped from under her dark sunbonnet, and she was totally ensconced in a maroon calico dress.

Mrs. Jenkins didn't look much like Etta Clark, but Elizabeth saw past the dark eyes and small-boned exterior, recognizing an inner warmth and tenderness that had made her grandmother Clark so charming. Memories flooded over Elizabeth, and she put her hand to her throat, willing her racing pulse to slow.

"The miner's fund was barely enough to cover these expenses," the woman went on. "Generous citizens provided the wagons and a few blankets."

"Yep. Some of these kids was pickin' the town dry. Had to git rid of 'em some hows," a pock-marked driver snickered.

"Mr. Adams, please!"

"These wagons is barely worth spit," Dodie mumbled, examining one of the tires.

"Joe! Check out these contraptions," David called.

"I have. Axle's need greasing; got a cracked bow back here."

"There's tug rot on this team's leathers," Don Suthers put in as he limped around the scruffy horses.

"Let's fix what we can," Joe said.

"Oh, gracious me, trail people are so nice." Mrs. Jenkins glowed with relief and praised their generosity. "We met buffalo hunters two days ago and they gave us a handsome amount of meat. Such nice men," she went on.

"Have you come far?" Elizabeth asked Mrs. Jenkins. She wanted to pull the woman aside and say: I'm a woman; Please, talk to me. Let's sit somewhere and smooth lotion on our hands—use quiet voices.

"From just south of Trinidad. About three hundred miles from here, I suppose." Mrs. Jenkins smiled at this wistful looking boy.

"Is that anywhere near Fort Union?" Elizabeth asked.

"About a hundred or so miles this side. Is that where you're going?"

The figures quickly whipped together in Elizabeth's mind and her shoulders drooped a bit. Fort Union was over four hundred miles away. More distance than she had already endured.

"Yes. I'm—. The wagons are going to Santa Fe."

Elizabeth looked back toward her own wagon camp. A thick fog of dust had blown up, making everything look dingier than it was. One of the children cried out as the dust devil swept around the soddy, and Mrs. Jenkins hurried off to help with the organization. Elizabeth was glad. She had come close to asking if she could ride back east with these wagons. But closely behind Elizabeth's thought came a vision of Johnny Tillison's horrified surprise when she shot him.

A smiley-faced girl of about eight brought her up short. A beautiful child with dark hair and shoe-button eyes, she stood out among the other lanky, light-haired children as they carried bedding back and forth to the soddy; it was real obvious one of her parents had been Mexican.

Al Guzlowski strolled up. "Who are they?" he asked.

"Orphans," David said. "Kids of miners and such been killed in accidents or whose folks have been taken by cholera. They're being sent back east to relatives."

Elizabeth looked back to the happy little girl, a certain pain joining her. And how will you survive, little one? she thought. I hope you won't be wandering the country a few years from now with no real home.

"Zee, go back and get Jorge to whip up some pan bread for these folks," David said. "Anything else he can think of, too."

His words drew her away from her melancholy thoughts, but her attention was caught by one adolescent boy who still sat in the second wagon staring straight to the back of it.

"What's wrong with him?" Elizabeth asked the wagon driver. "Why hasn't he gotten out?"

"Uh? Oh. He's tied to the wagon. We'll move him after we get set up."

"Tied!"

"Only way to keep him from running off. He claims his kin back in Missouri is a den of skunks and he don't want to be with them."

Elizabeth walked beside the wagon and looked at the youngster so intently it drew his angry gaze.

"What the hell you starin' at?" the boy asked.

David Hastings snapped, "Zee! Get on back and talk to Jorge, like I told you."

"Yessir," Elizabeth responded.

The children's situation got to everyone, one way or another, and when Hastings' people had done all they could for the Jenkin's wagons, Joe headed the freight wagons west with plans to travel for another three hours. Talk between drivers was about their own families or their own plight as orphans (five of them had been so before they were twelve). Elizabeth sat her horse, absently moving from one conversation to another. Casey rode up beside her. She pretended he wasn't there.

"I don't know what I'd do if something happened to Louella," Don Suthers called to Bill Porter who was driving the team three strides to his off side. "She keeps that family together. 'Specially in bad times like now, with me havin' to take trail work." Don had three children, ages five, six and eight.

"Sometimes I think about settlin' down," Bill responded. "But I already raised my two brothers and a sister. My pa run off when I was thirteen and Ma. She was never good for much. Had prairie fever most of the time."

Prairie fever was a general term for the kind of dottiness that struck folks who had trouble enduring the endless wind and rigor of the plains. Bill had grown up along the Platt.

"Maybe if I'd run across some strong-type woman—one who wasn't subject to no faints an' all."

"That makes me think of the Johnsons," Elizabeth said to Casey before she could stop herself.

"The family that hid you in Ellsworth?"

"Um hum." She scowled, but was glad to be talking to someone. Her self-imposed exile from the rest of the crew had started to chafe. "They seem like Western perfection: the strong adaptable woman, the hard-working man, and they've taken in two kids. Jemma's parents were servants to a family moving West; they both died of cholera. And then little Boudine got left with them by some prostitute. She said she was going to come back for him, but—." She laughed ruefully. "Not too many folks want to put up with a breed."

"Like that little girl with the Jenkins wagon. I saw you watching her. But she was such a sweetheart, I don't know how someone could not love her. To hell with her background."

Elizabeth's charity was slim to none. A fat lot you'd know about it, she thought of Casey. A stubborn mule wandered off from the small remuda and Elizabeth angled toward it. "I have to get to work," she said. She loped the gelding out.

She was surprised to hear the other loose mules coming along behind her, and looked back to where Casey was urging them away from the train toward where Elizabeth had caught up to the loner.

"What did you do that for?" Elizabeth asked, although she felt she knew why he did it, so they could have some privacy. Her heart thumped and she fiddled with the reins, then pushed a straggle of hair back under her hat.

"We haven't talked in a while," Casey said.

"There's nothing to talk about." Elizabeth wasn't sure why she didn't just ride off, move to the other side of the herd.

Casey was quiet. A pensive air surrounded him. "I think about settling down sometimes," he finally said. "But I'm sort of like Porter. I've got to find the right woman."

"I guess that's always the way," Elizabeth said. Now here it comes, she thought. Since I can't find the right woman, won't you take a roll with me? She glowered at the cloudy red sunset that spread along the horizon like spilled stalks of ruhbarb and wondered how long it would take him to start demanding, or threatening to expose her identity.

"My mother set quite a standard of independence for me. I mean, for what I look for in a woman," Casey went on.

"Yes, when you spoke of her, she sounded quite independent."

"Yes." Casey glanced around.

Elizabeth did, too, wary to see the wagon train far enough off that the wagons were just small blobs in the twilight. The tail lamps made white dots on the night, and the canvases glowed from the head lamps which hung behind the drivers. A hump of land slowly blotted them from view.

"I've never met anyone with her kind of grit, until you," Casey went on.

She blinked, shifted in the saddle. Her gelding slowed and walked sedately beside Casey's spotted horse. "That's a nice compliment, Mr.—"

"Casey."

Elizabeth nodded, giving him a shrewd look. "But I'm not the kind of woman to be turned foolish by a nice comment." She couldn't keep the harshness from her voice. All right; here it comes.

"I hope what I'm planning to say won't sound like foolishness, Elizabeth. Well—. I'm going to be establishing a business in Santa Fe."

Jitters started in her stomach and kept her breathing short while he continued, "and I realize, since meeting you, this is my time to really settle down. I know you don't think much of detectives, but—."

"Mr. Pritchard—."

"My name's Casey."

"Mr. Pritchard, what do you mean, settle down?" Elizabeth shook her head.

"I mean, settle down! Like Suthers and Porter were talking about. Like you and me in a house and—."

"No wait." Elizabeth could barely believe he was speaking so boldly. She glanced at him wide-eyed, and stopped her bay. Her thoughts stumbled as she realized he didn't intend any behind-the-bush encounter, and she took in his appealing features and sincere eyes which looked pleading, now, rather like a pup wondering if it were going to get a reprimand or a pat.

"I guess this is pretty presumptuous. I don't know for sure how you feel about me, but I assumed—. From the other night. From the way we can talk and all—."

"It is nice to have someone to talk to. Someone I can trust."

"No more than that? I thought—."

"Well, yes. I like you, Casey." Saying his name was easy, and felt good to her. A rush of warmth, the physical excitement from their night at

Fort Dodge all flooded through her.

"So you see. I'm not talking foolishness."

To Elizabeth, his proposal was as shocking as a pig flying. She jerked from the pleasantness, gritting her teeth and startling her bay when she quickly demanded that it move. It took off at a fast jog, and she could hear Casey coming behind her.

"Wait! Hear me out!" Casey called.

Elizabeth's mind catapulted through various scenes: her smiling and melting into Casey's arms, saying "Yes, yes!" Then they were in Santa Fe, in a little clapboard house (since she didn't know what housing looked like there), Casey riding off on his spotted horse to do detective work, while she waved and started baking sweets. Unwittingly she imagined them in bed together, following through on the passion that had filled them both nine nights ago.

Casey's hand was on the reins of the bay, urging it to a stop. "NO!" she said viciously. The horse whickered, ears back, as it danced under her. "Don't. Don't!" Elizabeth said. Her sensual thoughts had faded and practicality set in.

"What are you so upset about?" Casey demanded. "If you think I'm trying to compromise you in any way, you're—"

"Right."

"Elizabeth."

"Zee. I'm Zee Clark. A boy working with the wagon train. Don't talk to me like this!" She pulled the bay from his grasp.

"I'm talking about later. When we can just be a man and a woman, and keep on with what got started—"

"Stop it! I did not take up this trip to get involved—"

"But we're attracted to each other. There's nothing wrong with that."

"Yes there is. I'm Negro, Mr. Pritchard. Don't you know what that means?"

"I don't care! And does that make the way we feel for each other any less real?"

"No, but it makes it more dangerous. Mr. Pritchard, please. I have enough to do just keeping myself together on this wagon train without you complicating things more." She leaned on the pommel, not daring to look at him, for she couldn't deny that he was the most desirable man she had ever met: pleasant, educated, and with a smile that made her legs rubbery.

"I don't expect an answer tonight," Casey said gently. "I just want you to know how I feel."

"You're just intrigued by my situation, that's all."

"No."

"When we finally get to real civilization, you'll get things straight." She relaxed a bit, certain that was true.

"And what about you?"

She looked up at him, then couldn't look away. As if she would lose her sight within moments, she drank in the smooth, square jaw, brassy blond hair that wisped from under his brown hat. The sunset gave his skin a rich golden tone.

He walked his horse closer. "You've got on more layers than a Boston matron," he said, his hand moving against her side and up toward her breast. His lips brushed her cheek.

Her horse snorted and Elizabeth, breathless, kneed it from Casey, putting distance between them. She looked over his shoulder toward the rise of land that separated them from view of the wagon train.

"What if someone rode up right now?" she said. That helped her overcome the heady moment. "Or had been listening in all this time." They scanned their surroundings. Nothing in sight but mules and darkening land.

"Better push these critters back toward the wagons, or Mr. Hastings will think I've gotten lost," Elizabeth said in her rough Zee Clark voice.

"Will you think about what I said? We'll talk about it later."

Elizabeth nodded, not trusting her voice. She hazed the mules toward the wagon train, riding a bit in front of the little herd with Casey at the back. She could picture Casey sitting straight on his spotted horse as if he were still before her. He would change his mind when they reached a place with other women—eligible white women.

But her subconscious nagged at her, worried about how she would—should!—respond if he proposed again. She slapped the lead mule to a faster pace, wanting to outrun the thoughts.

Twelve

Trail life is going okay, but I am moving in a state of dread. Fearful first that I'll never get to New Mexico, and with a growing distrust of these plans I've made. Sometimes I wonder if I'll ever see Daddy again...

23 August

The Mountain Branch of the Santa Fe Trail may have been safer from Indians, but it was a more strenuous trek. In the miles since Fort Dodge, even when the road seemed to be flat, the wide rutted trail had climbed nearly two thousand feet in elevation, creating an almost constant four percent incline—not an easy thing for ten mules to negotiate when dragging four to five thousand pounds of laden wagon behind them. The mule's sides were wet from their effort and they often fussed and brayed complaints. Whips cracked and the men hollered.

In the morning, as the sun heated up the trail from behind and scorched into the backs of the J. Murphy drivers who didn't have wagon canvas to shade them, most of the teamsters were too bleary-eyed to be sociable. Dog liked to run, chasing whatever its keen eyes could spy: horny toads, prairie hens, rabbits. Jorge always felt good and would sing to his mules. His singing signaled that all was right with this stretch of the world. With her moccasins off, Elizabeth would lay back in the mess wagon hammock and fall asleep to his pleasant voice. She usually slept until the nooning, then she'd take over herding duties from Mel after dinner and stayed up most of the night. Mel slept from midnight until dawn—if there weren't any problems, and there hadn't been. It was as if leaving Kansas had put an end to Elizabeth's worries and any troubles for the wagon train.

She did have Casey to think about, and his proposal. When they were both in evening camp, she found herself fumbling with things when he was two strides away. He seemed more attractive each time she looked at him, and it grew harder and harder to remember her resolve of disinterest. But the strenuous work drained her energy and she didn't have any trouble falling to sleep.

She woke up fast, too. That was how it was on the twenty-third when Mel Burns rode up. "Pull over! Got to go back!" Mel had to yell to be heard over the creaks of the wagon, the jingling traces and Jorge's lively rendering of "Jesucita."

"*Que pasa?*" Jorge asked.

Elizabeth reached for her rifle before her eyes were barely open. Tom Dawson's constant teasing about her inefficiency the night the mules were rustled kept her ever on the alert.

"Got a wagon down. MacGrin says to circle back and set up camp. We're going to be a while."

"*Si no hay uno es el otro,*" Jorge muttered.

The hammock rocked and swayed as Jorge turned the team; the brake sound chafed the air as they went down the slope. Elizabeth couldn't get back to sleep, though. Jorge was fussing now, not singing, all about the men expecting to be fed, and tough beans. When the wagon stopped on the north side of the trail, Elizabeth had already pulled on her boots and stuffed her shirttail into her pants. She looked out of the wagon back, across the attached supply cart, onto the forming camp while she tied the big bandanna around her neck.

"Don't know why we never camp down there by the river," Sim grumbled. He was helping to string a picket line. Wind gusts slashed grit around him. "Got trees down there."

"Them ain't trees. Just fat-trunked weeds," Dodie said.

"Got mosquitoes down there, too. Damn insects is so thick you can spread 'em with a knife," Ledbetter said.

"That skinny ol' face of yourn be pocked all over red with blood in less than five minutes," John Bradshaw put in. He piled rocks around the base of a tall iron rod he'd just fixed into the dry ground. Dodie and

Ledbetter strung the picket rope.

Mel had the loose animals' necks haltered and tethered in two bunches. Elizabeth jammed on her hat and stepped into the drenching brightness of sunlight and went to help him get the teams unhitched.

"That looks like Mr. Cross's wagon down. What happened?" she asked, leading in a pair.

"Singletree split. Part of it's jammed over the axle." Mel rammed his elbow into a mule's side to get it to stop crowding. It brayed—flapped its ears. "You shoulda heard Mr. Hastings holler. Cussed Horace a blue streak for not keepin' check on his equipment. The only extra pieces we got are the short tongues they picked up at Fort Larned. Don't know how they're going to fix it."

By the time they finished with the animals, sweat rolled down Elizabeth's cheeks and into her shirt collar. Some of the men unloading Horace's wagon had come out of their shirts and their sun-browned faces and hands were odd contrast to their pale torsos. Sun-baked plains with tufts of parched grass was all she could see. Ethereal swirls of dust spouted up from the dry ground, twisted, whirled in frantic columns, died down. No clouds in the sky.

Elizabeth helped rig a lean-to off the mess wagon for shade. She carried water to the sweating men, collected dried dung for Jorge's fire. With all these toilsome endeavors, she wasn't inured to the vast land around her. Some people didn't like seeing so far or being capped by so much endless sky; but for others, the plains could weave a magic, snaring them to suspect secrets in its panorama. Elizabeth had been so caught.

The first time men stopped yelling at her to do something, she saddled her bay and rode up the trail. It seemed the land would end on the edge of a bluff at any moment—just fall away to nothingness, but it kept on. The slight crest that she finally reached after a mile, revealed land sweeping in gentle rolls and dales on to where it seemed flat as a board. Along a crease of undulation, a swathe of dark brown patches stood out against the tan background. Elizabeth squinted to see better. To the south, the thick brown merely faded with the land against the horizon. North, it curved like a single line, out of sight behind low hills. Elizabeth's mouth dropped open in awe.

The gelding swung its head to look back and whuffled a low greeting.

Horses trotted up the steady grade: John Bradshaw, Amos Ledbetter, Pete Hayward, and Mel riding and leading a mule.

"There are bison down there!" Elizabeth said, pointing. Youth and innocence shone from her face.

Pete Hayward smiled. "We finally get to see more than their shit."

"Yep. Figured so when I heard the shootin'." Bradshaw reined up beside Elizabeth. He spit tobacco juice into the dust.

"Shooting?"

Ever so distant against the breeze came a sound. Like an ax blade whacking into hardwood. Not often, not regular. Elizabeth hadn't noticed it until now.

"Sounds like somebody's got quite a stand," Pete said.

"I swear, I've never seen such a herd," Mel Burns said, leaning both hands on the pommel and staring.

"It's the time of year, with ruttin' and all," John said. "All the bulls and cows gettin' together, goin' south. Got the spring calves in thar."

"There's thousands and thousands of them!" Elizabeth declared. Twenty of the plains buffalo would have impressed Elizabeth since she had never seen one.

Ledbetter chuckled.

"MacGrin figures we can get some fresh meat off the runners," Pete said. "Come on with us, Zee. Maybe get to see the shaggies up close."

The route John Bradshaw led them on didn't get them much closer to the herd until after another two miles. John used to hunt buffalo and Elizabeth had heard some of his stories about when he was a mountainman at the end of the era in the early '50s. He angled his little party north along the face of the low hills, cheerfully explaining about buffalo and the men that made their living off the herds.

"If they see ya, they'll run. If they smell ya, they'll run even harder." John spat tobacco juice. "That's why we're stayin' up wind and far enough away not to spook 'em."

"Yeah. Be hell to pay if those runners thought we'd messed up their shoot," Ledbetter put in.

But the herd became distinct: brown humps, amber-colored calves. The gunshots were louder, closer, sounding like small cannons.

"Got three runners, sounds like. Pickin' shots real good." John's voice had gotten quieter and he held up his hand for them to stop. A huge beast at the edge of the herd seemed to be staring at them. "We'll jest sit here a minute," Bradshaw said. Finally the creature started grazing again.

Mel hunched forward, tapped Pete and pointed to his right; Elizabeth looked that way, too. Five horsemen were walking their mounts south along the hill, sunlit from behind. By their lean profiles and lack of saddlery, the quivers bristling with arrows on their shoulders, it was obvious they were Indians.

"Arapaho, most like," Bradshaw said. He spit.

Elizabeth's first-hand knowledge of western Indians amounted to the horror stories she heard as a child during the Santee Uprising. She had also read columns in *Harper's Weekly* and in newspapers that fluctuated from 'Lo, the poor heathen' types of articles to pieces about snarling, cannibalistic savages. These men neither looked like pious refugees nor mad dogs, but Elizabeth's heart beat so hard in her chest she couldn't swallow.

The Indians acted like they were the only people out there, and never even shifted their eyes from the buffalo herd.

The buffalo stepped along more briskly. A big bull swerved at a jog toward the herd; a cow raised her head, grunted. The Arapaho hunters angled their wiry ponies down the hill only a few rods behind Elizabeth and the teamsters. Elizabeth watched them until gunshots volleyed and got her attention. More grunts from the buffalo, then a low bellow. They were off, careening one way then another, right and left. A group of them veered out from the main herd and angled around a hummock toward the humans. Elizabeth kicked her bay up the hill, Mel right with her. Ledbetter fired his .44 into the air. The buffalo swerved back to follow the curve of the land.

The ground vibrated and the brown bodies blurred with sudden speed. Dust billowed and the deep snorts and flurry of activity got the horses fidgeting. High yips and yodels came from the Arapaho, and then that sound was lost in the heavy, continuous rumble of the running beasts. Elizabeth tied down her hat, pulled her bandanna up over her nose and followed John Bradshaw at a lope. Ten minutes of the buffalo running south with the people riding north before the herd was gone.

"Used to be herds like this all through central Kansas!" Pete hollered.

He had grown up in Kansas, his family one of those to pioneer along the Republican River. "Now there ain't more than nine or ten huge runs between here and the Rockies."

In short time, the Hastings' teamsters rode up on two men just turning a cow carcass on its skin. The air, already rank from offal, sweat and dust of the passing herd, now had the added scent of fresh blood and two men who hadn't bathed in a couple of months. Elizabeth could barely catch her breath. The leather chaps the workers wore over filthy canvas pants were stained dark with old blood and dirt; she could hardly see the print on the calico shirts because of the grime, and their greasy hair drew flies. Her rough-shaven sweaty comrades took on certain refinement when compared to these fellows.

One dirty man cut a seam up the carcass belly and began tossing entrails aside with abandon. The putrid scent of intestines wafted around him and blood soaked his clothes. Elizabeth backed her gelding away, nauseous, and joined Mel who had kept his distance from the start.

"The holy hell, you say!" the other man raged when Pete mentioned getting some meat off them. One eye was partially closed from an old scar and two days growth of whiskers made his face look even dirtier than it was. He cut the hide down the inside of each front leg. His partner was doing the same on the back. "We ain't givin' away nothin'!"

"Goddam, I'd ruther it rot in the grass than give it away," the other added. He grinned at them, even though there was no friendliness to his tone. The five teeth in the front of his mouth looked like brown snaggly posts. Elizabeth wondered how the man could eat.

"Had those fuckin' Injuns down here a while ago, tryin' to beg off us," said the scarred man. They peeled back the heavy hide, their knives deftly trimming sinew and fat from the inside. They had twelve animals to skin and butcher and weren't wasting time on socializing. "Anybody who thinks we'll jest hand over this hard work is pissin' in the wind."

"We don't object any to buying it," Pete said.

That got the rotten-toothed skinner's attention. "Buy, huh." He grinned. "Got to see Brian Mills at the main camp. Yes sir." He and his partner grunted from strain as they rolled the large carcass and tugged loose the hide. The man took time to wave his arm north, however. "Ol' Brian be glad to take yer money!" he giggled.

It was a relief to ride away from there and breathe fresh air, but two miles away, Elizabeth smelled the camp before she saw it, with skin lean-tos swarming with flies, a trash pile of garbage and empty tin cans perfuming the area. Two wagons were down-sided and heaped with cured buffalo hides. Smoke oozed from the edges of a makeshift, smoke house. But what got Elizabeth's attention was pegged hides that checkered a half acre area.

"They've killed all these?" Elizabeth asked in awe.

"Yep." John spat over his horse's right shoulder. "Buffalo's big business. Fer hides, at least."

"Land-o-mercy," Mel breathed, staring at the scene. More than forty hides were stretched to dry, already clean of sinew and fat.

"When I was in St. Louey last, I saw the new machines they got," Amos said. "Big ol' things that can handle a tough buffalo hide like it was doe skin. They're makin' buff clothes and hats, and furniture."

"But this camp's killed so many!" Mel said.

"Them buffalo ain't gonna run but a few miles, then stop and eat—puttin' on winter fat. The runner'll be on 'em again tomorrow. A good marksman can take another couple o' dozen and not be more'n fifteen miles from this camp."

"With a herd this size, bet there's outfits strung from here to Sand Creek," John put in.

"Halloo the camp!" Pete called out as they stopped their horses on the camp perimeter.

The man who knelt with a scraper over a green hide didn't look up to Pete's call, but Elizabeth stared at him. He was dressed as raggedy as the others had been, clothes the color of smoke and grease, but he wore a short blue coat and the cocky blue billed cap of the cavalry which seemed uncommonly clean and cared for. Not only that, but the man was black.

A paunchy fellow dressed in a filthy frock coat and checkered pants strode around from one of the lean-tos, a beaver-skin top hat on his shoulder length white hair.

"We come to talk about buying some meat!" Pete called. "One of the skinners said to talk to Brian Mills."

"Tha'yad be me. Come on and light."

They stepped off their horses.

"Was he really in the cavalry?" Elizabeth asked, glancing again at the man curing the hide.

"'Spect so, sonny. We found him last year fer daid in a burned out Kioway village. Thay'id stripped the buttons off his coat and cut out his tongue. He's sorta addled, but kin sher tan a hide." He turned to Pete. "You in the markit fer meat, is ya?"

"Yep. Got a freight train hauling to Santa Fe. Men got a belly full of venison; thought buffalo might be a change. What's your price?"

"Oh, dollar a pound sounds about right."

"A dollar!" Ledbetter roared. "Prime beefsteak ain't more than five cents a pound in Chicago!'

Mills just smiled. "You-all ain't in Chicagy."

Mel backed off and eyed the area, expecting some hard-case gunmen to appear to enforce Mills's position. No one showed themselves.

Elizabeth had dropped her reins and made her way to the worker who was humming "Rock of Ages" in a wavery baritone. His music stopped when his side-vision gave him a glimpse of moccasined feet. He jerked toward Elizabeth, eyes squinted in his very black-skinned face. The way he held that sharp curve-blade scraper made Elizabeth stop.

"You were with the cavalry?" Elizabeth asked.

The man's age was hard to judge since his thin hair was white and his inch of beard thoroughly grizzled. Wrinkles weaved across his dry skin like netting. He looked over his shoulder to where Mills was talking to the others. "Rock of Ages" started again in his throat. He turned back to his work, sunlight glinting on the sharp blade edge before he struck it to the fleshy hide, and he didn't stop humming even when Elizabeth asked.

"With the Ninth or Tenth?"

She squatted beside him, then remembered his tongue was gone and started again. "Were you maybe with the Ninth?"

The humming stopped. He scraped diligently at the hide.

"My daddy's with the Ninth. I was wondering if you knew him."

The man's hands halted in their work as if frozen by a sudden blast of cold air. He scowled at Elizabeth, studying her sharp features, sun-tanned complexion, and edges of smooth hair bleached to reddish gold. Elizabeth nodded to confirm her words. He was frowning hard now.

"His name is Fortune. Samuel Fortune. I'm going south to meet him, and—"

Explaining why she wanted to talk to this man was hard for Elizabeth. It might have been that she suddenly wasn't trusting the validity of her trek, or was worried that her father may have met some disaster as had this man, or worse. She wanted some assurance that yes, Samuel Fortune was with the Ninth, was healthy, and that she would find him.

It was lucky that this man couldn't talk. He could have told her that he had known Samuel Fortune, but his animosity toward him, who he considered an Uppity Nigger, wouldn't have made Elizabeth feel too good. This trooper thought the reading and writing, Injun-Negro was a trouble maker—one of those leftover radical Republicans who had threatened him to a drubbing if he didn't go to vote. In fact, this fellow was certain Samuel Fortune's rabble rousing was why his own company got sent out to winter battle against the Kiowa. They got shot badly, their white officer killed and himself captured. He had lived a year with the Kiowa before the 7th Cavalry rode over the village, and him, too. That was all the background for his actual thought: It makes a lot of sense that Fortune would have some near-white kid; lousy bastard.

The brief moment of his scathing look made Elizabeth's insecurities grow. "He's alive? Do you know. Just nod. Is he alive?"

If the man could have spit just then, he would have. As it was, he merely went back to his work and started humming again. This time the tune was "Go Down, Moses."

Elizabeth was fumbling for words when Pete called to her: "Zee!"

She looked around, blinking to keep her hot eyes from spilling tears. Mills waved her to them, too. "Come on up here, sonny! We need yor hep."

The ex-trooper never even looked up when Elizabeth went away.

"Seems your bossman here don't trust me. So I'll let you do this to show its fair."

Pete and Mills were crouched beside a square of oiled canvas. A deck of cards was in the center and with a quick second glance, Elizabeth's trained eye could see the cards were marked on the edge. Small creases that could have been grime, but Houston had introduced her to this novice marking job when she was thirteen.

"What's going on?" she asked. Ledbetter's face was tight with rage, Mel looked bewildered, while Bradshaw was scowling thoughtfully.

"We've dickered down to a price of thirty cents a pound. Mills here says we don't get anything without a hand of poker. If I win, we pay nothing. But we pay three times the price if he wins."

"Hell. We don't need the meat anyways! Forget the bastard!" Ledbetter growled.

"He's got a trick up his sleeve," Bradshaw said before he spit.

"Like I say. Let your boy here deal it." Mills rolled up the tattered sleeves of his coat and grinned, showing gum on top where teeth should have been. "Ain't nothin' up my sleeve. Jest tryin' to add a bit-a variety to my day. We'll play it cold, nothing wild."

His hands were a lot cleaner than the rest of him and the cards weren't the small one-and-a half inch pocket size like men on the trail usually carried. They were casino size and relatively clean.

"The deck looks short, to me," Pete said.

"Go ahead 'n count 'em." Mills fanned the cards on the mat. Elizabeth picked them up, thumbed the edge of the stack. She fumbled them in a clumsy attempt to shuffle and noticed Mel frowning with surprise. He was used to her easy card style when they played on night herd duty. But Elizabeth's feigned ineptitude allowed her to get a good look at Mills's cards.

Pete scratched his graying sideburns. "I don't know about thi—"

But Elizabeth hunkered down. "I'll deal them," she said, pulling off her gloves. "Who's going to shuffle?"

Pete shuffled once, the slovenly Brian Mills shuffled once, neatly splitting the deck and setting up marked cards with his deft fingers. Elizabeth made the last enfolding so that things stayed as Mills wanted them to. But like Phyllis Johnson had said, anything to do with her hands, Elizabeth did well.

"Face down, right?" she said to disguise her knowledge of the game. The men nodded.

With great deliberateness, Elizabeth dealt the first round of cards. She felt clumsy doing it slowly, but carefully placed the next rounds. Even with all the rough work she had been doing, she could feel the notches on the edges of the cards. Mills frowned at her hands. But he couldn't say what he suspected without tipping his own deceitful game. It was his deck, after all. When all five cards were dealt, Pete had three queens, a king and a trey; Mills had two fours, a jack, a ten and an ace. Elizabeth saw the smile fade from Brian Mills's face as Pete turned over his cards.

Twenty minutes later, the teamsters had 150 pounds of smoked and fresh meat strapped to the pack mule and were headed out of the buffalo camp without paying a dime.

"That Mills still can't believe what happened," Mel was laughing as they jogged along.

"I'm not too sure myself," Bradshaw said. "The deck was bound to be stacked."

"It was," Elizabeth told them. "The cards were marked, too. I just dealt him the hand he had expected to be yours, Pete."

Pete grinned admiration and disbelief.

Ledbetter slapped Elizabeth between the shoulder blades nearly knocking her into her gelding's neck. "Whooeee!" Compliments came from all around.

"Let's make tracks before his friends show up and take exception to our winning," Bradshaw declared. He struck a bee-line course for the wagons.

🐎

By the time the whole of this got repeated (and amplified) around the wagon camp that afternoon, it did a lot to strengthen some people's opinion of Zee Clark. Jorge was more convinced than ever the boy was no ordinary boy and had experiences they all might cringe over. The woman of my heart! thought Casey Pritchard. And Willie MacGrin (who that day had stalked the buffalo herd, tried several shots and got nothing) was bolstered in his opinion that Zee Clark was a real snot.

David Hastings took it all as one more thing to worry about. "Get those damn hide hunters coming up here after us, doing that. We didn't need the meat badly enough to take that chance."

"We just played by their rules and won, is all," Ledbetter said, still grinning.

"But we're going to have to tighten up the watch around here even more."

Casey, surprisingly, agreed with David, but for his own reasons. "I had a bit of a run in today myself." And he told about the Arapaho hunters he had met who had lost a horse while hunting buffalo and wanted to trade their buffalo kill for his fine mount.

"I see you're still riding your horse," Dodie Watson said with a grin.

"Most definitely." Casey sipped from his coffee cup. "They didn't take it too well."

"How many dead Arap did you leave back there?" Amos asked.

"None." Casey said, an ominous tone to his voice. "So I suggest we keep our weapons loaded and quick at hand."

"Mules will be grain fed and tethered to the wagon tongues," Joe said. "And we'll picket all loose stock."

Casey looked pensively at Elizabeth, knowing that not having night herd duties could be a problem for her.

But thoughts of covetous Arapaho didn't make night herding sound so pleasant to Elizabeth, and she cringed with the idea of meeting one of those nasty hide hunters in the dark. The humming trooper came to her mind, only as a melancholy puzzlement.

They got through that night with no problems at all, and Joe had Elizabeth ride with him on his scouting in the morning, that way he allowed her the privacy she needed by standing lookout while she took to the bushes. Elizabeth found this a bit embarrassing, but knew he meant well.

The wagons were back on the trail that morning, with Cross's wagon sporting a cottonwood splint on the broken singletree. They made good time, passing the Big Timbers area that used to boast thirty miles of huge cottonwoods. The trees were all but gone due to the thousands of cuttings done by travelers over the years. The bottom land was still lush, and there was plenty of buffalo sign, with the herd at one point being only a quarter mile away. Willie was all set to go shooting, but John Bradshaw reminded him that the herd could overrun the wagons if it got started in the wrong direction.

"We've got enough meat now," Joe said. "No point in killing for the sake of it."

It griped Willie plenty that they had enough meat because of Zee Clark.

They saw two other hide outfits in the distance and once heard the faint whap of gunfire. To David's enjoyment, they covered eight miles before dinner.

Casey, however, was getting nervous. A kind of sixth-sense nervous that made him insist the night guard be continued. He told Joe and Joe told the men: "We'll stand five men on night watch now, three-hour shifts."

"All this for a few broken down Arapaho bucks! Hell, we saw them," Ledbetter said. "They didn't even have a carbine among them."

"Well, besides the Injuns and hide hunters," Joe said. "We're in an area where we got bandits to worry about."

"That Fortune gang I saw the flyer about?" Horace called. He had read about the gang during his unauthorized fling at Fort Dodge. "Sounded like they was workin' east, way the hell behind us."

This was the first Elizabeth had heard about a Fortune Gang and she looked around for Casey to ask him about it. He was out scouting their back trail, as usual. She sidled toward Joe.

"We're in Colorado Territory now and there are some road agents around here. So just keep your weapons ready. We'll close in the wagons at the first sign of trouble."

"This mean we don't have to push these bastard mules in the dark no more?" Sim called.

"Not late, at least."

"Yahoo!"

The men checked carbines and rifles, and strapped on pistols. When Joe started to his horse so he could scout the road ahead, he nearly bumped into Elizabeth.

"What's this Fortune Gang Mr. Cross mentioned?"

Lots of possibilities scurried through her head, most concerning her father and who else might carry the Fortune name.

"It's a group working for Elizabeth Fortune back in Kansas. It appears they robbed the Wentworths and all," Joe explained.

It didn't take any time at all for Elizabeth to put that together. "Tillison!" she said between clenched teeth.

Joe gave a mirthless laugh. "Yeah. That's what Casey and I figured. Well, that's a long way from here. I don't think you need worry about them catching up with you." He patted Elizabeth's shoulder and then was face to face with Willie.

"Wait a minute!" the young man growled. "Is this asshole wanted by the law or something? God damn, I might have cut a few capers, but nothin' that serious. And here you treat him like he was silver lined!"

"Shut up, Will. You don't know what you're talking about." Joe tried to move by his son.

"The hell, you say! Clark gets the lightest duties and the best of everything from you and Jorge both. And now I find out he's—"

"You found out nothing!" Joe gave Willie a shove in the chest. "Look, son. I don't know what your problem has been on this trip, but I sure as hell hope you snap out of it soon."

"*My* problem! You don't know shit about my problems! You spend all your time kissin' this kid's boots!"

"Don't you have something you're suppose to be doing?" Joe's even voice didn't give a hint to the frustration he felt.

Elizabeth wondered if they ought to explain the situation to Willie, but settled against that, certain he would tell it around camp as fast as he could.

"Yes, sir. Oh, yes Sir!" Willie wheeled away from his dad and stomped to his horse.

Elizabeth left the area, too, feeling guilty for the position she had put Joe in. She grabbed up water buckets and slid her way down to the sluggish Arkansas to fill them. At the river, she had to dig a hole in the silt so the water would get deep enough to fill the buckets. She did this with her hands, jerking at the wet earth and cursing mildly to stifle her discontent while she waited for the slow seep to slosh over the oaken rims. Mosquitoes buzzed and bit even though she kept slapping her neck with her gloves.

When Elizabeth returned from the river, she was surprised to see David Hastings waiting at the edge of the camp, rifle in hand and a scowl on his face. She nearly passed out from worry that Joe had been forced to tell Hastings who she was, but that wasn't the case.

"Nobody's to go anywhere unescorted," Hastings snapped when she got close. "Weren't you listening to Joe? You don't even have a gun with you, damn it. Now learn to follow orders!"

"Yes, sir."

Willie might have been mollified if he had heard all this. He would have especially liked Zee Clark's meek response with downcast eyes, but he wasn't following orders, either—out plundering the dry washes, taking bead on lizards and feeling like his best friend was giving a party and he hadn't been invited.

Night watch took on more portent now, and the men went to their shifts grumbling, but their frowns were more from worry than complaint. First watch went from sunset to eleven o'clock, second until two, third until dawn when they would start hookup. Elizabeth stood second duty along with four others, one of whom was Casey Pritchard. He was across camp from her watching toward the rocky slope of the Arkansas; she looked toward the treeless plains. The night air was cool this late in August and the guards weren't allowed fires.

"No cigars, no singing," Joe had told everyone. "Don't do a thing that would tip off you're sitting there."

"Sittin' there freezin'!" Sim had complained.

"It's like bein' in the damn army again. Shit," Dawson said.

"Shut up."

That call from Ledbetter who had no affection at all for Tom Dawson since the man had tried to knife him at Fort Dodge. Joe had changed the order of the wagons to keep those two men far apart, and also to keep Guzlowski away from Cross. Mel Burns rode on the opposite side of the trail from Willie; Willie avoided Zee. With all this emotional heat, it wouldn't seem anyone would worry about staying warm.

Wrapped in her blanket, Elizabeth alternated between moderate comfort and flushes of worry. Two things were nagging at her. One was her attraction to Casey which she couldn't fully abate. But if Casey had stolen over to her to ask if she were warm enough (and he was considering it); and if he'd put his arms around her (he pondered that, too), he would have been in for a surprise because Elizabeth would have resisted. She was determined not to let her heart overrule her common sense. Casey's thoughts seemed to touch her, however, and twice she jerked and looked over her shoulder to study the deep shadows toward the camp.

Once Dog crept out to her and waggled his stumpy tail when she jumped. She shooed him away, not wanting a new batch of fleas in her blanket.

Her other worry concerned the moon. Looking at the moon wasn't anything new—a good way to tell time; but for Elizabeth the moon phase took on special significance which she hadn't even considered back in Ellsworth when she signed on as a boy. That curved sliver of light she was now seeing meant a near new moon, and that was her time of the month. She hadn't figured out how she was going to deal with that and she damned her own act-now-think-later character that had gotten her into this predicament.

The moon was half way through its western arc when more than Dog or her imagination crept up behind her. The hammer on her derringer clicked loudly as she swung around.

"Ho up there, Zee." Bill Porter held out his hands. Sweat had formed on his neck and forehead like water to a fresh well when he heard the gun action. "I'm takin' over for ya." He lowered his voice. "Seen anything?"

"No." Elizabeth eased down on the hammer and started rolling her blanket.

"What's that over there?"

This lump Porter indicated had caught Elizabeth's attention several times in the past three hours. Once she could have sworn it moved. "It's a juniper. The shadow makes it look bigger than it is."

Joe had reminded everyone that this desert land at night could play tricks on the eyes. "Do more listening than looking," he instructed.

"We know that. We ain't no damn pilgrims," Bradshaw had grouched. Tobacco juice streamed with vehemence.

Elizabeth was used to being out at night, but she had always counted on the mules and her horse to do the watching. Last night, even an owl had spooked her.

"Seems to me we're slinkin' around here for nothin'. Watson said that no self-respectin' 'Rapaho would ever attack at night. Comanch, neither." Porter scratched at his ragged beard and spit tobacco juice into the dark.

"It's road agents we're guarding against."

"Oh. Yeah." He shifted uncomfortably. "Hell, I prefer the idea of Indians. At least then there would be a pattern to go by, some regular style of attack. With bushwhackers, you never can tell."

Since Elizabeth had no experience with either one, she didn't reply, just gathered her things to leave. Bill said, "Joe said to tell ya that Hastings and him is goin' on watch."

Elizabeth knew what the message meant: Joe and Hastings shared a high-walled tent; she could take it now. Hastings even had a chamber pot in there and a wash stand. Not that there was any extra water for washing. The previous night, however, Elizabeth had taken real pleasure in using that tent rather than sleeping under the mess wagon between Jorge and Dog. Dog could snore nearly as loudly as Horace Cross.

That second night, those loud sleepers were the only disruptions Elizabeth noticed. Lots of things could have happened, though, since Clive Williams fell asleep during his watch; Dodie Watson saw a moving shadow beyond the east end of the wagon circle and almost shot before he realized it was Mervin Gaynor out to take a crap; Hastings watched the clear sky and cursed the fact that they were sitting rather than moving along the trail. He even thought about rousing folks to action so they could pick up a few miles. Casey Pritchard tossed in the darkness, thinking about Elizabeth alone in Hastings' tent. He nearly had to tie himself to the wagon wheel to keep from going over there. So with the portent abounding, it came off a rather calm stretch of time.

Another place on the prairie was calm, too. Another camp without fire; another group of men sleeping with their rifles close at hand. Both groups were up before dawn. Both groups skipped breakfast. Only the wagon-train people didn't really know what was going on.

THIRTEEN

Daddy always said fortitude and the Fortunes go together, and when times are meanest, you have to prove up on your best abilities. I surely hope I don't have to prove up anymore like I did today. I can't believe this mess I'm in...

26 August

"Stretch 'em out!" Joe called. Dog barked steadily like he was giving orders, too.

They took to the trail before the morning chill was out of the air and stayed to it until after midday. At the nooning they closed the wagons into a tight circle, and unhitched the mules. Two spans at a time, the animals were led to the river to drink, extra men standing guard over the operation. The sun poured out relentless heat like it was mid-July. No clouds. Flies.

Porter and Cross got into fisticuffs regarding scorpions, with Cross arguing that they were all poisonous. Elizabeth had slumped in the shade of the mess wagon, her hands chalk dry and her lips chapped. Dark stains marked the fingertips of her right hand from the tobacco she had been using on the insect bites. Her nails were dirty. Elizabeth sighed, wondering that if her father had ridden up right then, would he even recognize his little girl.

And this is the person Casey Pritchard wants to marry? she thought with a disdainful chuckle. She glanced to where he was talking with David Hastings and Joe, his clothes thoroughly rumpled, dust making white lines in the creases of his forehead and around his lips. Sweat stains darkened the crown of his brown hat.

At three o'clock, Hastings urged them off again. "We've got to make twenty-five miles today," he said to Joe from atop his grullo gelding. "That'll put us just a day's drive from Fort Lyon."

"A hard day's drive," Joe said. He reined his horse away from Hastings. "Haven't you noticed that we're going up hill?"

"I can't see that a soul is going to bother us here, with the fort so close. I say we push on after dusk," David went on.

"Why don't you leave that up to Casey. He's—"

"Pritchard doesn't have a store to run and people depending on him. My brother's wife could have had that baby by now. Lord knows Jake won't be much into working with a new youngster. I have to get there!" David would have really been in a state if he had known that Jake was still laid up with injuries from a bushwhacking.

Joe heaved a sigh and scowled as the wagons started past him. Jorge led off in the mess wagon with the supply cart attached, then Dawson and Hayward set their teams side-by-side, followed by Chambers and Williams. Ledbetter and Guzlowski were waiting to move their wagons on the trail along with Gaynor and Bradshaw. Suthers and Porter did some equipment checks then pulled in. Watson and Cross made up the last two wagons.

"Keep it close!" Joe called, riding down the line.

Close meant don't get strung out more than a quarter mile.

"Watch that left side over there!" Ledbetter called back to Suthers. "Got deep sand."

Even with the warning, Don's wagon lurched heavily through an unseen hole. Mules snorted and complained. The men cursed and whips snapped.

Elizabeth was one of the four guards, and gritty-eyed, she rode her gelding on the off side of the wagons near the head of the train, scanning to her right. It was hard for her to keep her mind on her duty because the panorama had again changed, now being drier, browner, with more sage and prickly pear. Against the horizon poked gray cloud-like formations that didn't move. When Pete told her those Sangre de Cristo Mountains were nearly 100 miles away, she was dumbstruck, not able to conceive of anything so large that she could see it from such a distance. Jorge assured her the white she saw was snow and that it stayed on the high peaks year around. He did this in a mix of Spanish and English, furthering her linguistic education. Once, Hastings rode up and yelled at her to stop day-dreaming.

Casey kept his horse at the front of the procession, the back trail being so broad and sloped there was little worry of a rear attack. Mel and Willie had the river side, Willie in the back.

"Eatin' dust, damn it," he muttered.

Dust was plentiful, too, churning up from the wheels, spurting from under the mules' narrow hooves. Wind gusted and swirled powdery particles through the air as the sun beat them down.

They continued that steady incline that had started at Fort Dodge, and they had been in Colorado Territory for two days. Nothing indicated this. Any geographical marker had either been trampled by buffalo or wild horses, or smashed up by Indians who didn't believe in federal borders, or stolen by whoop-it-up types who wanted a signpost to put over their bunk or to show to their sweety to prove where they had been. But after thirty years of steady use, the Santa Fe Trail was over fifty yards broad, and no one could get lost. They just trundled along the ruts of those who had gone before.

Riding ahead, Casey squinted into the late-day sun and topped a slight rise. He could see six miles ahead to where the land headed into the river breaks, with small hills and washes meandering like deep wrinkles. The road had curves in it to accommodate the hills and the bendingriver, which was marked by locust and cottonwood, some groves quite thick. Patches of green grass looked like blemishes on the brown land. It looked like a good place for an ambush to Casey, so he scouted a night camp a couple of miles to the east. The tension he felt as he rode had him flinching whenever his horse snorted.

Yet all his nameless feelings weren't enough to convince David Hastings. When Casey suggested that they bypass the trees, David exploded. "Bypass! That'd be another two or three miles. No, we'll go on through that tonight. Camp on the far side," David said. He sat his horse next to Casey's on the rise staring at the slight valley. The sun, an hour deeper toward dusk, burned like hot brass across the horizon. Joe faced his sorrel away from the sun on Casey's other side.

"Through it! Hell, man, that's probably where they're waiting!" Casey declared.

"Look, Pritchard. Back near old Fort Aubry was a great spot for an ambush. Nothing happened. I doubt anything will until we start that climb along the Timpas. There are so many hidey-holes in there, it's a natural."

"This isn't just some ordinary road gang we're worrying about. You say someone's out to stop *you*. They aren't going to follow a regular plan."

"Not so loud." David scowled around, although the wagons were still a quarter-mile on the back trail.

"I agree with Casey," Joe started.

"Who runs this outfit?!" David snapped.

"I run it. You just own it," Joe retorted.

"Damn right, I own it. And I'll say when we stop or not."

"Are you takin' over as wagon boss, Mr. Hastings?" Joe said.

"No, no." David huffed a big scowl and pulled a cigar from his inside vest pocket. "But the men are tired of all this night duty stuff. If we keep this up, they'll be worn to a frazzle."

"I'm tellin' you, it's going to be soon. I can feel it," Casey insisted.

"We'll push on 'til nine or so. There's grass down there and better water for the mules." Hastings jerked his horse away and rode toward the wagons.

In the hot evening, Casey squeezed tense hands on the reins and tried to relax. He again studied the land they were approaching, still uncomfortable.

"There'll be no changing his mind," Joe said. His horse stomped a back leg and whisked flies with its tail. "Shit."

"He's got a lot on him. His family, his brother. Lots of money invested in this from some hot-shot Illinois bankers," Casey said, hoping his argument would make him feel better.

"Yeah. Well, you warned him, though. If anything happens, it's on his head, not yours."

"If anything happens." Casey leaned heavily on the pommel and blew air through his dry lips.

Casey's acute worry should have been something David Hastings paid attention to. Casey Pritchard had been in some ticklish situations. Something was afoot, and he could feel it just as he had in South Carolina right before he was captured by Rebels; and once in The Nations the time when the Choctaw Mounted Police had run him down thinking he was a whiskey drummer. And there was Cassville. He thought of Darcy Goodhue, the man's anger barely subdued as Ox Lewis answered Joe's questions about their appearance on the wagon road. Casey had been one of the Pinkerton agents who infiltrated Cassville, and when his information got to the Union command, he had a feeling like this—that something wasn't right. The military had done the dirty work, but the results made him ashamed: the surprise attack, the slaughter, no prisoners. Goodhue was one of twelve who escaped.

But the wagon train trekked on, and true enough, most of the men seemed relieved to head toward that apparent oasis of trees where they would be protected from the continual gritty wind, maybe find some water that didn't taste like it had come out of a sluice pit. By eight-thirty, everyone was bone weary and they corralled the wagons under some trees, grumbling because Jorge hadn't hurried ahead with the mess wagon and started the cook fire so the meal could be ready for them.

"*Hay banditos aqui!*"

"Where? Ain't no *banditos*," Ledbetter scoffed. "I rode down here with Pritchard and scouted it out. You coulda been here a half an hour ago."

"It's food we want, Jorge *amigo*. Get with it!" Dodie Watson called.

"Eat shit," Jorge muttered. He made obscene gestures and slowed down at his work. Dog growled and bared its teeth at passers-by. "*Gringos tontos. Piensan solamente con las panzas.*"

He was right; their bellies did seem to rule their thoughts.

"Zee! Take these mules downstream and water them," Hastings ordered. "I told you there'd be no trouble," was his aside to Joe.

"Williams! Ride guard with Zee," Joe called.

Clive Williams grumbled and cussed, and no one noticed when Willie told Williams he'd take his duty. Casey was two miles away, reconnoitering the area to the west, or he would have had something to say about all of this, especially since he had just found sign of shod horses near an upstream ford.

In camp, little fires brightened the darkness and Jorge mixed his English and Mexican curses while he stirred a stew. Teamsters pissed and grumbled and spit; and three of them cussed mightily when Joe insisted they hoist rifles to go out on guard duty.

Elizabeth led tired mules downstream for water. When she realized the horseman on her flank was Willie and not the squatty Clive Williams, she frowned. She found a place for the mules and loosed them to their drinking, all the time keeping a wary eye on Willie. He reined his horse nearby as she got off and led her gelding to the sluggish river.

"Don't mind me," Willie said, also dismounting. "I just thought I'd tag along and take the easy route for once—like you always do. Shit. How'd you wangle riding at the front of the train while I'm on drag?" Willie's question didn't expect an answer.

Back at camp, Joe realized Willie, and not Williams, had gone out with Zee, and although Tom Dawson complained about baby-sitting two kids, Joe sent that man downstream to take Willie's place, certain his son was up to mischief.

Early starlight rippled on the brown water of the river and night birds called. Nervous, Elizabeth wrapped the reins around her hand.

"And I see you had a tent to sleep in last night while my ears filled up with dust," Willie went on.

The mules sloshed in the water, stomped, coughed, and Elizabeth worked hard to keep an ear on Willie's movements so she wouldn't have to look at him. Crickets started chirring, then stopped.

Willie asked, "Hey, Clark. You a bad guy? Jorge thinks you're a killer." He smacked Elizabeth's shoulder with the back of his hand. "Hey! I'm talkin' to you!"

The mules snorted. The gelding jerked up its head. Elizabeth flinched at a loud cracking in the air and yanked on the reins to keep her horse near. Mules were braying and bucking into the river. Her nerves felt singed; adrenaline flooded her system. Willie lay like a log at her feet, and only her dropping to her knees at his side saved Elizabeth from getting shot, too. A heavy caliber bullet slashed water behind her and sent the mules into a frenzied run.

"Willie!" She pushed his shoulder and leaned close to peer at him in the dim light. Brains and gore slid down the gravel from under Willie's scalp. Half his face was gone. Elizabeth slapped her hand to her mouth. A hot, sweet odor drifted by. She retched into her hand, stumbled away, still getting sick, towing her horse with her.

A galloping horse loomed along the river path. "Get down!" Dawson called as he clung to the animal.

Elizabeth didn't hear him, but her gelding got her to cover by tugging toward the river. She slid down the slope among fir saplings and cottonwood, her stomach in spasms, eyes watering. Dawson plunged his horse over the slight bank and slid from the saddle, tied the animal and hunkered beside Elizabeth.

"You hit?" he asked. He had a rifle strapped over his shoulders and pulled it around before squinting at Elizabeth. He glanced at Willie's still form, then shifted the rifle butt to his shoulder.

"The mules," Elizabeth muttered. "I thought he was trying to scare off the mules."

And other things raced through her head: how if she had been nicer to him, he wouldn't have come out here; how she should have let him win the shooting contest; how she was going to have to tell Joe.

"Get that damn rifle of yours, kid. We're under attack!"

A bullet ricocheted nearby, tree bark spattered. And from the distance sounded the heavy booms of the Sharps rifle John Bradshaw carried, quick staccatos of pistols, whines of bullets, and the steady blam blam from rifles. Most of the shots came from the outlaws. Thad Tillison had twice as many men, too, primed and eager for the slaughter. And now, one of them fired steadily at Dawson's and Elizabeth's position while the other was sneaking through the trees for a better angle.

"Snap out of it, Zee!" Dawson raged. He gritted his teeth as he thought of the boy's ineptitude with the rustlers.

Another shot slammed in close and when that bay gelding whinnied and tried to hightail it out of there, the jerk seemed to pull Elizabeth from her stupor. She blinked, gasped a breath, reality seeping into her.

"Oh. Oh, dear Lord!" The sound of gunshots filled her ears and she noticed the battle for the first time. She squirmed to her restless horse, tied the reins to a stout log and pulled the Winchester from the scabbard. Her gloves were slick with vomit. She tossed them away and levered up a cartridge. "They've attacked the camp!" Elizabeth flattened her back to the slope, staring to her right and listening to the sounds booming from the wagon camp.

"That ain't all!" Dawson growled, his belly to the slope as he peered across the trail to find his adversary.

Timber striped the landscape and dusty leaves drooped. Three strides away, a dead-fall marked the edge of the river. Bright stars and a faint moon hung reflected off the water and gleamed on the pale limbs of the cottonwoods. In this vague light, Elizabeth made out a moving darkness against the gray of the thickets. She drew bead, and clutched her rifle with the desperate realization it was a man she saw.

"Did anyone come out here with you?" she asked Tom.

"No, damn it." Dawson eased up the slope and squeezed off a shot. Two bullets whizzed back in return, but Tom had already ducked to cover.

Elizabeth's mouth was dry. "There's someone behind you—off to your left," she said. Her rifle was still at her shoulder and she kept it on line with the faint movement edging along the boulders eighty yards beyond Dawson. She levered the action.

"Take care of him. I think I got this other guy located."

Take care of him was just what she hoped Dawson would do, that was why she had mentioned it. Elizabeth gritted her teeth. Like target practice, she coached herself, not wanting to think of the dark form as a person. Or maybe it's Hank Tillison, came a malicious thought. Tom fired again, another shot came back, but the sounds seemed distant, as if in a dream. Elizabeth's chest ached and she narrowed her eyes. A hole horde of Hank Tillisons out there waiting to get me, she thought.

A vague glint made her tense. The outlaw had raised his rifle. Her breathing stopped. Clenching her teeth, she pulled the trigger of the Winchester. She heard the report of her piece just as the outlaw's bullet stabbed through the left sleeve of her shirt, whisking off a quarter-inch of skin before it drove into the gray dirt of the talus. The dark silhouette of the outlaw slumped over; the rifle fell into the river.

"Got him!" Dawson cried about his target. No more shots came their way, but to the west, the battle went on.

Elizabeth slowly lowered the rifle, still staring at the slumped form near the boulder. She had killed someone. The realization of that trembled through her like a bodily earthquake.

And I wanted to do it. She again thought of Hank Tillison—of Johnny Tillison.

Night sounds started up around her. The distant gunshots continued. Dawson went off to check on their assailants, who he found quite dead. When he slid back down the slope, carrying a few extra weapons to where the tied animals were, Elizabeth still sat there, unmoving.

"You got him clean. Rifle was in the river, but I got his handgun and the pieces off the other guy. Thought we could use them."

Elizabeth moved a bit and scowled, her strength returning. "What did he look like?" she asked. If only it could be that horrid Hank.

"What?" Tom squinted at her, puzzlement obvious.

"Was he a dark-haired fellow? Square jaw?"

"Uh, no. Blondish. Long-boned." Tom finished priming the loads on the Navy Colt pistol he had taken off one of the men.

Elizabeth's shoulders sagged and she rubbed her forehead with the back of her hand. Then the sounds of the wagon-camp fight assaulted her. "We've got to help the others." She started to her horse.

"Wait a minute. We can't just ride in there!" Tom grabbed her arm and pulled her back to the slope. "I been thinkin' on it. Listen." He pressed the readied pistol stock into her hand and she tucked it into the back of her pants as he spoke.

The plan Dawson came up with included the mules. It took a good a bit of time to round up a decent number, and shots kept coming from around the wagon camp. Elizabeth took time to pull the blanket and saddle from Willie's horse. She got the dry heaves when she approached the body. So did Dawson after seeing Willie's grotesque half-smashed face. They placed the blanket and saddle across it. Then to the mules. Dawson rode ahead and determined where most of the outlaws were. They headed the mules in that direction.

Thad Tillison didn't think much of the bunch of mules coming from the east. Part of the plan had been to get the herd. The full plan was to rub out this train, all of them, especially David Hastings. He was tired of playing legal games and having to win sympathy in Trinidad. He intended to end the Hastings meddling now. A few things hadn't gone as he figured, however. Like the wagoners pushing on past dark and holing up in the grove. This attack was suppose to happen at dawn, right after they started along the trail. Yet it seemed to work out all right. He had them in a clearing backed up to the river, while most of his men were concealed behind two hummocks. The others were scattered in the thickets and trees that ringed the camp. The bright cook fire had made their prey easy pickings, too, until one teamster got wise and smothered the flames. Thad felt certain the plan would work. The merchandise in the wagons would become stock for his Trinidad store, and his outlaws would get whatever they wanted from whichever dead body. All the loot in the tent would be divvied up; they'd cut cards for the horses, and the supplies in the mess wagon, along with a mule or two, would keep them eating for a couple of weeks. He had sent a couple of his crack shooters to take care of the two wranglers and bring the mules back. They would need the animals to move the wagons, and could sell the beasts for a tidy sum over in Pueblo.

What Thaddeus didn't expect was the sudden swerve the twenty or more animals took, the gunshots that came from behind them, or the torch someone threw into the thickets on the west. That brightened up quite an area when the flames took hold, and the stampede routed his men from their cozy positions. The tables were turned. When the outlaws bolted for their horses, the teamsters launched their own attack. Mules dashed about braying, kicking, dodging trees, avoiding the brush fire, crashing over people. One outlaw writhed toward the river, flames spouting from his clothing like orange wings. Don Suthers shot him.

Elizabeth trotted her gelding into camp at the end of ten minutes of fusillade which drove the enemy into the dark. This rout had left her shaken and hollow feeling. She had watched men yell out with pain, fall, and some from her shots. But if she hadn't shot them, they were most definitely going to shoot her. That thought kept things in balance for her, although her nerves were raw, head aching, arms and legs wooden with shock and weariness.

I can survive this, she thought. I *have* survived!

The brush fire cast an eerie orange flickering across the camp. Elizabeth's hands shook as she worked ten new cartridges into the Winchester. Jorge crawled from inside his wagon, Dog in his arms. "Señor Zee! *Gracias a Dios!*"

"Casey. Where is he?" Elizabeth asked. That her first thoughts had been for him didn't really strike her. He was a warrior, he was her closest friend here; seeing him would have given her a reassurance she couldn't explain.

Jorge stared around, overwhelmed by the scene. Men were calling out and scurrying in the dark with only a few lanterns lit. Moans came from shadows.

Elizabeth switched to awkward Spanish. "*Señor* Pritchard. *Donde es?*" She slid the rifle into the saddle boot.

"Uh? *No se! Toda la tiempo estoy en la carreta porque los banditos tirán en por todas partes y el perro era espanto, y*—."

Elizabeth rode off as he continued in Spanish about the fight that he didn't know much about since he was in the wagon protecting Dog the whole time.

"Zee!" The sound of Joe's voice pulled Elizabeth bowstring tight. "You're all right. Thank God. Where's Willie and Dawson?" The lantern he carried bobbed yellow light in a circle around him.

"Dawson. He's there." She pointed to where she had last seen the man. "Willie. Willie, he—" She slid off the horse, her face cold with re-membrance.

Joe raised the lantern to get a good look at her. The anguish in Elizabeth's eyes, the pallor of her skin, shortness of breath, gave him his answer. "Where is he? Does he need help?"

Tom Dawson saw the two talking and went over, hoping to spare Zee Clark the grief of telling. He thought the kid had held up pretty well, considering.

And Elizabeth was holding up again—had already gotten it out by the time Tom reached them.

"Where?" Joe demanded. He set down the lantern.

"About a half mile downstream. Mr. MacGrin. I'm sorry."

It came out like a whisper and Joe had already bolted for his horse, his heart slamming in his chest. Remorse and a passel of regrets joined his grief and shaped it to near madness. He whipped his startled horse to a gallop, a boulder of coldness filling his insides.

Trembling, Elizabeth sniffed back tears. Her arm stung as much as her eyes and she rubbed at it, realizing for the first time she had been wounded. "Oh, God." She clenched her teeth and her fists to control the shaking.

Tom was impressed by the kid. He put his hand awkwardly on Elizabeth's shoulder and patted a bit. "It'll be all right, Button," he said.

But one glance at the disheveled camp told both Elizabeth and Dawson that his words weren't even close to being true.

Fourteen

...I have killed, and died, and die again rethinking it all. At least Casey is still here. I just wish I knew what to do with myself now that everything is in shambles.

26 August

In the era when people were showing fortitude by settling Western land and taking off alone or as single families to search for gold or space of their own, road gangs were gathering together in big bands, dependent on the resources of others to make their way. Their meanness seemed to be generated by some need for power, and some larger desire not to take the risks the general populace apparently gloried in. A few lobos got excitement and reputation from being vindictive loners, but for the most part road agents were pack-oriented and cowardly—a handful of non-directed souls who let others (like Thad Tillison) convince them they knew the easy route to the good life everyone else was toiling for.

Which was why Thad Tillison's gang lit out like they did that night of August 26th. Five men had been rubbed out by the teamsters, including two of their best riflemen—put under by a couple of kid mule herders, no less (or so they thought). Four others had gunshot wounds that would lay them low for several weeks, and Thad Tillison himself was among the six who had been caught in the mule stampede. He could barely see straight for the pain in his leg where one of the frantic critters had kicked him. Then there were the two with bad burns from that sudden fire that flared when someone (Casey Pritchard) tossed a flaming limb into the thickets. In all, things had not gone as planned and these bandits weren't sticking around to have the situation get any worse, no matter the venomous exhortations of their leader. The idea had been to rout the wagons, collect loot and have a little fun; not to lose their lives.

§

At the wagon camp, four teamsters had been put under by the marauders' gunfire: Dodie Watson, Bill Porter, Horace Cross and John Bradshaw. Mervin Gaynor was so badly wounded, no one expected him to live until morning. Sim Chambers and Al Guzlowski were also injured, along with David Hastings.

Mental injuries, that no one could see, abounded.

Clive Williams experienced a mix of agony and relief that *he* could have been shot rather than Willie; *he* had been the one ordered to accompany Zee. Several of the men walked by the dying Mervin Gaynor and wondered why they had never really talked to the man; they worried that he had kin someplace they didn't know how to contact.

"Jorge! Bring that medicinal over here!" Pete Hayward called from Hastings' tent. Mel Burns and Don Suthers worked at beating down the brush fire.

"Is he going to make it?" Casey asked. He squatted at the open door looking in at David Hastings prone form. Casey wished he had been more forceful against David's plans, then maybe this wouldn't have happened.

"God damn bullet's still in his shoulder," Pete said.

A livid streak marked the forehead of the unconscious David Hastings, and a hole from a ricocheted .45 slug was near his right collar bone.

"Can he be moved?"

"We got no choice! He needs a doctor bad," Pete said. "There's others wounded, too. Guzlowski's shot in the arm. Clean wound. Chambers ankle got broke when he was running in the dark. Zee got nicked by a bullet."

"Zee!"

"Nothing serious."

Casey's pulse thrummed so hard in his ears he could hardly hear.

"*El jefe*. He will live?" Jorge asked, handing in the big whiskey bottle.

"*No se, amigo*. Go cook us up some java, would you?"

"It is all right now to make a fire?" Jorge asked. His original cook fire had been the first to be put out, by Jorge himself, before he scrambled into the wagon with Dog. Now Dog, tied to the wagon wheel, yelped protest that it couldn't get to the remnants of stew from where a mule had knocked over the teamsters' supper.

"It's all right. We've got a lot of work to do. Coffee will help," Casey said.

"You think they might come back?" Pete asked as Jorge hurried back to his wagon.

"Not tonight. We got them pretty bad there at the end, and groups like this aren't much for fighting lost causes. We've got the night."

"Ledbetter figured that, too," Pete said, somewhat reassured.

"We'll pull out for Fort Lyon at first light, so we need to round up as many mules as possible."

"I don't know that there's but six men who can drive," Pete said.

David Hastings moaned when Pete poured some whiskey into the shoulder wound. "That's a good sign," Pete said.

"Where's Joe?" Casey asked.

Pete's deliberate movements as he laid a damp cloth over Hastings' shoulder and stood up had Casey's limbs feeling icy even though he knew Joe wasn't one of the bodies laid out for burial under the big cottonwood.

"Willie bought it," Pete said. He stepped out of the tent into the cool air with Casey. "The boy rode out with Zee and the mules. Got shot down before he knew what hit him. Dawson saw the whole thing."

Dread filled Casey for what could have happened, and his eyes searched out Elizabeth. His insides knotted. He was sick with himself for that faint relief that it was Willie, not her, that got killed. Then a flood of dismay hit him as he thought of Joe out along the river tending to his son. He had gotten close to Joe in the past three weeks since they joined in Elizabeth's plans.

"Somebody needs to be with him." Casey started for his horse.

"Ledbetter already rode out," Pete said.

Casey drew a long breath, a new realization joining him. With David hurt and Joe out of camp, that left overall management to him. He gritted his teeth and appraised Pete. "There's a lot to be done, and Joe won't be up to it."

"I'll do what I can."

Grateful he could count on Pete, Casey nodded and strode off. He ordered Dawson in from guard duty for the grave digging detail. Had to yell at Sim Chambers to get him to stop his blathering, shouting at him that he was pretty certain the outlaws wouldn't be back that night. "Those thugs have wounded to care for, too," he insisted.

He sent Williams out to find the rest of the mules (the man didn't complain and took the possibly-dangerous assignment like it was his due), and then Casey examined the dead outlaws rolled in the thickets. One of them was the well-built, insecure, Tillison lackey, Billy Joe Shenby. A .50 caliber hole in his neck had let him die quickly, but the information his corpse gave Casey was a lot. The lurking suspicion that Gabe Tillison was involved in Hastings' problems loomed firm and large, although the motivation still puzzled him.

Finally Casey had a moment to approach Elizabeth. She sat cross-legged beside a horse-high sagebrush about five hundred feet out of camp, her eyes sweeping the openness around her. Although attracted by her tenacity and independence, Casey's latent manly thoughts expected, maybe even wanted, the stoic Zee Clark to give way to a quaking Elizabeth Fortune in need of consolation, so her straight posture and watchful manner surprised Casey. He could tell she heard him coming as soon as he left camp, not the dazed response of the inconsolable; she was holding up better than Sim. And when he stooped beside her, her dry eyes and impassive expression baffled him.

"Here. Have some coffee." He handed her a tin cup.

"Thank you." She took it and he noticed her hand tremble a bit. In fact, Elizabeth was trembling inside just as she had been since Willie got shot.

"How's your arm?" Casey asked.

"A little stiff. It will be all right."

That slight throbbing was nothing compared to the emotional pangs that were with her, and she had to talk about it.

"I killed two people tonight," she stated.

The words came out in a rush and Casey gritted his teeth. He sat down.

"Someone at the river after Willie got—." She shuddered. "And then, when we drove the mules into camp, a man lunged out of the bushes. He had a pistol."

The man had that pistol pointed right at her and had grabbed the reins of her horse with murder in his eye. Shocked, Elizabeth had pulled her horse around, kicked at the man, and then…

"I—I shot him."

The outlaw had shot, too, but the shifting of the bay had ruined his aim. Elizabeth would find the hole in her hat brim the next morning.

Casey swallowed hard, thinking of the dangers she had been in. "I wish I could tell you the first time is the worst, or that you'll get over it," he said.

"I won't get over it. I know that."

The cup of coffee she held seemed the only warm thing in the world right then, and Elizabeth put it close to her face so the steam would loosen her tightness.

"You've experienced this already, haven't you. I mean—you've had to kill," she said.

"I was in the war." The two guards in South Carolina flashed to Casey's thoughts and the sniper in Arkansas when he left the Confederate headquarters. Casey had also been in the battle of Pea Ridge.

"Yes. The war."

To Elizabeth, that equated with *I'm alive*. Mere existence had become a war to her. The War had been the beginning of events which put her into this circumstance in the first place; and then there was the ongoing war between cultures and races—that nasty war that had set Hank Tillison, and thereby his family, against her; and there was the mental war of being caught between and among the other wars.

"Has Mr. MacGrin come back?" she asked after a sip of coffee.

"No. I'm going to ride out there."

"When the shot came, I thought it was Willie trying to scare off the mules and get me in trouble. He tried that once, back near Fort Larned." She fiddled with the cup. "Maybe if I'd told his dad then about Willie's jealousy he wouldn't have kept on like he did—wouldn't have followed me out there tonight."

"We lost five men in this fight and I doubt they would have been saved by changing how they lived or acted a few weeks ago. Even Mervin Gaynor's going fast, for all his piety."

Elizabeth wasn't impressed by Mervin's supposed righteousness and she nodded slightly, finished her coffee.

"And I thought enduring my grandfather's dislike was bad." She gave a harsh laugh. "That seems a small thing, now. It's survival—that's what it's all about."

Pragmatic responses were not what Casey had expected, and he gave her a careful look, wondering how long she could hold herself together. He would have been shocked by how deeply her hardness had reached. Like soldiers in the field and with most humans in life-threatening situations, remaining alive where others had not strengthened Elizabeth's need to live and tightened her reactions into a knot of wary zeal.

Not that Elizabeth wasn't repelled by the bloodshed she had been part of and witnessed, nor did this response imply a loss of sensitivity. When Casey's strong fingers rubbed at the tension at the back of her neck, she was grateful; and when his other hand stroked the back of hers, she didn't resist.

"I—I was worried about you," she said to Casey. "I didn't know where you were, and—"

"I was worried about you, too."

"I mean, you're the best friend—the only friend I've got out here."

"It's more than that," he said.

The sound of her shaky breathing seemed to blot out other night sounds. If the setting had been different, Casey would have kissed her as an expression of his deep concern and caring, and if he had, Elizabeth would have allowed it, would have accepted his intent and relished the closeness when she felt so totally alone. She wouldn't have given a single thought to the racial disparity that otherwise plagued her.

But the night-swept prairie, with death and dying all around, was not the time or the place to risk exposing Elizabeth's true identity. Even for her to put her head on his shoulder could seem quite curious to the other men; and there was still work to do. The fact that Joe and Ledbetter hadn't returned to camp with Willie's body worried Casey, and he reluctantly excused himself. After a few moments, Casey's spotted horse trotted east along the river trail. Elizabeth heard it, but didn't look. Her hand balled to a fist.

In 1870, Fort Lyon was one of the best laid out forts in the West, with spacious sandstone quarters, hospital, chapel, and two commissaries. Relief of arriving there on the late afternoon of August 27th exuded from the remnants of Hastings' wagon train like sap from spring trees. But an undercurrent of depression accompanied this relief. From the original crew of eighteen, six men were dead, three were injured. What would happen next was anyone's guess.

Dog wasn't guessing. His immediate future became better defined the closer they got to the fort. Pungent odors of other canines scented the air, and one he sniffed bespoke strongly of a bitch in heat. Dog's stumpy tail waggled with joy as he trotted from one revealing sign to the next. Soon would end Dog's lonely days and his nights of distrusting the luring scent of coyotes. This impending doggy gathering totally put aside his confusion over the actions of his accompanying humans.

It had started before dawn when Joe MacGrin, who usually called "Stretch 'em out!" left camp alone on his horse. Casey Pritchard lit out after him about an hour later as the mules were being hitched. It was all part of Joe's grief, which Dog didn't understand, and which had grown since the previous night along the river bank when Joe tried to dig Willie's grave with his hands. Jorge had ridden out there near midnight and talked some sense into him. But Joe had nursed that grief into a real big anger by morning and struck out alone to track down the outlaws. Casey had recognized this, even if Dog hadn't. But that's why Pete Hayward, who Casey had left in charge, started five freight wagons out in the morning with a grouchy "Let's go." Dog had barked insistently and ran in circles trying to get them to realize that they had left most of the wagons setting at the camp.

Dog's master didn't sing this morning, either, but two men moaned from the hammocks in the mess wagon. The little caravan stopped around noon, right before they were joined by the cavalry patrol Dawson had ridden ahead to get. They put a man who had stopped moaning into a hole in the ground. Dog had wanted to investigate that, but the people piled the place over with rocks and spiny brush, so it wasn't worth his while.

All that odd behavior didn't matter anymore with the promises that lay ahead. Dog raced past the sweating laborers who were building stone portals at the fort gates and sniffed each big tree along the curving road that led to the main buildings, overjoyed by this return to civilization. He was soon greeted with various yips and barks, and two well-fed mongrels growled and paced him with their tails high. For Dog, this would be a glorious time.

Pete stopped the wagons to make camp on the broad meadow beside the cavalry stables. Staccato notes of trumpeters rippled around the fort grounds as the soldiers were recalled from drill practice. The sight of the mountains was lost behind murky clouds. Beyond the stables, the conical tips of Indian lodges poked against the cloudy sky, and a few blanket-wrapped natives stood near the commissary. Elizabeth took it all in, strangely unmoved by the nearness of so many people. It seemed foreign and crowded, especially when young boys and some of the laborers gathered around the wagons asking questions, curious for details about their plight. As the large population and the business of the fort seeped through to Elizabeth she felt slightly irritated that she was no longer in the middle of the plains, her only community being sixteen men on a wagon train.

Pete and Ledbetter rode off with Jorge and the mess wagon, taking David Hastings and the two injured to the post hospital. Elizabeth started helping Mel picket their meager stock, but he waved her off.

"Set a while, Zee. That arm must be botherin' you enough as it is."

"We're all tired, Mel." Her upper left arm was stiff and throbbed like it might from a bad bruise. But she had been shot. This was a bullet wound, keeping fresh in her mind the peculiar circumstance she was in. "Let's just get this done."

While she tethered and examined mules, her thoughts shifted between Joe MacGrin and Casey, who she was certain were chasing the outlaws, and what she was going to do next. *Do* on a long range basis. Casey had already told everyone that they wouldn't be leaving the fort until David was well enough to travel, which could be a week or more. Don and Mel wanted to get on to their families in Santa Fe. With the cash on hand, there was enough money to give a few of the surviving men at least half of their expected wages. Even if she could get her full wages (a dollar a day), Elizabeth knew she wouldn't have enough money to see her on to Fort Union where the majority of her belongings would be. All I've got, she thought. In a few trunks from Indiana.

With the stock cared for, she turned to her bay gelding. It whickered and pushed its soft muzzle against her shoulder. She scratched its solid jaw. "You're about the only thing from all this I'll really miss," she told the horse.

She was lying to herself. For all their aggravation, Elizabeth had developed genuine friendships with some of these men: quiet Mel who had talked a lot about his younger sisters, mother and invalid father (crippled by a Union bullet); Amos Ledbetter, as raunchy as any of them, but likable with a hearty laugh. That Dodie Watson and John Bradshaw were dead still stunned Elizabeth. They had seemed perennial, mostly because they had been the oldest and full of stories about how the plains use to be before "all these damn pilgrims moved in."

She combed her fingers through the horse's mane and sighed.

But melancholy didn't overwhelm her. As soon as work allowed, she headed the gelding along the road for the post headquarters to see if any civilian jobs were to be had. Gongs and bells sounded from the barracks, announcing evening mess. Indian people, none of whom seemed to have horses, shuffled toward the fort perimeters. Children were being called home from play, and the screened porches of the houses looked cool and inviting. The presence of children made Elizabeth wonder about schools. Getting a job as a teacher or governess would include her resuming identity as a woman, however. Right then, that offered more problems than it solved.

At a corner house, a young woman was being helped from a hack, the officer with her looking dapper in his blue frock coat, neatly trimmed sideburns and long mustache. The woman carried herself in the gloating way of a gambler just won on a bluff, smiling and waiting for admiration. Three troopers who were riding near Elizabeth, grinned and touched the brims of their caps. Elizabeth was merely surprised that this woman could act so haughty when the pinch-waist dress she was wearing, with full hip and back bustle, had been out of fashion for three years.

The fort had two laundry facilities with four sink houses. Ten separate living quarters for the women workers set on the back lots behind the various sandstone barracks and quarters. Officer housing was under construction and a drainage system was being laid out to keep the parade ground and housing area from getting boggy during the rains.

But no jobs, the graying major-sergeant answered Elizabeth's query. He eyed this wiry, weathered boy and wondered why the recruiting captain hadn't yet talked him into signing up.

Outside the office, men paid Elizabeth little mind, but the gelding came under admiring scrutiny from some of the construction laborers. As she headed the horse on the long route back to the camp, past the commissary storehouse and up the short row of infantry barracks, several non-coms, lounging under a tree, studied the handsome stock of that Winchester which protruded from the scabbard by Elizabeth's right knee. She made the turn in front of the officers' quarters and saw an older Negro man leading two horses toward a small barn. Elizabeth contemplated riding over and talking to him, and that was why she didn't notice the two girls who strolled along, their calico sunbonnets tied at the neck and hanging with their long hair down their backs, even though their mothers had told them not to be so brazen. They stared at the dark-eyed boy in moccasins who sat his horse as would an army scout—shag of hair bronzed from the sun, sensitive mouth. Their shoulders bumped each others'. They giggled and looked back after he passed.

On the next lawn, a little girl fretted and tried to escape the aggressive playfulness of a very dirty dog. The dog was Dog, still euphoric over this magnificent oasis of entertainment. He had already been in two fights, found the bitch, chased her, mounted her, snuffled lunch out of a bountiful garbage pile, and found the bitch again.

"Get away from here!" A woman rushed from the house holding a broom aloft like a hoe. "Go on! Shoo!"

Dog avoided the swat, leaped about, snatching at the child's dress hem.

"Get away!"

He was having a great time!

"Dog. Stop it!" Elizabeth ordered as she dismounted the bay; then "*Borron!*" (That was Dog's real name—Spot). "*Bastante! Ven aca!*"

Orders in his first people language and from the human he liked most except for his master got his attention. He loped, tongue wet and pink from the side of his mouth, to where Elizabeth stood.

"Is that your cur?" the woman demanded. She pulled up her crying child and glared at Elizabeth. Behind them at the door of the house, stood a middle-aged Negro woman whose complexion was just a shade darker than Elizabeth's sun tan. Her head was bound in a white cloth and she wore a pale apron over her gray dress.

"You get that mongrel out of here or I'll have someone shoot it!" the incensed mother continued.

"Yes, ma'am." Elizabeth grabbed hold of Dog's ruff with her right hand, studied the servant and thought about getting a job as a domestic. Dog yipped and squirmed. "*Callate!*" Elizabeth ordered, dismissing the idea.

"And you keep away from here, too, you lousy foreigner!" The woman marched to her house.

Very little could upset Elizabeth anymore and she chuckled at the woman's ignorance, found herself muttering *bruja*, then chastised Dog in English and Spanish she had heard Jorge use (she would have been surprised at some of the meanings) until Dog was sufficiently settled down to trot beside the bay back to camp.

In camp, Elizabeth tied Dog to the wheel of the mess wagon. He flopped down in weary contentment. When she took her horse to the picket line, she frowned because no black and white spotted horse was yet there. The many dangers Casey and Joe could have met pounded through her head, and the extent of her worry refueled her consternation over his irrational proposal.

He wants to marry me. And I—. She wasn't sure, although having Casey injured or dead, certainly wasn't the answer.

Elizabeth's concern for Casey was unwarranted, however, for he was, at that moment, entering the military garrison with a cavalry patrol. He had worries of his own enough for five people: over Joe's belligerent gloominess, and evidence that the outlaws had returned and looted the wagons. He wasn't even certain whether David Hastings and Elizabeth were all right, or if the remnant wagons had even reached the fort.

He had caught up with Joe that morning and forced the man to go back to camp. They arrived when the Fort Lyon troopers did and the wagons had already been plundered. Joe insisted on riding with the blue coats as they followed the bandit tracks south into rough country of hard-rock arroyos. There, the outlaws had scattered, each with at least two mule loads of booty. Joe had wanted to push on, take a chance, follow any trail.

"We can't run 'em down with a patrol this small," the lieutenant had said.

"Be damned, then. I'll find them!" Joe had started his horse forward and Casey rode with him.

"Joe, what are you going to do? Follow each trail?"

"If I have to. I got to get them."

"On foot? Look at your horse, man. You pushed him hard this morning as it was. He's worn out. You haven't got food, just a canteen of water."

"I got to get the bastards. I got to—" But he had stopped his horse, patting the wet-dark neck of the hard-breathing sorrel, the lining of its nostrils showing bright red from exertion.

"I know, Joe. I know. But think, man! How good are you going to be at getting them like this? I sure as hell don't want to have to go to Lucinda and tell her both you and Willie are gone."

"Pritchard." Joe's breathing was as if he had been running a race. "Pritchard. They shot my boy. My first born. They—"

"We'll get them, Joe. With more soldiers, trackers, we'll run them down. But you got to be fit to do it. Come on, now. Come on."

Even as he had talked the older man to turning back, he had watched him sink deeper into angry remorse.

Now, at Fort Lyon, the sight of the familiar mule remuda and Jorge's wagon at the camp area, lightened some of Casey's burden. Jorge could help Joe with this depression.

"The wagons made it in okay," he said to Joe.

"Yeah." Joe just stared at the camp.

"Which way to the post hospital?" Casey asked the corporal. He got quick directions then turned to Joe. "I'm going to find out how David's doing."

"That stupid bastard. I hope he's in hell!" Joe jerked his horse away.

"Joe—"

"What, Pritchard? You going to take his side after he ordered us into that ambush? You warned him and he wouldn't listen. My son's gone 'cause of that fucker." Joe slapped his big sorrel with the end of the reins and, tired though the beast was, it jerked a quick trot toward the wagon camp.

But it wasn't a matter of taking sides. Casey realized that Joe figured the wagon train would be disbanded and his credibility as majordomo undermined, but Casey still had a job. David had hired him to discover who was sabotaging efforts to start the new store. Protection was only part of it, and Casey was close to finally getting some facts. When he was in Fort Dodge, he had requested that any information about Jeffrey Bragg be sent here to Fort Lyon. Something could be here by now, some clue about Bragg or his wife that might shed light onto the situation. He knew Bragg had been a CSA officer, and expected Fort Riley would have come up with something. And then there was the suspicion that had been dogging him since the mule rustling attempt: Gabe Tillison. When he mentioned Gabe Tillison to the Fort Lyon troopers, the patrol lieutenant knew part of the name.

"They ran a Tillison out of North Texas last year for pulling these kind of jobs. Can't recall his name was Gabe, though."

Puzzle pieces began sliding around in Casey's head, almost fitting together. He was certain there were two Tillisons. "And around here?"

"This is the first wagon train to be hit east of the fort since last fall. Even the Injuns has been quiet. Most of the trouble comes along the Timpas or over by Pueblo. Robbing the traffic down from Denver and the rail lines."

The lieutenant didn't consider the rovings of a gang that had something personal at stake. Casey did, however, and although it was possible that Gabe Tillison had gotten his band of no goods out on the trail from Kansas ahead of the wagons for this attack, Billy Joe Shenby's involvement substantiated the two-Tillison theory. No one had recognized any of the other dead outlaws. They weren't from Kansas, but Shenby had been in Ellsworth, had been at Fort Dodge. Had, perhaps, ridden ahead to meet with the former North-Texas Tillison to set up this attack.

In the civilian ward at the post hospital, Casey found David Hastings unconscious and looking quite pale. The bullet had been removed and luckily, medical procedures were a few years past leeching, so rather than removing infected blood, the doctor was trying to restore the system with warmth, rest and rich broths. David would recover.

So Casey headed off to reduce his worries further by finding Elizabeth and learning how she was.

"Glad you're back," Pete said when Casey rode into the wagon camp.

"I was startin' to feel really on the spot as the camp leader." Pete grinned, but Casey could tell the man was serious. "Joe didn't talk much, but I take it you didn't catch nobody."

"No, we didn't." Casey stepped wearily from his horse and looked around. "Thanks for pitching in like you did, Pete. It's been a big help."

"Uh. Well, I'm glad you're back."

Joe and Jorge were in an intense conversation in Spanish. Dog slept. Don Suthers and Mel Burns were piecing together a meal at a small fire with Sim and Al Guzlowski.

"David'll be laid up here at least a week. I've got to get word to his brother, though. Jake was expecting the wagons to pull through Trinidad real soon with the store supplies." Casey tapped his right fist into his left palm. He was a bit nervous about those supplies. Those were the wagons he had left at the attack site, only bringing to the fort the merchandise Hastings had consigned to carry to Santa Fe. It had been a hard decision, but he decided this third-party merchandise would net a bigger financial gain than the loss of supplies—a loss Casey hoped to avoid by solving the store mystery. "What I'd like is someone to go up to Trinidad to talk to Jake and do some eavesdropping in cantinas." He studied Pete. "What about it?"

"Me? Hell, Casey; I don't think I'd be too good at detective stuff. I know wagons, but—"

"Well, somebody needs to do it. Take Hastings' things back—yeah. Act like he was killed. Some hoodlum is sure to start bragging his exploits."

"This could be just some random attack," Pete said.

"No." Casey ran his fingers through his wavy hair and resettled his hat. He scowled around the camp again. "Where's Zee?"

"Rode over to Las Animas with Williams and Ledbetter." Pete scratched his whiskers. "Dawson's over there, too. They've probably gone a-whorin'."

Casey sighed and, imagining the predicaments Elizabeth could fall into, pulled back into the saddle.

"The kid's all right," Pete said. "Let him be. After what he's been through, he needs a little fun."

"Right." Casey adjusted his hat against the freshening wind and rode out.

FIFTEEN

I'm caught in the middle of so much, not allowed to be myself.
I'm not even sure anymore about myself. Everything I do is de-
cided and shaped by someone else's threats or demands...

27 August

Las Animas was on a fertile wedge of land south where the Purgatoire fed into the Arkansas. Back in '66, one of William Bent's boys joined with other enterprising folks and designed irrigation for the semi-arid land. That touch of civilization, the relocation of Fort Lyon (it used to be twentymiles down river until '67 when it was moved because it kept getting flooded), and ample speculation about the railroad caused Las Animas to spring up in '69. A year later it was still in its raw stage.

Casey crossed the river on the military-built bridge into a rough area of tent facilities and shanty living. The sullen sunset cast long shadows from the trees, making everything look worse.

"Hey mister! Mister! I'll tend your horse for two bits."

This call from a dirty-faced pale-haired urchin of ten. Casey's instincts made him want to toss the kid a coin, but he'd be broke if he did that for every poor child he had seen in his travels. He waved the boy off.

A partial wooden building erupted with drunken cackles and coarse voices. Closer to town, women displayed themselves to the men who rode by. The dusty street was barely wide enough for two wagons to pass and was littered with muck. Dogs trotted aimlessly and nosed at garbage and a drunk who lay in a filthy alley. This time of day, the family folk of the area had been to town and left already, so the people on the street were mostly troopers, a few plain-dressed workers and burly buffalo runners, with their big Sharps and smelly hide coats thrown in. The only women were wanton, and the hitching rails in front of the six saloons (tent-walled and wooden based) were near capacity. Casey rode along slowly, looking for Elizabeth and her bay horse.

He saw Clive Williams first. The flabby man had just taken a leak beside the general store and stepped back into the street buttoning his twill trousers. He waved to Casey.

"Where's Zee?" Casey asked.

"I'm gonna meet him and Ledbetter at the restaurant up the way. I stopped to git me some licorice." He held out a bag. "Want some? Ain't had no licorice since we left Ellsworth." Clive swung onto the back of a small mule.

"No, thanks."

"You think Joe's gonna let us all go?"

"Can't really say." The way Casey saw it, Joe wasn't much good for running anything. Unless David recovered consciousness real soon, that kind of decision would be up to Casey.

"I figured to check out the jobs over here, but I don't know as there's much to be had," Clive said as they rode. "A camp town, seems to me. Suckin' a livin' off army tits."

Two drunken troopers slammed through a bar door and careened, laughing, into the street. Casey's horse snorted and fiddlestepped.

"Seems the only kind of town I ever see," Clive complained.

"Hey, *Señores!*" a brown-skinned boy called to them. "You want *mujeres?* Fine *mujeres.*" He waved his hands through the air in outline of a voluptuous woman.

Casey shook his head at the boy.

Pistol shots rang out and eight cavalrymen charged their mounts down the street from the river bridge. The boy's face brightened and he moved toward the horde. It was Saturday, and in a few hours most off-duty troopers would be over here. More pistol shots, and Casey kept his horse near the buildings to let the rowdies pass.

The restaurant was a decent structure with covered boardwalk and glass windows. "TILLEY'S" declared the hanging sign on the wooden false front. Elizabeth's bay was tied at the rail along with Ledbetter's brown mare. The well-lit restaurant contained two distinct, very clean, sections: one with a bar and bare, rough pine tables; in the other, beyond an ornate balustrade, the finished hardwood tables sported cloth coverings and candle center pieces. Officers brought their wives here, or entertained some of the European expatriates who had begun filling up the West with style. Several well dressed businessmen now occupied the tables, their mustaches and goatees neatly groomed. Casey made a useless swipe at his dusty shirt and sighed.

"He has to leave right now!" rose a tenor voice. A mustached man in black corduroy pants, and white shirt with sleeve garters stood beside where Ledbetter and Elizabeth sat at one of the pine tables. "Out!" the man insisted.

Casey and Clive thought Amos was being ordered out, which they didn't understand since he was no more poorly dressed than others on the peon side of the establishment. Casey saw the glint of coin on the table, too. He walked over as the man declared, "We don't serve heathens."

"What's going on?" Casey asked.

"He thinks Zee's an Injun," Ledbetter said. His look of amazement was outdone by Elizabeth's look of bewilderment.

"He's Cherokee. I can tell. But that's no different from Pawnee or Arapaho. They dress up like white and go to school, but it makes no difference!"

"Hold on a minute," Casey began suppressing a chuckle. He found a certain amusement that Tilley's bigoted eye had seen Elizabeth as nonwhite, but failed to recognize her sex.

"Do I have to call the sheriff?" Tilley went on.

Elizabeth got up, took up her rifle.

"Zee, come on." Ledbetter reached for her arm. She avoided him. "The man's a donkey's shit end."

"The boy knows I'm right," the man said, shaking his finger. "I can spot Indians in a heart beat."

"All right. I'm leaving," Elizabeth said.

Ledbetter's mouth fell open and Clive seemed to stand up straighter. Elizabeth headed for the door, hot with anger and flushed with embarrassment over the stares she was getting.

"You got no right!" Casey said to the man.

"I got every right. It's my restaurant. I'll serve who I please."

Casey hurried after Elizabeth who had just jammed her rifle into the saddle boot.

The restaurant man came to the door. "Indians aren't allowed in town after dark," he declared, his voice shaking with a strange fury. "You just go squat out there by the fort like the rest of your kind."

"You go to hell!" Casey raged.

By saying those words and trying to keep himself from punching the man, Elizabeth had a head start down the darkening street. When Casey got into his saddle, loud voices and thumpings from the restaurant stalled him a bit more. He kicked his horse to action when Ledbetter bullied himself into the street a second later, hurling invectives at the restaurant door.

Elizabeth was almost to the bridge before Casey caught her, and to his surprise, she looked at him and laughed. Not a happy laugh, though.

"The ridiculous thing is," she said to his puzzled look. "He was right. My grandma was Cherokee." She chewed on the inside of her lip, her indignation slowly being quelled, softened, stuffed away with years of similar incidents. Not forgotten, but helping to form a thick wall of stalwart emotions that her white contemporaries wouldn't understand.

"I can't believe how narrow-minded some people can be," Casey growled.

"I'm used to it, although this is the first time my Cherokee background has ever come up."

"As if any of that makes a difference in what a person is really like!" Casey raged.

"If he'd known about my grandfather Fortune, he probably would have committed mayhem." Elizabeth would have found it more ironic if she had known that Grandpa Fortune had been one-quarter Tuscarora—not 100 percent African at all.

"The man's a fool. All of this because of your grandparents. Your mother was white! for God's sake," he declared.

"Yeah. It's weird how that recent white blood gets shrugged aside," she said with another bitter chuckle. "It's sort of a useless power my people have, for a black or Indian grandparent to override a white mother's input." Her eyes narrowed, and she gritted her teeth. They were now inside the fort, and she urged her bay to the wagon camp, diverting her thoughts by wondering if Jorge had any food left since she hadn't eaten. Casey pulled in beside her, quiet and thoughtful.

Jorge had managed to get everyone fed while Joe MacGrin was off buying a bottle of potent whiskey. Joe wanted little to do with the camp and insisted that Jorge had no reason to cook for the others. But Jorge felt obligated. Don Suthers and Mel Burns gravitated to Jorge's wagon, while Sim and Al, with their injuries, stayed close to Casey's fire so they could keep tabs on management and how they would be cared for while they healed.

Elizabeth hadn't yet lost a job. Casey, stoic and pensive, asked her to separate the remaining mules into two groups, the larger of which he hoped to sell to the army. Besides his mental stew over Elizabeth's treatment and her unexpected reaction, he was fumbling with strategies of how to contact Jake Hastings, how much to pay which men; how long to stay at Fort Lyon.

The wind, which had been riffling the cottonwood leaves all afternoon, became stronger with night-fall. Later it turned into an icy gale and howled loudly, rattling anything and everything. Joe had yet to return from the saloon. The injured Sim and Al got priorities on sleeping in the tent. Pete joined them.

"Got room for you, too, Zee," Pete had said.

"No. Thank you." She'd rather chance the elements than be packed in with all those men.

Casey also refused, laying out his bed-roll on a layer of pine boughs near the banked fire. Elizabeth set up a low lean-to with a sheet of canvas and that, both of her jackets, slicker, and blanket kept Elizabeth warm. Dog curled up by her legs. Every time Elizabeth awakened, she pushed sticks into the fire to keep it going. Casey did the same from his side of the fire. He wanted to share his body heat, but didn't dare suggest it.

The clanking of wind-forced equipment and the creaking of the tree limbs kept all the sleepers ignorant of when Joe was dumped in the camp by two soldiers. She drew herself up tighter and slept on when Dog left Elizabeth in that frosty pre-dawn to help Jorge settle his drunken friend in the mess wagon. In the morning, a light frost tinged everything and made the vegetation look gray, and Joe MacGrin was a sodden wreck in his bed-roll.

"I have seen him this way before," Jorge said. His words left a fog on the air. "It will be a few days, but he'll be better."

"A few days!" Casey fumed. Over his wool flannel, he pulled on a leather shirt with fringe. "I need him in charge here, now!"

"It will have to be you, Meester Casey. Just a while longer," Jorge said as he poked at the coals under the cook fire. The big soot-blackened coffee pot set over the flames on a grid between two rocks.

Elizabeth sat up on her pallet with her blanket around her shoulders extremely worried about Joe's excessive drinking and her contribution to it. If Willie had known who she was, or, more importantly, if Joe hadn't figured out her identity, Willie might not have goaded her so, or he and Joe might not have been so estranged from each other and the horror of Willie's death wouldn't be weighted with that extra burden of unresolved family tension. She jackknifed her legs, trying to hold in as much warmth as possible, wishing for some instant remedy for her guilt and the situation that caused it. She rubbed at the healing bullet wound.

Al Guzlowski, arm bandaged close to his side to protect his shoulder, paced in front of the tent, his cup in his free hand. "MacGrin, he blames Mr. Hastings for all this mess—for Willie," he said.

"Seems to me it was gonna happen," Sim said. He sat hunched on a three-legged stool near the tent door, his injured leg stuck out in front of him. "They were ready for us, no matter what we did."

"That's how I figure it, too," Don said.

"It's real bad about the boy, though," Pete said, scratching his sideburns. "A real shame."

Casey sighed loudly, not allowing himself to think about the men who had died, or Joe's grief. He took stock of the situation, wondering which man he could trust to the work he needed done. He glanced at the two lean-tos on either side of the freight wagons where Tom Dawson and Amos Ledbetter were each still rolled in their blankets. Casey didn't trust Dawson to follow orders or not get into trouble. And Ledbetter was the only other experienced muleskinner left, besides Pete. When they got a chance to move the wagons, Casey needed Amos here.

The coffee Jorge had started began perfuming the air, and the men gravitated toward the fire. Tom Dawson emerged from his lean-to, and a few moments later Ledbetter crawled out of his, scratching his belly and pulling into a heavy plaid-wool jacket.

"Anybody seen Clive?" Casey asked, wondering how much of a bonus the lazy little man would want to go to Trinidad.

"Clive. Shit." Dawson spit into the cold ground.

Ledbetter just shook his head, looking disgusted.

Pete ambled over to Casey, sharing his concern. "Looks like you'll have to send the stuff with a letter on the stage," he said.

"What stage?" This was Elizabeth asking.

"It's due in here from Kansas at noon," Casey said. "I sure as hell hate writing to David's brother about this," he went on to Pete. "Be so much better if there was someone to explain—to reassure him."

"What about Don or Mel. They're thinking about pullin' out," Pete said.

Casey nodded, turned toward the to Santa Feans. "Mel, would you ride on to Trinidad and—"

"I'll go," Elizabeth said.

Casey looked at her and frowned.

"Well now, Button," Pete started. He scowled at his boots.

In a way Elizabeth was running. Running from facing Joe sober and the guilt-edged grief. Running from this situation of a static camp where keeping her role as a boy was so much harder. She only hoped Casey realized her reasoning and supported her.

"I sure wouldn't want to go alone with bandits out and about," Mel said, getting in his indirect refusal of Casey's never-finished question.

Elizabeth got up with the blanket around her shoulders. "I'd ride with the stage and its escort." She scrounged her coffee cup from her haversack. "I'd need to have my horse, though," she went on.

"Yeah. You would," Casey said.

Pete stiffened up like he was wearing frozen long johns. "With saddlery, that's a fifty to sixty dollar horse!"

Elizabeth was well aware of the value and although she was fond of the bay, she had already planned to sell it in Trinidad to pay her stage fare on to Fort Union. From there she would wire Fort Davis and find out where her father was. "It would be my payment for doing this, 'cause I wouldn't wait for you all to catch up. I'd go on my way."

Casey gritted his teeth, not anxious to be parted from her, but recognizing why she would be more comfortable away from this wagon camp and the prejudice around the fort. She couldn't do the spying he had in mind, but then, Mel wouldn't have been too good at that either. "That sounds like a fair deal to me," he said without even blinking.

Pete scratched his sideburns and frowned.

"By Jove, that's a good idea. The boy's earned it." This from Tom Dawson, and to everyone's surprise, his statement was seconded by Amos Ledbetter.

"Hastings probably ain't payin' him decent wages no how," Amos said.

"It is for sure Zee has done hard work," Al Guzlowski put in.

"Did Hastings give him a bonus when he saved Seth from gettin' smashed?" Sim asked. "Seems he deserves somethin' extra."

"Looks like everyone's in agreement," Casey said.

Pete ruffled Elizabeth's mop of brown hair and gave a nervous grin. "Looks like you got yourself a horse, Zee." He wondered what Joe would have to say about this when he found out, or worse, David Hastings.

Elizabeth ducked her head from his rough affection, both relieved and surprised that they had all agreed to her plan.

By mid-morning, although the wind had slowed to a breeze and the sun warmed people out of their jackets, Elizabeth still felt the morning chill frosting around the edge of her thoughts. While the army livestock officers perused the herd and decided which of the mules they might be willing to buy, Elizabeth was reviewing her actions with a critical eye. And this was something she didn't often do. For Elizabeth, it was usually full steam ahead into whatever she had pointed herself; to hell with the rest. It made for a nervy existence. Elizabeth was beginning to see the pitfalls in that attitude. This contemplative nature was what got her to Jorge's wagon at about the same time the Kansas stage was approaching the last dusty incline to the fort.

"How is he?" Elizabeth asked Jorge as the industrious cook put together a midday meal for the men of the train. From inside the wagon came a low moan.

"How is any *borrachon* the next day?" He grinned, but sobered when he realized Elizabeth's true concerns. "For the other." Jorge shrugged, his long face full of sorrow. "It will be time. *Mucho tiempo*."

"Where's the god damn bottle?" came Joe's grumble.

Jorge crossed himself. "*Y para mi, mucho tiempo.* I was too hard on little Willie." Jorge's eyes brightened with sudden tears, and he brought down his big machete-like knife on the sliced onions with great industry, deftly dicing them for the stew.

It surprised Elizabeth that someone else harbored guilt about Willie. She didn't know about the tirades Jorge had showered on the young man, all about how he was bringing down the MacGrin family name and that his mother wouldn't be proud of his laziness, that his father had rights to be ashamed. Not that Joe had been ashamed, exactly. More like perturbed by Willie's lackadaisical and argumentative manner. But the Estévez family had been friends with the MacGrins since before Willie was born, and Jorge had taken his "uncle" role to the hilt.

The growling from in the wagon grew worse. Jorge poured a dipper of a warm brew into a tin mug. "I'll take it to him," Elizabeth volunteered.

"He will be mean. It's my remedy, not his liquor," Jorge warned.

Elizabeth took the mug, her nose wrinkling to the vinegary smell. But the heavy odors in the wagon overpowered the steamy mug. Joe lay dissolute on the cot over the canned goods. He was shirtless and stains darkened his gray Union suit from where he had been sick. He lurched a bit when he heard Elizabeth approach, but when she was beside him, he closed his blood-shot eyes and grimaced.

"Get out of here," Joe growled. Elizabeth winced as if stabbed. "I ain't fit for you to be looking in on." With a sinewy hand, he clutched a wool blanket further up his body. "Get on, Elizabeth."

Elizabeth darted a quick, worried look to the wagon entrance. "Mr. MacGrin, it's Zee. Zee Clark!" she insisted.

He groaned a sigh. "Uh. Zee. Yeah."

She set down the mug on the small crate that served as his bed stand. "Here's some—ah—remedy." Now that she was in here, she wasn't certain what she was going to say.

"Jorge and his god damned remedy." He grunted. "I don't want that. I want—. I want—." He gasped and pounded on the wagon wall with his left hand.

"I'm sorry, Mr. MacGrin," Elizabeth choked out. She couldn't keep the tears from rolling down her face and when she tried to sniff them back he squinted over at her.

"Your pa." He took her hand in his callused one. "He better be glad to see you, after all you come through. He better!" His grip tightened, then he lurched to the far wall where a noxious bucket set for his use.

Elizabeth bit the knuckles of her right fist, shocked by his strong words. She backed away, not wanting to be overwhelmed by his nausea or add her own to it.

"It is not pleasant, no?" Jorge said when she stepped out.

"It's fine," Elizabeth said with a sure voice. She was more relieved by the results of her too-meager talk to Joe than the fresh air she took in. New tears stung her eyes as she realized Joe didn't blame her.

"Zee! The stage is in!" Pete called out.

"So. You will be going," Jorge said. He sighed. "I will not tell Joe why," he said sagely. "Anything that is to help Señor Hastings now makes him loco." Jorge put a slim hand on her arm. "But in Santa Fe, we will see you again, no? When Meester Casey *empieza* his business, you will be there."

He spoke this with a confidence that made Elizabeth frown at him, wondering what Casey had said to him and what Jorge suspected. But Jorge still assumed that Zee Clark was a hired gun and would continue to work with Casey Pritchard. He hadn't been the least surprised that morning when the young man volunteered to go to Trinidad, impressed with the excellent play-acting both Casey and Zee had done to make it all seem spontaneous.

The stage from Kansas arrived with two passengers and the driver complaining about the lack of activity. But he also complained about taking on more cargo, claiming the pull up the draws would be hard. He cursed the military that was slow at forming up, then sat in the shade and dozed while the teams were changed and things were loaded. The stage guard went off to the commissary for a meal and a drink.

Half an hour later, all of David Hastings' luggage was tied atop the stage, including his tent and other travel gear; his horse was in tow at the back of the stage. Elizabeth had helped strap the baggage up there, ensuring that the three pieces tagged for E. Houston were secure among the others.

"It's a wonder those weren't stolen by the outlaws," she muttered to Casey after she jumped down from the coach roof.

"They were in the supply cart with David's gear. I made sure they got packed in here to the fort," he said.

"How did you know?"

"I'm a detective. It's my job to know."

The air around them bristled with unsaid emotions. Elizabeth was afraid he would blurt his true feelings, and she ached with her thought that she wouldn't see him again. To steady her nerves she asked, "Why are you sending *all* of David's things to his brother?"

"A decoy. I'm hoping the outlaws will think the worst and get careless. So if anyone other than the family asks, don't tell that David is still alive."

"You think the outlaws are in Trinidad?" Elizabeth's eyes widened.

"A good chance of it. Or at least someone to keep tabs on David's brother."

"This is why he hired you, right? Because he expected something like this?"

"Sort of. Someone's trying to stop them from opening a store in Trinidad."

"Well, it looks like they've succeeded."

"But I intend to find out who they are." He took off his hat and smoothed his hair. "Eliz—Zee." He glanced at the nearby men, then steered her aside by the elbow. "I'll be coming to Trinidad as soon as Joe or David is recovered enough for me to leave here."

The intense study he gave her made her heart pound. She took a step back, stared toward the stage where the passengers were boarding.

"I'm going on to Fort Union," she said. And then further south from there, she thought.

"Selling the horse?"

"Yes. Except for this luggage, all I own is at Fort Union." She thought of the ivory-trimmed sewing box that had been her mothers; a bag of marbles from her father's boyhood, the series of little tin animals her grandfather Fortune had fashioned; the silver-backed hairbrush and comb grandmother Clark had given her when she turned thirteen. Houston had made certain that was packed, even though Mr. Clark had said to leave it. "What else can I do?"

The cavalry men mounted up.

"You could wait for me in Trinidad," Casey said.

"Casey, it won't work."

"Stay up at the Hastings place until I get there," he urged.

"No!" She shook her head. She went to her horse and checked the cinch.

"Forward!" called the sergeant with the escort detail.

Relief at leaving welled in her along with a deep anticipation of the rest of her plan: changing identities. Her own clothes, no more imposed pretenses, to exist as Elizabeth Fortune seemed the solution to keeping her frazzled emotions in hand. Getting away from Casey and pure physical attraction she felt for him would be good, too. She needed space.

She pulled into the saddle and was suddenly surrounded by men. "You take care now, Button," Dawson said.

"Luck to ya, Zee," Sim said. He braced himself on a wooden cane, keeping weight off his damaged ankle.

"You're a good one to ride the river with, and that's the gospel," Ledbetter added. He pounded a strong hand on her leg.

"*Vaya con Dios*, Señor Zee," Jorge called.

Pete scowled to hide his concern about the boy being off on his own.

"Ho-oO!" the stage driver called. A short whip snapped and the coach lurched forward as the four horses began the pull. In Trinidad another horse would be added to make three abreast up front and two on the pole. This needed to get the horses up the steep climb of Raton Pass.

"Zee!" Casey called as she moved her horse out. The glare of midday made his hair look brassy. "I'm going through Fort Union, too. I'll look for you!"

She nodded and waved, wishing her father would be at Fort Union, and then picturing Casey striding through groups of Negro troopers to get to her; of Casey declaring himself in front of all those white officers and their wives. The odd thing, she *could* imagine it.

Dogs barked, kids ran beside the road waving and whooping. The stage grated and crunched loud on the rocky road; horses coughed and clomped, saddles creaked.

Elizabeth's frayed nerves were on the edge of unraveling. She glanced back through the dust at the small clot of teamsters. Al waved, but too many people were missing: Horace Cross, Dodie Watson, John Bradshaw, Bill Porter, Willie—all dead. Joe was still abed with drink, and Dog ran the fort, not even here for a goodbye. She rubbed her nose, swallowed the growing lump in her throat, and urged the bay to a canter.

Sixteen

I am forever surprised by the incredible diversity of the land and its people; but mostly by the depths of my own reserves. Praise to this family trait that allows me to endure.

30 August

Along the steady incline of the Santa Fe Trail, the dry land was harsh, but each day in a different way. Sage dotted the tan, grainy land with the mountain peaks a continual backdrop. The dark rock foothills loomed closer, but open scrub grass and sagebrush filled most of the small dales along the route first scouted by the army back in '46. In '47, General Sterling had camped his troops in the verdant meadows beside the Purgatoire River near Raton Creek. That had been when he was marching to Santa Fe to restore order after Mexicans rebelled against United States authority and killed Governor Bent. There hadn't been any permanent settlers in the area then. Settlers didn't happen until twelve years later, and now their sheep and cattle dotted the hills where, on steep sections, rocks protruded from beneath the scant cover of soil.

On the descent from the slopes into the valley, Elizabeth could see the streets of Trinidad striped out north and south from the trail road which was Main Street. While the stage and its outriders picked up speed down the hill, two farm wagons and a high-wheeled freighter full of wood from the new lumber mill rumbled out of town. The drivers waved at the stage while their teams strained with the steep climb. *Jacales* dotted the pine studded hillsides and faces bloomed at open windows; children stopped to stare as the stage passed.

This was the busiest town Elizabeth had seen since she peeked out of the baggage-car doors of the K & P train in Salina, Kansas. The sudden noise and activity jolted her out of the stunned feeling that had been with her since leaving the fort. A chorus of whinnies started up from McCormick's corrals, joined by barking dogs which started a chain reaction to the newly-built Park Stables by Pilgrim House and on to the Taylor's U.S. Corral further up by the U.S. Hotel. In this livery lot beside the hotel, the stage was brought to a clattering halt. The cavalry dismounted. The driver yelled out instructions to workers and told the passengers they had thirty minutes.

Elizabeth stared at an elegant carriage driven by a Negro man. In the back of it, under the green and black canopy, was a well-dressed heavyset man with goatee. As Elizabeth dismounted her bay, she ogled at least three prominent merchant houses among the adobe buildings on Main Street. Signs along the walkways told of shoemakers, a silversmith, lawyers, a big placard for Templar House hotel and the International Order of Good Templars. Her grandmother Clark had been active with that organization, although the woman could never get Mr. Clark to participate.

Elizabeth clambered atop the stage. Her bullet-nicked arm ached, but she tossed down to a burly worker below, Hastings' and E. Houston's things. New plans had already sprouted in her mind: To deliver Hastings' belongings, change identities, and get a job in this bustling town. She could have her other belongings sent here from Fort Union, and then earn her passage to Texas.

"*Señoritas? Hay señoritas?*" A ten-year-old boy had ridden into the livery yard on a burro. "Meester Conners. *Hay señoritas* on the stage?" He slid off the fuzzy-eared beast.

"What you want with *señoritas*, boy?" the worker growled. "You barely old enuf to piss right."

"No! *No es* for me. *La Señora* Crawford. She send me. *Tiene salas...*"

"English, boy!"

"*Sí.* She has rooms for *señoritas.*"

"We know that!"

"She send me to ask."

"We know that, too," grouched a fleshy-faced man in jeans and plaid shirt. "Jest look around, Dominguez. You see any women?"

The boy's dark eyes darted quick looks. "No sir."

"Get on with you then." The man named Conners went back to the harness lead he was checking at the stage. "I swear. You'd think Eula Jean was tryin' to start a crib house, the way that boy keeps asking," Conners grumbled.

"Wish she would," the worker said. "Fresh loins would be nice around here."

"I will tell the señora that. You will give me a nickle to tell her?" the boy asked, grinning.

"She paid you to come down here and ask!"

"No. I will tell her about a creeb house—fresh loins." The boy giggled.

"Why, you better not!"

"You little thief." Conners swung a leg at the boy, who dodged and laughed, and leaped back on his burro.

"There is anyone here who needs a message delivered?" he called, riding for the gate. "For just a few coins."

Elizabeth thought about the task ahead of her and the message she had to deliver. "Hey, Mister," she said to Conners. "How do I find Jake Hastings?" Her voice was tired and harsh, coming out just like life was treating her.

But for all her despondency, she didn't miss the silence that descended on the area like a pall. The sudden intense scrutiny Elizabeth got from Conners and other people made her skin tingle.

Conners spat tobacco juice. "And what's your business with Jake Hastings?" His blue-eyed gaze was hard as hail.

"I—I work for his brother. Have some things—."

"His brother?" The man didn't believe a word she said and his budding anger came through to Elizabeth like thistles through muslin. The approach and words of the bandy-legged cavalry sergeant, who had been with the escort from Fort Lyon, eased the moment.

"Clark, I just found out Hastings lives up the mountain a ways," the sergeant said. His talkative frieindliness had been a boon to Elizabeth on this two-day trip, keeping Elizabeth's mind off her future.

"Up the mountain?" Elizabeth scowled at the tree-darkened slopes.

"What's he got for Hastings?" Conners asked the sergeant, still not sure about Elizabeth. Others in the livery moved in closer so they could hear.

"He's bringing back personals," the sergeant said. "The wagon train got hit by bandits before it reached Fort Lyon. Lots of men killed."

"God damn!" someone swore and stalked off.

"Ain't that the luck of it."

"Getting what they deserve, trying to steal that store from the widow lady."

"That ain't so. That Hastings family's been hit hard, I tell you," Conners shook his head.

"What do you mean?" Elizabeth asked, alert to the dissension.

"Jake, why he got shot up and left for dead just two weeks ago. It's a miracle he's still alive. Now this about his brother."

"Those Hastings folks just need to move on," someone else muttered.

Conners spit tobacco and glared at the man. "There's a team and buckboard here you can borrow," he said somberly.

"How much will that be?" Elizabeth had ten dollars Casey had given her and no more.

"No. That's okay, kid." He shook his head.

Not much later, Elizabeth was setting off west along Main Street in the buckboard. The livery man, Mr. Conners, hadn't wanted any fee for the rickety conveyance, but insisted on keeping Elizabeth's horse until she got back. Without that four-legged friend, Elizabeth felt more alone than ever.

Once across Raton Creek, the houses set on sloped lots with corrals and livestock sheds pitched at steep angles along the mountainside. Then switch-back roads were close with trees and chill with mountain air. The shroud of trees aggravated her mood, and Elizabeth felt she had traveled tens of obscure miles before she arrived at the level clearing. Having just begun to think she had somehow missed a turn, Elizabeth was relieved beyond comprehension to see a small pasture with a few milch cows and sheep. Chickens clucked from a shack under a lone box elder.

She hailed the house and was questioned by a stocky Mrs. Flanagan before taken inside. There, Elizabeth met the beleaguered Hastings family: Jake's wife Caroline was as pale as a mistletoe berry and heavy with the coming baby. David's young children looked wan like the refugee kids with the Jenkins wagon; and Jake, his right shoulder bandaged, broken left leg wrapped and elevated, the bullet line that creased his ribs itching something fearful, attempted brave smiles, but his eyes were hollow with fatigue and despair. The only thing keeping the place together was the staunch leadership of Mary Flanagan, David's housekeeper. She asked four times if "the mister" would be all right.

"Yes ma'am," Elizabeth answered, maintaining her Zee Clark role and not wanting to say too much. "Mr. Pritchard hasn't given up in his efforts to find out who's responsible," she went on.

"A good man, that one. A lot of experience," Jake said. He shifted a bit on the big mattress. "David told me Pritchard worked his first job for Pinkerton when he was only seventeen. Got captured in South Carolina. Escaped and stole North with runaway slaves."

Elizabeth listened, eyes wide and a bit upset with herself for wanting to know more about Casey Pritchard. That part of her life was over—done with.

"He's got quite a war record, too," Jake ended.

Elizabeth thought of the battle at the wagon camp and the men killed, the suffering. She tried to imagine that on a larger scale. It chilled her.

Mary Flanagan offered Elizabeth a meal and a bed in the nearby *jacale* with the two hired men. Elizabeth refused both. The orderliness and genial warmth made her certain if she took a meal here she'd end up crying her true identity and begging the right to sleep in the house. She was certain that Elizabeth wouldn't be received well by Mrs. Flanagan. The woman would certainly agree with Lost: that it wasn't right actin' mannish.

Back under the trees, away from the clearing, the buckboard rattled loudly without David's gear. Images of her own personal clothing hovered around Elizabeth's desperate desire for warmth and comfort, and worked at her like an itch she couldn't reach to scratch. Finally, after about a mile of driving in the fast-cooling evening, she whoaed the horse. The padding that had helped her win her job went flying; off came the twill britches; she tossed aside the straw hat that was nearly black around the crown from sweat and dirt. She dampened her work shirt with water from her canteen and wiped the dust from her face and neck before she pulled into pantaloons, a chemise and blouse. The skirt was badly wrinkled, but she shook it out and stepped into it.

Elizabeth was thinner than when she left Ellsworth and the skirt hung loosely at her waist. She had to tie on the bustle pad to help it fit.

She buttoned the blouse, tucked it in, too much aware of her callused, grimy hands. She scrubbed at them with a damp cloth and tears came hot to her eyes. By putting on Elizabeth Fortune's clothes she had hoped to be transformed into that optimistic young woman who had set out to find her father. No mangled Johnny Tillison or his hateful brother Hank, no dead Willie to remember, nor two corpses she was responsible for. No roving detachments of Ninth Cavalry to make her trek seem worthless.

The cold night bit to the bone before she got back into the wagon. From her portmanteau she took a cotton shawl and pulled it around her shoulders. Then she had to trust that the horse knew its way back to Trinidad, because it was too dark to see the road.

It seemed to be the nature of well-planned events to go awry, or so Elizabeth thought. All the bitterness and hindsight replanning of desperate desires couldn't change what was here and now. Elizabeth knew this and proceeded, as always, the best way she knew how. Obtaining the wherewithal to get further south was her major priority. To do that, she needed to refurbish herself as an educated woman and get a job. So on that late evening of August 30th, when she came upon a small sign near the road reading "Crawford's Boardinghouse," she took her luggage out of the buckboard, tied the reins to the foot brace, smacked the horse with a stout stick, and headed to the lamp glow she saw up the westerly hill.

A bit passed noon the next day, she soaked in steamy water in a galvanized tub in her room at the adobe boardinghouse of Eula Jean Crawford. Flames crackled pine wood in the fireplace, popping and sizzling on the wet spots created by morning frost. The room was warm and pungent. Elizabeth could barely smell the bath salts she had put in the water. On the round pegs set in all the thick walls, Elizabeth had hung her clothes. Her few notions of bath salts, cocoa butter and a rose water-glycerin decoction stood on the small wooden vanity beside the rope-slung bed. The mattress, filled with cedar chips, corn husks and down had allowed Elizabeth her good sleep, and although her discouragement from the previous evening didn't seem as intense, despair perched at the edge of her thoughts like ravens beside a motherless calf.

After becoming nearly euphoric in the first moments of soaking, she now soaped her arms and neck for the third time. The sun had returned her deep honey coloring, tanning her through the long-sleeved shirt, and even a bit on her legs. Only a wide band where her chest binding had insulated her skin remained pale. She laughed at the stripe, then carefully wiped across the puffy red welt of her bullet wound. It stung under soapsuds. Elizabeth clenched her teeth, the memory of the battle against the outlaws fresh to her mind: the man beside the river; the man in the bushes who had tried to take her horse, his angry face and wide eyes when she shot him. Like Johnny Tillison. Such surprise! She flinched and drew a shaky breath. No one ever believed they would get shot. Elizabeth certainly never thought it would happen to her.

"This rinse water's just the right temperature!" Eula Jean Crawford called from the wide brush-covered breezeway that connected the main house to the three rooms she leased out. In the Mexican part of town this hall would have been planted with flowers and herbs, and vegetables that couldn't take hot sun. For Eula Jean it was just a breezeway, and she kept kindling at the end that butted the mountain slope; the other end opened toward the narrow yard where a domed earthen oven stood. Eula Jean used that for a chicken coop.

"Taking it" (she meant the water) "straight from the well is like jumping into an icy stream." The stocky woman moved briskly, even though she was lugging two coopered buckets filled to sloshing with warm water. Her arms were thick with muscles under the cotton work dress, and all the veins stood out in the backs of her hands. She thumped the door with her elbow and then kicked it open with her foot. She wore a well-used pair of low-cut shoes, three buttons on the side: garrison footwear like the cavalry used for fatigue duty at the forts.

"And I brung you some vinegar, too. In case you want to rinse your hair. The smell goes away right quick."

"Thank you." Elizabeth scrunched down in the oval tub. The water was still hot around her shoulders. "Just set it close by." She had washed her hair first while the water was cleanest, and now the brown strands lay straight and thick along her ears and neck.

"Ummm! That smells fine." Eula Jean inhaled deeply of the steamy air around the tub as she set down the buckets. She gave Elizabeth a sidelong look.

Eula Jean hadn't been eager to let Elizabeth the room the previous night. The woman thought she was some low-life when she struggled to her door dragging the portmanteau, her face haggard, hands dirty. But today, seeing the variety of middle-class accouterments Elizabeth possessed, the woman's attitude had changed.

"Now this is a great looking dress, this wool one here. You'll be needing that in the next month or so." Eula Jean fingered the hem of the burgundy dress. "You lookin' to stay that long?"

Elizabeth didn't reply. She couldn't give out information she herself wasn't sure of. Eula Jean walked around the room studying Elizabeth's well-made clothes. Across the quilt on the bed, the woman smoothed the skirt Elizabeth was going to wear, still waiting for an answer.

"Few folks stop here in Trinidad. Usually just passing through to Fort Union or Santa Fe," Eula Jean finally went on. "You got business in town?"

"Ah. Not at the moment." Elizabeth hunched forward to rub her wash cloth over her callused feet.

Eula Jean fiddled with the pins that kept her long light-brown hair in a fat bun on her head. "How'd you get to town, anyway?"

"The stage from Fort Lyon."

"Really!"

Eula Jean's tight-lipped smile got Elizabeth worrying, and then she remembered the boy at the livery yard when the stage arrived. A boy looking for señoritas to stay at Crawford's Boardinghouse. She peeked at the woman past strands of her wet hair, seeing a puzzled expression.

"Mrs. Crawford, if you'll excuse me, please. I'd like to rinse off and get dressed." Elizabeth wrung out the wash cloth and laid it over the tub edge.

"Oh, surely! I'll just be in the kitchen stirring up some biscuits. Coffee's hot already." Eula Jean bustled out the door.

After a quick dry off and dressing in the loose fitting skirt and blouse, Elizabeth managed to pull up her short hair and pin it into a twist on the back of her head. She trimmed the front to loose bangs. She tried on her shoes and walked around the room in them. The little heels and pointy toes were too uncomfortable. She set them aside and pulled into the tall moccasins, not caring what any one might think.

She set up her writing tray on the small table near the door and thought about a letter to her father. She had to assume he had received her earlier letters—knew she was traveling West—even though she hadn't gotten a reply.

Dear Daddy,

I know I should have written sooner, but I've been detained in my travels. Be assured I am in fine health and will continue on to Ft. Davis within the next month....

She had no delusions that he would be able to rush to her rescue, and she found that she was more concerned about his possible worry than the particulars of when they would be reunited. She paused over that realization, feeling years older than she did when she left Oberlin—even than when she left Ellsworth. So much had happened.

I'm certain this all seems rash to you, but I truly didn't expect the trip to take all summer.

As with the letter she wrote from Oberlin, she refrained from mentioning the money she suspected Mr. Clark was misusing. She knew the amount, and the cost of her tuition, and had calculated that the proceeds from sale of their farm shouldn't be all gone. But she wanted some sort of proof before she mentioned it to her father or confronted her grandfather about it. Her father's resultant anger could put him in an awkward situation, bound as he was by the army. What could he do, except seethe and send angry telegrams?

Well, I'll tell you all about this trip when I see you.
With affection and Fortune fortitude,
Elizabeth.

Just sealing those words into an envelope relieved some of her tension. She sighed and took another sheet of paper from her dwindling supply. She dawdled a moment, addressed the envelope to Casey Pritchard, blotted it. She wanted to tell Casey, I'll be here when you get here. But she didn't—couldn't! She wouldn't make herself any more vulnerable to him than she already was. Upset with herself, she put down the pen and turned to the cool bath water.

Galvanized tubs weren't the height of bathing luxury, but they had one advantage—the metal gray hid dirt rings. Elizabeth felt so much cleaner, she expected the water to be dark brown like the Arkansas. It wasn't quite that bad, and she tossed buckets full out the side window into the yard that sloped up to the mountain.

"Señorita! Señorita Houston! *Ven.* Come with me!" The excited young voice accompanied the knock on her door.

Houston. Her current name. She had to remember who she was—or who she wasn't, as in this case. That was the name on her luggage tags, and last night it had seemed prudent to use that identity. Safer, too. With all that had happened, she still worried that she might be in Tillison territory. Frowning, Elizabeth set down the empty bucket by the half-emptied tub, and opened the door. The boy, Dominguez, who had been at the livery yard the previous day, stood outside, his eyes bright and excited. "It eez the sheriff, Señorita. He wants to talk to you."

Elizabeth's heart pounded and she wondered if Eula Jean had called the sheriff since the woman realized Elizabeth had lied about coming to town on the stage. And how will I explain my arrival if he questions that? She hoped it wouldn't come up.

"Dominguez, calm down!" Eula Jean called. The woman was standing with a portly Mexican man in denim pants. The metal badge glinted six points on the pocket of his plaid shirt.

Elizabeth smoothed her hands along the brown calico print skirt and fingered the buttons of the long-sleeved brown blouse as she walked along the breezeway and into the yard. I should be wearing black, she thought. And not just for her grandmother Clark, but for Willie and Dodie Watson and the others. She decided she would at least take off the lace that fringed the collar and cuffs. It felt scratchy and foreign anyway.

Dominguez skipped ahead, often grinning back at her over his shoulder.

"Oh, Dominguez. He's made such a to-do about this." Eula Jean shook her head, but smiled fondly at the boy. "Sorry to bother you Miss Houston, but—."

"The sheriff, he eez looking for information. A person eez missing! Last night, and you—"

"Dominguez!" Eula Jean said sharply.

"Your pardon, Miss. I am Sheriff Tafoya, sheriff here in Trinidad, and the boy, here, tells me you arrived late yesterday evening." He held his hat and bowed slightly as he spoke, his brown eyes studying her quickly. His English, spoken in a burly voice like he had to clear his throat, held only a slight accent.

"Yes, that's right." Elizabeth fiddled with the lace cuff of her right sleeve.

Eula Jean stepped forward. "You didn't by chance notice anything odd or hear nothin' when you was comin' up here last night, did you?" she asked, overriding the sheriff's cautious approach.

"No. Why?" Wariness hollowed out Elizabeth's insides.

"There was a buckboard," the sheriff began. "It come in empty to the livery barn late last evening. From this direction. When Dominguez told me the time you arrived, I thought mebbe you had seen or heard something?"

Elizabeth gulped a quick breath. "Well, no." She bit her lower lip. She hadn't considered that empty buckboard would be a problem.

Eula Jean huffed a sigh and put a hand on her ample hip. "Well, they figure somethin' bad musta happened, 'cause the man left his horse at the stable yard till he got back. And didn't you say this fellow was going to the Hastings'? Lord, they've had trouble."

Elizabeth tried to stay calm. She had forgotten about her horse and how Mr. Connors had kept it for collateral.

"It may not be connected with them," Sheriff Tafoya said.

Eula Jean shook her head. "This town just keeps growin' into trouble. A few years back the mexes and whites was fightin' so bad they had to call the troopers in to get it settled down. Right at Christmastime it was, too. Then there was the Coe gang runnin' over a hundred strong and stealing cattle and anything they could get their hands on. And we change sheriffs around here 'bout every season or so, too. Ain't that right?" She gave the man a sly look.

His facial muscles tightened because Eula Jean certainly had her facts straight. Tafoya had been in this job for less than a month; his predecessor holding the office for less than a year, and come New Years, it would all change again. "You will frighten this señorita. She will not want to stay in our fine town," he said, turning his hat in his hand.

"Oh, pshaw. All towns is the same. Fights most every weekend after the races."

"And people get shot! Boom!" Dominguez said, edging in front of Eula Jean's broad skirt, his arms gesturing emphatically in the air.

"But we do not know that anything bad happened last night," Sheriff Tafoya said. "Do not make up stories, chico." He smoothed his well-groomed mustache. "I am sorry to have troubled you, Miss. And do not be too upset by the rumors you hear."

"Yes. We do not want you to go!" Dominguez said. "The señora, she needs her rooms filled, and—"

"Dominguez!" Eula Jean cuffed him playfully and he ducked away, laughing.

"Señorita." Sheriff Tafoya nodded and smiled graciously at Elizabeth before starting his stout frame around the house to his horse.

"You see the sheriff out, Dominguez," Eula Jean ordered. "And then get back to town for those groceries I sent you for two hours ago."

"Sí, Señora."

"That boy." Eula Jean shook her head.

"But it's true, what he says. People do get shot." Elizabeth studied Eula Jean, wondering how much the woman could tell her. "I heard it in town."

Eula Jean started for her kitchen. Elizabeth followed along, eager for her words. "That happened a couple of weeks ago," Eula Jean said. "A Hastings, too. Oddest thing. These brothers come to town claiming to own Jeffrey Bragg's store, Lord rest 'im. And his wife shows up—Bragg's that is—sayin' she's running things now, and there was no record of Bragg having sold."

That news hit Elizabeth hard. The men of the wagon train had been driving under David Hastings' constant pressure to get to Trinidad. To a store he didn't own? She wondered if Casey knew, then wondered if Eula Jean had her facts right.

They entered the neat kitchen that smelled of sourdough and coffee. A green checked cloth covered the small table, and matching curtains hung at the window. With all the orderliness of the room, Elizabeth blinked her surprise at seeing a fat red hen nested on the window ledge—inside on the window ledge. The hen clucked and Eula Jean patted it. Her fondness for the barren layer defied explanation.

"These men. These Hastings people didn't really own the store?" Elizabeth ventured.

"It's under dispute." Eula Jean waved her to a chair and pulled cups from a thick pine shelf. "They claim its down in black-and-white somewheres. Hired lawyers and everything."

Elizabeth sat in a worn cane-backed chair, her breathing coming a bit easier. By now it is certainly all straightened out and legal, she thought. She accepted the coffee Eula Jean poured for her, remembering injured Jake Hastings and the wan Caroline.

A shrewd idea came to her. If she helped unmask the culprits who were creating problems for David Hastings, he might be willing to pay her stage fare to Fort Davis. This of course was a long shot and Elizabeth didn't pin any hopes to it, but it gave her something else to consider when she went out to find employment.

Eula Jean sat down across the table from Elizabeth and kept talking. "Then the younger brother gets shot up somethin' awful. Left for dead. Lots of folks think the Mexes did it, saying that they're spiteful and all. I don't believe that none. And now I hear the older brother's been killed. Terrible thing, I tell you."

"The older one killed? You mean murdered? Right here in town?" Casey's plan had worked! and Elizabeth was alert for more information she could put in her letter to him.

"No, no. Out on the trail somewheres. He had gone back east for supplies for this store he don't even own—Kansas is where they hail from—and was bringing back this wagon train of goods and don't you know they got attacked by Indians."

"Indians!" Eula Jean was a fountain of information, but Elizabeth knew she would have to listen carefully to glean fact from fiction.

"Burned the wagons, put near killed everyone." Eula Jean shook her head and clucked her tongue.

"You don't think the train was attacked by whoever shot the other brother?"

"I 'spect it was Indians, like they're sayin', or some of the white boys that dillydally around the pleasure houses some times. Lord only knows where they get their money."

"These men spend a lot? Do they hang out together all the time?"

Elizabeth endured Eula Jean's speculative look. The woman frowned. "You don't look to be the type to carry on with a seamy lot. I was hopin' you might stay a while—I've been shy on companionship of recent, as well as I could use the income. But if you think you can have men up here all hours of the night and day, well—"

"Mrs. Crawford, that's the farthest thing from my mind!" Elizabeth drew a long breath. Eula Jean's innuendoes and between-the-lines readings weren't any different from those of some of the gossips who would stop by her grandmother Clark's parlor on weekday mornings. To get on their wrong side was to have that whole social circle down on you. "I intend to find employment quite soon," Elizabeth quickly added.

"Well, I surely hope so," Eula Jean said. "Here. Have a biscuit."

Elizabeth accepted the puffy round of bread. She hadn't eaten since before the stage reached Trinidad. Eula Jean pushed a small crock of jam her way, produced a plate with sliced ham on it—added another biscuit. Elizabeth tried not to stuff the food in her mouth, and listened while Eula Jean went on about how the town had changed in the past five years. The woman ignored Elizabeth's voracious appetite while she expounded on the influx of merchants and the hope they all had for a railroad. Elizabeth finished all the food presented and Eula Jean had brought area history up to 1869. Elizabeth's coffee cup was filled for the third time. Eula Jean cleared away the dishes. The woman was starting in on her time as a laundress at Fort Garland.

"Mrs. Crawford. I hate to interrupt, but I do have to go now. I've letters to write and things to fix up."

Eula Jean held up her hands. "Oh, of course. Me runnin' on so," Eula Jean walked with her to the door. "I've not had much company of late."

"Thank you for the food. I hadn't realized how hungry I was."

"I should think. You slept through dinner. I'll have supper ready a bit before sunset, but if you want somethin' before then, just give a holler."

"Thank you, I will." Elizabeth smiled at the woman, liking her friendliness, even if she was more garrulous than any woman Elizabeth had ever met.

Back in her room, Elizabeth sat again at her writing table, knowing she had to inform Casey of the bad state of the Hastings family.

After blotting the letter and sealing it into an envelope, she rinsed the steel nib of her pen and put away the small jar of ink. Then she returned to the tedious work of emptying the tub. The grating on the plank floor as she pulled the tub to the portal got Eula Jean's attention, and the woman (who just happened to be on her way to the wood pile at the end of the breezeway) rushed over.

"My land, girl! I can't have my tenants doing that work. Get on with you!"

Elizabeth wanted to empty the tub herself, dismayed to let someone else see the abundance of grit sloshing in the bottom, but Eula Jean would have none of that and sent Elizabeth on her way with directions to the mail depot and the names of disreputable establishments she expected Elizabeth to avoid.

Elizabeth relented and glanced around the room, making certain her Winchester and work gloves, her extra boy's clothing were locked in her portmanteau. She was certain Eula Jean would snoop. After tying on a dark brown bonnet that shaded her face much more than the hat Zee Clark had been wearing, she collected the letters, put her shawl around her shoulders and started to town.

SEVENTEEN

I am hoping for life to become normal, and I don't even know what normal *is. A regular ebb and flow. Predictability. But it seems my very being repels all that leads to that.*

31 August

The prosperity wrenched out by Trinidad's old pioneers, Mexican and white, was evident to Elizabeth as she made her way down the rough road from the town's newly developing south side. The primary income came from ranching both sheep and cattle, and many of the white families were third generation in the area. They generally had ranch houses in the hills north and east of town, while well-to-do old Mexican families had adobe homes in town with plank or tile roofs and many rooms, with separate kitchens and servants' quarters laid out around large courtyards. Felipe Baca had just built a two-story dwelling right down on Main Street, not too far from the Catholic church. Baca also put money and labor into the new convent that was under construction, and he brought in Navajo Indians to work his big farm.

Elizabeth hoped this growing town would provide her the opportunity she needed to make her way. A decent way this time. Although she still used an assumed name of Eliza Houston, she was tired of pretense and work on the edge of danger. She wanted something safe and sure: a governess, perhaps, or store clerk. She knew her figures and had a good hand; she might be able to scribe for a legal office.

A group of Mexican carretas was passing over the river bridge when she reached it, the two wooden wheels of the ox carts creaked loudly from the load of goods as they shambled toward Main Street. A goose honked loudly at her from a crate on the back of the last wagon, and that got all the poultry in tow in an uproar. At the bridge edge, where the slope dropped off to a large arroyo, Elizabeth wrinkled her nose against the smell of garbage. The closer she got to town, the more noxious odors she smelled. Cow flop, urine, sweat, tobacco combined to make Eula Jean's remote location quite pleasant. Town noises supplanted the sound of thrush and breeze that had been up the slope, too, with hammers on metal at the wheelwrights, vendors with small carts calling out their wares. She could understand smatterings of the Spanish that seemed to flurry from so many mouths: children calling as they ran, a woman yelling at a dog, an old man joking with a friend over a checker board. On Beech Street, she scanned the store fronts. Sheriff Tafoya's office dominated a corner—a log structure with iron bars on the windows. Between the wool broker and an insurance office she saw the freighter's sign Eula Jean had told her to look for. "U.S. Mail" was stenciled on the window over the door.

"Hey, *muchacha*!" came a call. The fellow in calico britches and a colorful serape made kissing motions at her from under his long mustache when she glanced his way. She gave him a vicious look, drew her shawl more tightly around her shoulders and went to the freight office to send her letters.

"When will these go out?" she asked the balding man at the counter.

He squinted at the envelopes. "With both of them going to forts, they'll go with the first stage or courier that comes along." He tossed down her letter to her father. "For this one, the southbound stage from the rail line in Colorado is due in here day after tomorrow. Don't know about the other one."

"You don't know?" She couldn't keep impatience from her voice.

"Fort Lyon. That's a might off the routes most folks are taking these days, what with the railroad and all."

Elizabeth let out an aggravated sigh as she worried about how soon Casey might get the information she had written him.

"Send a telegram, if it's so important," the man scowled at her.

"There's a telegraph in Trinidad?"

The man chuckled then quickly sobered. "Sorry, ma'am, but from your accent, I take you for an easterner—surprised 'cause we have a bit of modern inventions in the West."

Elizabeth just stared at him, wondering what he meant about her accent.

"Do you want to send the telegram to Pueblo and then on to Fort Lyon?" he asked, holding out the letter to Casey.

"No. No. I've found that everything in the West costs considerably more than it does in the East." She dug a few half dimes out of her coin purse, paid the man and went outside.

After paying for the letters and the two day's rent she had given Eula Jean, Elizabeth had six dollars and change left of the ten dollars Casey had given her. She had to find employment and she decided to walk the town that afternoon until she did.

Horses clomped by, spattering dust on her skirt as she reached the top of the hill at the corner of Main. Going east, she passed the large emporium of Prowers and Hough and one owned by Maurice Wise which even had a bakery in it. She wondered how Hastings thought to compete with those places. Three businessmen walked by and they tipped their hats to her. Elizabeth gave a faint smile, while inside she was very pleased to be given this cordial deference. It seemed like years since she had been treated like a woman—except for Casey.

At Bridge Street she was attracted by the traffic. The narrow, curved street was alive with horsemen and heavy freight wagons going to and from the adobe establishments with wooden false fronts. Vague sounds of bouncy music flittered from open doors. Saloon doors. Elizabeth swallowed hard, realizing this was not the street she wanted to be on. She hurried along the street, grateful to see two conservatively dressed matrons, their high-brimmed bonnets tied securely at the chin, carrying packages out of a millinery; a young mother with a little boy in tow was studying merchandise in a furniture store window.

Around the corner on Plum Street were more shops, but the essence of bawdry didn't pervade as it had on Bridge Street. Elizabeth relaxed a bit and scanned the street as she walked. Ahead, jutting over the walkway, was a large hanging sign with painted black letters "Bragg's Mercantile." The store David Hastings thought he owned. Curiosity drew her to the gray-painted wooden structure. The attractive, broad-fronted building had two multi-paned windows on either side of the front door. When Elizabeth got closer she noticed a sign filling one of the twelve-by-twelve inch panes. There, in black on white, were ten letters she had been looking for: "Help Wanted." Help wanted, and in the very store David Hastings claimed as his.

She blinked a few times, not believing her sight. Here was her chance to make the money she needed and possibly get more information for Casey's investigation.

But Elizabeth had plunged down so many lanes of hope, she subdued her elation, thinking of the many types of help the owner could be hiring: a load man to lift huge crates, a sweeper to clean the floors and wipe up muck and tobacco spit, a—teamster. She shuddered and moved closer, then her heart pounded with expectation. "Clerk," read the small word under "Wanted."

Inside the building, the spacious room was well-laid out with the long part to her left holding a fine display of tools and hardware, farm implements, seed catalogues. A pot-bellied stove and two chairs marked the edge of that section, and directly before her by some thirty feet was another door leading to a store room. The other part of the room displayed clothing and household items, and held a long sales counter. In front of each window were two tables unused, but Elizabeth could imagine them with wares on display to be seen from the outside—a lure to customers. Elizabeth smiled, suddenly realizing what David Hastings was hurrying too.

A pleasant-voiced woman was speaking: "Stop back next week," she said to two of the three customers. "This was just a partial shipment and I expect more soon, although it's hard to say when, as dangerous as the highways are these days."

"Ain't that true!" responded a sunbonneted woman. The little bell over the door tinkled brightly as the women left.

The store clerk gave Elizabeth a quick smile and perusal before she turned to the other woman in the store. "And how may I help you?" The woman smoothed a wisp of blonde hair back with a decorative comb which she fixed with practiced precision behind her ear. In her mid-thirties, her black high-collared, long-sleeved dress didn't hide her buxom beauty, and her direct manner appealed to Elizabeth. Her hopes edged up a notch.

A few vanity items on the shelves near the walk through to the back storage area caught Elizabeth's attention. She walked to them while the blonde woman helped the customer to a pound of sugar and a tin of white vinegar. But Elizabeth's interest in the neat array of mesh and lace gloves was diverted by what she saw on the shelf below. Bolts of material.

Elizabeth's heart lurched up to her throat, pounded ferociously. Blue silk moire and Valenciennes lace!

A whole lot had happened to Elizabeth since Ash Creek, but there was no way she could forget this material and David Hastings' concern when he thought it was going to fall into the mud. She stepped closer, put her hand out and gingerly fingered the magnificent fabric. The exquisite cornice tatting with a broad swirl that resembled a peacock tail was the same. The material was the same, which meant—.

"That's fine stuff, ain't it?" the store woman said, coming over. The doorbell rang as the other woman left.

Elizabeth felt hot and cold all at the same time. She swallowed hard and faced this woman. "Ah—do you own this store?" Her voice was cramped by her flux of feelings. Thoughts of dead Willie, John Bradshaw, Dodie Watson, Horace Cross slammed into her mind and swirled with the defeated expression of Jake Hastings and his pale wife.

"Why yes! Well, it was actually my husband's, God rest him. Died this winter. I'm Lola Bragg." She smoothed her small chapped hand over the silk.

"Where did this come from?" Elizabeth's voice still had a far away sound.

"Some place back east, I suppose. The sheep herders around here surely don't make anything like this."

"Of course not—but." Regaining her composure was of utmost importance, and Elizabeth sensibly walked to another part of the store, working hard to quell the anger rising in her. "Where do you get something like that? You. For your store. It must cost a fortune."

"Well, that it does. I'm selling it for just a little over cost—fifty cents a yard. But I've found it's worth that bit extra to keep the customers happy."

The pleasant, smiling face of Lola Bragg looked quite sincere, but Elizabeth was certain that this woman and her store, were connected with the attack on the wagon train—part of some collusion against David Hastings.

"Now I'll tell you. One of the Gutierrez girls came in here just this morning and saw that material. She's got an eye for beauty and the pocketbook to buy what she wants."

"It might be sold? Soon?" That material couldn't leave the store if it was to be the evidence Elizabeth intended.

"Well." Lola shrugged and smiled a merchant's smile that suggested she recognized the acute interest before her.

"I would need six yards of each," Elizabeth said impulsively. "Yes. Six yards."

"That would be twelve yards total. Six dollars," the woman said.

Elizabeth's heart pounded. That's all she had was six dollars. "Oh," Elizabeth stared down at the floor, trying to come up with a plan.

"I know, that's a lot of money. But if you want to put a little bit down now, I can hold it for you. For a few days at least."

"You could? Oh, that would be best." Elizabeth went to the counter to open her purse. "I'll give you two dollars now—."

"Three," the blonde said. "Fifty percent down, the balance before the week is out."

"All right," Elizabeth swallowed hard, hoping that would be enough time. She took the money from her purse, smoothing each bill carefully on the counter. "Can I have a receipt or something?" She was certain this woman's unscrupulous nature would not hold her to this oral agreement.

Lola smirked. "Sure, honey." She tore off a piece of wrapping paper, scribbled on it in pencil. "Got the date on there and everything."

"Thank you. Thank you very much." Elizabeth clutched the paper and started for the door.

"Now you hurry back," Lola said.

"Yes, I will." Elizabeth forced herself to turn and smile. "Goodbye," she said, "Nice meeting you."

"Sure, honey. See you soon."

With her back to the closing door, Elizabeth's eyes narrowed and she had to force herself not to run up the street as she contemplated going to the sheriff, telling him about the wagon-train robbery, and the material in the store.

She crossed Bridge Street, hurried passed the back of the Catholic church. A horse whinnied at her from the paddocks beside the stone building. She stopped, suddenly realizing complications. *How do you know?* the sheriff would ask.

I saw the material. I was with the wagon train dressed as a boy.

No. That wouldn't do. She stood a moment, unable to form a way to get him to believe her—too get *anyone* to believe her.

Except Casey.

Re-energized, she made her way back to the postal office. But the agent wouldn't retrieve her letter to Casey.

"I'm sorry, Miss. It's already in a bundle with a bunch of others," he said, barely looking up from his ledger. "I'm not sorting through them."

"I will, then. Please!"

"No ma'am. That's in the care of the U.S. Mail service now. Private citizens got no right—"

"All right!" Elizabeth glanced around for a stationery counter. Back east, a counter with paper, envelopes, pens and ink was often a standard item in a post office. Finding none, she walked out and slammed the door. She'd have to write another letter, come back down here, pay another twenty-two cents to get it sent.

As she walked back to the boardinghouse, frustration churned in her like fresh whey to a hard paddle. There was nothing she could do with the information she had learned, other than to contact Casey Pritchard. That and keep the material in the store so her claims against Lola Bragg would be valid. She would like to know more about Lola, too, and how she got the goods for that store.

The vision of the Help Wanted sign flashed to her. She shook it away. She had covered only a small portion of Trinidad's downtown. There had to be other places looking for workers.

Eula Jean was hanging out wash to the late-afternoon sun that barely reached her yard. "Well! Did you get your letters mailed and all?" Eula Jean smiled broadly, her pudgy arms upraised to the clothesline, a bleached baking cloth lapping against her in the slight breeze.

"Yes. Thank you." Elizabeth pulled the thin, cooling air into her lungs. Her legs ached from the hike up the curving hills to this place.

"I thought you'd be gone longer. See some of the town?"

"I walked around a bit," Elizabeth said, still moving to her room.

"I got coffee still hot! Would you like some?" Eula Jean called, hope in her voice.

"Not at the moment."

Once in her room, she glanced around, trying to see what Eula Jean may have tampered with while she was out. Nothing seemed out of place, only because Eula Jean was very careful. Elizabeth sat a moment on the edge of the bed, and it felt so comfortable, it was all she could do to keep herself from laying back and closing her eyes to fatigue. It seemed the whole month's worth of strenuous work and worry had piled onto her right now. Right now, when she had so much more to do. Sighing, she went to the table and set out her writing tools. *Dear Casey*, her letter began. (The last one had greeted Mr. Pritchard).

In the cool dining room at the main house, Eula Jean set the large table for three. She served a hot supper of fried squash, mixed with onions and tomatoes, and side meat with plenty of hot cornbread.

"Ummm! This is so good!" Elizabeth complimented. Dominguez looked at her and grinned. "I haven't had this kind of bread since—for a long while." Her grandmother Clark had made it like this: light and cakey, made with eggs and milk.

"Well, I'm not partial to tortillas. Since I got the eggs and the milk comin' steady, I like to fix my cornmeal this way." Eula Jean spooned some more squash mixture on to Dominguez's plate.

"This you cannot roll and fill with food," Dominguez said.

"Got no need to roll it and stuff it if you use a knife and fork," Eula Jean retorted.

"When one is in a hurry, there is not always time for a knife and fork," the boy said. He sounded like a sage, dispensing this trail wisdom to them. Elizabeth laughed.

"And where do you have to go in a hurry?" Eula Jean quipped.

"*No se. Pero* when I have to—."

"Then I will make tortillas," Eula Jean said.

She picked up the heavy crockery pitcher, shaking her head and looking irritated, but this pretend argument was a usual thing between them. The boy actually lived at Eula Jeans, his father having died, his mother disappeared. Eula Jean had been vague when she mentioned it to Elizabeth before dinner. "He feels better about hisself to be my hired boy than my just carin' for him. So I play along," she had muttered when Dominguez was out getting more kindling for the stove.

"Now, Eliza. You figured out how long you might be stayin'?" Eula Jean poured more herbed honey-water into Elizabeth's cup.

The words jolted Elizabeth back to the problems facing her. "No. A while, I guess. I'm not sure."

"You must be short on finances," Eula Jean said. "Did you look for work in town today?"

Elizabeth frowned, then spoke impulsively. "I found a job. At Bragg's Mercantile. Would that bother you if I worked there?" As she said the words, she knew she would get that job. What better way to learn of the store owner's involvement in the Hastings' problems? If she hadn't been so upset when she was in the store, she would have asked for the job right then.

Eula Jean set down the pitcher. "Bother me?"

"Ah! *La viuda* Bragg," Dominguez said. "She is *mujer muy bonita,* no?"

"We aren't talkin' about how pretty the widow Bragg is," Eula Jean said, frowning at the boy.

"You told me about the situation with that store and all," Elizabeth went on, "But you didn't really say which side of the Hastings-Bragg situation you were on."

"Goodness. I don't take sides in nothin'. It's much more interestin' to sit back and just watch the goings-on."

"Señora Crawford is *como un arbitro,*" Dominguez said. "She could run the best court in the land."

Eula Jean ignored him. "Clerking in a store is a fine position for a young lady. Good you found something."

Elizabeth was suddenly anxious for the next day so she could return and get that "fine" position. She was hoping it would net her a lot more than a decent wage. She started clearing her dishes from the table.

"Now just stop that!" Eula Jean said. Elizabeth halted, dish in hand. "You're a paying customer here, even though we did eat kinda casual. I can't have you cleaning up after yourself."

"The señora is afraid you will not want to pay her if you also do work here," Dominguez said.

"I ain't afraid of nothin', Dominguez. And you're the one who's being paid to work!"

The boy laughed and took the dish from Elizabeth. Elizabeth smiled and started for the door of the small dining room.

"I keep coffee hot until an hour after sunset," Eula Jean said. "Come get a cup anytime. Anytime at all."

"Yes. Thank you."

In the cooling evening, Elizabeth made her way back along the corridor to her room, feeling much more at ease now that she had decided how to proceed.

Cottonwood leaves had barely begun to yellow, but Elizabeth, in a green crepe dress with black trim and matching bonnet, was attuned to the soon-changing season as keenly as she had been as a child. The brightness of the morning seemed symbolic to her that she was doing the right thing. She laughed at the tinge of superstition which that idea stemmed from and hurried across the river bridge into town. Her first stop was at the freight office, where she left her second letter to Casey with the grouchy postal agent. As Lola Bragg raised the draw shade on the paned-door and turned the latch key, Elizabeth had just rounded the corner off Animas Street onto Plum. A church bell rang, signaling it was eight o'clock, and a bevy of Mexican children scurried, laughing along the street toward the Catholic church. When Elizabeth crossed Commercial Street a closed wagon lumbered up outside of The Butcher Corral. The driver's call "Ice man!" to the store startled her.

A slant of yellow sunlight shimmered along Plum Street and ahead was the Bragg store with its Help Wanted sign in the window and the incriminating evidence of wrongdoing on the shelves within. Elizabeth went up the steps and pushed open the door.

"Well, good morning!" Lola said, her surprise evident. This day she was dressed in navy blue with a scoop neckline filled in with a print scarf. "Back so soon? You must have raided the egg money for coins for that material." She smiled good-naturedly.

"Not exactly." Elizabeth smiled back. "I will have difficulty getting all the money, because I haven't employment, and I know you need a clerk, so I thought if you hired me—."

Lola laughed and came around the counter. "You know, when you came in here yesterday, I thought it might be because of that sign. And I just put it up yesterday, too. Have you clerked in a store before?"

"Yes," Elizabeth lied. "At home. Back in—," Elizabeth forced another smile as she sought to win this woman over. "Tennessee," she finished, certain she had heard a bit of Southern turn to the woman's speech. The war years were close enough that people were still swayed by their sympathies during that conflict.

The blonde woman's eyebrows quirked toward her hairline and she pursed her lips. Elizabeth looked away and tried to sound more southern. "Ah did bookkeeping and everythin'."

"Well, I don't need a bookkeeper." Lola's gaze swept Elizabeth, hairline to boot toe—lingering a moment on those moccasins. "But I surely could use a good clerk. One who knows figures and can help me talk to these Mexican people. You speak their lingo, don't you?"

Elizabeth looked up, surprised.

"You look to be part—or maybe some Ute in you?" Lola shrugged. "I don't really care. Got no hard feelings for these people. Well?"

"I—I only speak a little bit of Spanish. Not much at all." Elizabeth's wariness made her tense.

"What brings you to Trinidad, anyway, Miss—ah. What was your name?"

"Houston. Eliza Houston."

The woman gave a slight laugh. "A Tennessee girl with a good Texas name. How could I turn you away?" Lola Bragg didn't believe her, but the lies appealed to the woman as she saw Elizabeth as a kindred, misdirected soul.

Elizabeth laughed with her. "I've been trying to get to Fort Union to find my brother," Elizabeth said. "I have just plain run out of funds, though. Stage fare is so expensive out here!"

"That it is. So you'll only being staying long enough to earn your fare?"

"Well, no." Elizabeth furrowed her brow. She had lived a most difficult lie for over a month, so this next little fib came easy to her. "Since I started my trip, my brother's been killed. I—I just learned of it before the stage reached Trinidad."

"Well, don't that beat all." Lola nearly smirked.

Elizabeth continued as if she hadn't noticed. "His patrol was ambushed, I guess. It happened nearly a month ago."

She wiped an imaginary tear from her cheek with her gloved hand; Lola clucked her tongue and patted Elizabeth on the back. "You're really something, honey. To keep on like you do."

A thumping came from the back of the store, then a door opened and slammed closed.

"Lola?" called a deep voice. "Hey. I got some stuff out—." A man limped through the small walkway and stopped, staring at Elizabeth with pale blue eyes. "Oh. Didn't realize you had a customer."

"She's my new helper," Lola said. "Eliza, this here is Mr. Thompson."

He whipped the dirty black hat off his scraggly blond hair and nodded. Elizabeth clenched her jaw, wanting to back away. Her vague unease was caused by the man's features, which seemed familiar, as well as his build in gray calico shirt and striped denims.

"I'll just wait back here." He returned to the storage area, favoring his right leg.

"Does he work for you, too?" Elizabeth asked, trying to shake the discomfort he brought.

"In a way. Handles the freight and all." Lola went to the front and took the sign from the window, but she hesitated when she turned. "I close the store for dinner at eleven-thirty, reopen promptly at twelve-thirty. That's when the other stores close," she said with a smug grin. "I can only pay you twelve dollars a month," she stated. "What with my husband's death and all. Well, I've expenses and—."

"That's an admirable amount, Mrs. Bragg," Elizabeth said, although she thought it a paltry sum.

"Then it's good to have you working with me, Eliza."

After the jobs in which Elizabeth had most recently been employed, working as a store clerk seemed incredibly simple. She went at it with an enthusiasm and energy borne of someone accustomed to hard work, and also as a way to keep at bay the thoughts of what she hoped to prove.

While Lola was in the stockroom talking to the freight man, Elizabeth re-examined the blue silk material and its companion bolt of lace. Behind the counter, she tucked her purse and shawl on the broad shelf that held the extra roll of brown wrapping paper and a shotgun, then went from one display to the next, taking in the contents and wondering how much of it was from the Hastings' wagons.

The bell rang at the door. Elizabeth, standing behind one of the display tables in the middle of the room, smiled and turned to greet her first customer.

"Oh." The middle-aged woman, weather-tanned with deep lines around her eyes and mouth, stood stiffly at the door in her faded calico dress and matching sunbonnet. She looked around and frowned. "Who are you? Where's the owner?" Her brusque words dimmed Elizabeth's smile.

"She's in the storeroom. Would you like for me to get her?"

"That's Mrs. Bragg, you're talkin' about."

"Yes."

The woman relaxed a bit. "Thought for a minute you was with those others—that they had taken over the store."

"Those others?" Elizabeth had an inkling as to what the woman meant, but wanted to hear it said out; wanted to gauge the sentiments in this town against the Hastings brothers.

The woman merely peered at her, her thin cheeks going tense as she inspected Elizabeth, squinting slightly from tired gray eyes. "You're not from around here, I see. Oh, well. You got any dried fruits? I need some apples and raisins. These are the lowest prices in town. I don't know how she does it and makes a living, too. But I always stop here just to see what's on the shelves." The woman walked around the store, stiff-legged, her posture as tight as an angry rooster's.

Elizabeth remembered where the grocery items were, found the dried fruits. The bell rang as she asked the woman how much she wanted. A mother entered with her two young children who stomped and yelled like they were on a school playground. Elizabeth wrapped the pound of apples and the half-pound of raisins while the little boy whined for some hard-rock candy.

The bell rang, announcing an elderly man in a rumpled brown suit.

He wanted cigars. "Some of those new ones you got in just the other day," he said.

The bell rang. Lola came from the back to help. A slit-eyed burly man lounged in the store-room door, glowering around the room. "He's my load man," Lola said casually.

Elizabeth got the cigars, which looked just like the fat smelly ones David Hastings always smoked. Men came in and looked over implements hanging on the hardware wall. A dapper fellow examined the suits displayed on a rack with other clothes.

And so the morning progressed, with Elizabeth impressed by the number of customers. As she made orders, she noted that the coin payment was considerably less than she would have expected. On her meal break at 11:30, she visited Wise's store and Davis and Baraclogh's and confirmed that the ten cents Lola Bragg was charging for a two pound tin of crackers was a very low price. Other items were equally reduced.

The day passed quickly, with a moderate flow of customers and Elizabeth helping Lola shelve the new items she had received that morning. More canned goods, an assortment of notions from papers of straight pins to darning eggs, a small selection of baby clothes. Elizabeth wondered if those could have been gifts David was bringing back for his brother's expected new baby. Lola made a listing of the items as Elizabeth placed them on shelves. A system Elizabeth found curious, as if the woman didn't know what she had until the items were unwrapped and Elizabeth called them out to her. The "load man" disappeared around two o'clock and when Elizabeth hoisted a keg of nails to her shoulder without a second thought and carried it to a customer's wagon, both the man and Lola were impressed.

By the time Lola dismissed her at four o'clock, Elizabeth was even more convinced that the entire store was being stocked with stolen items, and that Mr. Thompson was probably a thief, or working with thieves.

Elizabeth stood a moment on the street listening to wagon sounds and horses near and far cough and whicker and stomp. Sweet heavy smells came from the brewery a block away, and she could hear the chuffing of engines from the mill near the Purgatoire River. She folded her shawl over her arm and sighed. The climb up the long hill to Eula

Jean's was something she didn't want to deal with right then. Elizabeth missed not being able to pull into the saddle and be carried wherever she wanted to go.

Thoughts of her horse headed her along Plum Street and onto Maple. This route would avoid Bridge Street, with its rowdy houses that this time of evening were just beginning to crackle with activity. On Main near the U.S. Corral, she wondered how she could regain possession of her horse without drawing too many questions. She dodged some running boys and a rickety buckboard driven by a man who would have as soon run her over as not, crossed Main, and slowed her stride at the livery paddocks. The bay stood eating at the feed bin near the loafing shed. Elizabeth smiled. She couldn't call to him, for she had never given the gelding a name, but seeing him assured her that he was well taken care of.

A heavily laden wagon from Quick Step Mill rumbled out of the livery gate preventing Elizabeth's passage. She squinted her eyes and looked away from the dust that fogged up from around the wheels. This had her looking across the street, and she blinked hard. The wagon headed up the street. Elizabeth stayed on the boardwalk, unmoving and staring through the settling dust at a rider turning his mount onto Bridge Street A black horse and a man dressed all in black, a pistol on each hip. His back was to her and then he was lost in the shadows cast by the buildings.

Elizabeth caught up a handful of skirt and jogged across the street, her springy stride much more suitable to Zee Clark than a demure young-lady store clerk. At the corner she stopped, seeing the man get off his horse outside of the Senate Saloon. Yes. It was Darcy Goodhue. He paused after tying the horse's reins to the hitching rail and seemed to be looking right at her. Elizabeth forced herself to turn slowly, not wanting to attract attention by whirling away. Two steps and she was out of his sight beside the Fisher Building Bookstore. Her heart thumped so hard in her chest it hurt and she made a quick perusal of the street, expecting to see the mammoth Ox Lewis on his big horse. Only shoppers and businessmen were on the street.

She headed resolutely along Main toward the sloping street that led to Eula Jean's, and her logic subdued the panic that had struck. This wasn't much different from when she had seen Darcy Goodhue on the

Kansas trail. He didn't really know her. Even if Ox had been around and looked right at her, he wouldn't have recognized her either. She was certain he hadn't been in Lady Faye's the evening she shot Johnny Tillison; and that night in the hotel—. She gritted her teeth. No. Neither of them knew her.

But new worries joined her like ticks on a bear. Casey Pritchard would arrive in a few days. Darcy Goodhue was certain to recognize him, and that man in black had promised a showdown with Casey.

Usually Elizabeth had no trouble finding solutions to problems, albeit they were often extreme solutions, but outside of putting on her pants and old shirt, sneaking into town, stealing her own horse and riding out to intercept Casey, she could think of no answer to this problem. Except the telegraph. She could send a telegram, and then not have enough money to buy the purloined material. She could ask Lola Bragg for an advance—. How ridiculous! And chances were she was making more of seeing Goodhue than need be, transferring her own panic to Casey's situation. But then the venom of Goodhue's tone when they were in Kansas came to her again and her worry returned.

The mental debate of the various possibilities consumed much of her evening, prolonged because, rather than taking dinner with the talkative Eula Jean and Dominguez, she stayed in her room, feigning exhaustion from her first day's work. It was a mistake not to give herself a break from this numbing dilemma. Weariness finally tugged at her. The wind made a constant hissing through the pines. She fell asleep with the lamp glowing from the bed table and the two windows securely closed.

EIGHTEEN

*…Near the house a great horned owl is making its gloomy call.
Grandma Jannie* [Fortune] *always said they muttered omens,
talked of death. Does this owl know something of my future?*

2 September

Sometime during the night Elizabeth's body relaxed and put itself on cycle. New moon six days gone, and her identity as a woman was truly complete. In the morning, she dug out the necessary cloths from an oiled stuff sack in her portmanteau and spoke discretely to Eula Jean who nodded and supplied her with a rinse bucket and showed her where to toss the water on the manure pile behind the livestock shed. When Elizabeth started off to town to her job, her positive frame of mind was back and she attributed her previous night's consternation to the start of her present physiological condition.

That's not to say that she totally discounted the circumstance of seeing Darcy Goodhue. But she decided he could be well on his way down the trail by now, headed for Santa Fe, most likely. When Casey came through, she would warn him to be on the lookout.

Elizabeth tromped across the bridge well before the store opened, remembering that Lola Bragg had mentioned another shipment of goods would arrive today. Elizabeth wanted to be there to peruse the new items and see if she could identify anything else.

The "Closed" sign was still in the window at Bragg's store, but the front shades were up indicating Lola was there. Elizabeth started down the wagon path that ran between the store and the barrister's office toward the back door. When she passed under the window of the storeroom, Lola's voice came easily through the pane of canvas and stopped Elizabeth mid-stride.

"Oh, Thad. The man ain't been dead a year. It wouldn't be proper for you to be coming and going from his house."

Elizabeth could smell coffee and cigar smoke. A sparrow flittered from the gutter on the lawyer's building, chirped, flew to the eaves of the store.

"Well, I'm sure gettin' tired of this back and forth stuff."

That was the voice of the freighter Lola introduced her to the previous day. Elizabeth glanced back at the street, not fond of eavesdropping, but hoping to learn something about this store operation.

"Maybe now that you hired that girl, we can take a trip up to Pueblo or something," he continued.

"It sounds great. I'm sure damn sick of wearing mourning clothes, but I don't want to go anywhere until things are settled with Hastings."

Elizabeth definitely wasn't leaving now. She inched into the deep shadows of the alley and her dark blue dress, the one with the white trim on the peplum, made her nearly invisible.

"Uh. Could be he's dead. That's how rumor has it, at least."

Lola laughed. "Yeah. You got him good in that attack. So now the poor widow lady can keep her store without anymore hassles."

Elizabeth clenched her teeth, wondering what Jeffrey Bragg had been like to have a wife like this.

"That bastard hurt us, too. And I got men pullin' out."

"I thought they were pretty content."

"Yeah. Until Foster died; that made seven we lost. And then with Goodhue showin' up yesterday."

Elizabeth tensed.

"He was talkin' about Gabe gettin' run out of Kansas."

Elizabeth's heart pounded. There could be lot's of Gabes around, but she knew of only one, and in Kansas, too. The one for whom the man named Goodhue seemed to work. Tillison. She had hoped to never hear that name again, and now this. As if he were following her. The bitter coincidence of it galled in her throat.

"Darcy seems to be a lot of talk, to me," Lola said.

"I don't know. He says Hastings has a god damn Pink workin' for him. One of them that set up the raid on the Cassville headquarters in Arkansas. You know, Darcy was caught in that—lost a lot of friends—

he'd remember. Anyway, I think we need to clear the Hastings' stuff out of the store. That's why I come here this morning."

"That would leave me with empty shelves. Hit another wagon train, get me some supplies."

"I got men still injured, Lola!"

"So find some more men! And send someone else for a load man. That guy yesterday was chasin' customers away, he was so ugly."

"Aw, Lola. My boys don't want to be loafin' around this store when they could be at Skelly's with a drink in hand."

"Look, Thad. We got to do this right. This is the ripest situation we've had in a long time."

"I don't know."

"Come on. Don't get so jumpy. Gabe probably sent Goodhue out here to get rid of this Pink dude. After that, we've nothing to worry about."

The man's grumpy sigh came to Elizabeth. She glanced again at the street, hoping no one saw her standing there.

"And if he doesn't?" the man grouched. "Or if he thinks vengeance first and doesn't do the job right?"

"There'll be time then to move stuff. Besides, who's going to identify bags of beans and nails and the like?"

"Well, there's a few things," Thad began.

"Oh, yeah, but I could stuff them in a gunny sack and throw them in the trash. Come on, Thad. Hum?" Her voice mellowed into sort of a coo, and the man chuckled. Lola giggled a bit.

Elizabeth hurried back to the edge of the alley, a sense of outrage filling her as she thought about her dead friends—killed because of these two. And they were somehow connected with Gabe Tillison.

She turned west along the street, going back the way she had come and trying to decide how was she going to keep working for that woman. She gripped her clutch bag, feeling the hardness of the derringer inside. And this man wants to move merchandise, she thought. The only way to keep tabs on that silk and lace and the baby clothes was to stay on at the store.

I can't do it. Her brisk steps carried her across Commercial Street and to the corner of Convent, where she stopped, fury still churning in her.

And what if a Tillison should show up? She put her fist to her mouth—horrified.

But Elizabeth couldn't let these people get away with the murder, the theft, the deceit. That they could be connected to the Kansas Tillisons added another point of wanting to see them put to justice.

Elizabeth flinched when the church bells rang for morning mass, and she looked back toward the store, eyes narrowing with concentration and contempt. It wouldn't be hard for her to play the forlorn young woman, destitute without a family. That wasn't even a lie. And her actions would be advantageous for more than just her own benefit. It could save the store for David and Jake and Caroline, and bring murderers to justice.

The necessity of it forged Elizabeth's strength and she grabbed up the corners of her blue skirt, striding resolutely toward the store.

She knocked at the front door of the store feeling a perverse pleasure, knowing she was probably interrupting Lola and her thief of a lover. Poor widow lady, she thought as she knocked again. She drew a long breath and forced herself into the role she was playing. When Lola arrived, brushing at wisps of hair, a sticky smile on her face, Elizabeth wanted to laugh.

"Eliza," Lola said, opening the door.

"Sorry I'm late," she responded. "I imagine you were doing books or something. Go right ahead. I'll take care of things out here." She began folding back the cover cloth on the tables of merchandise in front of the sales counter. "Goodness me, things collect dust even inside and covered. I'll have everything looking fresh in no time." She shrugged out of her shawl and put it with her clutch bag on the shelf behind the counter. She thought she heard the slow creaking of the back door hinges that would indicate Mr. Thompson sneaking off, but gave no indication, merely picked up the feather duster and started to work.

Lunch time. She didn't want to leave the store, but Lola insisted. It had been another busy morning, and Elizabeth felt she had wrapped more packages, tied more twine than seemed possible. The material still set on the shelf, although the Gutierrez sisters had come in, one speaking rapid Spanish, her dark eyes excited as she showed the fabric to the other.

233

Elizabeth couldn't make out much, although it had something to do with a *baile*—a dance. They were plump women, and Elizabeth imagined it would take nearly all the material to make a dress for one of them. She breathed a big sigh when the heavy-jawed women left the store after only purchasing two tins of crackers.

So she left for lunch, not intending to stay away from the store very long for fear something important would happen. Her steps took her to Main Street, where she again examined the conditions for her horse before she perused the busy street, looking for Goodhue or Ox Lewis. She recognized no one.

Staying on the east side of Main, she hurried to Templar House, a reputable establishment for a young woman. The small restaurant had a reasonably priced menu and an interesting lobby complete with daguerreotypes of groups of Good Templar members: the men in pinched waist coats, black pants and shiny shoes; the women with lively expressions in puff-sleeved dressed with bustles and scooped lace-trimmed necklines. A large framed certificate dated 1868, proclaimed the establishment of Good Templars had been initiated by a Third Cavalry unit out of Fort Lyon.

Elizabeth munched on the roast chicken sandwich she had bought, wishing that had been the Ninth Cavalry; wondering if a telegram to Fort Davis might not be the best way to next contact her father. As soon as I get some money, she thought as she finished her dill pickle and went back outside.

"*Hola,* Señorita Houston!" came a happy call.

Elizabeth smiled and waved at Dominguez riding up on his burro.

"There is *un coche* soon arriving. I will maybe find more company for you and the señora."

"Mrs. Crawford sent you down?"

"She will always send me until her rooms are filled. But most gringo ladies no want to walk so far to town, like you do not care."

"The hill is steep."

From the north came the excited barking of dogs, heralding the stage's passage down Prairie Street. This was the stage from Pueblo that ran every two days—a stage that had gotten to Pueblo from the rail line in Kit Carson, Colorado at the Kansas border.

"I will make a little *carro* for my burro—and carry señoritas back and forth."

"And how much will you charge them? Too much, *es verdad*?"

The chorus of barking grew more insistent. The stage from Pueblo rolled into view, careening around the corner from Prairie onto Main Street and toward the U.S. Corral.

"Who is to say what is too much?" Dominguez called over the rising clamor. He laughed and kicked his burro to a jog.

Elizabeth laughed with him.

"Elizabeth."

Her name came from close by, spoken by a man. Her eyes widened.

"My God, I've been worried about you." Casey Pritchard dismounted his spotted horse at her side, his attractive face mellowing into a pleased smile. "Look at you. You look terrific." His brown eyes sparkled as he took her in.

"Oh, Casey!" The flood of happiness on seeing him quickly waned. She stepped back and shot a worried look around to the clots of people, many of whom gravitated toward the livery to see what and who the stage brought. "We can't talk here. Not out on Main Street." She started across the dirt road that was Beech Street.

"Elizabeth."

She ignored him and veered onto a steep footpath that led up the rough hill, knowing Casey would follow.

"Or it's Eliza, right? I should have guessed that. I heard that boy call your name—Houston. But when I got to the Hastings' last night and they told me the messenger boy I'd sent had disappeared—."

"You've talked to them? You know what happened to Jake?"

"Damn right. David knows, too. Someone at Fort Lyon wondered if he was related to Jake. Told him all about it while he was lying there in the hospital fuming." Casey's horse blew loudly through its nostrils as it walked.

"So Mr. Hastings is all right?" She continued to climb, feeling less panicked in the deep shade of the towering pines and occasional stands of aspen where downtown Trinidad had not yet expanded. Main Street noises lost definition.

"Mad as a drenched cat, but he's doing well. I can't imagine him staying at the fort for much more than another few days. You know how he is. Would you stop!" He gave a brief tug on the sleeve of her dress.

Elizabeth's pulse quickened and she stepped onto the deep cushion of needles on a level place beneath a Douglas Fir, before glancing suspiciously through the thick evergreens back toward Main Street where everything seemed to sparkle in the bright sun of noon. "You shouldn't be in town," she told Casey. "Darcy Goodhue is here, and he's friends of the outlaws that attacked our wagons."

"What? How can you be sure?"

"I overheard one of the bandits talking about him—how Goodhue is going to settle with you for Cassville. It even sounded like Gabe Tillison had something to do with it." Elizabeth drew a deep breath, and sent furtive glances around the isolated place. The horse yanked a mouthful of elder leaves, content at their side.

"And he's here, huh?" Casey scowled. "How the hell did you find this out?"

"You didn't get my letter? No, you couldn't have, so soon. I found the material, Casey, right there in Bragg's store!" She gripped his vest, realizing his lack of comprehension. "That special lace and silk that was on Mr. Hastings' wagon train is now on a shelf in Mrs. Bragg's store! And from what I heard this morning, she's working with the outlaws. She knows the goods are stolen!"

"I'll say she does," Casey growled. "That's what brought me to Trinidad so soon. I finally got word that Jeffrey Bragg was never married. This woman's an impostor."

"That explains a lot! Well, this morning the outlaw, Mr. Thompson, wanted to get the merchandise out of there, but she told him no. And I saw baby clothes, and cigars like David smokes."

"Wait a minute! How are you doing this?"

"I took a job at the store, and—"

"You what? No, great Lord. Well, that can end. I was on my way to the sheriff about this when I saw you." He grinned at her. "Great detective work, though. We'd make quite a team."

Elizabeth flushed and pulled her shawl close around her shoulders.

"We've got something else to talk about, you know," Casey went on. "And there's no time like the present. I can't believe my luck that you're still here."

Elizabeth's heart pounded, wanting to put off that "something else." She kept her tone business-like. "Um. Well, I've found out that going on to Fort Union may not be enough. My father is probably back at Fort Davis by now."

"Down in Texas?"

She nodded, consternation returning to her about what her father must be thinking.

"Selling the horse might have gotten me to Fort Union, but I couldn't be certain I'd find a decent job there." She shrugged. "So I looked for one here."

"And ended up at Bragg's store, putting the capper to my mystery." He turned her toward him and bent to kiss her.

Elizabeth pulled back. "No, Casey."

He leaned toward her again and her skin tingled, breathing became short. "Don't," she whispered.

"It's okay. You're a woman, I'm a man."

She jerked away, her resolve coming on her like a shield. "It's not okay. I'm a black-Indian and you're not." Elizabeth said in the same quiet tone he had used.

"Elizabeth, just because the rest of the country is backward and big-oted, doesn't mean it has to dictate our lives." He sighed impatiently. "I don't care!"

"That's easy for you to say. You're white. You won't have to make all the changes."

"But whose going to know?" he said with exasperation.

"Casey, you're fooling yourself. You see a high-yellow gal with straight hair. You wouldn't feel this way if I had some real color."

"I would have been attracted to you if you'd been black as coal. It's your carriage, Elizabeth, your verve and independence."

Elizabeth shook her head. "I may not have been independent and full of stupid verve if I'd been dark skinned. I'd certainly never have been given a job at Lady Faye's. Never have shot Johnny Tillison and gotten myself into this mess."

"I probably wouldn't have met you, then."

"Probably not. But what's done is over," she said, looking at him squarely.

"Just like that," he snapped. "Then you're saying you don't care for me, that what we've shared is gone?"

Her heart pounded and she bit her lip, unable to hide her caring for him.

"I didn't think so," he said, a slight smile on his face. He took her arms, pulled her to him.

His kiss brought back memories of Fort Dodge and the pulsing eagerness she had for him then and still felt when she thought of him. His arms around her seemed good and right, but—. She pushed back on him, trying to get her breath and clear her senses.

"Don't, Casey. There's more to it than this—than just the physical." He continued to hold her. "Casey, listen! I don't mind being Negro. More than that, it's important to me." She squirmed from his grasp. He frowned at her from a flushed face. "Casey, the times I've had to pretend I was white have left me—pretty unhappy. It's too much to think you could make up for that. It would be quite selfish of me."

"Elizabeth, we'd be living in a community with people from all kinds of backgrounds. Santa Fe has everyone; Spanish, French, Indians—"

"But I'm certain that New Mexico law is just like all the other states—forbidding Negro people to marry white. So I would be pretending and lying."

"How is this any different from what your parents went through?" he growled. "Or don't you have their fortitude to deal with it?"

Elizabeth glared at him. "When they were married, they had someplace to go. Indiana didn't allow mixed marriages, but the Northwest Territories had no such ordinance. My mother's parents were upset, but neither of my parents had to totally give up their identity!"

Casey raked his fingers through his hair and started to protest. She held up her hand. "Wait, Casey. Think! What if we had children?"

It was a bold statement, but they had been through so much together and she had already told him things she would have never dreamed she could speak of to a man.

He didn't seem the least flustered; rather, a soft smile came to his face; he reached toward her. She drew herself away.

"Little brown-skinned babies, Casey. Could you deal with that? Maybe a boy would be dark like my Grandpa Fortune. Even if we lived like hermits, I couldn't stand to see you turn on them."

"I wouldn't."

"You don't know that. And if we were living this lie of my passing for white, what would I mention of my family? Would my father be able to visit us? I couldn't tell my children how their grandfather was one of the first Negro Cavalrymen in the West; or about their great-grandmother who was Cherokee and the African great-grandfather tinner and how they helped build a new community in Indiana. I'm proud of those things, Casey, just like I'm proud of my mother who had courage to stick to her convictions. The only wrong thing, neither my father nor my mother realized how hard life would be for their children. I know. And what I'm living through I don't want for mine."

The little girl with the Jenkins' wagon came to mind, and Elizabeth knew the resentments that could build in that child. Resentments Elizabeth had never felt until she was thrust upon her white grandparents in conservative Indiana; her brother Houston had confided to her the pangs of guilt he suffered for passing as white, and even Scott showed the pressure at times. The confusion and alienation they often felt couldn't be weighed and measured, but it was a burden Elizabeth would never be rid of.

No matter how much he wanted to, Casey couldn't ignore the fervent passion of Elizabeth's words. It locked them both to unhappiness. His hands moved over her back. He had been certain he could give her a happy life, knew his own liberal convictions were true, but he didn't know how to convince her or how to refute the gripping logic of her argument.

Tears of longing burned her eyes and made her throat hurt. She shook her head, raising her chin, blinking hard. "I have to go," she said, pulling her shawl around her.

"Not yet. We have to figure this out."

"I already have, Casey. We cannot get married. I cannot lie anymore, I won't! I love you, but we cannot—."

"Damnit, Elizabeth. Don't do this!" He reached for her. She backed away.

"I have to go back to work." She knew he was angry. At the situation, maybe even at her. But she couldn't debate it with him any longer. If I just walk away, he'll believe me, she thought. "I'm late as it is." She started down the steep hill.

"To work? You mean at that store?" Mention of it seemed to refocus his thoughts and redirect his anger. "I don't want you to go back there. It's too dangerous," he said, coming behind her. His horse whickered and skidded a bit on the slope of slick pine straw.

"I want to be certain the evidence stays in the store."

"I'm going to get the sheriff now. With what you told me and the information I've got, the sheriff will close the place down."

"Go on ahead," Elizabeth said, seeing the horse at such a disadvantage. It snorted and tossed its head. "I'll talk to you later. I'm staying at Crawford's Boardinghouse. Up on the hill." She pointed south.

With the horse sideways on the hill, Casey mounted. "Don't go back to that store," he called. "Promise me that. And this other. We'll find a way. I—."

"Go on. Go get the sheriff," Elizabeth said.

The horse needed a faster pace to handle the steepness, and Casey gritted his teeth, didn't say anymore. The horse, nimble though it was, skidded up a cloud of dust during its decent. Elizabeth waited a few seconds, and headed back, not even considering how her and Casey's disappearance together to this secluded part of town, and their subsequent reemergence at separate moments, could have started some busybodies talking. Luckily, Eula Jean was at her boardinghouse, so Elizabeth wouldn't have to endure that woman's cold-eyed reproach. Even Dominguez, who had queried the stage passengers (the two who got off in Trinidad were men) had left the area.

Several men at the corral and three or four along the store fronts took note, however. Spotted horses weren't often seen in this region, and as ranchers and sporting men, they took interest when Casey collected his horse and walked it to the street.

Another man was more interested in the spotted horse's rider.

"Pritchard!" The word cracked like a springtime ice.

Elizabeth, just reaching level ground and brushing the dust from her skirt, was locked in a brief moment's paralysis on hearing Darcy's voice. Then she ran to the street.

"Mr. Goodhue," Casey was saying when she reached the boardwalk by the hotel. He turned his horse to face where the angular man stood, legs wide spread, beside the livery fence. Many people still ambled along

Main Street, unaware of the tension blooming like a thunderhead just to the side. But a few others saw what was coming.

"Go get the sheriff," a businessman said to a boy sweeping the planks in front of the hotel. Without hesitation, the youngster moved away to do as suggested.

Darcy eased forward, his hands hanging beside the black handles of his pistols. "I want you folks around here to know that because of this bastard, I watched four good friends get gunned down," he said. "And lots of others shot in their beds when the Union raided Cassville." He was playing to the curious bystanders, his Southern speech thick with contempt for Casey.

"That was during the war, Goodhue, and I had no control over the officer's orders. I wasn't military." Casey's voice was moderate and reasonable, but Elizabeth saw his right hand clenching the pommel of his saddle, his left laid casually across his lap toward the forward thrust of his Adams pistol.

"No. You weren't military. You were worse! A Pink! A goddamn spy playing like one of us 'til you got the information you needed."

Elizabeth ached inside, recalling Casey's painful memories about his part in the Cassville raid.

"The war is over," Casey said. He turned his horse away.

Against the businessman's whispered protests, Elizabeth had moved out to the hitching rail. With her hand in her clutch bag, she gripped her derringer. At this range of sixty feet, accuracy of the little piece was suspect, but she would shoot if she had to.

"Damn it, Pritchard! Get off that circus horse and fight somebody in daylight, face to face!"

Casey urged his horse away from the man.

"I'll shoot that fat-assed creature if it takes another step. Get off, I tell you!"

Casey stopped his horse.

Women skittered into the bookstore across the street and peered through the broad front window. A man in a black frock coat and low-crowned hat moved among the male bystanders taking wagers. Casey dismounted on the off-side of his horse so his back remained to Goodhue. With this much of a crowd, Darcy wasn't going to shoot anyone in the back. Casey spanked his horse smartly on the flank and yelled "Git!" The animal snorted surprise, jerked a quick trot away from Casey. A boy grabbed its reins and pulled it into a side street.

Casey turned; Darcy's hands closed to his pistols.

Three shots in less time than an eye blink. Elizabeth jerked spasmodically from the suddenness. A dog barked frantically and horses neighed in the corral and raced to the far shadows. Elizabeth's derringer was out, ready to use.

Darcy Goodhue, was crumpled on his knees, one of his pistols in the street four yards behind him, his left hand trying to raise the other pistol out of the dirt. Blood spread like oil across the left front of his shirt. Elizabeth took aim with her derringer, but the man fell on his face.

Elizabeth bolted around the hitching rail and dashed to where Casey, propped on one elbow, sat in the street, gun arm steady and aimed at Goodhue. Sweat beaded his forehead, and the right shoulder of his shirt was already wet with blood. Elizabeth put away her little pistol and knelt beside him, offering her legs as a prop.

He winced with pain, gave her a brief grin. "I couldn't let him shoot my horse," he said.

She wanted to laugh, but tears crowded her eyes. "Oh, Casey," was all she could get out.

"Damn lucky you're a good shot," a man said, kneeling and taking over the support Elizabeth was struggling with. "Him with two pistols."

"Folks'll carry two, but they usually only know how to use one," Casey said, grimacing. "How bad is he?"

"Oh, you nailed him, yes sir! If he's breathing, it won't be for long." Darkness clouded Casey's face.

"It couldn't be helped, Casey," Elizabeth said.

He tried to get up. "Steady there, fella. Somebody's gone for a doctor," the man said.

"Got to get to the sheriff," Casey said.

"Sent for him, too," another man said. "Get up here by the hotel, out of the sun."

Elizabeth took a canteen someone offered and carried it along.

The crowd grew steadily larger, pressed in close. Darcy had been turned onto his back and lay limp like a rag doll; people peered at him.

The doctor, in brown suit pants and white shirt—suspenders, got up from Darcy's side and shook his head. He walked to where Casey was being settled.

"Don't know why the bloke isn't dead yet," the doctor said. "Nothin' I can do for him though." He readjusted his glasses and frowned at Casey. "Now let's see about you."

Casey's shirt had been ripped away from the shoulder wound. Elizabeth held the canteen while he drank water from it, then she dampened part of her shawl and wiped his forehead. "Isn't the sheriff here yet?" Casey asked. "Got to get up there."

"Bullet passed completely through. That's fortunate," the doctor said. "My office is across the way, and we can get a proper poultice and wrap on that. A sling would be more comfortable for you."

"I have to talk to the sheriff!" Casey insisted.

His concern suddenly came through to Elizabeth. "She'll find out Darcy didn't kill you; and the evidence—." Elizabeth was on her feet, galled by the prospect that Lola Bragg and her Mr. Thompson might get away.

"Elizabeth, wait," Casey tried to extract himself from the doctor and another man who were herding him toward the doctor's office.

"I'm just going to be there. They won't do anything if I'm there!" she called as she started off.

Elizabeth's movement up Main, across the broad thoroughfare onto the connecting Maple Street that led to the Bragg's store was going against the flow of pedestrian traffic. "Somebody said there was a shooting!" and excited young man said to her as he passed at a jog. "*Que pasó?*" a tortilla vendor queried.

"*Vea. Sangre,*" whispered a girl to her friend. They looked directly at her, and Elizabeth glanced down, surprised to see her right hand smeared with Casey's blood. It was on the cuff of her dress and she noticed another streak along the fold of her blue skirt. She stopped near the shoe shop and rubbed clean her hand with her damp shawl.

By now the frantic haste that had spurted her from Casey's side had pooled out. She kept that calm on top, while underneath her mind was working, working, deciding what she would do if Lola started moving the evidence. She could buy the material—part of it at least—if the woman would sell it, which she probably wouldn't since she knew it could possibly be identified as part of the Hastings' shipment.

Suddenly Elizabeth realized she was going into a dangerous situation. She glanced over her shoulder, hoping against hope that Sheriff Tafoya's stocky form would be turning off Main Street behind her. No one. And four strides away, was the store.

The "Closed" sign was still in the window from lunch, but Elizabeth saw Lola behind the main counter, leaning on her elbows and smiling. Bold as a blue jay, Elizabeth marched onto the boardwalk, turned the door knob and walked in.

"I'm sorry I'm late, Mrs. Bragg. I stopped at Templar House and they had the best chicken sandwiches. You should have let me—."

"It's her!" someone exclaimed.

"Well, I'll be damned," came a low male voice.

NINETEEN

...Life goes in circles, Grandmother [Clark] *always said. I hope to hell this circle is finally closed.*

4 September

Elizabeth's energy ebbed to her toes, threatening to pull her to the floor in a dead faint. She stared at Hank and Johnny Tillison, and wanted to rub her eyes to make the ugly apparitions go away. But they were real, loafing there in Bragg's store like they belonged. Elizabeth jerked toward the door, but Hank got there first, barring her from leaving.

Hank's grin was malicious, his brown hair looking longer and stringier than before. Three faint scars were high on his jaw and Elizabeth knew they were from her nails, inflicted a month ago almost to the day. Hank's arm whipped around, the back of his hand catching her solidly on the cheek and staggering her back into the room. Everything lost color, but Elizabeth forced herself to stay aware. She had to stay on her feet and think of what to do.

"What the hell are you doing!" Lola was around the counter and at Elizabeth's side, glaring at Hank. Elizabeth gasped a frightened breath, wondering if this woman would help her.

"She's the one, Aunt Lola," Johnny began. The right arm of his green wool shirt was tucked up and tied off with a piece of rawhide. His pale blue eyes still held an edge of pain.

"I don't know what you boys are talkin' about. She works here! Now just settle—."

Johnny grabbed Elizabeth's shoulder and jerked her toward him. Elizabeth flinched, held her breath. "She's the lousy bitch who shot off my arm!"

245

"*She* shot you? I thought you said it was some nigger," Lola said.

"She is. Can't you tell? Look at her!" Hank growled. He grabbed Elizabeth's cheeks, pinching and holding her face for Lola's inspection. "Don't you see it, Aunt Lola? Uppity house nigger thinks she can be white and shoot people."

Hank gave Elizabeth a good shove into the high counter. As she fell back, Johnny grabbed her purse and yanked. "Bet she's got a gun in there. She likes guns."

Hank was pulling down the shades on the windows and Elizabeth's brief hope that Lola might protect her vanished with the woman's next words. "I knew there was something about her." Lola, arms akimbo, strode over to her. "And you lettin' me believe it was Mexican or somethin'. All this time I've had a damn nigger in the store!"

"Don't let them," Elizabeth's voice was faint. Scream, she coached herself. Run!

Hank seemed to know her thoughts and hit her again; he grabbed a cloth and stuffed it into her mouth—just like before.

"We have some plans for her," Hank said. "They been brewin' a long time." He unfastened his belt and pulled it out of the pant loops.

"Yeah. You go take a walk, Aunt Lola. We'll handle this." Johnny was saying.

Lola's laugh was mean. "I think I'll just go up to Templar House and get one of those good chicken sandwiches." She snatched up her purse from behind the counter. "Take her in the back room, boys. I don't want the store messed up. I'll lock the door when I leave."

Hank grinned as Lola left. "Now you'll see what you were meant to be," Hank said, grabbing her left arm. Johnny took hold of her right. The front door closed, locked. Elizabeth kicked first at Johnny then at Hank while her mind searched for escape.

"This is what should happen to her, right? Like you keep sayin', she deserves this, right Hank?" Johnny was asking.

Hank laughed. She twisted against their hold and made gargly noises, desperation tensing every muscle and surging adrenaline through her. They shoved her into the long alcove onto the army cot beside the office desk. She fell on her back, the two men standing at the open end of the narrow space, blocking her way out.

"You take her first, Johnny. It's your right. Then—" Hank pulled a sharp knife from out of the sheath on his boot.

Panic sent bile to Elizabeth's throat. It burned and seemed to fuel the cord of anger that was knotted all through her fear. When Johnny leaned over with a rope to tie her down, she kicked out, her left foot catching firmly on that empty right sleeve and connecting with the tender healing tissue. He yowled and reeled away. Elizabeth scrambled to her feet.

"You stupid bitch!" Hank said, lunging toward her.

She grabbed a heavy leather-bound ledger from the desk, whirled it at Hank, whacking him full in the face. His nose bled, but he shook his head and kept coming. Anything loose, she threw, sending a barrage of papers, a ruler, books. Johnny got up, rocking and rubbing the cloth of the empty sleeve.

Elizabeth, her back to the wall, wedged herself behind the metal end of the cot and shoved the bed like a sled into the man. He staggered back. She churned her legs, pushing until Johnny fell over, then whisked up the pillow when Hank came at her from the side. The tip of his knife slit through the pillow, and she jerked back, sending a shower of feathers into the air. Leaping over the end of the bed, she wallowed across the soft mattress, gasping and pulling at the gag in her mouth. Hank was behind her now. Big black-handled scissors hung on a nail over the desk. She grabbed them, hurled them at Johnny so she had a chance to get out of this dead-end place. He twisted away and fell again.

"I'm bleeding. Hank," Johnny cried. He was on the floor, having fallen on his healing stub.

The gag was loose, but Elizabeth had no time to pull it away from her face. Hank grabbed her arm. She whirled, fist knotted, and threw a round-house punch which struck the man below his ear on the neck. Hank's knife ripped, belly high, across her body, she fell back, felt the subtle snagging of her dress, heard material tear. Her head pounded.

There was other pounding, too, but the frenzy of her need to survive blotted it out. Hank paused. That was all she needed. She bolted for the front of the store, jerking loose the gag as she went. Johnny pulled his pistol. Her purse, containing her derringer, was on the floor. But no time.

Johnny's gun popped, sounding loud in the confined space. She didn't feel anything and kept moving. Hank was behind her, cursing. She scurried behind the counter.

Johnny's pistol went off again, splintering wood right by her hand as she ducked.

The shotgun was there, on the shelf. The irony of it glinted in the corner of Elizabeth's mind. This is how it all started, she thought. How it will end. Crouched behind the counter, she grabbed up the weapon and instinctively checked the load. Both breeches were ready. Hank and Johnny seemed oddly still.

Then she heard the pounding on the front door. "Open up in there!"

"We gotta get out of here," Hank declared. "Out the back."

"Break it down, boys," came a muffled sound from outside.

"Get her! They won't shoot her," Hank called as he headed for the back.

There was a scraping sound to her right. Still crouched, she jerked around, shotgun and all, and had Johnny Tillison centered with the big barrels. The look on his face. Eyes shocked, scared. It was a month ago and Johnny was reeling back against the wall, blood splattering.

And I've killed two men since then, Elizabeth thought. She pulled back the hammers. "Drop your gun, Johnny." she said, more aware of his terror than her own.

The thumping on the front door. Steady bang, bang. Glass broke. The pistol fell from Johnny's hand. He raised his arm. Shots came from the back room, then a flurry of footsteps.

"Hold it right there," was a husky call.

Elizabeth stood up slowly as the front door collapsed to the battering. A long mustached man rushed in, star on his shirt pocket and pistol drawn which he immediately pointed at Johnny Tillison where he hunched, staring at Elizabeth and the shotgun. "You can put that thing down now, ma'am. I'm Deputy Rifenberg. We got 'em."

His smug sauntering way irritated Elizabeth, and she didn't move, not sure she could trust him.

"Get 'im handcuffed boys," Rifenberg said.

"Sure thing, Rife." Metal clinked. "Might be a little hard with this one," the man laughed.

"Elizabeth."

Hearing Casey's voice started her trembling. She lay the shotgun on the counter and leaned on it as he came to her from the back room, the white sling on his right arm looking bright against his dark undershirt.

"She was gonna kill me," Johnny whimpered as a man pulled him up by the collar. He cried out from the pain in his right stub.

Through the window Elizabeth could see Lola Bragg, a deputy standing beside her. The men in the room were staring at Elizabeth, taking in her torn dress, the swelling bruises on her face. She tasted blood.

"I'm tellin' you, I don't know why you didn't shoot this one, after what they tried to do to you." It was Mr. Conners from the livery, his eyes hard on Johnny.

"I shot him once before. And it was Hank that started it all, not Johnny," she said.

"That other one's dead, ma'am. Tried to shoot his way out the back."

The relief Elizabeth expected to feel wasn't there, and she bit her lip as Casey holstered his pistol. She didn't ever want to know his part in Hank's death. He put his arm around her.

Sheriff Tafoya came in, looking around. "You're late, Juan," Conners said with a sneer. "Rife had to do the work again." Tafoya looked dejected.

Johnny spit when he was pushed past Elizabeth. "Fortune. That's a hell of a name. You're nothin' but bad luck, bitch."

"Shut your mouth, boy!" Conners jerked him toward the door.

"Elizabeth, are you hurt bad?" Casey asked, smoothing her tousled hair.

"No. Just tired. Very tired."

"Pardon, Señorita." Sheriff Tafoya came to them, alert and with an intense gaze on Elizabeth. "He just called you Elizabeth, not Eliza. The *hombre malo* said Fortune, as if it were your name." He scowled. "You are Elizabeth Fortune?"

Elizabeth stared at the sheriff from the shelter of Casey's right arm. No more games, she thought. "Yes. I'm Elizabeth Fortune."

"Ah. Señorita. I'm afraid I must take you to the sheriff's office." Sheriff Tafoya drew his gun.

"What the hell are you doing?" Casey demanded.

"This woman. She is wanted in Kansas on many charges," Tafoya told Casey. He looked back at Elizabeth, still frowning. "You are under arrest."

It was a bit ironic that the previous month when Elizabeth actually shot someone, she didn't get arrested, and now, when restraint had dominated her actions, she was hauled off by the sheriff. But it all proved out to the best. Bragg supporters were chagrined that Lola wasn't a poor widow lady, but was married to a known outlaw. Everyone was a bit disgusted with themselves that Thad Thompson hadn't been recognized as Thad Tillison, about whom they had all heard the previous year and been warned that he might be coming in their direction. Hastings supporters were smug in this final proof that Jake's and David's claims to the store were valid.

No one was particularly impressed with Sheriff Tafoya's catching Elizabeth Fortune, and he sent her up to Eula Jean's under house arrest, a deputy went along to keep an eye on her.

Eula Jean was more concerned over Elizabeth's abused condition than over the possibility that she might be an outlaw—a Negro outlaw at that. Johnny Tillison was letting everyone know, hoping it would make the people of Trinidad less sympathetic toward Elizabeth. It didn't, especially since most people didn't believe him.

Sheriff Tafoya, being a meticulous man, if not the speediest at his work, sent telegrams off to Kansas to learn the truth behind the month old flyer and how he should proceed. Casey was at his elbow, every step of the way, looking out for Elizabeth's interests. And that was how he found out that Gabe Tillison had been arrested and that Ox Lewis, a former employee of Gabe's, had admitted that Elizabeth Fortune had nothing to do with the Elizabeth-Fortune-Gang crimes.

Tafoya's telegrams also got a response from another source, but Elizabeth wouldn't find out about that until many days after Eula Jean killed a chicken and steamed it up with a luscious gravy; she served it with cornbread, and stewed tomatoes and squash. Casey, who was leaving the next morning to go back to Fort Lyon and report to David Hastings, ate at the boardinghouse that night with Elizabeth and Eula Jean and Dominguez, their celebration that Elizabeth had been cleared of those onerous Kansas charges.

"And all this time you was lookin' for your pa, huh?" Eula Jean said after Elizabeth told a few details of her trek. "And I thought you was an out-of-work actress." Eula Jean shook her head and picked up the empty casserole dish. "Thought I had met myself a real live play actress!" She stalked off to the kitchen.

"I guess in a way, I have been an actress," Elizabeth said, sobering. She and Casey walked outside. "Pretending to be first one thing and then another." She shook her head. "It's going to be hard to realize who I really am."

"I can help you out there," Casey said, taking her hand. The trees on the hill seemed etched against the twilight. "You're the spunkiest, most beautiful woman I've ever met."

"Casey, don't."

"No, I'm not going to beg and plead and tell you how miserable my life will be without you." A look of melancholy swept him. "I won't do that. I understand and respect your decision." It was hard for Casey to say that and thereby defer to her arguments. He squeezed her hand, walking with her to the shelter of a tall fir. Goshawks called through the woods, crickets chirped. "I surely wouldn't want to hide any of your family history, and every kid needs to hear about his granddaddy. I want to brag about him already, and all I know is how he raised you. Which is almighty fine."

He wanted to pick her up and twirl her around, but with his arm in a sling, that wasn't feasible even though Elizabeth didn't weigh much more than one hundred pounds. Instead, he bent and kissed her, moving his lips softly from the bruise that was diminishing on her cheek, to the cut on her other cheek.

She put her arms around his neck. "You like women who are beat up, huh?"

"No. I just like you. No matter what your condition. And just remember. I'll always be around if you ever need me—want me. When this world mends itself, or you see a ray of hope. Whenever! I'll be here for you, Elizabeth Fortune. That's a promise."

His knack for saying the right words was getting to Elizabeth, and for all her staunch moral principles and unselfish thoughts of the future of their children, she was realizing more than ever that she could really love this man—seriously and in every way.

That night she wrote in her journal: *"Maybe I could be his paramour."*

EPILOGUE

Casey was in Santa Fe when Elizabeth's life next changed. While bunking in with the MacGrin family, he had found an office for his detective agency and already had two clients who had heard reports of how he handled the Hastings' affair. He pushed aside the pain of that accomplishment—the lives of six men, the loss of the woman he loved—and settled in to build his new career.

Elizabeth in the meantime, was still in Trinidad, where, as a material witness, she had to stay until the Tillison trial at the end of the month. Not a totally negative occurrence, however. Hastings kept her on as clerk in the store; she received one hundred dollars from Barlow and Sanderson stage company for her part in the capture of the Tillisons, and another sixty dollars from Casey. He told Elizabeth it was reward money from David Hastings, although it was really part of his own pay that he was more than happy to share with her since Hastings was such a skin flint (Hastings was only paying Elizabeth fifteen dollars a month to clerk). With these funds Elizabeth had wired her father at Fort Davis— to no response. She had her trunks freighted from Fort Union and bought several pieces of new attire, including a pair of brown riding boots made specially by a local cobbler.

Early evening on Wednesday, ten days after the Tillison capture, she tried on a recent purchase, a tan, trimly-cut, split skirt with a hem a few inches above her ankles.

"The practicality of pants, and the comfort of a skirt," she muttered. She slipped her hands in the deep side pockets and strode around the room, her moccasins silent on the worn plank floor. The skirt pattern was simple, and she had already decided which of her old skirts she would cut and alter to this style.

"Señorita Eliza-Elizabeth Houston-Fortune!" came Dominguez's eager call. He liked giving her the Spanish-style long name, and would have gladly added in Zee Clark if Elizabeth had told him about it. "Señorita!"

Elizabeth opened the door and Dominguez came running as if blown by the chill wind which gusted through the breezeway of Eula Jean's boardinghouse. "Señorita! *Ven*! There are soldiers here looking for you!"

"Soldiers!" Elizabeth stood for a moment, surprised by the idea, then hurried through the slant of late-afternoon light behind Dominguez to the front of the boardinghouse.

The two blue-coated men standing in the yard nodded when Elizabeth came in view. "She is here," Dominguez said. "The Señorita Fortune." He gestured to Elizabeth.

"Oh!" The older of the men frowned. "I guess we have the wrong place," he said, stepping back toward his horse.

"Dominguez said you were looking for Elizabeth Fortune." Elizabeth said.

"Ah, yes. But we're looking for a colored girl, ma'am. Sorry to have—"

"I *am* a colored girl," Elizabeth snapped, her hand going to her hip.

If Casey had been there, he would have enjoyed the soldiers' flustered expressions.

"What is this about?" Elizabeth asked. Fear suddenly caught in her chest. "My—father?" She clenched her fists under her chin. "About my father?" she repeated.

"Is your father Samuel Fortune?" the younger man asked, his eyes wide with curiosity.

"Yes. He's in the Ninth Cavalry." Her voice faded. Eula Jean came from her house, frowning at the men. She had two other boarders now, but felt a real fondness for Elizabeth.

"When did you last see him?" the older man barked, his voice suddenly gruff.

"What's this all about?" Eula Jean asked, not liking that man's tone. She stepped beside Elizabeth.

"Samuel Fortune's a deserter, and we're checking—."

A brief moment of relief washed Elizabeth, "He's not dead? Oh—."

But Eula Jean roared, "A deserter?"

Elizabeth focused on the words, stunned. "That's not possible. You must have him confused with someone else."

"Samuel Fortune, out of Waseca County, Minnesota. The only one in the Cavalry—in the Colored Troops at least."

"You mean he's missing," Eula Jean put in, sensing Elizabeth's dismay. "Captured, or something."

"I think the Army knows the difference between missing and desertion," the gruff one said.

"No. You're wrong. Daddy would never just up and quit." Elizabeth said, becoming more alert.

"Or run," the younger man suggested.

"No!" Elizabeth exploded.

Later that evening, Elizabeth stared into the orange flames that lilted in the fireplace of her room. What the soldiers told her ached within her, along with the heat of a simmering anger. How dare they accuse her father of desertion—he who had always taught integrity and dependability. "No matter how bad things seem," he had told her time and again. "They'll only get worse if you quit."

Eula Jean had offered sympathy; and when Elizabeth didn't show up at the dining room, Dominguez brought supper to her. Elizabeth ate only part of it, then took out her writing utensils with several possible letters in her mind: a friendly, courtesy letter to kind Mrs. Holcum, in Oberlin; another newsy letter to the Johnsons; an outraged note to the War Department, demanding that the charges against her father be dropped. That one churned through her brain. What proof? they would want to know.

"He went out on a dangerous patrol," the younger soldier had told her. "Only two of seven troopers returned. Four were killed."

"That doesn't mean—," she had begun.

"He ran. The two survivors were witness," the older man had said.

"They're wrong," she seethed as she opened her journal. "I know they are." She dipped nib into ink.

I often wonder at the caprice of my family name. And yet, there must be a reason for the way things happen. Perhaps I was meant to come west, just to take responsibility for this situation.

14 September [1870]

She dusted that with sand, set it aside, and feeling more focused with her plans, smoothed a sheet of paper.

Dear Houston,

I wanted you know I am in good health. I have endured incredible events, some of which I may tell you about sometime. Enclosed is a bank draft for part of the funds you loaned me. Thank you. I will send more in a few weeks.

She drew a long breath, gritted her teeth and kept writing.

What I have to tell you is very painful, but I feel you should know. Daddy is missing. Missing and accused of being a deserter.

She hoped Houston might have some word of their father. Over the past five years, Samuel had been writing to Houston, too. Elizabeth also wondered if her grandfather Clark already knew about this, the lie giving him the impetus to cut her loose. That wasn't so, however. Although Wilson Clark would soon learn of Samuel's alleged desertion, even *he* wouldn't believe it.

This isn't true, of course, and I intend to get all the facts of the case, and repudiate this calumny. I am well-heeled, and have employment for as long as I wish at Hastings Brother's General Store. But as soon as possible, I am proceeding southeast.

Once again her optimism burgeoned.

I know that once I find Daddy, it shouldn't take too long to clear our family name.

Not to worry. I'll write.

Your loving Sister,
Elizabeth

THE END

AUTHOR'S NOTE

Although the main and active characters of this novel are fictitious, the following people actually lived and worked in the positions in which they have been portrayed or referenced:

Sheriff Sieber, Ellsworth, Kansas

Dr. Duck, Ellsworth, Kansas

Miss Squirm (real name withheld), Ellsworth, Kansas

Dr. Liang, Fort Larned, Kansas

Henry Booth, Fort Larned, Kansas

Outlaw Gangs: Dalton, Younger, and Coe

Snively's Raiders

Perry Hodgsen, Ellsworth, Kansas

Sheriff Tafoya, Trinidad, Colorado Territory

Don Felipe Baca, Trinidad, Colorado Territory

The Gutierrez family, Trinidad, Colorado Territory

Deputy Rifenberg, Trinidad, Colorado Territory

And family quite similar in makeup to the Johnsons' existed in 1870 Ellsworth, Kansas.

With the exception of Lady Faye's, Tilley's, Bragg's and Crawford's Boardinghouse, every named establishment and environmental landmark truly existed.

ABOUT THE AUTHOR

Kae (Karyn) Follis Cheatham has been a research analyst, livestock photographer, math and history tutor, sports editor, fundraiser, political media coordinator, soccer coach, print model, university adviser for Native American recruitment, administrative assistant, and choir director. But she is first and always a writer.

Pleased (and relieved) to be of Afro-American and Native American heritage, she was born in northern Ohio and has lived in several states. She has a college background in English and history, and boasts two children (who are grown and gone). After many travels throughout the West, she has recently decided to freelance from Helena, Montana.

Kae's writing and photography have appeared in a national rodeo magazine, and her editing skills have been used by Athlon Sports Communications and several national publishing houses. Kae has published articles and numerous poems (in *Pikestaff Forum, Crosscurrents, ART/LIFE,* and other literary journals), and four books of fiction; her 1997 juvenile's biography of Dennis Banks was a Finalist for a 1998 Spur Award. Although two of her books are contemporary young adult books, her primary interests are in the historic West 1830–1870. She shares her time with a dog and two horses.

FICTION/WESTERN/MULTICULTURAL

When Elizabeth Fortune is forced to quit school and find a way to survive, she must rely on all her personal resources. For a young woman in 1870, that's hard enough, but for someone of mixed Native American, African American, and Anglo American heritage, it's a challenge that few could survive.

"High adventure as Elizabeth Fortune, a woman with as much integrity as beauty, is disowned by her white grandfather. Doubly disguised as a boy—and white— she hires on as a teamster to hunt for her father, a Buffalo Soldier on the frontier. … [The Adventures of Elizabeth Fortune] leaves us hoping for the further adventures of one of the most intriguing heroines this reader has met in years."

—Jeanne Williams, past-president of Western Writers of America, winner of four Western Writers of America Spur Awards and the Levi Strauss Golden Saddleman

Dealing with the complex issues of race and gender that still confront us, *The Adventures of Elizabeth Fortune* captures the essence of the post-Civil War American West through historically accurate, often breathtaking description.

K. Follis Cheatham is the author of four books, including a biography of Dennis Banks for young readers that was a finalist for the 1998 Spur Award. Cheatham, herself of African American and Native American descent, is a freelance writer specializing in photos and ads for equine enterprises and rural activities. She lives in Helena, Montana.

Blue Heron Publishing
$16.95 USA / $23.50 CDN

ISBN 0-936085-44-4 $16.95

9780936085449

Sparkling stories about Jesus

90 STORY SERMONS FOR CHILDREN'S CHURCH

MARIANNE RADIUS

Where can a teacher or children's church worker find stories that are highly appealing to children, true to the Biblical narrative, and Christ-centered? Here in this book – ninety chapters written in a graphic style which children can readily understand and which preachers can easily adapt and deliver from the pulpit.

To children, who, like parents, face loneliness, discouragement, insecurity, temptations, **90 Story Sermons for Children's Church** presents the good news that God cares. It invites the child to open his heart to the Savior, to put his hand in God's hand, and to walk with Him in love and trust.

In these chapters, the people who met Jesus come alive. The places He visited become real. His words speak vividly across the centuries.

BAKER BOOK HOUSE, Grand Rapids, Michigan
Canada: G. R. Welch Co., Toronto
South Africa: Word of Life Wholesale, Johannesburg
Australia: S. John Bacon Pty. Ltd., Melbourne
New Zealand: G. W. Moore Ltd., Auckland